To Jill

I hope you enjoy it!

Archibald Fly
The Thegn's Daughter

Joy Kenward

Published by FeedARead, 2011

A CIP catalogue record for this title is available from the British
Library.

Cover image by Karen Gunning
Email, karengunning@btinternet.com

About the Author

Joy Kenward's writing interests reflect her academic background in Literature and History. She has won national competitions for her short stories, and has been teaching Creative Writing for ten years. *Archibald Fly, the Thegn's Daughter* is her first published novel, based on her most successful fictional character.

For Bob

Acknowledgements

I want to thank the YouWriteOn people for their good advice and enouraging comments, and especially to Edward Smith and the publication team for their help and support. I thank my dear friend June Dauncey for her support from the moment Archibald's character appeared in my head. I also thank Ann Merrin for reading the story and for being a true friend. I thank Louise Kavanagh for the great portrait photo of me. A great many thanks also to Karen Gunning, author and artist, who created the splendid image for the book cover; and to Paul Gunning for his generous expertise. Most of all, I thank Bob, for his patience and for sharing with me those wonderful days of research that took us to Cadbury, Sutton Hoo, West Stow, The British Museum and Glastonbury.

Author's Note

This is a fictional story. The setting is broadly in the times of King Arthur, a figure who the historians do not believe ever existed. Similarly, the characters and events in my story never existed, nor are they based on any real living or historical people.

It is unlikely that Anglo-Saxons ever rode to battle on horses, preferring to fight on foot. Nevertheless, Archibald, Finric and their associates certainly do go to battle on horseback in this book.

In writing this story, I was enthralled and captivated by many of the history books I read in order to gain a 'feel' of the times between when the Romans left Britain and the Norman Conquest. Meanwhile, the story of Edith, Archibald, Kyneth, Mother Werberga and the rest grew in my head. It is not truly a historical story. My Beornwine never existed; scholarship was rare in those days; Archibald is not even strictly a Saxon name. I make no excuses: In the end, the 'story' was more important and more real to me than the 'history'. Here it is. Welcome.

Chapters

The Fly Family and 0ther Characters

FINRIC FLY: freeman of Mercia
HYLDA: his wife
HEREWARD, ELDRED, HESTANandGODWINE (the twins), ALVAR, FARIN, HARALD, ARCHIBALD, EDITH: children to the Flys
ORIN: an enemy of the Flys
MIRETH: the maid abused by Orin
ELANOR: Finric's second wife and step-mother to his children
SIRIC: Elanor's brother, Keeper of the hostelry at Beornwine
GYTHA and ALDYTH: Siric's daughters
WULFRED: Chief of Beornwine
MORDETH: Wulfred's wife
WULFIRTH: Lord of all the Ufer lands, including Beornwine; Son of Chief Wulfred
CWENA: Wulfirth's wife; kinswoman to the King
KYNETH, OSRED and LEWITHA: the Wulfirth's children
ALFRED: Chief Wulfred's younger son
MOTHER WERBERGA: herb woman of Beornwine
FRITHA: Hereward's wife
ELDRIC and HYLDA: Hereward and Fritha's children
HERIN and JUDITH ELFRITH: Fritha's parents
ALICE: Alvar's wife
ROSE: their daughter
MYTHWYN and INEGARD: women whom Farin got with child
MAY: Farin and Mythwyn's daughter
HEATH and BEBBE: Finric Fly's adopted son and his wife
PEPIN HEATHSON: Heath and Beebe's son
BERON and WORIK: bondsmen to Finric Fly
MAGBA: Beron's wife
GRANT, DAVY, GLADWYN, INA: Welshmen that join Finric's household
TORHELM: Thegn and Lord to HestanandGodwine
PRINCE CENRED: Torhelm's elder brother

ROB OF DALE: a travelling merchant and minstrel
JENETH BROWN: a bondsman to Chief Wulfred
REDHELM: a warrior
GARTH: a warrior
BROTHER DAVID: of the Holywell Abbey
THE LADY LEOBA: Abbess of the Holywell Abbey
THE LORD TOBIAS: Abbot of the Holywell Abbey
FATHER MALDON: of the Holywell Abbey
CARAU, ENYA, BROTHER CARL: folk of the Abbey
HALBERT: a Saxon thegn
BENCARAD: a kinsman to Siric
EBEN FREEBORNE: Captain of the Lord Wulfirth's huscarle
ETHELA FREEBORNE: his daughter
ORWORTH: bondsman of Chief Wulfred's household
HERON FREEMAN: bondsman to Kyneth
RHIAN and ENID: girl's at the Holywell Abbey women's school

1

Nightmare

What I remember is this.

A cushioned jolting, fast gasping breath and a headlong rumour beneath me that I knew to be the pelting of horses hooves – galloping.

My family was escaping – fleeing on a night of sparse moonlight on horses that did not know the road. I was not more than three years old but safe, bundled up on the saddle of my brother Archibald, my saviour, whose arms surrounded me as he grasped the harness of his horse and beat its sides with his heels. We fled with our father and elder brothers away from enemies who would harm us, away from our home, away from sights and sounds that made that home a terror to me.

I should have been left behind. As a girl, they assumed that the witch-blood was high in me. The evil ones would have me killed. And, living, I was a danger to my family. But my brother Archibald, who was nine years old, loved me. Otherwise I should have met the same fate as she who loved me more - she, gentle and wise, courageous and kindly; she who healed and counselled and brought other women's infants safe through birth. She, my mother.

And as we galloped, waking and sleeping, I relived the last sight I ever had of my mother. It was a sight that still rakes my memory with horror, even now, even after all these winters.

2

Forest Home

My father was a Christian and a Free Man. He kept his house in a pleasant valley close to forest in the country of Elmet of the Mercian kingdom. His name was Finric Fly and he had many times ridden as mounted huscarle to the Lord Ulef, who presented him with the seax as a sign of freemanship long before I was born. He granted him also the right to hunt in the forest and work the land where we lived to our family's own benefit forever.

Father carried that seax always, hanging from a belt at his waist. Although, handle and blade, it was no longer than his own forearm, it made for an invaluable tool and weapon, always to hand. Even when - in times to come - he became a powerful and prosperous man, visited by Lords and princes, my father never failed to keep that ordinary-looking blade by him. As for myself and my brothers, from a very young age we looked on the seax with pride, knowing that it denoted not only Father's freedom, but that of ourselves, his children.

The Lord Ulef was Chief in that country. His mother was kinswoman to the Welsh Kings and brought Christianity into our region of Mercia. My father had served him well in the wars, for Father was a great warrior and skilled in battle. It was unfortunate for us that Father's battle spirit remained in milder times, so that his fiery anger would cause him to beat us and raise his fist to our mother also. He never struck a blow upon her though, and I learned later that he had already heard her called a witch, and his fear of her powers stayed his hand. Indeed, our mother's will saved us, their children, from dire injury at his hand, for my father was a stormy man in those days.

Much of Father's war-prize gold was spent on horses which he loved. He was a great huntsman, in which skill he trained his sons. He also grew wheat and oats, and my mother's garden was a wonder of herbs and plants of all kinds with magical properties of healing and nourishment. I was the youngest of their nine children: the only daughter, and my mother took delight in me. In my very first memory I was in her arms as she climbed swiftly and lightly through the breezy green of a tree in full summer leaf. Below was darkness, for my father was thundering in a rage, but my mother laughed and made me smile with merry words as she climbed. We stayed aloft awhile and she sang songs to please me, until father's anger was calmed and it was safe to descend.

I grew straight and fearless, like her, and became an intrepid adventurer in garden, field and woodland. In truth, however, I rarely adventured for long or far, because my eight brothers were glad to be my steeds and carriages, and ladders into the trees I loved to climb. I was also always accompanied by our friendly house-dog, Broch, whose job it was to guard me when I walked abroad. So I could never be lost for long, and wanted for nothing.

My favourite brother was Archibald. He was nearest to my own age (but, as for that, even he lived six winters before I was born), and my usual playfellow. My older brothers spent all day hunting with Father or working in our fields. It is true that Archibald also had his tasks, but they were nearer to home, keeping the fuelhouse stocked with logs and tending the fowl and stables. He had a way with him that made animals love him, and the horses would follow him around. Even Thunderer, our father's steed, would nuzzle Archibald's hand and push him in the chest until the boy spoke to him kindly and stroked the great head which was almost as big as himself.

Archibald always had time for me. He lifted me onto a pony and taught me to ride as soon as I could easily sit. And he shared with me the secret place he had built in the fuelhouse. It was a little hidden den, a space with walls of logs and a log roof, where two children could sit together and keep treasures and secrets. There we would hide away from Father when he was angry, and there we kept possessions such as Archibald's toy sword (when we did not need it for questing), a stash of apples stolen from the family store, and my collection of feathers - jay, woodpecker, magpie and any others I could find.

That fuelhouse den, which began as a playhouse and retreat, was eventually to be the refuge which saved my life.

Perhaps because of Father's reputation as a fighting man, every one of us, his offspring, were wild to learn the ways of the fighting thegns and longed for a life of questing. My early memories include sitting by firelight with my whole family, listening to Father tell of riding into battle with his Lord. He carried a great healed wound like a bird's beak above the wrist of his shield arm, as well as other smaller scars, and the top of one ear was flat where it had been sliced off, along with a finger's breadth of scalp, leaving a livid scar where no hair grew. This last was the source of one of our most favourite of Father's tales.

"Tell us about the Welsh raider, Father!" someone would say.

And Father's eyes would light with a mix of pride and humour, which was joy to me, because this was his best mood, when all his family seemed to please him, and he would even sometimes take me onto his knee and let me touch his scar as he spoke. And I remember seeing Archibald across the fireside, his eyes wider than any as he listened.

"It was my first time riding with the Lord Ulef's company," said Father, "when I was younger than Hereward here." He paused as everyone glanced for a moment at my eldest brother, slim as a young linden tree, and imagined our father as the soft-skinned, bright eyed boy of his youth.

Father shifted slightly, rubbing his thumb over the polished end of his seax handle. "I was cleaning my Lord's sword by a stream near our encampment," he said, "When I heard a sound behind me. I turned, and a huge man twice my size stood above me on the bank, his face twisted with hatred and his spear already half-way to my head. It struck a great blow that knocked me to the ground and I thought I was dead."

Father stopped; every eye was on him, every breath caught in wonder and dread (though all had heard the story before).

"The certainty of death gave me courage," he said, his voice broadening. "Although I could only see out of one eye because of the blood over my face, I took up my Lord's sword and swung it, double-handed, at the raider. He did not expect anyone to rise up from such a wound and I caught him with his shield arm up and took him underneath it, across the heart. He fell heavily and did not move. I approached him carefully, but he made not a sound except for the soft bubbling of bloody air escaping through the hole in his side. He was dead."

Father looked around at us all. We knew the rest: that his own wound was of the flesh only and had healed quickly; that he was praised by Lord Ulef's chief huscarle warrior, who had seen it happen; that he was taken into the Lord's huscarle from then on and eventually granted his freedom. He became a trusted favourite of the Lord Ulef, who dubbed him 'Fly' because he was as quick and keen to fly into battle as an arrow from his own bow. This was, of course, a matter of pride to all father's children, and we all felt honoured to bear the name 'Fly' for ourselves.

Then Archibald spoke softly from the fireside, "And the three rules, Father. Tell us of the three rules."

Father put up his fist with one finger raised, "First!" he said, "Never leave your back unguarded in a strange country."

"Next! Never assume a fallen enemy is no threat."

"Last! Take with you into battle the sure certainty of death. Only there will you find full strength and courage, and the freedom to use it!"

Although we all feared our father's temper, we believed him the greatest warrior in the world. Such maxims, heard from his own mouth, entered into our souls as truth. When I heard them first, I must have been too young to rightly understand everything he said, but even as a tiny infant I lay at the heart of my family's disposition, reading their emotions through my body, as all babies do, and I became one with my brothers' aspirations from that time onward.

It was when the Lord Ulef died and his son Orin succeeded him that our troubles began, for Orin disliked my father and resented the love Ulef had born him. And Orin was an evil man. Men feared him, and women too.

3

Saved

I was very young, and so my memories of those early times are sparse. Yet one day stands out clearly in my memory, as defined as a rider on a skyline hill, seeming larger and closer than is truly the case. It was a day when trouble came to our house, and I remember it because I brought the trouble there myself, on the back of my own pony, Fellow.

It was summer and I was awake with the daylight that morning, for my brother Harald had told me there were wild strawberries ripe in a clearing only a little way into the forest, and I had a fancy to breakfast on strawberries. I opened my eyes. There was no sign of anyone else stirring.

The whole family slept in the long room which was the main part of the house. My parent's bed was at the far end, divided from the rest by a fine wooden screen that my eldest brother, Hereward, had made to replace the cloth curtain that had hung there previously. Here, in a corner next to them, was my own sleeping place: a cot which (it seemed to me) was becoming rapidly smaller every day. I had not mentioned this phenomenon to anyone, but each morning I measured the diminishing space by lying flat and placing my head against the board behind my bed, then stretching my body out so that my feet reached towards the end of the cot. This morning confirmed the findings of my earlier experiments – it was easy with the balls of my feet to touch the wooden rail, which only a few weeks earlier could barely be reached with one toe. I suspected that the whole house might well be shrinking. No-one else seemed to have noticed – even my mother who was quick to observe most things (such as the removal of even the smallest honey-cake from the covered shelf where the food was kept). I resolved to speak to her on the matter very soon. Mother was always kind and wise – and apt to set my mind at rest over most puzzles and problems. So for the moment, I put it out of my mind, in favour of my quest for strawberries.

I crept out of bed as stealthily as I could, so as not to wake my sleeping parents. I glanced at their heads, side by side on their feather pillow. My father was turned towards Mother, with his face – less stern in sleep –half hidden in her dark hair. His hair and beard – the colour of year-old thatch - had a few white hairs in them and I would dearly have loved to examine one closely – for they stood out stark and coarse among their softer neighbours. This seemed a good opportunity, while Father slept, and I stood there for a moment, considering whether he might notice the loss of just one white hair if I plucked it out now. Instinct told me to leave well alone and, with a sigh of regret, I stepped beyond the screen.

In the half-light that filtered through the roof-thatch, I could see my eight brothers lying sleeping in their long shirts upon the two raised platforms covered in fleeces and woollen blankets that served them as beds. With the exception of Archibald, all my brothers were well grown and like men to me. Even Harald was eleven winters and rode to hunt with the others. Thus, it seemed to me almost that I had seven fathers beside my own parents. Some I loved more than others, and some I was wary of, but there is no doubt that because of them I felt safe from any dangers that might lurk outside the family, dangers that – although I did not know it that innocent morning – were soon to enter into my life with fury and alarm, so that I would never feel such security again.

I stood at the threshold of the house door, looking back again at my sleeping brothers. There was a beam of soft light lying over the faces of the twins, HestanandGodwine, as they slept side by side – beautiful and alike as a pair of doves, their blue eyes hidden under matching violet lids, even their golden hair lying in symmetry, as it seemed, upon that shared couch. Then my glance happened to fall on the bone-white face of Alvar, who slept close to the twins, and as if he knew I was watching, he opened one eye which stared straight into my own. Without raising himself, he crooked a finger, beckoning me to approach him. I stepped back into the shadow of the doorpost, pretending I had not noticed. Then I turned, opened the door just enough to pass through, and was free.

Broch, our house-dog, circled my legs joyfully at the prospect of a walk, for it was his job to guard me should I go beyond the home yard. The tethered yard dogs and hunting dogs greeted us with waving tails, but lay down again as we passed through them and on to the forest path beyond.

Harald's directions had been good and I soon found the wild strawberries in a clearing close to the path, where the summer sun came high enough to reach and ripen the little berries. Even at this early hour, the sun was risen and began to filter through the leaves in a way that was most pleasant. Broch lay down to complete his morning snooze while I picked strawberries. My intention had been to collect them in the pocket of my tunic dress to share with my family for breakfast, but it seemed that every berry I picked found its way into my mouth instead of my pocket. I did not notice this at first, but soon by an act of firm will, I ensured that every second berry at least was saved to be carried home again.

I had collected a small number of strawberries when Broch put his head up and sniffed. Then, with a joyful yelp he ran to greet my brother Archibald, who always seemed to have a wonderful instinct for my whereabouts, and had come to find me. He held out his hand.

"Come," he said, "Mother calls you to breakfast."

I felt guilty that I had so few strawberries to share, "I need some more," I said, "There's not enough for everyone," and I showed him the sparse collection in my pocket.

But Archibald said "We'll come back together later and collect enough for supper." He gestured with his head, "They're off on a hunt this morning," I knew this meant that Father would be in a brisk and impatient mood. I put my berry-stained hand in my brother's and we ran back to the house with Broch trotting at our heels.

I had been gone for longer than I realised, for the home yard which had been quiet when I left was full of life and preparations for the day. The fowls, out of their shelter, were pecking busily in the yard, and the stable door was open with the horses tethered outside, ready for the hunt. I could smell the scent of the morning's baking, which made me eager for my breakfast, despite my stomach already being half-full of strawberries.

I made for the house door, but Archibald stopped and murmured, "Wait." He stooped to pick up a small sharp stone from the ground, took it to Father's horse Thunderer and, lifting one of the great feet, tucked the stone firmly into the hoof. I was puzzled by this operation, but the horse, perhaps more familiar with animal husbandry than I, looked down mildly, nuzzling at Archibald's head in a friendly way. I held out a strawberry and the huge animal took it delicately from my hand, nibbling with his soft hairy lips. Archibald hugged him quickly, then gestured to me to come and we opened the door.

As we entered, the family were all seated around the table. Mother glanced up at us and then over to Father, who was breaking bread, so I knew we had missed the morning prayer, and were in trouble.

"What is this?" Father's voice boomed, so that I was arrested in making my way to my place next to Mother and was unable to move my legs or my eyes, only looking down at the floor, faintly hoping that if I didn't move, Father would cease to notice me. Father's chair scraped against the floor. I heard Mother draw a sharp breath and stand also. She would protect us, as always, if she could, but I sensed the impatient force of Father's anger, and knew he was going to strike us – Archibald and me – but still I could not move. Then I heard Archibald's voice, pure and clear as a blackbird's call before a storm.

"Father, Thunderer's lame."

There was a ringing silence. I dared to look up. Father's expression was of shocked concern, whilst his complexion – late to catch up - still bore the ruddiness of rage.

"He's moving badly. I looked at his leg, but couldn't see any wound." Archibald, his face a study in innocence was standing between me and Father who pushed him, not roughly, out of his way and strode outside.

"Where have you been?" hissed Alvar, while there was a general groan around the table:

"If Thunderer's lame, Father will want Willow," said Hestan mournfully.

"He might prefer my horse, Archer," mused Godwine with open pleasure, "I'd be honoured if Father chose my mount!"

My eyes moved quickly between HestanandGodwine, and indeed it was true that, despite their uncanny similarity of face and figure, their characters were as opposite sides of a quarter-moon – Godwine always smiling, pleasant, cheerful, while Hestan was doleful and surly. Thus, it was usually easy to know them one from another. They were rarely seen apart and, together, were excellent huntsmen. Father often praised them to the detriment of Hereward, who (as the eldest) Father believed should lead in this skill.

Now Farin pouted "No, Lancer is by far the better horse. Father will take Lancer, and I'll be stuck here."

Hereward shook his head, "I'll suggest River. He's the stronger mount, and I've plenty to do here."

"Father won't allow you to stay," pointed out Eldred, *"The eldest son's the hunter."* This was a favourite saying of Father's, particularly when Hereward suggested missing the hunt in order to work on the farm or household. Hereward shook his head and smiled, passing bread to me and Archibald, whilst Mother poured a beaker of milk for each of us.

"Wash your hands and come to table," she said quietly. We dipped our hands in the bowl by the door and took our places, eager to be out of Father's notice when he returned.

Mother's hand-washing ritual was something the whole family was accustomed to. She had a natural respect and awe for all the works of nature and of human life, and believed that all activities should be given our best attention, untainted by previous tasks or concerns. She said that to wash our hands upon finishing one task and beginning another would give proper pause, and remind us to offer a courtesy to God in our work. Therefore every morning she would draw a fresh bowl of water from our well, add a prayer and a handful of rubbed herbs and set it just inside the house door. We were used to coming in and washing our hands between tasks, although I regret that I often forgot to do so unless I was reminded. However, this became a tradition in our family – a tradition that lasted well beyond my mother's life, was carried by my brothers into their households and, eventually, by me into my own.

Perhaps Mother's odd ways did indeed please God, for it was certain that our family was blessed with rich harvests, fine hunting and good health. Indeed, we were generally spared when others were cursed by diseases of agues or shits or wet coughs. If ever we were ill, Mother would cure us with special prayers and infusions or compresses of herbs, which grew plentifully in her garden. Our animals benefited too, and we rarely lost a calf or foal when my mother had the care of them. Mother's wisdom and powers were well known in that area. People would come to seek her advice, and she was often called upon to attend a birthing, bringing her own herbs and refusing any payment, but offering help by the generosity of her own nature.

My brothers were still discussing who would have to give up his favourite horse to Father, and I was eating hungrily when Father returned. His face was clear with relief.

"It's nothing," he said. "He's only picked up a stone in the hoof." He swiped lightly at Archibald's head as he passed him, "I thought you had more sense boy."

I stopped, my mouth full of bread, and stared at my brother Archibald, with the realisation of how he had saved us both from a beating.

After breakfast, I stayed with Mother in the house and helped her to clear the platters from the table while preparations for the hunt continued outside. Mother did not ask any questions, but only looked upon me in such a kindly way that my words tumbled out in my eagerness to confess my morning's adventure. I presented to her the remaining berries in my apron pocket and she accepted them gladly and admired their flavour so much that I felt a warm satisfaction in my own stomach which was most pleasurable.

I took the opportunity of our being alone to broach the subject of my shrinking bed. I was fearful, for indeed it was a strange tale that I doubted even Mother could explain. She sat in Father's big chair and took me on her lap.

"Listen to me child. It is not your bed that shrinks, but your own little body that is growing," she said, "It is time perhaps for Hereward to make a larger cot for you."

I looked at her in wonderment, and my voice trembled, "But what will happen when I have grown too big to fit inside the house?" I asked.

Mother smiled, and I knew all was well. "Oh but that will never happen," she said, "For when you are as big as I, you shall be a woman and then you will cease to grow." She laughed, and laughter on my mother's voice was a wonderful thing, kind and warm and dry as brown moss. There is little left to me of my mother, but that hour when she made the world right again, chasing away my fear, has stayed with me in a memory of her voice that I would know anywhere on earth, and sometimes I still catch myself listening out for it, although I know truly that I never shall hear it again while I live.

4

Dangerous Guest

It was with a lighter heart that I joined Archibald about his tasks in the home yard after the hunt had left. I fed the fowl with grain and scraps from our table while he cleared the old straw from the stable and fetched fresh hay for the horses to eat on their return from the hunt. I did not forget his promise to come with me and gather more strawberries for supper. I had a notion that it was important to provide food for the family, and wanted to bring something for the table, believing it would add to my own importance in the family. I was disappointed then to find Archibald taking up his bow to practise archery.

"Can't we go to get strawberries now?" I said.

"Just ten arrows," he said, "Let me shoot ten arrows and then we'll go."

"But I want to go *now*." I had a strong will in a little body and had not yet learned patience, (indeed patience was never an easy lesson for me and I still lack it in great measure). I wanted us to be gone to the forest straight away and, forgetting I owed him gratitude for saving me from a beating at breakfast, I felt the need to have my own way swelling so greatly inside me that it was necessary for me to stamp my feet and shout at the top of my voice, in order to prevent my head bursting with rage.

"You *said* we could go and I want to go *now*."

Archibald did not answer me but stared with his pale eyes down the flight of his arrow and carefully released the string of his bow. It was a good shot, which did not improve my mood and, as he reached for another arrow, I got there first and tried to pull it from him, damaging the feathers with my hot hands.

"Edith. Leave it. Let go of the arrow." Archibald raised his voice, which was rare, and this brought Mother out to the yard.

"Edith!" It was Mother's voice of authority on a high, sharp note, and I could not disobey. "Come child," her voice softened. "Have you washed your hands ready for the strawberry gathering?" I shook my head. "Well then, come now and I shall give you a basket to put the berries in. By the

time you are ready, Archibald will have finished his archery practice."
Distracted, but still simmering with misplaced indignation, I followed her
into the house.

~ ~ ~ ~ ~

*The mother's gaze rests on his face for a long moment. The boy was born
under a noble star and his parents had the good judgment to recognise it,
naming him Archibald "The true brave". There are ways to prevent the
quickening of a child in a woman's belly and this mother was a wise one;
she wanted no more babies after this boy, and made sure that none other
came – until the little daughter was conceived out of joy and gaiety. Then
she was glad, because Archibald loved the infant and made her his own
care. She trusts him now to watch over the girl, but will give him this
space first for his bow practice. She turns her attention to little Edith, who
is bubbling with wilful passion, and she smiles, beginning gently to
distract her with interesting tasks. This mother rarely stoops to physical
chastisement; there is enough of that from the father. Out in the home
yard, the boy breathes clear streams of air. Every arrow strikes home.*

~ ~ ~ ~ ~

I washed my hands and, under Mother's guidance, offered a prayer
for the strawberry picking. Then we prepared a little basket, lined with
soft grass to protect the berries and stocked with a small loaf and
earthenware jar of milk. Thus Mother kept me busy whilst Archibald
completed his archery in peace.

When I emerged into the light of the home yard again, Archibald was
leading Fellow, the old pony, out of the stable. The sight chased away the
last of my bad humour, for this was a game I loved. Archibald lifted me –
basket and all - onto the pony's back and solemnly handed to me his toy
sword, laid flat across both his palms. I took it graciously as befits a thegn
well served by his squire, and Archibald led the way into the forest.

We soon found the spot, and I picked strawberries with a greater
conscience this time to fill the basket than to fill my stomach. Archibald
did not help much, for he had taken to lying on his back in the clearing,
staring at the sky through leaves, while Fellow munched grass. I did not
object, because it suited me to do the strawberry picking myself, and I felt
it a fine thing to be occupied thus on a sunny day, with my brother close
at hand. In turn, this brought the remembrance by contrast of the awful
scene at breakfast that morning, when I stood as rooted to the earth floor

of our house in the expectation of a beating from Father. I turned towards Archibald.

"Why is Father so angry?" I asked, and saw Archibald's face darken, although no cloud covered the sun.

"I don't know," he said.

"He is always angry."

"Not always."

It did not suit me to be contradicted, and I pulled disconsolately at a couple of strawberries and stuffed them into my mouth.

"Besides," Archibald had rolled onto his side and was looking at me, "It is not fit for a warrior to find fault with his liege Lord."

I nodded slowly, for this was a truth I would not dispute. "And yet I wish he was more kind than cross. I think he does not love me – nor any of us." This thought made my eyes sting a little.

"He loves us," said Archibald and nodded his head firmly, as though to persuade himself as much as me. "He loves us, but God gifted him a great burthen of anger, so Mother says, and it is for us to have a care not to weigh it down any further on him."

I had not thought that God might bestow such a gift and it made me feel differently about my father, and a little guilty for loving Mother and Archibald much more than him, for he must surely be a great soul thus to be trusted with such a burden. I vowed to present my whole basket of berries to him, in the hope that it would please him and so ease his soul.

I did almost fill the basket, and then we set about eating the bread and milk that Mother had prepared for us. I was sitting on the grass in a patch of sunshine, losing to my brother at pick-a-straw which we were playing with some twigs, and feeling ready for a little sleep, when Archibald suddenly dropped his twigs and turned his head in the direction of the forest road, which was no more than fifty paces distant. He glanced at me and lifted a hand to his ear. I listened, and heard a sound like a human voice whimpering or sobbing. It was coming our way. Archibald stood up and went to Fellow, taking his halter.

Very soon a figure came into the clearing. I knew her straight away. It was Mireth, a young slave-servant of Orin's household, whom I knew from the errands she made to my mother. I liked Mireth well enough and was usually glad to see her, but now she was making a sorry sight on that fair day, for her clothes were ragged, her arms scratched, and her face and body marked with livid bruises. We approached close, as children do, and stared at her. The sight of us clearly did not please her, for her sobbing increased and the tears poured down her face.

"What is it?" said Archibald. "What has happened to you?" But Mireth did not speak, only wept the more. She seemed thin, so I thought I knew what would cheer her, and offered her a hand-full of strawberries from my basket. To my surprise, she shook her head and turned away.

Archibald said to me "We'd better take her home. Mother will know what to do." To Mireth he said, "Come with us. We'll take you to Mother Fly." She nodded in gratitude, although she could not speak for the tears still streaming down her face.

Archibald led Fellow to a fallen tree and encouraged Mireth to stand on it and so climb easily onto the pony's back. I declined to sit with her, but walked behind my squire, who bore the basket of berries as well as leading the pony, while I followed with my sword, guarding the lady that we had rescued from dragons.

Mother was in the home yard as we came out of the trees, and she hurried towards us. Mireth almost fell from the pony's back into her arms.

"Oh, Mother Fly," the girl wept, "Help me. I know not where to go or what to do." Mother led her gently to the house, with Archibald and me close behind.

It was summer and the fire was low in our hearth, but Mother rarely let it burn out, for wood was plentiful and she kept the fire for cooking and the brewing of healing draughts. She sat the maid on a stool and gave her a drink. From the smell, I recognised this as the strong camomile infusion which she kept for grief or sleeplessness. While Mireth sipped the brew, her sobs quietened, and Mother bathed her wounds, never questioning, but murmuring gently as she did when coaxing me to sleep. It was warm by the fire and time for my nap anyway, so I set my basket of strawberries carefully on the board by the window, then curled up on a sheepskin and was lulled off to sleep by the sound of my mother's voice.

I was too young to understand much of the maid Mireth's trouble, and by the time I awoke, she was dressed in one of Mother's simple robes, and was calm. I knew the look on Mother's face, which was a condition of both anger and determination. Shortly afterwards, when Father came in with my older brothers, she got up and put herself between him and the maid.

"Finric," she said, "We have a guest who needs our help."

"What guest?" Father's face was open and pleasant. I guessed the hunting had gone well, but I knew his mood could turn quickly so I took care to appear still asleep, and squinted between half-closed eyes, my ears alert for every word.

What Mother told him was this. The Lord Orin had taken Mireth in his lust and then outcast her when she showed to be with child. He had his bully henchmen take her into the forest and beat her, then she wandered lost for a day before finding the forest road and making her way towards our house. She knew that my father was no friend of Orin and hoped for refuge in our family. I thought this would be well for Mireth, as Father was like to take her part, being against Orin. And yet he seemed wary and reluctant, which surprised me, whilst Mother seemed to expect it.

"Let the maid rest here," he said, "but she cannot stay. It would be bad for us if we cross Orin in this."

The smile fell from my mother's face. "Finric Fly!" she cried, "What sort of man are you that delivers a helpless woman into the hands of your own enemy?"

"Hush Hylda," he said, "There is no question of that. The maid may find shelter somewhere else, no doubt. But I must think of my own family." I could see Father was discomforted by Mother's censure, and could hear both shame and fear in his voice as he drew her to one side, away from Mireth, who had begun to whimper again, but closer to where I lay on my sheepskin, so I could hear him even though he lowered his voice. What I heard made me wish that I was truly asleep, for little children take meaning from tone of voice and manner, even when they do not really understand the words spoken. It was the first time I had heard the word 'witch' but I liked it not, for it sprang bitterly from my father's lips and brought a pallor to Mother's face that was like a foreboding of death itself.

"No neighbour will support us against Orin while his men speak openly of you in this way," Father was saying, with Mother's eyes large on his face, "They say you work sinful spells and hold yourself with unseemly pride and power."

Mother drew herself up, "And you believe these evil words? You, who have seen the good I work with my herbs?"

There was a sneer on Father's face that made my little soul quake as he denied her, called her 'unwomanly' and 'shameful' and raised his hand against her. I shut my eyes tight because they threatened to flood with tears and give me away. I could not stop my ears, however, and the sounds of my brothers' movements in the house stilled. All were listening to Father.

"It was a bad day that I took you to wife," he said, and his voice thundered so that I was shocked into opening my eyes. "My family is tainted!" he cried, "It is a pity the girl-child was ever born. She will carry the witch blood and we are cursed!" His eyes were upon me and I cowered in dread. But my brother Archibald, who was the bravest being I have ever known, came and sat beside me and took me in his arms, so that we stared together into the twisted face of our own father, and I was not alone.

"None of this is true!" Mother's voice was high and wild, "If you listen to Orin and his men, you are as bad as they." She took two breaths, slow and tremulous, and then continued in a calm and light voice. "I am a true Christian wife to you, Finric Fly, which well you know, and little Edith is a child of perfect innocence. No evil spells are wrought in this house, only prayer to earth and heaven, and healing by God's will, through the lore of herbs and good sense."

Now I believe that Father knew the truth of this, and was in fact subdued by his own terrible words. His white anger abated without its normal course, which was to beat anyone foolish enough to stay close to him in a temper. Thus our evening meal took place peaceably, with the maid Mireth joining our table without any comment from Father. I did not forget that I had pledged my basket of strawberries to him, and now it seemed more urgent than ever to ease the pressure of anger on his soul. I was sorely afraid of him and doubtful that I should bring myself to his attention, being his tainted girl-child. But the misery I had been brought to by his words had given me some kind of bleak courage and, when we had eaten our meat, I slipped without asking from my stool and fetched the basket from where I had set it by the window. It seemed heavy now to me but I carried it past all my seated brothers and Mother and Mireth, and lifted it high onto the table in front of my father.

"They are for you." My voice emerged from my mouth at no more than a whisper.

Father looked at the basket in an expression of puzzlement. "What is it child?" he said, and bent his head down to me with his brow puckered. But it did not seem to be his usual angry frown, so I guessed that the strawberries were already easing his soul of anger. I found my voice and managed to tell him that I had picked them all myself and that they were all for him. My father gazed at me with an expression of gentle puzzlement unlike his usual fierce visage. Then he lifted me off my feet and seated me on his own lap, where on his instruction I divided the strawberries between all of us who sat at table, carrying them by the handful to each person's place.

I shall not forget the happy air in our house that evening, when Father seemed altered, just for a little time, from the fearful figure I knew. Perhaps he was shamed by his former words, but I liked to think it was the strawberries that caused the change. And it is true that the strawberry is a fruit for easing of the soul. I have used it often since that first time.

29

But I do not think anyone at that table could easily forget the particular bitterness of Father's former words, which were more terrible than any of his rages. As for me, I shall always remember, because the events of that evening are bonded forever to what happened not many days later, when the innocence of my early life ended and the journey was forced upon me which set the mark of travelling in my soul.

5

Beast

It was a fine, dry morning and Father had ordered another hunt, which was his favourite occupation. The work of huntsman was only less noble than that of warrior, in his judgment. (Indeed, I have found no better test and training in horsemanship and weaponry than the hunt.) So, that dawn, all my elder brothers were making ready, flighting arrows and sharpening knives, while Archibald helped prepare the horses. Father was in his usual mood at such a time, which was short-tempered and volatile, and I thought it best to keep out of the way. So I took myself off to the secret den in the fuel-house, and awaited the departure of the hunt.

Now the fuel-house was roofed but open at the sides, and Archibald had made the den at the centre of the wood-pile, which was rarely touched. The passage within was only wide enough for a child to enter, and yet the den itself afforded a good view all round, whilst disguised by its surrounding of logs. I settled myself down on the earth floor and nibbled one of a small store of apples hidden since last autumn. The apple was shrunken and wrinkled but sweet. I became sleepy, as little children will, and was unaware when my father and brothers left for the forest.

The sun was high when I awoke, disturbed by Broch's warning bark, together with the clatter of strange horses' hooves, and the gruff voices of men. I opened my eyes and saw a tall man on a fine horse riding in to our home yard, followed by six or seven more horsemen. One of them carried a black standard which had embroidered upon it a white sun with zigzag flames radiating out from a central disc. The form of that standard is one of the dread images that branded itself on my mind that day and has never left me. I have never forgotten it, though I saw its like again but only once, and that not for many years to come.

Mother and Mireth were in the garden, tending herbs, and Mother straightened as the horsemen approached. The tall man rode straight up to her and I thought it was badly done, for his horse's hooves were trampling on the garden plants. Broch gave a low growl and bared his teeth at the horsemen, but Mother spoke to him and he crouched at her feet.

"Mother Fly," said the man, "Where is your husband?"

"Greetings, my Lord Orin," said Mother, "My husband is hunting in the forest, as is his right. He will be back soon."

Now, I knew this not to be true, for the hunt would certainly last all day, as usual. I thought to call Mother and remind her of this, but something in the demeanour of the men held me silent. Mother asked Orin to move his horse away from her garden, but he only laughed and rode around with his bully-guard following on their horses until there was not a plant left uncrushed and the air was filled with the pungent scent of bruised herbs. Mother watched in silence, but Mireth began to whimper and then to weep. I heard Orin mock her and then Mother's voice rose up clear and fearless.

"How dare you taunt this poor maid?" she said, "You treated her most ill, and against Christian law. The least you should do is to leave her in peace!"

He turned his horse and faced my mother; Broch could no longer contain himself but leapt up with a ferocious growl, making the horse shy. At that, Orin took a hammer hanging at his waist and swung it at Broch's head, taking the poor dog off his feet. Broch yelped once and then lay still. A scream gathered itself in my stomach, but never reached my throat, for what happened next deprived my body of any breath.

My mother was standing with her hands to her mouth, staring at poor Broch's bloody head. Orin said coldly, "And who are you to teach me Christian law?" and then he used that terrible word I had last heard on the evening of Mireth's arrival in our house. The word was 'Witch' and as he said it I saw him reach down to my mother, take hold of her robe, and tear it apart with a great ripping sound.

~ ~ ~ ~ ~

The boy has been in the forest, collecting kindling. He is called home by something that might be second sight (for he is indeed a blessed one) or might be the scent of herbs, viciously bruised, carried on an urgent breeze. He starts to run when he hears the sound of horses' hooves, but wisdom holds him back at the forest edge. He sees his mother, half naked, bound in the rags of her dress and tied to a tree. But Archibald, the true brave, is as strong in mind as he is in courage. He knows the futility of running to her aid, surrounded as she is by so many armed men, and he but a boy of nine winters. He vows instead to save his little sister, for

*there is no sign of her, and he guesses where she is. He curbs his will to
act and remains hidden, watching and listening.*

~ ~ ~ ~ ~

They fetched a smoldering brand from the house and set it to my mother's
hair. She never cried out, only watched their faces in haughty distain,
even while her hair was burned away, even while the terrible smell of it
reached me, her child. Now I saw the evil ones turn upon the maid
Mireth, but while Mother had stayed silent under their torment, Mireth
gibbered with terror as they questioned her.

"They're away in the forest," she said, the words spilling out of her in
a chatter of fear, "Master Fly with Hereward, Eldred, Alvar and all. The
little one too. All in the forest. We're alone, but for the infant girl, Edith."

"A girl? A daughter?" said the beast, with his hand in the maid's hair,
wrenching her head from side to side.

"Yes!" she shrieked, the tears pouring down her face, ready to tell
them anything to save herself.

The man released her with a blow, throwing her to the ground.
"There's a girl-child." His voice was loud and menacing, "A witch-child.
Find her!"

In my hiding-place, I gasped. It was all too much terror for me, so I
put my fists one in each ear to try to stifle every sound, and closed my
eyes tight shut. When I opened them again, it was to the soft touch of my
brother's hand. His eyes were big in the dim light of our den, and he
placed a finger to his lips, warning me to keep quiet. He scooped up those
few withered apples that lay in our store there and put them in the fold of
his shirt, together with his flint arrow-head. He crept out and I followed
him silently, with not a glance of regret for my feather collection or the
toy sword, and we left behind these playthings as we left behind the
innocence of our childhood.

Most of Orin's men had gone into the house, searching for me, and
the others were still in the home yard. Only one was near us. He was
tethering his horse loosely to a post, not three paces from our hiding
place. The man walked to the forest edge, a look of concentration upon
his face. He stopped by a tree, pulled down his breeches and squatted.
The man's arse was fully in our view, and my brother observed carefully,
choosing well the moment to make his move.

Quietly, with me beside him, Archibald approached the horse, a fine
big animal, all harnessed, with a leather mask and a good fleece-saddle.
He offered it an apple and patted its nose as if we had all day to wait and

there were no evil men nearby, intent on killing. The animal nuzzled him, and he gave it another apple, talking in soft, muttering tones. And the horse stood quietly, its face close to my brother's chest, for it was Archibald's way to make all animals love him. Then he lifted me on to the saddle and quickly climbed up behind me. And the horse stood calmly as if it had been carrying us all its life.

With a squeeze of his legs, and slight pressure on the reins, Archibald urged the animal to a gentle walk in the direction of the wood, making as little sound as possible. But suddenly there was an enraged shout, and the horse's owner was on his feet, lunging towards us with his breeches around his ankles. There was no more reason for stealth; Archibald loosened the reins, nudged the horse's flanks with his feet and called "On!" in a loud, firm voice. He was a born horseman, my brother, and thanks to him, a horse's back was as natural to me as my mother's lap. I plunged my fingers into the thick mane and clung on. That horse might have been keener than we to escape his old master, for it broke quickly into a canter, and then a gallop, making for the trees, and Archibald guided him with one hand and held on to me with the other.

What his former master had called that horse none of us knew. But after that day we named him 'Swift' and well so, for he left all Orin's men far behind in a short time, and before the sun had moved very far in the sky Archibald was able to bring us to a place in the forest where he knew Father and our brothers would pass on their way home from the hunt. We did not wait long, for my brother Harald was nearby, keeping the horses while the others continued the hunt on foot. He heard us approach and, after listening to a few words from Archibald, told us to stay while he galloped off to find the others. We were still mounted on our horse when first the hunting-dogs bounded up to us, followed by Father and the others. Father had an expression of puzzlement and anger on his face.

"What is the meaning of this, boy?" he said, taking hold of Archibald's tunic and almost pulling him from his seat. But he soon loosed his hold when Archibald spoke. Father was filled with rage at the sound of Orin's name, but then blanched as he heard about the treatment of our mother. I saw fear on his face then, stronger than the anger. Without a word, he mounted Thunderer and galloped back homeward, with all of us following. But we smelt the smoke of burning wood, and something more fearful, long before we entered into the sunny glade that had been our home. Father turned quickly on his horse and told Archibald to take me back under the trees and wait there for him. But he was too late. I had already seen the wreck of our home – the house a heap of smoking ashes, our orchard ruined and, most terrible, two blackened figures against a charred tree. I knew Archibald had seen it too, for as he turned the horse away he tightened his arms around me and sobbed pitifully with his head against mine. But I was silent, for the horror was too great for me to bear. I only stared ahead into the forest, my eyes stretched wide, but seeing nothing, and I clung to my brother, knowing with my child's wisdom that he was now my chief saviour and protector, for my mother was gone.

6

Wounds

We did not remain in that place for long. Father, bidding my four eldest brothers to stay with him, ordered the rest of us back to the forest, and we waited where the kill from that day's hunt had been stashed in the branches of an elm tree. They joined us there within the hour, with the grime of soil on their hands, and all my brothers were weeping.

The day was lengthening to dusk before anyone looked to themselves. Father, who had stood darkly alone after dismounting, began himself to make the fire. He prepared a small hind, tending the meat as it roasted, not allowing anyone to help him. It was a small enough meal for eight tall men and boys, and two children, yet there was meat to spare at the end of it. I could not eat, for my throat and stomach were stuffed with what felt like a bushel of dry corn, which only grew bigger when I thought of our mother.

I thought Father was angry with me, and with Archibald for bringing me, for his eyes were fiery red and wet, as when he was in a great temper. I remembered his words that last time I had heard him rage at our mother, *"The girl-child will carry the witch blood. We are cursed!"* So I knew I should not be there and tried to stay small - hidden behind Archibald - hoping not to catch Father's attention. He knew where I was, though, for he approached me – to beat me, as I thought, but he only brought me tender morsels of meat on a leaf and left it in my lap without a word. But I could not eat.

After a little time, my father got to his feet, "You have eaten and rested," he said, addressing all of my brothers, "And that is well, for now we have work to do. Put away your sorrow. Now is not the time for mourning. Now, I charge you to use the force of your grief as kindling for battle-rage in your hearts."

"I ride now to avenge your mother's death. I ride to kill Orin."

He sprang onto his horse, and my elder brothers did likewise. Archibald was on his feet, at the side of his new horse, but Father bent low in the saddle to speak to him. I heard not what he said, but Archibald held his horse and did not mount. When he had watched them all ride off into the dusk with the great hunting-dogs alongside them, he came back to where I sat. His face was white and streaked with tear-tracks, but he looked calm and determined. Checking that Swift's tether was fast to a tree, he took the fleece saddle and then held out his hand to me.

"Come," he said, "We must stay hidden until they return." He led me into thick undergrowth, some distance away. Then he cleared a small space with his knife and spread the fleece saddle there for us to sit. Our arms and legs were scratched by brambles and my face too was sore where a big thorn had made a deep scratch. I never cared about such small injuries, either then or now, but Archibald wetted a corner of his tunic with spittle and rubbed it gently over my wound. The action was much like my mother's own when tending one of my hurts, and suddenly the knowledge of her loss struck me like a heavy blow, and at last tears of grief sprang into my eyes. I cried and wailed until Archibald murmured, "We must be quiet, Edith, lest anyone should hear and know where we are." He held out his arms to me and I curled up close to him, shivering and weeping quietly with my brother's own tears dropping softly onto my head.

That evening became night and day and evening again before they returned. Neither of us had eaten – nor could we have done. But the thirst induced by our tears drove us from hiding to fetch the leather water bottle attached to Swift's harness. We were near him, drinking, when my family returned. Above the undergrowth that almost covered my head, I could see my eldest brother, Hereward, astride his horse, leading the others. Harald was missing and, over the front of Hereward's horse was lying the body of my father, with a great wound slashed through his tunic at the breast across to the top of his arm, with shiny red flesh gaping through cloth and skin like a silk lining. I blinked at what I saw, only understanding in slow seconds that this was my mighty father, hacked through like meat. The wound ouzed a steady welling overflow of blood that spattered in stormy drops on leaves and grass. Hereward dismounted and, with the help of HestanandGodwine, gently lowered Father to the ground. Father made no movement of his own will, and I might have thought him sleeping but for his eyes that were semi-open.

I never feared my father more than then, when I thought him passing to the realm of death, and I clung so hard to Archibald that I left him with a leaf-shaped scarlet pinch-mark upon his arm which eventually turned black, but never left him. In the quieter days of the years to come, Archibald looked on the mark as a sign and reminder of that day.

I stared at Father, and there came a sobbing, keening sound that filled the clearing where my furrow-faced brothers gathered. Then my brother Godwine came and took me out of Archibald's arms.

"Look Edith," he said, "Father took a blow to the head that has made his consciousness faint away. But he lives; he lives, and we will find a safe place where he can recover from his wound." Though Godwine's face was grave, his constant nature lent clear light to his features, like a glimpse of sky on a stormy day. He calmed me, and the terrible keening sound quietened. Only then did I understand that it had come from my own voice.

Eldred had a bloody bound-up wound of his own on the thickness of his arm, but he took a needle and thread, and sewed up Father's injury. I had seen such operations performed before, but only by my mother. Eldred had learned from Mother, but had not her level of skill. However, in time, the long wound was sewn together, and the blood oozed only slowly from the stitched gash. Hereward sat with Father's head on his lap and tried to pour a little water into his mouth. We were glad to see Father swallow. Then his eyes blinked and opened fully, and he said "What is it?" in a loud, clear voice.

"Father, you were knocked out," said Hereward. "Be careful to move; you are wounded, but Eldred has sewn you up."

Father struggled to sit, then groaned and collapsed. Hereward spoke to him urgently. "We should flee from here now, Father. You and Eldred are wounded. We have not the strength between us all to prevail against Orin's force." He paused, "All our dogs were killed or scattered in the battle, so we can have no good warning of enemies approaching. If we are not all to be killed, we must flee now and take our revenge on Orin another time, when we have some hope of prevailing."

Father gave a grunt of rage, but nodded with pain-filled eyes, "You are right boy. Help me onto my horse." As they held him upright he half-fainted again but, between them, Hereward, HestanandGodwine managed to get him onto Thunderer's back and Hereward sat up behind to hold him on.

I remember nothing more but night-time and galloping, galloping, Archibald's arms around me, and a new horror in my head, for my sweet brother Harald was dead – left at the scene of battle where he had fought as valiantly as any of my brothers, though they were overwhelmed by the strength and numbers of Orin's men. Father had been off his horse with the dead Harald in his arms when he was attacked and had his own wounds inflicted. He was only saved by Hereward who, though no great warrior, was as noble and courageous as any. Hereward had reached down from his horse and grabbed Father by his sword-belt - calling to my other brothers to follow - and ridden swiftly away. It was some time before they realised that Orin's men were no longer behind them. But no-one thought we could be safe for long. So we set off through the trees on narrow paths, away from the main forest road, galloping where we could, for the night was dry and there was enough moonlight for the horses to make way.

Thus began our long journey away from the Mercian lands. On we travelled and I could not regret the widening distance between myself and the scenes of terror and ruin that had been my home. By the motion of Archibald's horse, I jolted between waking and sleeping nightmare – preferring the waking state, for there was my brother protector with me. Sleeping, I saw Orin's standard before my eyes –a stark white sun on a black background, and heard his rough-edged voice strike through my soul, "*Witch-woman, witch-child, Witch!*"

Whenever I awoke we were galloping, until at last the sunrise was at our left, the forest behind us, and I could hear the music of a stream nearby.

We were many miles from the old country and there was no sign of habitation nearby. My brothers deemed it safe to make camp and sleep in the lee of a big rock close to the stream. One of them (I did not know which) helped me from Swift's back, but I would not be taken away from Archibald who, too weary to move, was also carried gently from his horse, and we were laid together on a sheepskin. I slept again, my hand in Archibald's sleeve. At one time I awoke to see our father crouching over us in his bloody tunic, his eyes shining, and I thought it was a dream. Somehow I was not afraid, and gave him what smile I could manage. He nodded, his face all mildness, so that I hardly knew him, and a big tear ran from his eye and splashed onto my face. He wiped it away; I remember his finger, warm and rough, on my cheek, and I knew that this was no dream. Then he put his big fur cloak over us. I slept again and, waking later, saw he was sitting close, shivering, but leaning on his spear and keeping guard over me and my brother Archibald as if we were precious things.

Father's recovery was short-lived, for by the morning he had taken a fever, and so had Eldred, whose own wound was deep. They were both racked with violent shuddering and their wounds were inflamed and swollen. My brothers knew that we could only wait and pray. It was summer and those few days were hot. Archibald and I were set to tend Father and Eldred with cloths wetted in the stream and placed on their faces and on their wounds to cool them. Hereward and Alvar remained with us, while Hestan, Godwine and Farin went to hunt, for we were now greatly in need of food.

Hereward took an axe and, with Alvar's help, set about felling a number of young straight trees.

"We must make a shelter for Father and Eldred," he said. "They need time to recover."

Archibald helped to collect boughs in full leaf for roofing, whilst Alvar split narrow branches into strips with which to fasten logs together for the walls of the shelter. Hereward and Alvar were not much alike in character, but they were both highly skilled with knife and plane. Hereward had built much of the fine furniture in our house. As for Alvar, he liked to work with a small knife, and had fashioned ornaments and other things for our family.

Alvar was the only one of my brothers that I feared. I would never be alone with him if I could avoid it. I had seen him, white of face, watching me and others with a silent intensity that puzzled and disturbed me. His great talent with the whittling-knife was well appreciated by the family, and he had made beautiful toys for me, notably a marvelous horse with legs that moved. Yet I never felt worthy of these gifts from Alvar. I never played with them much, for he watched them with possessive force, even after he had made a gift of them to me. I feared to damage those gifts.

Watching him working now with his knife, I remembered that all the clever things Alvar had made were now destroyed in the ruin of our home, and I felt both guilt and pity for him, but did not know why. He suddenly raised his eyes to me and I turned quickly to my task of bathing Eldred's hot face. Father was sleeping and Eldred also lay with his eyes closed and his face red and swollen, breathing heavily. I felt very weary also and, after laying another wet cloth over Eldred's brow, I curled up on the soft grass beside him and was led into strange dreams by the rasp and bubble of my brother's breathing.

At last my sleep became serene and I dreamed that I lay in a peaceful glade where a unicorn stood in a shaft of sunlight. Overcome by happiness, I got to my feet to approach the creature, but before I could reach it I was awoken by someone lifting me - none too gently - from my place next to Eldred. I began to wail immediately, grieving for the unreal dream happiness that was gone from me. And I found that everyone around me was also weeping. The hunt was returned, my Father had awoken with the fever abated, but my good brother Eldred was dead.

They buried Eldred on the grassy slope not far from the shelter that Hereward and Alvar had made. Although Father was still weak from the fever, he was resolute that he would dig the grave himself. Wild eyed and half dressed, he wielded the wooden shovel that Hereward made, slicing through turf and soil until I saw new blood spurting out of the wound on his arm which Eldred himself had sewn up.

"I left one son dead on the battlefield," he cried, his hand on the shovel slippery from his own blood which was running in crimson rivulets down his arm, "I will see this son buried with my own hands!" Turning towards Eldred's motionless body, Father's eyes stared wide and he gave a terrible howl. Then he set his shovel to the ground again with frenzied energy, hair and blood and spittle flying, as if assaulting the body of a hated enemy.

Very soon, however, weakness overcame him, the shovel fell from his hands and he collapsed onto the heap of soil that was to cover my brother's body. He was carried back to the shelter, where he went into a wild semi-sleep, bellowing our mother's name "Hylda!" time after time, in a fearful tone that brought into my soul a blackness so impenetrably deep that I could not honour my dead brother with the tears he deserved.

Over the hours that then passed, it seemed that I stood in a dim place that none of my loved ones could touch. I knew very clearly that my father would die and then, very likely, all the rest of my family. And I knew it was my fault, because of the witch-blood in me. I could neither eat, nor drink, nor even think. When my brothers spoke to me their lips seemed to move with no sound – or with sound that I no longer understood. I wanted Archibald, but found it impossible to ask or to reach out for him. When they lifted me up, my body was stiff. I could not know myself and I could not know them, for they were of the dead, and so was I. When they carried me into the shelter where my father lay, I was ready to see his dead body there, shortly to follow my brother into the ground. But Father was not dead, nor even asleep. He held out his arms to me and in my stillness I was given to him. In his red and haunted eyes I knew my own soul and, I believe, he knew his own in mine.

What true story can be told from the memory of a child of three winters? How can I recall the reality of those days? It is a matter of family history that my father was subdued into proper rest and recovery by the distress of his little daughter. All feared that if Father be lost, then I could not long survive.

"It was all too much for a little one to bear," Hereward used to say when recalling that time, and I would listen, glad to be the centre of the story and the cause of my father's recovery. But I felt, really, it was a tale of other people and other times, and I did not know which images and memories in my head belonged to the truth and which to story. Even my dream of the unicorn - against all your reasoning - still seems as true as reality in my memory.

7

Travelling

We remained by the shelter near the edge of the wood for another three moon cycles. At first I was laid on a little cot next to Father and we both slept, day and night, until my exhaustion and his wounds were healed. Whenever I awoke, Archibald was close, tending me with water or a little food and stroking my brow until I slept again. Later, I felt well and would roam around our camp, being watched over by all my brothers and "passed around like a talisman" as Father said. Father himself took longer to recover, but his vigour eventually returned and he began to ride and exercise his wounded arm until he was as strong, or even stronger, than before.

In my fear for Father's life I had become less afraid of his temper. Certainly, he seemed a different father from the one I had known. Whether it was the terrible mode of my mother's death and the loss of his sons that changed him, I do not know.

I saw him angry many times in the years to come, and sometimes hurtful and critical to my brothers or me, but my father never again struck any of us from the day my mother died.

Eventually, Father deemed it time to move on and, making a last farewell at the mound of turf that covered my dead brother, we left the camp by the stream that had become a little home to me. I believe we were travelling for some time, but I knew not the counting of days, and even one fort'night is a long time to a little child. Travelling, eating at a camp fire and sleeping under the sky became a natural state of being to me.

Once - when the air was fresh and bright with a sharp cold smell - we saw the Sea.

We had been riding since first light that morning and the sun was well risen when we came to a grassy cliff-top to look down upon a mighty bight of water – as wide and busy as a cloudy sky on a breezy day. It seemed marvellous and fearful to me, but all my brothers looked flushed and happy, as when they had been racing, so I put fear away from me and simply marveled. Father gazed out at the shape of the land, which curved around to the West before us, like the edge of a bowl enclosing the Sea. "It is as I thought," he said.

Hereward trotted his horse up to Father. "Is this a good place to stay?" he said.

"No."

"Why Father? We could become fishermen." Hereward laughed – and I saw him for the first time as a man – as tall if not as broad as Father. They laughed together, face-to-face, and it was the first carefree sound I had heard for many a day. Then happiness leapt up in my heart so suddenly that I could not contain it in stillness. I slipped from the horse and began to run and dance on the grassy cliff-top, spinning with my arms wide. Spinning, the Sea flashed past me, then my father's face laughing, then the Sea again, then Father, and at last the sky, for I had fallen flat on my back. All laughing now – with me or at me, I did not care - Father, my brothers, the sea-gulls, the splendid Sea itself and me – back to back with the grassy cliff-top. Hereward dismounted and picked me up, lifting me towards the Sea, and I held out my arms to the mighty power and freshness of the Great Water.

Archibald had ridden off with Farin to find the beach, so I stayed close to Father while he spoke with my older brothers about our journey and the reason why he wanted to travel directly south, keeping the Welshlands to our right shoulders and not crossing its borders.

~ ~ ~ ~ ~

On the sea shore, the boy and his brother see three fishermen, struggling to pull their boat with its heavy catch out of the turbulent surf onto the beach. He slides from his mount and runs to help pull the rope. After a moment's hesitation, Farin does the same. With this new pulling-power, the boat begins to rumble up the steeply sloping bank of pebbles. The fishermen are jubilant that this massive catch is safely landed, and are easily charmed by Archibald's guiless friendliness. They make a gift of three large fish to the brothers, who ride off waving farewell and calling good wishes.

It becomes a legend in that small fishing community – the unusually large catch out of season, the strangers who effortlessly heave the overloaded boat from the surf, and the boy whose smile fills the exhausted fishermen with new life. As the new Christian religion gains strength in this windswept outreach of Britain, the people there like to believe that they have been blessed by a visit from the One who chose fishermen as his most favoured companions. It was a harmless notion, and besides, there was none to tell them otherwise.

~ ~ ~ ~ ~

The cliff top might not have been the most suitable place to set up our camp, but I think even Father could not bear to leave the sight of the Sea. When Archibald and Farin returned with three wonderful sea-fish for our supper, we found a sheltered place behind a rock, made a fire and struck camp.

As the night came down, Father bade us keep the fire low, for we were in sight of the Welshlands which were inhabited by fierce and doughty warriors. "It is best we keep as quiet and invisible as may be," he said.

"Did you not travel to the Welshlands yourself once?" asked Hestan.

"Yes boy, when you were a babe. I went with the Lord Ulef to buy spears and arrowheads from the great Welsh armourers, and there had my own sword made." All eyes turned to Father's sword - a heavy, plain instrument which seemed to me at that time the mightiest and finest in the land. Father took up the sword and half drew it from its leather-covered scabbard. The blade gleamed in the sparse firelight. He always kept it clean and true.

"On that journey," he said, "We had runes of passage from the armourers, and from my Lord's kinsmen in that land. That generally gave us safety through the settlements and allowed us to travel the roads. But there were some natives in the land who had no love for the armourers and none for any travellers. We had to fight for our lives more than once."

My eyes were wide with wonder as Father began to tell of the battles he fought alongside the Lord Ulef, but I was weary and my eyelids soon drooped. When I opened them again, it was day and we were riding again, my blanket tied around Archibald's waist so that I might not fall. I scrambled up to kneel on the horse's rocking back and peered back over Archibald's shoulder, but the Sea was far behind.

8

Beornwine

We had been travelling on for several more days when we came to a settlement on a hillside with a river at its foot. It was a fair-sized place with many houses, barns and huts, around which a low wall had been built, surmounted by a wooden fence. On the outer wall was a hostelry – a building set up for travellers, with space for stabling.

As we approached, a little, scrawny man came out from the hostelry gate with two barking dogs at his feet. "What is your business here, sir?" he called to Father, flashing fearful eyes at this great man with his following of grown sons and boys (I was probably not seen, sitting behind Archibald with my arms around his waist and my eyes peeping from behind his back).

Father dismounted and walked, open-handed, towards the little man, stopping a fair distance from him so as to show no aggression. "I am Finric Fly sir," he said, "I travel with my sons, and we seek a place to rest – perhaps to stay - if we might be of use."

Father had hunted a good-sized hind that morning and he offered it to the keeper, whose expression changed from suspicion to approval. He spoke to the dogs who immediately ceased barking and began wagging their tails, jumping up to be petted. "Come within, sir," he said, "And all your sons. You are well-come. Come and take food here, and rest. I have room for all, and space for your horses. Well-come to all of you."

After tethering our horses where they could drink from a water-trough, he brought us all inside. There we were fed with bread and meat, milk and ale, while I made friends with the dogs and the man spoke with Father in a friendly manner. He told him that the settlement was known as Beornwine after the river and a great King who lived there many years before.

The hostelry-keeper's name was Siric, and his house was full large and long, with screened sleeping-quarters at one end and a loft above. There were plenty of benches, two large tables and a big central fire-place. Soon the room filled up with people - men and women come to see the strangers - and there was much adult talk.

I was warm and full of meat and bread, my head nodding on the table, when the door opened and a fresh breeze revived me. A man was standing in the doorway, his voice shrill and fearful and I thought he had been running, for his face was red and his breath came fast. Although his accent was rough, I clearly understood the words "Raiders. Thieves. Danger!" All the men in the room leapt to action (to fetch swords, spears and axes, as I soon knew, and to gather in the courtyard). Siric then looked at my Father and, reaching out a hand, grasped his sword-arm.

"Will you and your sons help us?" he said.

"We are at the service of Beornwine," said Father, bowing slightly, and a light came into his eyes that I had not seen for many days. He had his sword and my brothers their bows, spears and hunting knives. The little keeper took up a long spear and a mattock and, no doubt feeling the power of my family of doughty newcomers at his back, strode from the room followed by Father and my brothers.

Now, my brother Archibald was only a boy of nine winters, but had the heart of a noble thegn. He turned to me, putting a hand on each of my shoulders, "Stay here Edith," he said, "I'm to join the men."

"Don't leave me," I cried, and took his sleeve, holding it with all my three-year-old strength. I felt greatly fearful of being alone in this strange place after weeks of travelling, when Archibald had hardly been out of my sight.

"I must go," he said, and pulled his arm away. Yet my grasp was so strong that a scrap of woven wool was torn from his sleeve as he pulled it from me. He ran to the door, with me close behind, and I saw him leap onto Swift's back and make away after the others. I began to run after him, my legs pounding as fast as my will could make them go. I think I believed with my child reckoning that I could catch up with him, but as the distance between us quickly widened, I began to stumble and to weep with frustration. At last I stood there in the dust of his passage, wailing in rage, with the innkeeper's dogs accompanying me in a chorus of mournful howling.

Suddenly my watery view of the road changed. Someone had picked me up from behind and, speaking to me in kindly accents, was carrying me back to the inn. I fought for my liberty, but my strength was used up mostly by my weeping. In a gloom of humiliation, I gave in to my grief and found myself in soft arms, with a gentle hand wiping the tears from my face. It seemed expedient to stop for long enough to learn the mettle of my captor, so I ceased wailing and stared at the face of this oppressor.

It was a woman with her hair pulled loose from its cloth wrapping by my earlier efforts to be free of her grasp. She had a sweet face and her hair was a dark tumble over her shoulders, so that she put me in mind of my mother. This brought on more tears, as I was overcome by the remembrance of what Mother had been to me and my terror when I last set eyes on her. And now I wept in earnest, passionate sobs and allowed myself to be embraced and rocked like a baby.

The woman's name was Elanor Burhelm, and it came to pass that she would have the care of me through all the rest of my childhood and growing years. And Elanor became as dear to me, I believe, as ever my own mother could have been.

9

A New Home

When the men came back that evening, Father was at their head, riding on Thunderer. When they were heard returning, Elanor took me by the hand and we climbed on to the low earth wall near the inn. The Chief of Beornwine, a white-bearded old man named Wulfred who wore a purple robe, led the way and everyone gathered to greet the men returning. Elanor held me up and I counted my family back by name, every one – Archibald, Father, Hereward, HestanandGodwine, Alvar and Farin. It was with great relief that I saw they were all safe and whole. Some of the Beornwine men rode on horses, like my family, although most were on foot. None was badly wounded, but the raiders had been routed, and some of them killed. It was a fine victory. My brothers had given a good account of themselves and were much lauded by the local men, especially HestanandGodwine, who had fought fiercely side by side, as if they had been of one mind and no doubt making a fine sight together with their yellow hair and blue eyes.

That evening the hostelry was packed full of people – house and yard – all come to celebrate the victory. The old Chief Wulfred was given prime place next to the fire, and he asked to speak with my father to thank him. I saw the two of them talking, grave-faced, and guessed that the old man was learning the reason for Father's departure from his home country. Then my brothers were called before him in line and he clasped sword-hands with each of them, even Archibald, and gave them smiles and affable words. I, of course, was not far behind Archibald, and when the old Chief saw me, he took me onto his lap, and asked me my name.

"I am Edith Fly," I said, with certain pride, anxious that he should know I belonged to my father's family.

"And where were you while the Flys were fighting for my village?" he said.

"I had no horse of my own," I said, shame-faced, "I could not go."

49

My answer seemed to give him much pleasure, for he smiled broadly and then said seriously, "I thank you for your willingness to support us, little one, but I am glad you stayed to guard our good lady Elanor Burhelm."

Everyone was smiling, and, although I suspected he was making gentle fun of me, I did not mind. He kept me on his knee and fed me honey sweets and cordial while introducing me to all the people who were there. I was tired and my head ringing with all the sights and sounds of this new place, so I remembered few of the faces and names told to me that evening, only Gytha and Aldyth, the two daughters of Siric, the hostelry keeper. These girls, who were near to my own age, looked upon me in a curious but not unfriendly manner, especially Aldyth, who had a sunny smile and hair as red and glossy as a hazelnut. I should have liked to go and play with them, but I was enthroned on the purple-robed lap of Chief Wulfred; I knew the honour accorded to me, and I stayed.

The Chief then called my father to sit beside him, "My friend," he said, grasping Father's shield-arm, "I hope you and your family will stay among my people, for such gifted sword and bowmen are well-come to our village. The land here is fertile and makes good harvest. Much of it is in my power to gift. If you stay, I can grant you a good acreage on which to build and farm."

Father looked thoughtful, "I thank thee, sir. It is a fine offer."

"Stay with us, at least a little while. Rest yourselves and gather strength here at the house of Master Siric. Tomorrow I shall ride with you to the seat of my eldest son, the Lord Wulfirth. Beornwine and all of the lands in this part of Wessex are under his rule, by gift of the King." The old Chief smiled and spoke low into Father's ear, "For my son found favour at court, married well and is a King's thegn."

Father nodded respectfully, "Then I deduce the Lord Wulfirth is himself a renowned warrior, as I hear you were in your youth."

"Indeed, he is a son to be proud of."

All my family were made well of that evening. Archibald, who from horseback had sent a true arrow into the shoulder of a thieving raider, was much praised. Even I was paid tribute by being called the 'girl-warrior' because I had wanted to follow my brothers into battle. I was well pleased, even though they laughed.

It happened that Elanor Burhelm, who had been so kind to me, was sister to Siric the keeper, and a kinswoman by marriage of the Chief Wulfred. She was a young widow with her own house and land, but stayed that evening at the hostelry, where all the village – man and woman – came to celebrate victory. I was present when Father thanked

Elanor formally for taking care of his daughter, and there was sober respect in his manner to her, which made me glad. He raised her hand to his lips and I saw a blush come to the lady's cheeks.

The Chief Wulfred eventually left the gathering in favour of his own bed, and I settled down on the cushioned seat he had vacated by the fireside. Raising a last drowsy glance to my father before succumbing to sleep, I saw that his face no longer bore the haunted marks of pain and horror. He seemed a man in full strength and vigour, among good people. Archibald came and curled up beside me, as sleepy as myself. I was therefore wholly content and I slept, untroubled by any dreams.

A story often told with high satisfaction in Beornwine was that of Chief Wulfred's son, the Lord Wulfirth, and his wife Cwena, who was of a high family favoured by the King of Wessex. Theirs was a love match, which brought power and wealth to Wulfirth. He, of course, favoured his father's people, who benefited from his protection, and he and his Lady and their children were always much lauded when they came to Beornwine.

Wulfirth had been sent by his father, Chief Wulfred, to join the army of the King of Wessex in the Mercian wars. He fought valiantly and to great honour, and had been summoned for presentation to the King. There at the royal court Wulfirth met the lady Cwena, fell in love and boldly petitioned the King to grant that they might marry. The King challenged Wulfirth to wrestle with the Court's strongest man, in order to win Cwena's hand. The story goes that Wulfirth won the fight through the magic of the Goddess Freya, who took pity on the young man, for, though strong and brave, he could have been no match for the Court champion, and yet he had the man on his back in minutes.

It is a fine story, but my guess is that the King was testing the young man's courage and love, and bade his servant deliberately lose the fight. However it happened, Wulfirth came to find favour with the King, married well and was granted extensive lands in the region of Ufer, including Beornwine at its borders.

True to his word, the morning after our family arrived at Beornwine Chief Wulfred rode with my father to the Lord Wulfirth's Hall at Ufer Hill, which is half a morning's ride away, if the ground be dry. There, with due ceremony, Wulfred commended Finric Fly to his son. Such a meeting was vital because any band of armed men, even such as our family, could be thought of as likely hostile in a new country, and needed to have its allegiance established.

For his part, the Lord Wulfirth, on hearing of the events of the previous day, thanked Father for his help.

"Although you come from the land of our old enemies in Mercia," he said, "The recent evil done to your family there would show you to be in need of a new home and new people. I join my father in declaring you well-come to our country."

He got down from his high seat from which he had conducted that morning's business and stood at the same level as Father, clasping his sword-hand. "In truth, sir," he said, "Beornwine is short of experienced warriors. Except for the sort of skirmish that occurred yesterday, the land is peaceful at present. But strong and doughty men are needed to keep it so. I am occupied fully with matters here, and too far from Beornwine to be summoned to arms in much less than a day, If you have had your fill of travelling and wish for a new home for your family, there will be land at Beornwine for you, as my father has promised."

Father bowed low to the Lord Wulfirth, who then had food and drink brought to the hall, and introduced him to his wife, the beautiful Lady Cwena. Then they talked informally of fighting and hunting, which, as it turned out, were the favourite occupations of Lord Wulfirth, so he had much in common with my father. Without delay, a hunt was arranged, and Father returned to Beornwine that evening with a fine stag for Siric's hostelry and a new and powerful friendship made for our family.

10

Elanor

Father was married to Elanor within the month. Years later she told me it was on that first evening - when all the village was celebrating victory over the raiders and paying tribute to the help afforded by my family - that she had fallen in love with my father. I believe it was the same for him.

Elanor was a widow whose first husband had been killed in the wars. I sometimes heard other women call her 'the barren one' and it is true that she (who was surely made by God to be a mother) never had any children of her own. I think she grew stronger and happier in our family, and we all loved her. When they married, the Lords Wulfred and Wulfirth made Father a freeman of all the lands of Ufer and Beornwine, with license to hunt in any of the forest lands there.

Elanor's house was some distance beyond the walls of Beornwine, not unlike our first home in shape, but larger with high walls. It was strongly built with stones at the base, for stone was plentiful in that area. There was a long hall-room below and an airy loft above, well under the roof, for sleeping and keeping stores. Elanor's first husband had built it and Father and my brothers soon added wooden out-buildings and turned much of the land nearby to farm.

The long hall was the living room of the house, where my step-mother kept her hearth, baking oven and roasting spit. It was here our family would gather all together for meals, along with our bondsmen and women. These were hired by barter from Chief Wulfred to help on our land or household, for my father was a free man and soon became prosperous. The bondsfolk had their sleeping quarters in the outbuildings, but the family all slept together in the loft above the house. Father and my step-mother had a room of their own up there, divided from the rest by a wooden wall and door. Between that and where my brothers slept, I had a little partitioned area with my bed and a small wooden chest for my clothes and treasures.

I remember the day we moved in, before any of the alterations were made. I was running in and out of the house in excitement, examining every corner, chasing fowl and playing with one of Elanor's dogs, Spin, (a friendly yellow-and-black creature, fond of chasing his tail). I climbed the ladder-stair and ran back and forth along the length of the big loft, delighting in the sound of my feet on the wooden boards, and getting in the way of my brothers, who were making screens and building pallets for their beds. Spin was a gangling, almost-grown pup at that time and - scampering after me - he became excited and started to chase his tail with great determination. Twirling too close to the ladder-hole, he suddenly tumbled down with a yelp. Everybody laughed, but I hurried down to comfort him, sorry that the poor creature should be mocked for his antics. Shaken from the fall, Spin crept into my arms, but, with nothing much injured except his pride, he was soon running about again. However, the incident cemented our friendship, and Spin hardly ever left my side from then onward.

Because of all the activity and excitement, it escaped my attention that Father had not yet entered the house. Soon, however, I noticed him in the home yard working awkwardly with some wood and carpentry tools. With Spin beside me, I sat down to watch him. He had split a short length of thick log into a wide plank, and was fixing legs to it, one in each corner. My brother Hereward, our best carpenter, was nearby and I wondered why he did not help or advise Father, whose skill with wood-working was no more than common. But Hereward had some of the wisdom of our mother, and he let Father be, only glancing from time to time at the work as it progressed, and keeping the rest of us away, for Father's visage was determined and fiery.

When Elanor came out of the house with a pitcher of apple juice and walked straight up to Father, I feared for her. Yet he set down his tools, took the pitcher from her, looking into her eyes without a word, and they kissed like lovers. All my brothers looked away, with glances that were a strange mix of pleasure and pain and anger. I knew they missed our mother, but the space she had held in my life had become dark and I was only grateful and relieved that Elanor was filling that space now, too quickly perhaps, but with light. So I did not look away but watched as Father thus honoured his new wife. When he had finished with the apple juice and resumed his work, Elanor took up the pitcher and brought it to every one of my brothers and finally to me. Each of us took it from her and drank, and I believe her sweet smile and kindness warmed the soul of every one of us.

Father carried the rough table into the house and then Elanor followed him inside with a bunch of herbs and a basin of water drawn fresh from the well. I know now that Father had spoken previously to Elanor of Mother's hand-washing rituals, but at the time it seemed to me both natural and wonderful to see what was taking place. Father beckoned to us all and we followed him into the house. The new board-table was put next to the wall, near the door, and Elanor placed the bowl of water onto the table. Then she spoke a Christian incantation over the bowl and sprinkled the herbs into it. One by one, we all washed our hands, and then gathered to eat for the first time together there.

Thus, through the hand-washing ritual that she had established years before, my mother's spirit entered into our new home, and Elanor into our hearts.

To Hereward's great satisfaction, Father agreed that he could have care of the land. Usually, Hereward had Alvar to work with him, and my other brothers too, if they were not hunting with Father. To my disappointment, soon after we settled there, Archibald began to join the hunt. I missed him, but he loved to ride and, although he was young, his ambition to quest was as strong as Farin's and the twins'.

Hereward was a fine farmer and, over the years, we prospered as a family, insomuch as we grew wheat, oats, apples, pears, leeks, turnip, beets and other crops enough to feed ourselves and our animals. We also had our own large fish pond. Indeed, there was food to spare, and always meat at our table, not only from Father's own hunts, but also by the gift of our neighbours, who were grateful for the protection afforded by the fierce fighting skills of Father and my brothers, which helped to keep away enemies. It all made for a peaceful settlement in that pleasant vale between forest and river at the heart of the kingdom of Wessex.

As time passed, I found myself secure and content in my new home. Yet I did not forget the reasons for our coming to that place. Nor shall I ever forget, and although a small child might not be expected to understand all that befell her in that violent time, I was left with three very clear effects: First, the knowledge that my brother Archibald was my saviour, second, my sleep plagued by nightmares featuring a black standard with a white sun which flapped terrifyingly over my head; third, an irrational fear of one simple word so that hearing it could make me shake with dread and run to a hiding place or my step-mother's skirts. That one word was 'witch'.

My step-mother Elanor was as kind to me as my own mother had been. But even as I was small, I knew the difference between them, for Elanor's ruling star was duty, where Mother's had been freedom, and Elanor would look troubled at my wild antics, where Mother had laughed. But I loved Elanor, and tried not to vex her. I believe I was a good child, as far as my nature allowed, and she loved me, steadied Father with her gentle ways, and was mother to us all. She was a fine needle-woman and she made an embroidered cloth for my bed, with shapes of animals all fashioned in coloured wool. Among them was a unicorn - an animal I had heard of in hearth-stories as well as seeing them in the best of dreams. I was glad it was there on my bed-cover, for this proved to me that such creatures really do exist, Elanor being a woman of simplicity and truth.

Elanor also made for me a fine doll of close-woven cloth stuffed with straw, dried herbs and wool. Her eyes were cornflower blue and her lips red, and I named her Bertha. Unfortunately, my dog Spin was not a great friend of Bertha; he had been known to attack her with his fangs and was even once caught in the act of burying her in the ground. However, I was fond of her and she was my close companion for years, sharing my activities which included tree-climbing, fishing and other rough adventures. Often she became broken or torn, which caused me much grief and anger with myself for clumsiness and lack of care. It was then that Elanor began to teach me needlecraft, so that I could mend Bertha myself, and also embellish her face with a healthy flush of pink wool, or knotted pock-marks, depending on her state of health, which was most variable.

Because of Bertha's injuries and ailments, I became a needlewoman without noticing, for my step-mother was a fine teacher, which was to my great benefit in years to come. It was at Elanor's side that I learned cookery also, for eating was one of my chief pleasures. She allowed me to make the honey cakes I loved, and dumplings for the family dinner, which all admired and gave me praise. Now I understand my step-mother's wisdom in teaching me these tasks in such a way that I learned only with pleasure and willingness. It was much later that she taught me another skill of far greater import for my future life, and so I came to owe Elanor a debt beyond repayment.

11

Ice

The country was peaceful enough in those days and we did not even keep a guard on our homeyard. The dogs told us quickly enough if strangers approached, and there were plenty of strong men in our household – family and bondsmen. Any likely aggressors would keep clear of us.

A good number of travellers did pass through our land – some looking for work, some trading goods. A roving merchant might be likely to appear in our homeyard perhaps every two moons or so. Some would arrive with heavy wains loaded with a single product, such as pigs of iron for the forge. Others brought carts full of various non-perishable produce: plain iron knives and other tools, heavy cones of sea-salt, fair quality pots and jars, ropes of various lengths and thicknesses, bolts of rough-weave linen and other articles of practical use. All of these caused much interest in our household, but none so much as the light-travelling peddlers with their bundles of beautiful or unusual goods.

One such peddler was Rob of Dale, who came on a dappled-grey pony, a harp slung over his back and a single sack behind his saddle. Trotting into our homeyard dressed in his many-coloured cloak like a visitor from fairyland, he would throw small favours (such as painted beads) into the air and all we children would run to catch them. He would alight from his horse and, before taking any refreshment, sing a song and play beautifully on his harp, making big eyes at the comely maids of our household. For their part, they would buy his ribbons and beaded cords by exchange for a few eggs, a pitcher of fresh milk: "… and their hearts," as Godwine would say with a smile.

Rob was always most respectful to Elanor, bowing low as he showed her some carved box, or ivory comb or length of fine linen. Although Elanor's cheeks brightened, she would meet his flashing eyes with her own cool and dignified glance, never smiling as she bought some trinket that pleased her.

Rob would usually stay overnight in our household, sleeping in the men's dorter, where the unmarried men of the household lived and slept.

However, I think it doubtful that he spent the whole night there. I remember one morning as all our household's children gathered to wave him off, Hereward and Godwine were watching close by.

"So," said Hereward in a low voice, "It's likely a new child will be born by the spring."

"'Tis usually the case," murmured Godwine.

I turned to look at them, wondering what their meaning could be. But Hereward and Godwine simply grinned broadly at each other and then went off laughing together. I was left wondering what this new magic could be that Rob of Dale had wrought.

It was the case that occasionally one of our unmarried women would come to be with child, but all little ones were welcomed in our household, especially by Elanor. I was only a child myself, and was amazed and delighted by any birth, whether it be a litter of pups or a new baby. However, for a while after that visit by Rob of Dale, I thought all children came from some magical elixir brought by a travelling peddler.

Whilst we usually welcomed peaceful visitors, offering them food and drink generously, there were times when there was little to spare for strangers, even in a prosperous household like ours. One such time was the second winter after Father and Elanor were married.

Winter had come early, laying snow and ice on the land. This was at first a fresh diversion for us children, as we played in the snow, making snow-maidens with crowns of holly, pelting each other with snowballs and sliding on the iced pond. We would run indoors if we became too cold, and warm ourselves, for there was always plenty of wood for the fire.

But as the cold continued for a full moon cycle, and then another, the adults began to look grave-faced. "The grain-store is half-gone," Elanor said to Father one morning as we sat at our breakfast. "Normally we would hardly have touched it by this time of year. But the late turnips and beets can barely be got out of the ground with axes – and then they are all half rotten. We have to eat bread instead. And now the sheep are coming in off the fields, looking for food. The snow and ice is too hard for them to find any grass."

Hereward looked up at Father, "Fodder for the cattle and horses is depleted too." he said, "We can't start feeding it to the sheep."

Father nodded, "We must keep just the ram and three or four good ewes," he said, "We'll pen them and feed them with a little grain. We may as well kill the rest while there's still meat on them. With this frost, it will keep well in the underground store."

"I'll see to it today," said Hereward, "Will you hunt?"

Surprisingly, Father shook his head. "Hunting is poor," he said. "I found two hinds, dead of starvation, in the forest yesterday. It is not worth using the horses if we are to come back with nothing."

Father, my elder brothers and a group of bondsmen kept themselves warm that day killing the sheep, taking off the skins and storing the meat. I went with Archibald and some children who came over from Beornwine to play on our frozen pond. We had made a fine slide and there was much laughter and enjoyment.

But after that day the snow and ice ceased to be pleasant, even to me - much as I loved sliding. Elanor ordered a limit on the amount of bread we ate. Meat had to be rationed after one night when wild boar got into the store and took away half of the sheep-meat before our men chased them off with burning torches.

Another moon passed. We began to long for a thaw. Prayers were made to the Christ and to the Gods of Spring, but none were answered. A bondswoman who had recently given birth died, and her baby too. After that, others became ill. More died, despite all Elanor's herbal ministrations. All of us were thin, all hungry. I spent much of my time sleeping.

A time came when spring would normally have been well advanced. Still ice and frozen snow lay hard on the land, until one morning when I awoke and birds were singing; there seemed a change in the air and that was the beginning of a slow thaw.

The thaw helped little with the food situation. Still it was too cold for anything to grow. Every morning the ground was frozen solid, and only thawed little by the end of the day. The pond remained iced over, but had lost its attractions, for now we were forbidden to play on it as the slow thaw made it unstable. The sky was dull; the cold lost its crispness and became damp and bone-chilling. Elanor reduced our rations even more.

It was into our miserable, freezing homeyard that a skinny youth in rags came one day, begging to work in exchange for food. I was standing there, wrapped in one of Elanor's cloaks, double-folded, with Bertha under my arm and Spin at my feet. I looked at the stranger curiously, while the yard-dogs set up a chorus of barking. Worik, one of Father's best bondsmen, came out. "Ye'll have to be off," he said, not unkindly, to the youth, "We've little enough for ourselves here, and there's no work needs doing. Ye could try at Beornwine, over the hill."

The stranger turned, shivering, and moved slowly away. Spin took it on himself to run after him, but did not bark, only sniffed at the boy's hand. For his part, the boy pulled gently at Spin's ear in a friendly way, and was not bitten for his efforts. As I watched him walk miserably away, I felt hollow, not only in my stomach but also in my heart. I was constantly ravenously hungry and - animal-like - would eat every morsel given to me without a thought. Yet I felt my family diminished by our inability to afford charity to others. There was a loss of pride, a loss of virtue; it made me angry.

After eating my meagre breakfast, I wondered down to the pond with Spin and Bertha. I had been expressly forbidden, on pain of a beating, to go out onto the ice. Nobody was about, and I always considered forbidden activities as a challenge. However, the strength of the warning – which had come from Father himself – held me back. After a while I had the happy thought that no-one had forbidden Bertha from going on to the ice. Now Bertha was a timid doll, often reluctant to share my adventures.

"Come along," I encouraged her now, reaching out to put her down on the frozen pond. "See! Is it not a fine thing to slide?"

I pushed her a little. The doll lay there, impassive.

"Go on Bertha!" I ordered, "Slide!"

I grabbed her and slid her across the edge of the iced pond, then ran to where she stopped against the nearby bank. Spin was there before me, barking (for Bertha was not his favourite companion) and I had to wrest her from him. This was a fine game! I sent her off again, this time with much more force, but she hit against a static willow root above the ice, changed direction and slid off towards the centre of the pond. This was most irritating to me. Spin was barking, but he was too cowardly to set foot on the ice.

Faced with the loss of my doll, I looked around me. There was no-one to be seen. The ice looked as hard and thick as ever. I took a tentative step. It was perfectly solid and supporting. In another few steps I was reaching down to where Bertha lay. Suddenly from behind me there was the sound of a great crack - like a lightening bolt. I turned to find the source of it, but a massive sheet of ice was towering over me. My footing disappeared and I plunged into the icy water.

This was sudden and violent cold that I had never experienced. It took the breath out of my body. I could hear Spin barking, but faintly as if he was a far distance away. I thought to cry out, but could not open my mouth. I heard the ice shattering, but the cold had taken away the feeling in my arms and legs; it began to enter my heart and stomach.

Then, wonderfully, the terrible chill began to convert to peaceful warmth at my very centre – at my very soul. I relaxed; I sank.

But my comfort was disturbed. Rough, slippery, wiry hands grabbed my hair and my tunic. The feeling of peacefulness left me and I was in pain and shivering – shivering violently. There were voices; Spin barking and licking my face; someone carrying me.

And then I was in the house, safe with Elanor, who was rubbing me dry with rough woollen cloths, wrapping me in a fleece, seating me beside the fire and feeding me with warm honeyed ale. My father rushed in and knelt in front of me, tears pouring down his face.

"It was Bertha," I mumbled, my voice hardly restored. "Bertha **would** go out onto the ice."

Father nodded, smiled through his tears and put his arms around me. It occurred to me that I might not get a beating after all.

As the pain of returning feeling began to subside in my limbs, I noticed another casualty being given almost equal attention as myself. On the other side of the fire, wrapped in fleeces as I was myself, sat the skinny youth. Soon I was told that he had been close by when I was at the pond. He saw me fall in, broke the ice near the bank, and plunged in to save me. When Father heard this he turned to the youth, saying, "You shall join my household, if you so wish, and share what food we have left to outlive the winter."

The youth's name was Heath, and my father's decision to take him into our household was a good one, for the boy became like one of his own sons. He grew to be strong, clever and gifted in hunting and agriculture. Over the years, he became a valued member of the household and a close friend to my eldest brother Hereward. As for me, Heath was like another trusted elder brother to me, and I loved him unconditionally from the very moment that I saw what lay beside me next to the fire that day. It was Bertha; Heath had saved her as well as me. She sat steaming by the fireside for a couple of days, and I made her a fine new dress to replace her shrunken tunic but, sad to say, my doll never quite recovered her former robust condition.

12

Alvar

As I grew, our household could be counted a happy one, despite its small troubles and conflicts. As to that, there was never very much serious fighting between my brothers, because of an understanding that bonded their hearts, one to another, and which kept them from the serious conflicts I saw in other families. That understanding lay in the need to avenge our mother's death, and was never forgotten though rarely spoken of, and this gave a blade-edge to their eagerness for quest.

The rule of law in that land required one man from every household to fight in the wars, if wanted, and from a large household like ours, two or more would have to go. As my father himself was a great warrior, and all my brothers but Hereward willing if not desperate to have experience of warfare, we would send three or four: Father with HestanandGodwine and our armed bondsman, Beron. Sometimes Father would also take Farin, who, although young, was a better rider and bowman than Alvar. They would join with the other men of the Lord Wulfirth's company to fight where they were needed. This gained my father the high esteem of Lord Wulfirth, who shared with him valuable prizes in times of victory, and we became more prosperous and more powerful.

    It rankled with Father that Hereward, his eldest son, had little desire to ride to arms, or even to hunt. This was as unfathomable to me as it was to Father. Even so, I knew Hereward to be industrious and gifted in all matters regarding the raising of food and maintenance of buildings. He was also very kind to me. I thought Father's frequent criticism of Hereward unfair, but he seemed to bear it mildly. Occasionally, Hereward did spend a day hunting with the others, but he always fretted about the state of the farm whilst he was away and would spend the evening touring our land, refusing to rest until he had looked over all the animals and growing crops, even though there were trusted bondsmen and women enough to care well for them in his absence.

Like Hereward, my brother Alvar would hunt with the others when required, but did not generally have much aptitude for it. Despite this, he escaped Father's censure. Alvar's greatest skill was in intricate woodwork and he would spend long hours alone at this work. Father praised him for the fine results of his labour, but did not somehow seem to talk to Alvar on the same level at which he addressed my other brothers. I would see Father's glance slide away from his face as of some strange sight that he could not understand. In truth, I think it was the same for everybody except Elanor, who was as sweet with Alvar as with any of us.

When Alvar looked at me, his eyes would linger watchfully for a fraction more than I found comfortable. It would seem to me that he was appraising some animal that had no ability or wish to communicate with him. It was only when he was working at his wood-carving that his face looked naturally and pleasantly absorbed. Then I could see that he was as handsome as any young man could be. But if a friend or brother stepped towards him with a smile of welcome, praise or invitation, his answering smile always seemed to come more than a heartbeat late, and did not extend to the eyes. This was, I think, the reason for him being more solitary than my other brothers. They did not fight with him, as they might with each other, but neither did they seek out his company. Certainly, for myself, I tried never to be alone with Alvar. I did not have any good reasoning for this, only that he had a way about him - even when he smiled and gave me presents – that left a prickling sensation on the back of my neck.

Yes, Alvar was very much alone, and I did pity him for it, although as to that, he did not really seem to mind. I pitied him, but I could not love him, and for this I felt guilty. These feelings of pity and guilt on my part resulted in me finding myself one day in a situation of danger from which I emerged with a new lesson learned.

One warm autumn day I was walking with Spin in the hazel copse a short distance from our house. Elanor had sent me there to look for fallen nuts which would signify they were ready to be harvested. I never minded tasks that involved something good to eat, and hazelnuts were one of my favourite foods. Therefore I was seeking diligently, as any fallen nuts I found would, of course, go into my mouth. Spin also was fond of them and entered into the search in a serious manner. However, a blackbird landed close enough by us to be considered prey to Spin, who set off on a vain chase as it flew away in a flurry of feathers. I took little notice, knowing he would be back soon. I had bent down to examine a fallen hazel cluster, which I found to be barren, when I heard a step close by.

My whole body leapt with shock as I looked up to see Alvar standing suddenly before me.

He smiled his strange, disturbing smile. "Did I surprise you Edith?" he said.

My instinct was to turn instantly and run back to the home yard, but I immediately felt guilty for this reaction. It seemed cruel to show Alvar that the sight of him induced such an impulse. I therefore stood up and smiled back as naturally as I could, although my heart was still beating hard. "I did not see you," I said.

"That is because I was behind this tree. I only stepped out as you came by."

"Were you looking for some wood to make things from?"

He ignored my question and continued looking down at me with that smile on his face that I did not like. I wished for Spin to come back to me. Alvar reached down and circled my arm with his hand, which he could do easily, for I was a child of six at that time and he my elder by ten years. He pulled me towards him and, continuing to hold me by the arm, pinched and prodded my limbs and body with his free hand, both through my tunic-dress and underneath it. Some of these attentions tickled and some hurt, but I did not like any of them. However, I affected to laugh, as if he meant it all in jest, and indeed, I cannot truly tell you whether that was the case or not, so strange was Alvar.

"My," he said, "You are a soft little thing, are you not Edith?" and prodded me again in the ribs. I squealed despite myself, and he did it again, laughing like a baby with a rattle. This time it hurt badly and I shrieked and tried to pull away, but his hand was around my arm in a tight grip. He pulled up my tunic, the better to see the effects of his operations – though I wriggled indignantly - and he had his finger between my legs when there was a low and threatening growl behind us. We both looked round, and Spin was behind us, his lips pulled back in an unfriendly snarl and his hackles ridging his back like a birch-twig brush. Suddenly, I was free, but I remained motionless. Spin was not a large dog and, although he could inflict a nasty wound with his teeth, he was no real match for a man, even one as young and lean as Alvar.

"But Spin," I said carefully, "'Tis only Alvar, you silly dog."

I looked up at Alvar. The smile was gone from his lips and he was watching Spin warily.

"It will be supper-time soon," I said, "Shall we go back now?"

Alvar nodded slowly, his eyes still on my dog.

I began to walk back to the house and he came with me. I chatted away as we walked, thinking that if I behaved normally, then everything would *be* normal. "Elanor sent me to look for hazelnuts," I told him, "But I only found barren clusters fallen. I think it is not yet time."

He nodded slowly again, "A few more of these warm days will see them ripe," he said.

His ordinary reply had me bubbling with relief, and I gabbled on about nothing that I can now remember. I dared not look at Spin, fearing to remind Alvar that he was in danger from the dog, because that might put me in danger from Alvar.

When we reached the home yard, Alvar left me without a word. I looked for Spin, who was close behind me, his hackles still up as he followed Alvar a little distance, then came back to me, wagging and licking and generally making a fuss of me. I went with him straight to the little partitioned cell in the loft where I kept my bed. I pulled up my tunic and saw the red and purple bruises already beginning to rise over my ribs and stomach and around my arm. Then I held Spin close to me for a little time, but I did not weep.

Because I was always running and climbing and tumbling, cuts and bruises and scabs were more often than not decorating my limbs and torso to some extent. Nobody questioned me about the bruise on my arm, and nobody saw the ones about my body, for I kept them covered until they had faded.

The question I ask myself now is this: Why did I not tell Elanor or Archibald or Hereward or one other of my kind brothers about my treatment at Alvar's hands? It is true that I pitied him. But it was also my belief that he knew I did not love him, and this was the cause of him tormenting me. I felt guilty about the incident, and believed that my manner with Alvar when I met him in the copse was the cause of his behaviour, and that his treatment of me was my own fault. The strange notions of children are mysterious.

Spin did not leave my side for many days, taking the view that I needed more protection than usual. When we came across Alvar in the house or home yard, Spin would put his head down and give a low snarl. But this was rare, for Alvar would move away if he saw us near: he sat far from me at table, and did not approach me alone again for a good span of moons.

I did learn an important lesson from the incident, which was never to let either guilt or pity blunt my instinct for danger. I became more wary afterwards and this no doubt saved my skin many times in the years to come.

13

Conflict

Although my father counted himself a Christian, his family was not of the educated class which studied writing and holy texts. One exception was Elanor herself. Elanor could read and write. When she was a girl she had been taught letters by a priest who lived in her father's house. When the man died, the two holy gospel books in his possession passed to her. Elanor kept them in the locked chest in the bedchamber she shared with my father, but I saw them often, for she would sometimes read to us from them. One bore writings in Anglish, which was much like our natural tongue; the second was written in the magical Roman language, used by all the holy men and women. The first had a plain wooden cover and contained many closely-written velum sheets that seemed to me to bear a procession of many-legged insects across its pages. The other was rather larger and had a cover of fine leather with silver fastenings. The title letter of its first page was written large and beautifully coloured in red and gold. Its lettering was rounded and, when I was allowed to look, I could discern some repeated patterning in its beautifully inscribed lines. However, I was not permitted to touch either of the books or come close to them, for fear of damaging the precious markings with my clumsy child-hands.

HestanandGodwine, who aspired to become full fighting thegns one day, begged Elanor to teach them to read.

"What do you want with letters?" said my father when he heard of it. "Reading and writing
makes not a blade strike true or an arrow fly straight. It is of no use to a fighting man!"

"But Father," said Godwine, pleasantly, "A learned man brings credit to his family."

"And is of much use to his lord in time of war," added Hestan. "If we are able to read, we can relate and follow written messages."

Although my father continued to deride the magic of letters (as he did most skills in which he had no proficiency himself), the thought of the twins bringing honour to the family (and thus, himself) through learning was an idea that obviously worked on his mind. A few days after the conversation with HestanandGodwine, he announced that Elanor might teach the twins to read and write. And so it was. They were hard-working scholars, for their dream was to become thegns of the first order. Soon both could write the Lord 's Prayer, and read haltingly from the gospel texts. Father still mocked, but only lightly, and I knew he was pleased, for I heard him bragging about his learned sons to Elanor's brother Siric. With this book-learning and their fine prowess with bow and spear, my brothers were well set to bring honour to the name of Fly.

One morning at the time of harvest, some three years since our arrival at Beornwine, Father was preparing to hunt - although we had fresh meat enough for a week, with smoked and salted joints beside. At breakfast he bade Alvar, Farin, Archibald and the twins to get ready their horses to join him. Hereward raised his head, "but Father, that leaves us short-handed for the harvesting."

"You've Heath and twenty bondsmen and women. We don't keep them to get fat on our food while we work the land ourselves." Father spoke with a sneer, as if such work were beneath him.

Hereward flushed, but his voice stayed calm and reasonable. "It's the Grain Rite next week. The wheat crops must be in and drying by then."

It was an important matter, I knew, for all to be ready in time for the priest's blessing at the Rite, so that God would send good harvest the following year. Father only glanced impatiently from Hereward's face to the open door, for the air was fresh and sweet and fine for a day's hunting.

"Work hard then," he said, and his voice bore a dangerous clarity that forbade any further argument. Down the long table there was a stir and a stilling of the usual cheerful breakfast chat and clatter.

Hereward did not heed the note of menace in Father's voice. "But Father," said Hereward. "You do not need so many for the hunt. I will be hard-pressed, even with all our bondsfolk. The weather might break tomorrow and I cannot have the harvest in by then. Leave me HestanandGodwine. Their strength will be worth six men."

Father shook his head impatiently. He hated to be opposed, particularly when he knew he was wrong, "You cannot have HestanandGodwine, because they ride and they hunt and they fight," he said, his voice rising, "HestanandGodwine are men and do not grub in the earth for grain like base creatures."

With a kind of thrilled horror, I watched Hereward's face change from red to white as his self-control fell away from him. He stood suddenly and thumped on the table with his fist so that my wooden beaker jumped and tottered in front of me. "Do you call your own son a base creature, who works hard for you and the family?"

Father's look made my soul quake, for it was the look of cruelty, and I hated it. He turned to Hereward and said, "My true sons are valiant fighters and huntsmen, not *serfs*, who plough the fields."

Hereward made a dive over the table, scattering food and dishes. He was slim but strong from hard work in the fields, and he had inherited a portion of Father's own temper. He aimed for the face, but his arm was arrested by Father's left hand, with the right drawn back for a blow. Then I saw Father hesitate; in a heart-beat I witnessed the conflict between his will and his impulse. He stayed his hand; he paused. And the rage shivered out of him, leaving him looking weary and old. He released Hereward's arm and let him crash onto the table, overturning more dishes and spilling food and milk onto the floor. Then, without a glance even for Elanor, Father turned and strode to the door.

As the door slammed shut, I dived to the floor, trying to rescue a platter of honeycakes which Hereward's body had overturned onto the floor. But Spin was there before me, wagging his tail happily and gobbling honeycakes at a fearful speed. I grabbed three or four cakes and, as I was under the table anyway, decided to stay there and eat them in peace, for the room was in uproar after Hereward's outburst. Peeping from under the table I could see the four of my brothers that Father had ordered to hunt gathering weapons and making ready to follow him as quickly as they could, whilst placating or chiding Hereward (according to their nature); bondsmen and women were adding their voices to the subject (most complaining because they would have to work longer and harder because of the hunt); Heath was trying to reason with Hereward who was still full of unspent fury against Father; Elanor was calling the women to help clear up the mess.

Spin and I thought it best to stay where we were and, full of cake myself, I helped him to find other morsels of bread or meat and a puddle of milk that had trickled under the table, for I never knew a dog like Spin for having a seemingly endless appetite.

14

Harvest

I spent that day in the fields with Hereward, Heath and most of the bondspeople. Even my step-mother Elanor attended the reaping, for every possible hand was needed to bring in the harvest. As Hereward mowed the wheat-hay with his great blade, I followed behind with a group of men and women, gathering sheaves of hay as large as myself. These we carried to Worik, the bondsman who led the work of setting up the hay in great stooks to dry and then thatching each stook to protect it from rain.

I knew our bondspeople well, and was happy to work with them, for all were loyal to our family and kind to me. Heath was, of course, a great friend and, like him, many of the others lived all year in our household. One such was Worik, the son of slaves, who was known for his gentleness and his mighty voice. It was said that Worik, full-voiced and standing in our home-yard, could be heard on the other side of the Beornwine settlement. Thus Worik, like Heath, was a much valued bondsman. Both had their own partitioned place in opposite corners of the unmarried men's dorter, which they were allowed to make comfortable and private, as they wished.

Other men and women were bonded for short periods – at times of harvest or planting, perhaps. Some came only for a day in time of need. Just such a time was this day, but although Hereward sent out for extra hands, few came, for it was harvest for everyone, and fine weather. All households were mindful of the coming Grain Rite and few had any able-bodied people to spare. I found the work difficult, for the early fresh warmth of the day had given way to a burning heat. In truth, I was not accustomed to hard work as I was the youngest of a prosperous family, and tended usually to be indulged.

In the heat of the day, Elanor bade me go with her and two other woman to the house and we fetched pitchers of milk, loaves, cheeses and cooked meats to bring into the fields, as the workers could not stop long enough to return to the house for their midday food. A barrel of water had been set up under the shade of two big oak trees to keep cool. Elanor bade Worik give the call, and all gathered there to eat. Only Hereward did not heed the call; he was mowing the furthest field at the edge of our land. I told Elanor I would go to fetch him, but took a pitcher of milk and a small loaf with me, thinking that, should he refuse to break his work, he could take refreshment standing as he was in the field.

As I came up behind Hereward, I watched him for a moment as he continued his regular movements with the sickle to the sweep and fall, sweep and fall of the long wheat grass. Keeping my distance, I called to him, for I felt it wise to stay well back from that circling sickle. He stopped and turned and looked glad to see me, or to see the victuals at least, for he smiled and ceased his mowing. My brother was working without his shirt, as this was a mighty hot day, and his face and shoulders were streaming with sweat. He drank the milk at a single draught and asked whether I had brought any water, for the leather bottle at his waist was empty.

"I will bring some now," I said, taking the bottle from him and beginning to go straight away, for it was no short walk back to the water barrel, and then I must return.

"You are a good girl Edith," said Hereward. His eyes moved from my face and I realised that he was looking at something or someone behind me. I turned and saw a figure approaching us across the unworked land next to ours. It was a young woman I recognised, although I did not know her well. She was of the Beornwine community, although her father's land was at the southerly point of the settlement, whereas ours was to the north. As she came closer, Hereward greeted her, "God's day to you Fritha Elfrith," he said.

"God's day to you Master Fly," she answered.

"Go Edith," he said to me, "Fetch the water as I asked." But the young woman he had called Fritha was taking a water bag from a sling around her shoulders and offering it to him.

"Please," she said with a smile that made her thin face beautiful, "Drink from this."

He drank deeply, and I think there was some spell or thirst-slaking herb in the water for when he lowered the bag his eyes were shining with a rare light and I thought what a handsome brother I had. I knew I should go to fetch more water, but was reluctant to leave, for I wished to know more of Fritha and to see if she might work any other spells. Besides, Hereward did not urge me to go again. Indeed, I believe I might have become invisible for a few minutes, for all the notice either of them took of me.

Hereward passed the water bag back to her. "Thank you most kindly," he said with a little bow, "I was greatly in need."

There were smiles between them and then Hereward asked her, "Is your family not harvesting this day?"

Fritha shook her head and looked troubled, "There is only myself and my father, for my mother is ailing. I have been today to the Chief Wulfred to seek help for we cannot gather our harvest in time for the Grain Rite. That is what brings me here now. Wulfred bade me come and ask the Master Finric Fly if anyone might be spared to help us."

Hereward ran his hand through his hair and looked distressed. "We're short-handed ourselves today."

Fritha nodded and I thought her shoulders drooped a little. "I shan't wait then. We shall do what we can. I must not waste any more time."

Hereward looked deeply disappointed, but she began to turn away. Then she seemed to notice me for the first time and gave me a little smile.

I found myself crying out, "Don't go yet. Hereward has emptied your water-bag. Let me take it and fill it for you while you rest here."

Now it was a surprise to me when I heard myself making such an offer, for it was a good long walk to where the water-barrel was under the oaks. But now I think it was love and pity for my brother Hereward that made me speak, and he glanced at me then with a look that returned my love a hundredfold and filled me with a cool and happy emotion I could not explain but which carried me to the water-barrel and back again, even with two heavy water-bags, without complaint.

Father and the others had made a good hunt, and we sat all at supper in the heat of that summer evening, the harvesters too weary for much talk, the huntsmen pleased with their day. But even Father was subdued, I thought, and no-one in any mood for family fights.

When we had eaten our meat and I was considering curling up on a fleece with Spin to save me the toil of climbing the loft-stair to my bed, Hereward spoke, "Father, do you know how much land the freeman Elfrith owns?"

"More than he uses," said Father, "He works a field or two, and he has a cow on the common meadow."

"His daughter came today, seeking a hand to help with the harvest. I told her we could not spare any today."

"With only two fields, three of them should manage," said Heath.

Elanor spoke up, "Herin Elfrith is disabled with an old battle injury. His shield arm is all but useless."

"How did it happen?" asked Farin, always eager for any tales of battle.

"It was in the great war, when all the able men of Beornwine met the call to arms against the Mercians. We lost many of our men."

There was silence around the table for a space, for our family was Mercian before the great journey following Mother's death, and we knew that Elanor's own young husband had been killed in that war. I counted up to fifty of my own heartbeats (Elanor had begun to teach me counting and I was learning quickly) before she spoke again.

"Herin was brought home half dead with a terrible septic wound to his arm. He was in fever and ill for months, but Chief Wulfred sent the Frankish slave Judith to nurse him and he recovered. Afterwards Herin married her, with Wulfred's blessing." Elanor's face changed as if with a sudden troubled remembrance. "I believe Judith has been unwell," she said. "I meant to visit her, but there has been so much to do here that I forgot."

"If Fritha's mother is ill, then that must be why they need help with the harvest," I said, "With Fritha's father having only one arm to work with."

"And everyone else busy with their own harvest," said Archibald, whilst Hereward gave me a grateful look that puzzled me until I hit on the notion that just to hear Fritha's name was a pleasure to him.

"I'm minded to go myself and help them tomorrow," he said to Father respectfully. "With the hunt over, we'll have five men more than today."

"No-one can be spared tomorrow," answered Father, "But if we have a good day with our own harvest, I'll send one of our men to help them the next morning."

"That is good of you Finric," said Elanor and they smiled at each other down the length of the table. But Hereward had a look of defiance on his face that made me fear a scene of angry words and spilled food such as had occurred that morning. I let my eyelids droop and pretended to fall from my seat with weariness. I might have bruised myself but lucky for me I fell on Spin, who yelped but was unhurt and licked my face. This made it difficult for me to feign sleep, because it tickled. Everyone laughed except for Archibald who was up from his seat in a moment, to make sure I was unhurt (for I was still Archibald's chief care, even though we were together less often because of the hunting). I looked up at him and he nodded as if he understood what I had tried to do.

"She's mightily weary," he said, helping me to my feet.

My step-mother kissed me and I was carried off to bed by my brother Hestan. I knew it was Hestan for he looked at me mournfully as he set me in my bed and said a prayer over me asking God that I might not be stricken by any ague in the night and die. Fortunately, we were followed up by Godwine who kissed me and said a prayer of thanks to God for his pretty sister. Archibald brought me a woodpecker feather that he had found in the forest. Then Hereward came to me and smiled as if we had a fair secret together, and he stroked the hair away from my forehead until sleep took me over, which was very quickly. Thus I slept happy in the knowledge that I had made a good day and was well loved. No child could want any greater blessing.

I slept soundly and was only woken in the early morning by Spin circling on my stomach, which was his way of letting people know that it was time to awaken and let him out of the house. In truth, Spin was not supposed to be a house dog, but to sleep in the home yard with the other dogs. Spin had his own opinion on the matter and hid whenever possible – often in my own little sleeping cell. I never objected to this, for I liked the company, and in the winter Spin's body kept me warm, for he did not trouble to sleep on the floor, but joined me on my bed.

If Spin had not been with me that morning, I would certainly not have risen so early, for it was hardly light and I was indeed mightily weary from the previous day's harvesting work – and knew there was more to come this day. Also it was hot, even at this early hour, which made me want to sleep the more. But I dragged myself yawning from my bed, pulled on my daydress of light wool and walked down the long loft-room to the stair, with Spin's feet scampering on the wooden boards beside me.

As I passed my sleeping brothers, I saw that Hereward was missing from his bed. When I had climbed downstairs and opened the door out to the home yard, I saw him there, already mounted on Lancer. Now, Lancer was not our strongest or steadiest horse, but was certainly the noblest looking with his black coat and long mane. Hereward had on his finest cloak of coloured woven wool, fastened with a large brooch which I knew to be Father's. At his side was his scythe, wrapped in sacking, and tied in front of him across Lancer's back was a hind that had been brought back from the hunt.

Hereward looked down sharply when he saw the door open, but, on seeing me, smiled with that conspiratorial expression I had seen on his face the night before when he bade me goodnight.

"Edith," he called softly, and gestured for me to come to him.

I approached and stroked Lancer's nose while looking up at Hereward.

73

"I'm going to Fritha," he said with such a look about his whole body that I thought he would fly, rather than ride, to the southern Beornwine where the Elfrith fields lay. Indeed, Lancer seemed to catch Hereward's mood, for he lifted his head and scraped a front hoof impatiently, so that Hereward had to hold the bridle tightly to restrain him. Now Hereward, - though my brother - was as a man to me, for he was over twenty-one winters and full grown in height at least. Even so, I knew as well as he which man was the Chief in our house, and I knew Father would be full angry when he knew that Hereward had not only defied his order but taken his gold brooch and his best hind from the hunt

I opened my mouth as I thought to warn my brother of his duty, but found myself saying in a hurried and demanding tone, "Take me with you! I wish to see Fritha also."

"Not today Edith, I cannot. I shall take you another day, I vow."

I was about to object because, now that the idea was in my mind, it was growing bigger apace but, before I could speak, I heard movements in the house behind me.

Hereward said again quickly, "Another day, sweet sister," loosened his hold on Lancer's bridle, and they were gone.

I heard someone's step at the door behind me but I could not look around for my eyes were on Hereward galloping away and seeming to me as fine-looking as any noble thegn on his steed. I could have wished that he was carrying a sword, rather than his farmer's scythe, and wearing armour with a crested helm, such as the thegns that Father had told me of, but none could look braver, nor - or so I thought - be questing for more trouble.

15

Storm

"So Hereward has gone." It was Archibald standing behind me.

"Only to Fritha," said I. "Only to help with the harvest and take food for her mother and father." But in my soul I knew that Archibald was right and although our brother might return to us that evening, the greater part of his heart was away with Fritha's family, never to return.

Archibald and I met each other's eyes and were both thinking that there was no way we could save Hereward from Father's wrath when he returned.

"They are all still asleep," Archibald murmured, "It's best for us that we have not seen this. Back to bed with you, and me too."

We crept softly back up to the loft and I lay down on my bed, knowing that there would be no more sleep for me that morning. Thus it was a great surprise to me that the next thing I knew was Elanor smiling down at me with her hand on my face, rousing me gently, for Father and the whole household were below at breakfast.

It was a relief to me that all seemed to understand Hereward had gone early out into the fields to begin his mowing, and Father only urged those of us whose work it was to gather and stack the crop to not tarry but follow after Hereward as soon as we could. Archibald, whose morning task it was to feed and care for the horses, did not of course mention that Lancer was not in the stable. Father chose to take over the mowing of the fields that Heath had begun the previous day, telling Heath to begin with a team of bondspeople on the middle-land, and work outward, eventually meeting up with Hereward as he worked in the direction of the house.

"The rest of you go where you will to help your brothers," he said to the hunters of the previous day.

Archibald jumped up and fetched the scythes for Father and Heath, then followed Heath as he walked ahead of his team, out to begin his day's mowing. I ran after them and was in time to see Heath stop and look down at Archibald. I knew Archibald was telling him about

Hereward's quest to the Elfrith land - against Father's order - and was aware of the trouble it would bring.

Heath walked over to HestanandGodwine who had found two old scythes in the barn and were sharpening them with a whetstone and oiling them as carefully as any sword, Hestan working in the shadow of the house, Godwine next to him in the sunshine, beyond the rim of the shadow. Nearby, Alvar was busying himself drowning an unwanted litter of puppies in a bucket of water, and he walked over to us, one struggling puppy dangling by the throat from his hand. Heath told them quickly about Hereward's absence and the need to mitigate Father's wrath by endeavouring to bring in the harvest as quickly as if Hereward had been there. Godwine was most interested in Fritha and questioned me closely as to her appearance, whereas Hestan seemed to relish hearing more than once of the brooch that Hereward had stolen, and the hind.

"Father will be wrathful!" he cried, "There will be bloodshed in the family, I'll warrant!"

Godwine nodded vaguely in his direction, but looked down at me with light in his eyes, "Oh Edith," he murmured, "To think that Hereward should be the first of us to ride away for the sake of a beautiful damsel in need!"

Alvar said "What'll he do to her, do y' think?"

We all stopped and turned to him. His eyes were sharp and his lips wet over teeth bared in something shaming a smile. I did not understand his words, but a creeping chill entered my stomach as I watched him. Nobody answered, but Godwine walked over to him with a look of disgust on his face and took the puppy out of his grasp. He passed the little creature to me and I ran with it to the hut where its mother was tied up, crying for her babies. I knew that most of the dogs' litters had to be killed so that we would not be overrun with them, but still I hated it. This little one would live, for Godwine had reprieved it. The mother dog greeted it with a high-pitched whimper of joy, and the pup was soon suckling happily.

There can be few secrets in a household such as ours and, between my brothers and our bondspeople, Hereward's quest was soon known to everyone. The one exception was Father. No-one would easily bear the burden of communicating to him the truth of his broken authority. Also, it is my belief that Father was already feeling a little chagrined after riding off to hunt the day before, leaving the important harvesting to only Hereward and Heath, and had decided to make recompense by working especially hard. Our family's position of respect in the community could not come only from hunting skill and reputation at arms. The ability to rule and provide for a large household is a mark of rank and status in itself. Father sometimes acted foolishly but he was no fool. Yesterday he had given full rein to his desire to ride and shoot – which was his nature. Today he would pay for it by taking off his shirt and working on the land from morn until dusk. This was also his nature.

I believe Father was neither curious nor suspicious that day. He might be accused of disloyalty for his day's unnecessary pleasure, but would never have doubted Hereward's loyalty. And Father did not join us for our midday meal under the oaks, but remained working in the field as Hereward had the previous day. Someone had to carry bread and water to him, and I was chosen. Even Elanor feared to approach him in the knowledge of that of which he was ignorant. As the youngest I was considered most obviously innocent. I did not hold such a view myself, knowing my own misdeeds and some of my faults, but also because of words that had been spoken in the darkness of my past, barely remembered. However, I was required to make the errand and make it I did, taking bread, meats, cheese and milk through the heat of the day to my father.

"You are a good girl, Edith!" he cried as I approached. He kissed me, nor did I fail to feel guilty at his pleasure and kindness to me for my reluctant mission.

By the end of the day, all but the norsfeld (a small stretch of our cultivated land on a north-facing slope) had been harvested. Father returned to the barrel-oaks and took a report from all the work teams. Although his face looked burnt and weary and riven with sweat from his day of toil, Father seemed greatly pleased.

"It is finished," he said, "We shall leave the norsfeld to the horses and the gods," (for my father, though a Christian, was not above the superstition of the old faith which required offerings out of the harvest to whichever gods held dominion over them). He began to lead the way back to the home-yard, with the household following behind and, although we were weary and the late day come down heavy and dull with heat, all were glad of the fine harvest got in. Being young, I found some energy from the thought that I could rest on the morrow and look forward now to a fine Grain Rite in a few days.

I ran up to my father, mindful of his good mood and kind words to me when I had taken his food to him at noon. I smiled up at him and marched along at a fast pace beside his slow strides, and he returned my smile and put his great hand on my shoulder. As the shorn stubble and meadow grass passed my eyes, I saw myself walking, heavy with armour and responsibility, at the shoulder of my Lord King, his favourite named Thegn of Honour. As I was choosing the style and decoration of my sword and the mettle of my steed, it was natural that the memory of my brother Hereward, riding out so nobly at the beginning of the day, should come to mind. I glanced with apprehension at my father and thought I saw a troubled puzzlement fall onto his features. I did not wait to find out if he was about to ask me whither my eldest brother might be, but fell back in a cowardly manner not worthy of any Thegn of Honour, to find my brother Archibald and take his hand, whence I felt stronger, as I always did in his company, and was able to resume my dreams of noble questing.

A great board was set up in the home yard that evening, all laid out with cold meats, cheeses, oat cakes and apples, and pitchers of mead and new ale. Torches were lit and all the household gathered round. There was a mood of merriment among the bondspeople and my brothers too, which was spiced, I thought, with excited expectation, for Father could not much longer fail to miss Hereward. This general eager expectation of filial conflict only served to increase my own gloomy apprehension, as from an early age I had hated any quarrelling in the family. I got up from my seat and sought out my brother Hestan, confident that he would carry a mood more closely resembling my own. I was disappointed even there, for he only raised a beaker of mead between us and said with some excitement in his eyes, "A fight tonight, Edith – and a split in the family, I'll warrant!" as if such things were to be welcomed.

My own gathering foreboding was of a pace with the blackening skies and ever increasing press of heat. There was no wind, and the sun had disappeared so that the evening seemed hours ahead of itself. As we began to gather to eat, a great drop of rain splashed on to the board in front of me. Just then, Father came to his place. He was looking round through the dusk, with a frown on his brow.

"Where is Hereward?" he said.

But people were lifting their heads to the sky. More heavy drops began to fall and Elanor gestured to a woman who was coming out of the house bearing a board with a haunch of cold roast venison upon it. "Go back," she cried, "Back inside everyone! Quickly, bring all the victuals." All helped to carry in the feast as the rain crashed down, and there was much laughter, and some shrieking as a silent lightening began to flicker in sheets upon the underside of the low clouds. Very soon all the food was inside and on our table, the torches were hung upon the wall-brackets, and Father and the men began to bring the benches into the house. Then, a long rumble of thunder stilled us all, and in that moment I remembered two of my loved-ones who were yet missing and likely out in the storm. One was my brother Hereward; the other my dog Spin. I could not help Hereward, but guessed where my pet might be.

Now, Spin was a doughty dog, brave in defence of the Fly family and household. He was a keen snapper at the heels or hooves of any stranger to our home-yard who had not been introduced to him, and courageous in stealing a meal at any opportunity, even against his master's orders. In all, Spin was a dog with a mind of his own, more easily persuaded than beaten into order, and I loved him. His one weakness (besides honeycakes, mutton, oatcakes, venison, cream, apple syllabub, butter and cheese) was extreme cowardice in the face of a thunderstorm. I had last seen him just as the rain started and the victuals were being brought inside. Someone had let fall an apple from a platter and Spin had scampered after it under the make-shift table in the homeyard.

My father was standing in the doorway, looking out at the storm and I came up to stand by him. Beyond his legs I could see the rain coming down and, beneath the table in the yard, a small, shivering figure with its tail tucked well under its body. I did not fear thunderstorms and I stepped past Father and out I went into the rain, crawled under the table and gathered Spin into my arms. He was not a large dog and I could carry him, so with him whimpering like a pup, I peeped out from under the table and was about to make haste through the rain back to the house when there was a mighty clap of thunder and a fork of blue lightening only a few paces from our shelter. This shocked even me and I felt Spin's fur all standing on end like a brush. Instead of the house doorway, I decided to make for a closer shelter and wait for the storm to move on. Clutching Spin, I stumbled across to the nearby hut where the other dogs lived. They were all huddled together against the back wall and I sat down just inside the entrance with Spin in my lap. He would not leave me, but whimpered a complaint that we were too close to the outside. But I was determined to see as much of the storm as I could, so he had to be content with trying to bury himself deep in my arms – as far as a medium-sized dog can do so in the arms of a child of six winters.

Thus, in the shelter of the dog-hut I was hidden from view but able to see everything that took place when my brother Hereward came home.

The torches in the house were bright and, through a torrent of rain and hail, I could see Father still standing in the house doorway. Then two great claps of thunder followed one after the other accompanied by more forked lightening, and I felt my own hair rise on my head and body, although I was not afraid. When I looked back again to the doorway, I could see Elanor beside Father. His stance was of surprise and anger and I guessed they were speaking of Hereward. Elanor had her hand on Father's arm and was speaking to him in a calm, earnest way, which was typical of her, and which could steady Father out of even his greatest tempers. But Father's hands were in fists and over the rain's tumult I heard him roar. He strode out of the doorway, for such rage always needs action.

At that moment there was another mighty crack above and a finger of blue fire shot down into the middle of the yard, straight through the table where we had been gathering to eat only a short while earlier, and under which Spin and I had been sheltering only moments before. The whole scene was illuminated with a nightmare light that lasted for several of my wild heartbeats and I could clearly see Father standing stone-still, his eyes staring ahead with such fixity that I followed his gaze. Opposite him across the home yard was a figure on horseback, ghostly in that devilish light between fire and water. The horse was Lancer, a dark cloth covering his eyes, and the rider was my brother Hereward, his hair and cloak heavy with water.

Father roared, "HEREWARD!" and then something else that I did not hear for the storm and the rain and the thundering in my own ears. Hereward slipped from Lancer's back; Father leapt forward; I saw Archibald run ahead of him and thought he would go to take Lancer into the stable.

But the light had changed; now it was flickering and fiery. Despite the rain, the table in the centre of the yard was afire with great and crackling flames; and my brother Archibald was throwing himself into the centre of the blaze.

Father and Hereward both started forward at the same moment. Father grabbed Archibald with his great fist and threw him clear of the fire but dived into it himself, with Hereward there ahead of him. My mouth was open in disbelief. As it seemed to me, my family in the mass had been driven to lunacy by the storm, and I alone had kept my reason.

16

Merry-Making

How glad I was that the sky chose that moment to empty upon us a deluge to tame even that fearful blaze, but Father and Hereward were flailing about in the smouldering ruin of the table, and Archibald only held back from joining them by Elanor who had run out and was kneeling in the yard holding him with all her strength.

Incredulous, I stepped out of my shelter as the rain began to slacken. Spin slipped to the ground and crouched at my feet. Archibald and Elanor gave a cry together and in a moment I almost had the breath pressed out of my body as they embraced me. I felt this greeting out of balance with my very short absence, and I wanted to see what had happened to Father and Hereward, so I struggled out of their grasp. There stood Father with Hereward beside him staring towards us, their hands and faces and clothes wet and blackened with smoke and charcoal. As their eyes lit upon us, Hereward groaned and fell to his knees with Father leaning over him. Together they were weeping and shuddering and clinging to each other, while Elanor and Archibald made themselves wetter still with tears, and Spin joined in with some lusty barking. I thought it a most peculiar conclusion to Hereward's transgressions.

As Archibald explained to me through his tears, when the second great spear of lightening had struck through the table, Father and Elanor believed that I was still there, sheltering with Spin under the table. Father, seeing Hereward, had called to him that Edith was within the flames and, hearing this, Archibald had run to my aid, before being prevented by Elanor, while Hereward and Father took his place.

I was chagrined to understand that I had caused such trouble, but relieved to have their apparent madness explained.

Father and Hereward both had burns to the hands which needed bathing in a fresh infusion of herb-water but, fortunately, the last fall of heavy rain had prevented more serious injury. I considered in my mind whether I should feel guilty for their wounds and decided against it, for the cause was simply misunderstanding and besides, it had created a peace-making between Father and Hereward and bonded them closer than I had ever seen them.

When we were all attired in dry robes and Father's and Hereward's hands had been bound with cloths, the feast began again in the house, for the harvest was in safely before the rain, and the storm had passed, leaving the air fresh and the night-sky full of stars. All were merry, and four of my family were touched by that light-headed happiness that comes from relief. As for me, I felt glad enough to be the source of that relief and to have confirmed what I had suspected for some time – that my father loved me.

I was sitting between my step-mother Elanor and my brother Archibald, close to the end of the table where Father sat with his eldest son next to him, for Elanor did not deign to take her usual seat a long table-length from her husband, but wished to be close to him. Father and Hereward talked together like new lovers, speaking of the past and the future, life, love, the forest and the land. They were becoming sentimental over beakers of mead, when I heard Fritha's name mentioned.

"They are in poor straits," Hereward was saying, "for Fritha's mother is ill and her father has only one useful arm. I worked all day with him and Fritha, and we got in their harvest, but I doubt it will last them the winter."

"They can salt the hind you took to them, and there will be more – whatever they need," said Father with a magnanimous depth to his voice.

"They have land enough, but they cannot work it. This year they planted fields close to their house, instead of land on a southern slope which is also theirs but further away. It would have yielded a much better crop."

Father lifted his beaker of mead and with his other hand tapped Hereward's arm, "I will give them two bondsmen from our household, if that is your wish, and you shall go there yourself and husband their land. I will make do with Heath. He is a good enough farmer."

"Heath is strong and loyal and a good husbandman."

Heath was half-way down the table sitting happily next to a pretty young woman called Bebbe, who had been bonded to us from Chief Wulfred's household for the season. Bebbe and Heath had become close since she had been in our household, and they were to be betrothed at the forthcoming Grain Rite. I thought they had eyes only for each other that night, but now Heath looked up at the sound of his name and saw Father and Hereward smiling and nodding to him over their beakers of mead.

Father, his voice sounding as if he had not quite the mastery of his tongue (an effect of mead-drinking I had discovered) raised his beaker and said "To my adopted son Heath. A fine husbandman!"

All were happy to drink more mead, for whatever reason, but Heath's eyes were wide with surprise and his face flushed with more than mead at such words of tribute and regard from Father. I myself felt a glow of pleasure to hear Father honour Heath with the title of adopted son. Hereward also looked flushed with gratitude and pleasure for his friend.

Heath's forthcoming union with Bebbe was an extra cause of merriment around the table that night, and Father's tribute to him was the beginning of many more. I did not understand all the comments, but many caused laughter and made Bebbe blush like a rose. On the day of the Grain Rite, she was to travel with our household to Beornwine. There she and Heath were to be betrothed before the priest who was coming from the Holywell Abbey to preside at our Rite. After that a house of wood-and-thatch would be built for them in our homeyard, and Bebbe would join our household and be wed to Heath. It was to be the first wedding among us since Father and Elanor had themselves married and I was much excited at the prospect of the betrothal and the Grain Rite itself.

This harvest celebration and holy dedication of the land was called Lammas by some of the elder folk at Beornwine. Indeed, the name endures to this day, particularly among the pagan peoples of the north. But in those days I cared little for names; all I knew was harvest brought the Grain Rite and that meant feasting and celebration. I turned to Elanor who had been feeding me with enough honey-cake to satisfy my heart. "Tell me again what will be at the Grain Rite," I said, for I had little memory of the celebrations of the previous year, only general colour and noise of hooves and voices – and a great giant with a painted face who had set his eye on me and made me run in fear to my step-mother's skirts.

Elanor put her arm around me and counted out with her fingers all the mysteries and wonders of the Grain Rite, "First," she said, "will be the procession of our household, and you must rise early that day and fetch a fine sheaf of wheat from the stack so that we can bind it up to carry ahead of us in the procession. The Lord Wulfirth, Chief Wulfred, and the Holy Father from the Abbey will be there to meet us, and the Holy Father will bless all the sheaves of wheat and other harvest offerings. Then all the blessed food will be taken back to the Abbey with him when he returns."

"What will happen to all that food, Mother?"

Elanor paused, as she often did when I called her Mother, and then answered me gently, which was her way, "All the blessed food will be eaten by the holy men and women at the Abbey, and that is when the magic happens, for as they honour the best of our harvest by eating it, so that endows next year's harvest with the holy joy of God, which will spring up in our fields and meadows and animals in abundance."

"Is that why HestanandGodwine are travelling to the Abbey with the holy man?"

"Yes, a man from every family is to go as guide and protection for the Abbey cart. Last year your father went himself, but he says it is a young man's duty, and the twins beg to go together."

"A quest!" I breathed, wishing I could ride with them.

Elanor smiled, "Yes, but before that there will be betrothals and christenings, then feasting and music and testings."

"Testings!" Now I remembered, at last year's Rite, watching warriors riding against each other with spears and shields. "There will be warriors!"

"Warriors and giants and merchants with pretty things to buy."

"Will you buy anything Elanor?"

"I shall buy something for you because you are a dear good girl."

"Oh what?" said I joyfully, thinking of a small sword just the size for a child of six winters.

"Would you like some beads like these?" From a pair of brooches at her shoulders, Elanor had three strings of coloured beads hanging across the front of her dress, which I much admired.

"Oh yes, and perhaps a sword too?"

A great laugh went up and I realised that many around the table had stopped their own talk to listen to us. I joined in the laughter for the joy of it, and considered that very likely they thought me too young for the fine quality swords sold by the merchant travellers at the Grain Rite. I judged otherwise, but would make do with Archibald's toy sword for a few years more. He did not need it now, because Alvar had made him a full-sized wooden sword to use for practice, for Archibald had known twelve winters now and was half a man. Often he hunted now with Father, so that I felt lonelier than ever. But loneliness touched me not that night when I felt myself to be at the heart of my family, and Archibald there at my side, laughing with me.

17

The Herb-Woman

The next morning Hereward was to go with Heath and Warik to check how our stacks of wheat had fared in the storm, taking a bundle of good thatching straw to make good any damaged stacks. But at breakfast both Hereward and Father used their hands with edgy care and Elanor insisted on removing the cloths that bound them so that she might see the extent of their wounds. Both were fiery, with broken blisters over the palms. "They must be bathed again in herb-water" she said, with a look of concern, "but I would fain consult Mother Werberga as to the best herbs to use."

"Who is Mother Werberga?" I asked.

"She is a herb-woman, who knows much of healing; a wise-woman." This last Elanor spoke in the old tongue of her people, using the word 'wicca' for wisdom.

I brightened at this, "Our mother too was a herb-woman," I said, "She knew how to heal all wounds and sicknesses. She was a wicca-woman."

It seemed my voice had sounded into a sudden emptiness. I looked up; all around me was a quickening hush and, although nobody spoke, I heard as clear as a warning bell the word *witch* slicing the heavy silence. My flesh rippled with an old terror, but Elanor scooped me into her arms where I smelt the clean comfort of her soft woollen dress and heard her say, "So she was, child, and I would she were here to help us now; we'd soon have these men's hands all well again."

I nodded, my gaze clinging to her face that saved me from my soul's darkness. And now indeed there was also my brother Archibald, with his hand on my shoulder and a kindly light in his eyes.

"I'll go," said he, "I'll ride on Swift to Mother Werberga and ask for herbs and a good recipe." He tapped my shoulder, "Come with me Edith. Old Swift will carry us both without losing any speed."

And the darkness in my head slunk away as the hubbub of morning gathered again in the house, while Elanor made sure we knew what to ask the herb-woman. She wrapped up a fresh soft cheese as a gift for her, and another which she bade us take with a dish of cooked and honeyed pears to the house of Herin Elfrith for his wife Judith, who was ill. Archibald helped me to clamber up to the fleece on Swift's tall back and Elanor handed up the basket of pears and cheeses, tied round with a cloth so that none should be shaken loose. It was some time since I had ridden far with Archibald, although I sometimes took out a good-natured pony called Boy, who didn't mind carrying Spin and sometimes Bertha on his back along with me. But Elanor was nervous about me going far alone, and so my riding skills were weakening, for Archibald had little time these days to ride with me. It worried me, for I knew no fighting thegn could afford to neglect the regular practice of horsemanship.

Hereward came to us before we left. "Tell Herin Elfrith that I cannot ride because of my hands, but I will come soon," he said to Archibald. Then he reached up to where I sat on Swift's back and, although his hand was stiff with bandages and pain, he gently placed a yellow harvest flower in my basket. "Edith," he said softly, "Tell Fritha I shall see her soon. I shall see her at the Grain Rite."

Archibald leapt up beside me and we rode off across the meadowland, where the grass was grazed short by our own sheep – perfect for a gallop. Archibald spoke firmly to Swift, loosened the reins, and we were speeding along at a great pace. I held on tightly to my basket with one hand, to Swift's mane with the other and laughed for the joy of speed and freedom.

Archibald asked at Beornwine for directions to Mother Werberga's house and also to the Elfrith's. The man he spoke to pointed out a house about half a mile south of the main settlement. "That's Herin Elfrith's house," he said, "You can ask there for Mother Werberga's place. It's not much further distant, right down by the river."

The Elfrith house was earth-based, with low walls of wood and daub, and roof-thatch that looked old and neglected. It had not much of a home yard, with only a small area of flattened dirt with two or three low outbuildings in poor repair. There was smoke coming from the vent in the house roof and I could smell boiling meat. I guessed that they were preparing the hind Hereward had taken to them the day before. As we approached, they must have heard Swift's hoof-beats, for Fritha came out of the house to meet us. I think there was disappointment on her face to see that it was only me and Archibald, and not Hereward. But when she saw the fresh cheese and the dish of honeyed pears that we had brought, her face softened.

"This is such a good and kindly gift," she exclaimed. "These light foods will revive my mother better than anything," and her eyes filled with tears.

She asked us to come into the house, so Archibald tied Swift's halter to a tree and we followed Fritha through the doorway. It was a dark and lowly place such as poor people have, with little light entering from the outside. A fire burned on the floor in the middle of the house with a big pot over the flames where meat was cooking and the place was full of smoke so that I coughed. On a low platform against the wall lay a woman with grey hair loose about her shoulders. She made to sit up as we came in and greeted us warmly, although she coughed and looked most ill. I thought it would be better for her to be outside, away from the smoke, but she shivered with cold or ague, so perhaps she preferred to stay within the house, where she could be near to the fire. I wondered not for the first time why others did not have a funnel of straw and daub hanging from the roof over their fire, to carry away the smoke. My brother Hereward had made such a funnel at our first home and another in the large house where we lived now. It is true that we had to keep pails of water close by because the funnel might sometimes catch alight, but it was a fine arrangement and kept our house almost free of smoke. I guessed that not much time would pass before Hereward would build a funnel at the Elfrith house too, and make it a more comfortable place.

Archibald asked where Mother Werberga's house lay and Fritha's mother questioned us about why we were seeking herb-lore, so we told them all about the storm and the fire and Father's and Hereward's injuries.

"Hereward injured?" cried Fritha.

Afraid that she might blame me for Hereward's wounds, I made light of them. "His hands are not very bad at all," I said, "but he gave me a message for you," and I passed to her the little meadow flower and said what he had bade me tell her, that he would see her at the Grain Rite. Fritha's eyes lit up at this, and her mother smiled also, although weakly and then closed her eyes.

"My father is in the fields, said Fritha, "I must fetch him. He will want to thank you for these kind gifts."

I was curious to see the man with the withered arm, but Archibald urged Fritha not to disturb her father's work. "We must be on our way," he said. "I need to see Mother Werberga without delay so that I can fetch the healing herbs for Father and our brother Hereward."

Fritha thanked us again and her mother reached out a hand to us. Archibald went to her, and I beside him. "I wish you well, Mother Elfrith," he said.

"Thank you child," said she in a weak voice, "I think the foods you have brought to me will restore my health full soon." I could see that she had beside her a little box with a carved lid, which she worried at with her thin fingers until it opened. She took out two woven cords of coloured threads and tied a green one around Archibald's wrist; a red one around mine. I was much taken with the gift and thanked the lady, although her sickness made me timid.

Fritha came out with us to the clear air again and pointed to a copse down near the river. "You will find Mother Werberga's house within the trees on the river side of the copse," she said. Archibald lifted me onto Swift's back and vaulted up behind me. It was a grand thing to be riding again across open land on a clear day, having both given and received gifts. I thought my woven wrist-band very fine and believed it probably bore good luck for me. Then it struck me that the Elfriths were far poorer than we and that it might have been wrong of us to accept gifts from them. I voiced this to Archibald, but he said; "With every gift we give, it is beholden to us to accept another."

I thought then of how I had once sought to lighten my father's burthen of anger with a gift of strawberries. I had not known then that I was beholden to accept a gift in return. Perhaps that was why I had not understood that my father loved me for years afterwards, because I had not been prepared to accept the gift of his love. It was all very mysterious to me and I did not understand it all, but was glad of my new wrist-band.

It was many years before I truly understood Archibald's words concerning gifts and learned to give and receive willingly of life's gifts, and to welcome the changes it brought. But it seems strange to me now that Archibald, a half-man of only twelve winters, should have had such wisdom at that time.

Mother Werberga was, I think, the oldest person I had ever seen. She was sitting on a stool outside her little house when we arrived, tending a fire on an outdoor hearth. Archibald pulled Swift up to a walk, so as not to startle her. She did not get up as we approached, but smiled as if she knew us – although I was certain I had never seen her before. She was a fine-looking woman – tall with brown skin that was folded and creased about her face and arms. Her head was covered with a cloth of plain wool, but her long hair cascaded down beneath in supple shining curls that were as white as winter snow.

"Are you Mother Werberga?" said I before Archibald could speak.

"I am child, but it is custom to give your own name before taking another's."

I slipped down from Swift's back and went to her, for she was fascinating to me and, although she looked strange and beautiful, I did not fear her. "I am Edith Fly of Finric Fly, and this is my brother Archibald."

She nodded, "Finric Fly is the new man who takes on the household of Elanor Burhelm."

I shook my head, "He is married to Elanor, but he is not new. We have lived here since I was little."

"Ah, time travels as a slow horse for you Edith, but for me it speeds as a bird across the sky." She turned to Archibald, who had dismounted and was holding Swift's halter in his hand. "Bring your horse to this tree," she said, indicating one with a rope tied around it. "This is a good place for my visitors' animals, where there's a patch of grass for them to crop." When Swift was settled, she showed us to a log near her own stool, and invited us to sit. Then she asked Archibald, "How many winters have you lived in Elanor Burhelm's house boy?"

Archibald held his head high, saying "I am Archibald Fly and my step-mother answers also to the name of Fly."

"And how long have you lived in Elanor Fly's house?"

Archibald frowned, "Is it not then my father's house?"

"Who spends more time in the house, boy, your father or your step-mother Elanor?"

"Why, Elanor is more in and about the house and home-yard."

"Then is it not more really her house than his?"

"Perhaps." Then he smiled and decided it was meet to answer her question, "We have lived there full three winters and this spring and summer."

But I was thinking hard. "Why is it," I said, "that only a woman's first name belongs to her? Her family name is always a man's – her father's or her husband's name. Elanor had her first husband's name, and now she bears my father's."

"So what name would you have Edith?"

I considered the question. "Hylda was my mother's name and Elanor is my step-mother's name," I said, "but I want to keep Fly, for it was the name given to honour my father. The Lord Ulef gave it to him for being as quick as an arrow in battle and a great archer. All my brothers bear it too, and Archibald is a fine archer also."

"Is that so?" and Mother Werberga turned to Archibald with a smile.

But Archibald only shrugged in his modest way, "I like archery," he said, "So I suppose I aim well, because I practise often."

Then Mother Werberga walked down the gently sloping bank to the river and drew out of the water a pitcher that she had put there to cool, tethered by its handle to a willow bough. She brought out of her house three beakers which she filled from the pitcher and handed one to each of us. It was a delicious infusion the like of which I had never tasted before.

"What is it?" asked Archibald raising his head from his beaker and licking his lips.

"I make it from flowers and berries, honey and herbs," she said. We drank another beakerful of the delicious cordial and then I helped her carry the beakers to the river, where we washed them in the slow-flowing water.

Then I sat down beside her and could have happily stayed talking with her for much longer, but Archibald stirred. "Mother Werberga, we have brought you a gift from our mother Elanor and a message to ask for your help." He brought forward the basket and gave her the cloth-wrapped cheese. She pressed the cheese, smelt it and looked at its colour, and seemed mighty pleased with it.

"And is there something I can send back to your mother in return for her kindness?" she said.

I thought Elanor would be glad of anything that would heal burned hands. And so we told Mother Werberga about the storm and the burned table and my family's misunderstanding as to my whereabouts. She listened with a gratifying measure of wonderment, so that I found myself exaggerating the height of the flames, and my own action in rescuing Spin from the storm, so that I might see her eyes open even wider.

"But child," she said, "why should your father imagine you were under the table?"

I had to explain somewhat shame-faced that this was a common refuge for myself and Spin. I knew that admitting this made me seem much less valiant, but Mother Werberga only nodded, although her eyes sparkled suspiciously, or so I thought.

"You must bring your dog to see me some day," she said, "But now you will need a cure for burns."

She questioned us as to the appearance of Father's and Hereward's burned hands, whether there was any swelling, and the number and appearance of the blisters. Then we followed her into her garden and she gave me a basket to carry, into which she put a mass of flowering sun's wort, together with a sprig or two of wormwood.

"Now listen to me children," she said. "You must remember what I say now, so that you can tell your mother Elanor just what to do so that the men's burns shall be healed."

She gave us long directions, including prayers to the Sun God and Moon Goddess. She was particular as to the boiling of herbs and method of soaking binding-cloths. "Let not the injured man go outside or work until the cloths are quite dry," she said.

She told us this method again, and asked us questions to ensure that we understood. Then she made us both repeat it to her. Archibald did mention that ours was a Christian family, but Mother Werberga did not seem to well understand that Christians did not generally address the sun and moon deities. Neither of us thought it meet to instruct her, but kept our counsel and passed on her message word for word as far as we were able when we reached our home.

With Mother Werberga's recipe in our heads and her herbs in the basket, we prepared to go home. As I sat upon Swift with Archibald behind me, she came to bid us farewell. I smiled at her, for I liked her very much. "Thank you for the cordial," I said.

"Come again, child," she said, "Bring fresh butter and wheat-flour if you can. Then I will show you how to make a rich food better than cordial to take back to your family."

18

The Thegn

I had thought it unlikely that Father would follow Mother Werberga's directions so far as staying within the house while the wet cloths dried upon his wounds, but I was surprised that he complied. It is true that he was angered by the instructions, but made no attempt to disobey. It was not so with Hereward, however, for he walked out from the house after his hands had been bound. I thought he was gone to Fritha's house and feared for his wounds. Indeed, when he returned at sunset, he was in much pain, and had the added discomfiture of Father's rebuke to endure. "It's foolish to run against the advice of these herb-women," said Father, "It will come to no good."

But Father seemed to retain the good feeling he had found with Hereward after the storm and said nothing when, two days later, Hereward walked out again, the wet cloths still on his hands. I had a mind to follow him and not long after he left I decided to take a long walk. Spin, had been put out of humour when I rode off on Swift without him, and had sulked for more than a day until I stole a honeycake from the crock for him. I knew he would be glad now to be my companion, so I called him and off we went together.

Some of the time I could see Hereward well ahead of us across the undulating land. Much of the Beornwine harvest had been gathered and stacked, but there were still some fields high with crops, and I was pleased that indeed our household was well ahead of the village. Hereward bypassed Beornwine but I thought fair to go there and see Siric's two daughters, Gytha and Aldyth, who were near my age. Both the girls were busy with household tasks when I arrived, but they stopped to greet me, full of news and wanting to talk, while Spin went off to visit with the Beornwine dogs, who knew him well. I had been looking forward to telling the girls about the storm and the fire, but I had to wait, for their news was fresher. Gytha was a heavy girl – well fed from her father's hostelry and a good two winters my elder. She was a motherly type and always treated me like a baby, which I did not much like, although she was kind enough. Now she saw me and clasped me, her round face red as a sunset with excitement, and nearly had me over among the chickens she was feeding. "Have y' seen that thegn?" she said, her eyes wide.

I was straight away as excited as she. "What thegn?" I asked.

Aldyth interrupted, "Oh Edith, his name is Torhelm. He's so big and fine – tall as a giant all plumed and handsome in blue with a black horse, and the richest thegn in the whole land." Aldyth's tongue almost tripped itself in the attempt to describe the heroic personage before her sister could.

"His sword is covered all over with jewels," said Gytha, "and there are gold and silver bands around his arms; and when he got down from his horse..."

"... he got down and came straight into our house and spoke to me first ..." said Aldyth.

"... he gave me his sword to care for, and ..."

"... he told me I was a pretty maid. I think I shall marry him." Aldyth was all of seven winters and her mind turned to marriage, which was the way with many girl-children that I had met in Beornwine. But my thoughts were gone from her now and all my concentration was with Gytha, and her last words.

"You have his sword?" I asked.

Her face collapsed a little. "Not now," she said, "But he stays at our house until after the Grain Rite."

They dragged me into the hostelry, a very large house that, of course, I knew well, for had it not been the first place of shelter we had found on the day we came to Beornwine? Also it was the house most visited by my family, for of course Elanor was kin to Siric and the girls like to be my cousins. Now they towed me by an arm each to the far end of the house usually reserved for travellers. On a low platform in one corner, Siric had hung a fine heavy curtain of coloured wool, which to me was a wonder in itself that I had seen but rarely, for it was only brought out for the richest travellers. Gytha swept this aside; we peered within and the girls were silent for a minute, letting the splendour of the sight do its work on my admiration. The bed of straw mattress and sewn fleeces was plumped and neat. Behind it, propped against the wall, was a spear with a shining tip. On top of the bed was a bag made of leather with the finest silver clasp I had ever seen. Next to this, laid out reverently by Gytha and Aldyth was a comb, a mirror of polished silver, scissors, a woollen night-cap with scarlet tassels and a great cloak of black fur. This last Gytha reached out to smooth with her hand and nodded for me to do the same. It was marvellously soft, dark and shining. "It comes from a far country, brought by a rich merchant," she murmured.

"He told me that first, because I asked him," added Aldyth.

I could not help myself; my eyes were stretched wide with as much admiration as the sisters could wish for and, I fear, my mouth was open in un-thegnly amaze. I turned to Aldyth, but she was bent down slipping a wrap off something that lay half propped against the foot of the platform. And then I saw it. It was a round shield, taller than me, its four quarters painted blue and black, the rim of it bound in silver and the central iron boss also with silver plated upon it, all wrought in marvellous patternings and notions, most skilful and costly, no doubt. At the time I was all delight and awe, although any true knowledge of the bearing of arms would have told me that no fighting thegn's shield would be so prettily adorned, for it would likely be broken in any true fight. Shields are for fighting with and for protection; most warriors carry a spare if they can. I doubt Torhelm ever took this one into battle. I made to touch it with full gentleness and respect, but Aldyth covered up the bright thing once more, whispering, "We should not really have shown it to you, for we are the only ones who have the care of all his things in the house and no-one else is to see or touch anything, so don't you tell Father, or Elanor or anyone!"

I was about to assure her on my honour of my future silence on the matter, even on pain of death (although, in my mind, this did not include silence to Archibald from whom I held no secrets) when we heard certain noises from without that told of a small crowd with an unusual light clanking at its midst. The girls seemed startled with both guilt and pleasure.

"It is he!" they squealed. Quickly pulling the curtain across again, they ran to the house door, but not before me for I was ahead of them.

In the large home yard of the hostelry were gathered many young men and girls of the village (most of whom should have been working, no doubt, for not all the harvest was gathered). Behind them were smaller children – most that Beornwine contained (which was a goodly number for this was a blessed region, touched neither with famine nor plague in the time that I had lived there). At the heart of this melee strode a giant – so he seemed, for the helmet above the iron-clad shoulders was plumed with black and blue feathers and stood high above any common head.

This was the great thegn Torhelm, as Gytha quickly told me. The cause of the clanking was his armour, in leather-hinged plates of iron, shaped over his arms and legs and body. I remember the intricate make-up of it for I was fortunate enough to examine it in detail later, and I can say truly that never in my future experience and dealings with warriors did I ever see anything finer. Nontheless, had I in later years been given the chance of fighting in such a suit, I would have refused, for its weight would deprive me of the speed and skill that I believe often saved my life more readily than any heavy armour could have done. Rather, for protection, give me thick padding and a light breast-plate or mail shirt if I can get one; give me a quick and doughty steed. Give me youth and a noble quest and the future all ahead of me as it was on that day when, knowing nothing of fighting, I lifted up my voice and cheered along with the others for a young man with more money than valour who made a fine sight with his armour flashing in the sunshine and his sword bound at his side.

I had forgotten my earlier quest to follow Hereward and see him with Fritha, which had been such a great curiosity for me. The strange compulsion of ordinary young adults that will drag a pair of them towards each other despite storm or pestilence, whilst fascinating to me, did not compare with the attractions of a real fighting thegn.

Torhelm's hunger and thirst needed to be satisfied with Siric's finest ale and venison (probably a haunch from my father's own recent hunt). He unbound his sword from around his waist and it was indeed decorated with gold and silver and studded with marvellous crystal gems, the scabbard worked in silver patterning much like the binding of the shield that we had seen earlier. He hung the sword upon the wall by his bed. Then Gytha and Aldyth and myself were allowed to help him off with his armour, and he proved to be wearing fine clothes beneath, rather than the thick gambeson padding needed for battle. It was too hot for the fur cloak, and he put on a tabard embroidered with gold and purple thread (signifying noble lineage, so Gytha said), replaced the sword at his waist and sat at table, talking genially to all of us, the gold and silver bands on his wrists glinting in the sunlight that streamed through the open shutters. It is true that the hostelry table was fuller than usual, and many of the Beornwine folk came to drink ale and see the fine thegn, for the harvest was nearly done and no other visitors to the Grain Rite had yet appeared, so all had time for curiosity.

I saw Torhelm's beaker was empty and I brought a pitcher of ale to replenish it. He noticed me then and said, "Who are you, little maid?"

"She's Edith Fly, daughter to Finric Fly who is married to my father's sister Elanor," burst out Aldyth, and I nodded my concurrence while Aldyth added, "She has six brothers and they are all great riders and hunters."

Truly, before the arrival of Torhelm, Aldyth had shown a great interest in my brothers as husband-material, particularly Farin, who was tall and handsome. But Farin was cast off now, for all her interest was in the great Torhelm. Indeed, Aldyth seemed not a little angered that he had noticed me and she was now trying to ensure that I did not usurp her place. She elbowed me aside and poured the ale herself.

Torhelm thanked her for the ale, and then he said, "Riders, you say, and huntsmen?"

"Yes, for on the very day they came here there was a battle and all of them rode in defence of our village, even Archibald who was only nine winters, and they have been here ever since." She paused to draw breath and Torhelm opened his mouth to speak, but Aldyth was before him, "And that venison is from their household too."

Torhelm looked over her head to me. "Do any of your brothers have an interest in questing?" he asked.

"Oh yes, all of them!" said Aldyth and I in unison.

19

The Grain Rite

Now Worik of our household had heard of a voice-battle that was to be held at the Grain Rite and, the day before it was to begin he went away to a high field at the far edge of our land to test his voice. There was no doubt in our household that he would win the battle, for we knew of no-one whose voice could match his for volume and clarity. At breakfast time many of us gathered outside the house from where we could see Worik standing on high land several fields away. He cast his voice slowly and clearly to us, saying that he could see many horses and laden carts arriving at Beornwine, and flags and tents of all colours being set up both within and without the walls.

Archibald and I looked at each other in silence amid the murmurs and cries of our household who were giving praise to the quality of Worik's voice. We cared not for the voice but only for the message it brought. Without waiting for our parents' permission, which might not be forthcoming, we went into the house and out of a little door at the rear, then ran across the fields, free as two birds (although Archibald restrained his speed so that I could keep up with him). On a low hill opposite the village, we climbed a tree and watched the activity below us. Men and women, many of them dressed in coloured clothes, had come in carts laden with barrels and baskets; young men on horseback were arriving and camping outside the circle of the Beornwine buildings; and – to our great delight – we saw three armoured warriors on caparisoned horses being admitted through the gate. Soon they were joined by Torhelm, mounted on his horse. I recognised him by the black and blue plumes on his helmet, which he had doubtless donned to impress the newcomers, for they hardly posed any danger to him, their shields and swords being strapped behind their saddles.

We were watching Torhelm greet the warriors when another cart arrived. It had signs of the Christian cross painted on its sides and was driven by a man in a plain brown robe. As we watched, all four of the warriors dismounted and knelt on the grass, making obeisance to the plain man, which I thought odd, but Archibald said, "See Edith, the Father has arrived from the Abbey and the armed men pay tribute to him."

I was astounded, for I had expected the holy man to come arrayed in gold upon a silver horse, with light in a circle around his head. "That is not *my* idea of a holy man!" I cried with some scorn.

Then my scorn was turned back upon me in Archibald's face. "You know nothing child," he said, "Can't you see the warriors? It is one of the thegnly duties to be pious and to pray and follow the teachings of the Holy Church – see they all have the cross as part of their arms?" Indeed, all three shields were painted with a cross through the middle, although each had different symbols and colours on the four sides divided by the cross, and I reflected that Torhelm's shield was of a similar design. Archibald said, "And yet, see how they give honour to the plainly dressed holy man? They know he is greater than they in piety, and bow down before him."

It was a great mystery to me, and I began to feel my ambitions for thegnhood to be moving away from me, for there would be so much to learn. I knew I would rather look at the warriors than the ordinary-looking man on the cart. But I hoped he might prove more interesting when directly observed, and on the morrow I would see all.

That night I could hardly sleep, and I awoke to our cock, who would crow at the moon or a firefly as much as the rising sun. It was yet dark, but I lay awake, shivering with excitement. Very soon after, I heard movement among my brothers and saw candle-light above the screen that divided my bed from theirs. It seemed that some of them were as eager for the Grain Rite as I was.

Soon Worik came to escort me to the nearest of our harvested fields. There I chose a fine wheatsheaf, tied neatly into shape, with the fat ears of grain fulsomely arrayed along the top. This was to be carried at the head of our household's procession to the Grain Rite. I then picked a bunch of blue cornflowers with which to decorate the sheaf, and another for Worik's tunic. "Why, thank you, little one," he said, and carried me back to the house on his shoulder, with the wheatsheaf under his arm, where all congratulated me on a fine choice.

Breakfast was early that day, for Elanor also was up before the sun broke over the eastern hills. Bacon and fried oat cakes were cooking by the time I returned with Worik from the fields. Bondswomen were preparing baskets of meats, cheese, bread and beer to take with us, so that there would be no need to return before the day's end. I sat with a piled plate before me, then found that I could not eat after all, so Spin's breakfast was heartier than usual that morning.

After she had ensured that all were well fed, Elanor fetched a bowl of herbed water and carried it up to her room whilst Father strode around the home yard, ordering arrangements for the horses and instructing those who were to stay and guard the house. I thought it time that I made ready for my day. I followed Elanor aloft. She heard my footsteps and called to me.

"Edith, come hither child." I put my head around the door to the room she shared with my father. It was a fine room, the bed covered with a rich red cloth and embroidered hangings on the walls. Elanor had washed her hair and was combing the water out of it. Now she took hold of me and washed me all over with the herb water, to which I submitted without complaint, for the day was warm already.

"Go to the chest now," she said, "and bring what lies on top."

This was an oak chest which had belonged to Elanor's family for many years. It had an iron lock upon it and I was not normally permitted to open the lid. But this time, my step-mother untied the big key that she always wore hanging from her girdle and handed it to me. I fitted the key carefully into the lock, turned it using both my hands and pushed open the lid. Inside lay a new dress just the size for me made of finest wool worked all over with red and yellow thread in wonderful patterns. I took up the garment and held it out in my arms.

"Does it please you child?" Elanor was standing behind me.

"Why yes. It is splendid."

"It is for you to wear today. I worked it myself."

I could rather have chosen a tabard and hose set, suited to a young squire, but I could see that Elanor had hoped to please me, so I hugged her and thanked her most kindly for the gift. Indeed, I was pleased enough with the dress and doubted that either Gytha or Aldyth would have one so fair. So Elanor helped me to put it on and fastened it at the waist with a woven belt much like my wrist-band, and at the shoulders with two little silver clasps, which she said were a present to me from Father. Then she braided my hair with a red and yellow ribbon and her own with a blue one worked with gold and silver thread. Then Elanor took my hand and we went down together and found my father and brothers all finely arrayed for the Grain Rite, Father's wide silver bands around his wrists to show off his wealth.

All the household set out together, most on foot, but my parents and brothers and I on horseback, with my wheatsheaf tied on the front of Father's horse. Behind us Heath and Bebbe, who were to be betrothed, sat on a cart full of produce from our harvest. This was to be blessed by the holy man and (all but Heath and Bebbe whom, Father said, we could not spare) carried on to the great Holywell Abbey. I considered that we made a fine sight of it, for our household had swollen to over thirty in the past year. Archibald was on Swift and I was riding next to him upon a pony called Bracken which my father had obtained recently. And as I surveyed my family, so finely attired and supported by such a household, and as I felt the crispness of my new dress and the weight of the silver clasps at my shoulders, I had a new realisation that my father had become an affluent and powerful man. I felt it a fine thing to be part of this family. So much so that, for pure joy, I kicked at Bracken's sides with my heels and galloped ahead; whereupon my whole family did the same, soon outstripping me on their faster horses. They wheeled around and rode back with all speed and there was laughter among us all. Then a happiness rose up in me that has rarely been surpassed. For what is finer than to be young, well loved and to belong to a high family, riding to unknown adventure, with the greater measure of the day yet to come?

I have said that all my family were attired in their finest. Indeed, all of us wore new clothes that day. My step-mother Elanor had done all the fine needlework herself, but the materials, ribbon and thread must have cost my father dear on his monthly visit to the merchants who came to the Holywell Abbey. If we all made a fine sight, none was better than my brothers HestanandGodwine together. They were dressed in blue and white tabards with yellow embroidery and breeches and hose in red. With their fine figures and golden hair they seemed to me a double vision of nobility, and many heads turned in their direction as my father rode through the gates of Beornwine at the head of his family and household.

Inside the gates, we dismounted before a great booth beneath which sat Chief Wulfred, on his carved Chief's seat, which had been carried there for the occasion. His wife Mordeth was with him, and all their family, including the Lord Wulfirth, with the beautiful Lady Cwena and their two young sons, Kyneth and Osred, and little daughter Lewitha. Among them also was the Chief's youngest son, Alfred, who was to be betrothed that day. And all were in their finest raiment of dazzling silks and braids and furs, with gold and silver brooches, rings and wrist-bands about them. Father was greeted as a friend by both the great men, and then Chief Wulfred turned and presented Father to a small, plainly-dressed man who sat quietly nearby under a purple canopy. They both knelt before him, and then we also had to each go and kneel in the grass in front of the holy man.

"Edith, this is Father Maldon," said Chief Wulfred kindly to me as I took my turn after all my brothers. I knew I was to bow my head, as I had seen Father and Elanor and everyone else do before me. But I was full curious and could not help myself but to look into the face of this great holy man. He caught my eye sharply with his own and I bowed my head quickly, for he did not look in good temper. Certainly, his face did not seem suffused with the light of heaven, as I would have expected from such a blessed being. It was then my task to bring forward to him the wheatsheaf that I had brought from the fields with Worik that morning. With some difficulty I carried it to Father Maldon, who raised his hand in a blessing over the sheaf. He saw the blue cornflowers decorating it and reached out to them.

"I picked them, Father," I told him, then quickly bowed my head as I was not sure that I should have spoken. He did not answer, but someone took away the sheaf and when I looked up again, Father Maldon had fixed one of the cornflowers at the waist of his brown robe. He gave me another sharp look, and then suddenly winked at me. I decided that I liked him but feared him, which seemed fitting. I was well pleased when these formalities were over and I was allowed my freedom.

The day passed by too quickly, as is always the case with the happiest times. I spent most of my time with Gytha and Aldyth, and at first the three of us shadowed Archibald, although it seemed to me that he wished to shrug us off after he met up with some other boys of his age. So I hung back then and feigned an interest in the merchant selling beads, so that Archibald could make his escape from us. Elanor saw us at the beadsman's booth and joined us to buy a string of beads for me, and one each for Gytha and Aldyth too, so they were well pleased. We listened to the minstrels and joined in the dancing; cheered for Worik in the voice-battle (which he won); ate and drank our fill; and teased the giant to make him run so that we could flee from him, shrieking with delight (for having reached the age of six winters, I had outgrown my timidity of giants and dragons from which I had suffered a long year before. Indeed, I hoped for the sight of a dragon that day, but none came.)

The greatest pleasure for me was to see all the warriors who had come for the testing. Many would come to compete for the honour of it – and for the bag of silver which the Lord Wulfirth presented to the winner. All were a matter of wonder and awe to us with their noble or fierce looks, armour and weapons. Torhelm strutted amongst them, conspicuous in his rich accoutrements and plumed helmet. The three of us swelled with pride to see him for we felt that he in some small measure belonged to us. Indeed, he gave us smiles and errands to run, which we accomplished with as much speed and eagerness as any young squire to his master's command.

Before the main testings, many families gathered together to watch the boys' tests. In Beornwine, boys under sixteen were not allowed to be tested with blades or spears against each other, but there were spear-throwing and archery tests for the boys. In the archery tests, boys had to shoot five arrows from a standing position, and five from horseback with the horse moving at a trot. Now Archibald was mightily skilled with the bow and arrow and a practised horseman; Father had decided he should enter the test this year. When the time came, I went with Gytha and Aldyth to the boys' testing field. I soon found Archibald and it seemed right to me that I should play squire to him as in our old games. So I stayed close and silent as he chose the arrows for the tests. He had flighted them all himself and he smoothed the feathers now, looking down the length of every arrow to check for straightness, a frown of concentration on his face.

One of the Lord Wulfirth's men had been charged to oversee the boys' tests. He went to all the boys and made marks on their arrows so that they would know who had shot which arrow. He marked Archibald's arrows close to the flights with a mark like a cross.

When the overseer had moved on, I took Archibald's arm. I was surprised to feel that it was trembling, and I understood how nervous he was. I whispered fiercely to him, "You will win; I know it!"

He simply glanced at me in a way that made me loose his arm. Then he said, "Can you hold Swift?" and, without waiting for an answer, walked to the hay-bale where the other archer-boys were gathering for the standing test. I took hold of Swift's halter and the horse (who could have snatched the halter from my hand with a light toss of his head) bent to nuzzle my hair in a friendly way.

Eight boys had entered the test. Most of them were of fourteen or fifteen winters, and Archibald, at only twelve, looked small and slight against them. They had to aim at a wooden shield with a red circle painted on it, which had been nailed to a tree.

The overseer called "Shoot," and a flock of arrows flew towards the painted shield. Many of them went wide or short of the target and some hit it but fell out, but I was not looking at the target; I was watching Archibald. I had seen him practise with bow and arrow so many times that I had ceased to take any notice. But now, I observed the expression on his face – serene and yet fervent – all trace of nervousness gone, and I knew that every one of his arrows was speeding straight to the target.

As the overseer checked the arrows that remained in the shield, he called the name of the boy that each one belonged to. Only two boys had every one of their five arrows left in the target. "Jeneth Brown and Archibald Fly!" he called. "Only they shall compete in the horseback test."

Jeneth Brown was a tall, shock-haired boy who was the son of one of Chief Wulfred's armed bondsmen. While we were all cheering Archibald's success, Jeneth Brown looked at our family with an unfriendly air. He was strong and skilled with the bow, but he did not have a mount of Swift's quality – only a rough pony borrowed from the Chief's stables and I doubted he had much experience of horsemanship.

My parents and brothers went to speak with Archibald, but I was charged with the care of Swift, and knew my squirely duties, so remained where I was standing. I was surprised to see Jeneth Brown approach me.

He did not greet me in any proper or friendly way, but grunted and said "That's a small child to mind a horse of that size."

"Swift knows me," I told him coldly, "He will stay quiet for me." I pointedly took my gaze away from him, for his surly manner deserved no respect and after all, he was Archibald's rival.

In the next moment Brown had grabbed me forcefully by the arm, so that I loosened hold of the halter. He pulled me to him, squashing my face against his stomach, so that the breath was forced out of me and I could not cry out but only struggle for breath against the stink of his ill-preserved leather jerkin. Then I heard Swift give a startled cry and stamp his feet on the ground. The grip in which I was held slackened and I wriggled round in time to see my captor thrust a sharp stick into Swift's tender quarters. The horse cried again in protest, but did not run away, which must have been the boy's purpose. I could see that Swift had his ears back and head up, ready to bite, but holding back because I was so near to his tormentor. Brown pulled his arm back for another thrust, but, wild with rage at this cruelty, I sank my teeth into his arm. He yelled, flinging me away from him, and I sprawled on the ground. Swift took the opportunity of giving him another nip – much heavier than mine – then reared, preparing to kick, but someone was there at his head, and a calm voice telling him, "Swift, stay!"

It was my brother Archibald, carrying his bow, with a quiver of arrows at his belt. Swift was down and quiet, but still trembling. Archibald looked puzzled. "What happened?" he said.

Before I could answer, Brown said. "This stupid girl can't keep control of your horse, and the vicious creature bit me!"

I wondered whether the 'vicious creature' thus named was me or Swift, since both of us had bitten Brown. I began indignantly to refute his lies, but Archibald gave me a warning glance as he pulled me to my feet, so reverting to my role of squire, I stopped, keeping my rage within.

"Well, I am sorry for that," Archibald said calmly to Brown, "Swift is used to guarding my sister. Perhaps he saw you as a threat. But we must go now. They are calling us for the mounted competition."

"I doubt I can ride or shoot with my injured arm," said Brown with a childish pout. But Archibald had turned his attention to his horse, talking to him softly. Swift was still trembling a little, but he calmed as Archibald mounted. I thought it wise not to trouble my brother with my complaints before the competition, so I contented myself with leading his horse into the arena, which was really just a marked off section of a nearby field.

The two mounted boys had to start the competition side by side. Swift was nervous to have Brown so close to him, and side-stepped away. Archibald spoke quietly to him, and he stood still, but was trembling visibly and rolling his eyes.

With the overseer watching, Brown yelled, "That horse is vicious! It has been made to bite my arm so that I shall miss my mark!" And he displayed the livid bruise of the horse bite on his upper arm (not caring to draw any notice to the double crescents of human teeth-marks at the wrist).

As Brown spoke, Swift shied again and showed his teeth. Unable to contain my silence, I ran to the overseer, shouting, "It is not fair! It is not true! He hurt Swift! Look!"

In a moment Archibald was off Swift's back, more concerned for his horse than for any cheating on the part of his opponent. I pointed to the place where Brown had attacked Swift with the stick. The competition overseer strode over and examined Swift. Standing next to him, I could see two raised areas and a small trail of blood under the horse's back leg. I glanced at Archibald and saw my brother's face pale with rage, but the overseer turned to him, saying in a low voice, "The injury is slight; your horse has taken no great hurt. I counsel you to stand the test now and take your revenge that way."

Then he stood back, saying to Brown in a full voice that everyone could hear, "Well, you have a wounded arm, and Archibald Fly has an injured horse. That puts you in equal standing. The test shall begin!"

With a single cold glance at Brown, Archibald mounted and urged Swift forward with gentle pressure of his legs that few would even notice, so much in accord were horse and rider. At the same time, Brown kicked his pony into a sudden trot. Archibald, with the larger mount, soon overtook him, aiming one arrow rapidly after another towards the target. He was still a good distance away from the target, but three out of his five arrows found their mark. Brown, clearly not practised in riding, was jolting around like a sack of turnips; all of his arrows landed far wide of the mark.

"I declare Archibald Fly Victor of the Boys' Archery Test!" called the overseer, and a great cheer went up from our family and household. The Chief Wulfred himself presented Archibald with the fine jay's feather to wear in his cap. Everyone gathered round to congratulate him; and I thought I would burst with pride at my brother's achievement.

After the celebrations were over, Father took Archibald to the Chief's booth. There the Chief's son, the great Lord Wulfirth, presented my brother with a seax knife which had a small circle of gold on the hilt. It was in a leathern scabbard etched and painted with the shape of a blue feather. It was a wondrous gift that many envied and which Archibald always treasured, although we all knew that it was given as much to mark Lord Wulfirth's respect and friendship for our father as to reward Archibald for winning the boy's test.

As for Jeneth Brown, perhaps he considered that Archibald was too stupid or too cowardly to take revenge on the treatment of his beloved horse. He was wrong.

My family and household were drifting back to our own canopy under the trees. I was with Archibald who had let me hold his new knife, and I was turning it over in my hands, full of admiration and envy, when Jeneth Brown came swaggering along with a group of Beornwine boys. Archibald's eyes narrowed and he shouted, "Brown!"

The older boy turned to Archibald and laughed, "Do you want to fight me, little boy?" and his friends smiled with him, for indeed Archibald seemed no match for Brown, being a head shorter and much slighter than him.

Archibald gave his answer in action, running and launching himself at the sneering boy. Brown's expression changed to surprise and then pain as he fell over backwards under Archibald's attack. At the same time, I saw Brown's friends move forward; one of them picked up a stone and took aim on the back of Archibald's head.

I screamed and jumped onto the boy's back, one of my arms around his neck while with the other I reached out for the hand that held the stone, digging my fingernails into his wrist. He yelped and dropped the stone. The next moment I was plucked from his back by one heavy hand, while another grabbed the boy by the scruff of his neck. A deep voice said "You lads, keep away! If you do not, my sons will be glad to fight you also!" It was my father and standing behind him was HestanandGodwine with Alvar and Farin.

Wide-eyed with respect and fear, the Beornwine boys backed off, joining the circle of watchers which was forming around Archibald and Brown. I thought Father would stop the fight. But he just set me on the ground, keeping a firm hand on my shoulder while he watched the fight.

Archibald had not waited for Brown to recover from his initial attack, but fell to the ground with him, raining blows upon his face. Brown bellowed and began to fight back; there was a rolling tumble of arms and legs; Archibald had one fist in Brown's hair with the other pummelling his face; Brown was trying to reach for my brother's throat. He yelled again in pain as a burst of blood sprayed from his nose under Archibald's fist, and he began to roll away, then to kneel and to stand, still with the much smaller Archibald clinging to him and attacking with fists and feet. At last by sheer strength Brown pushed my brother away from him and began to run. Archibald was only prevented from going after him by Alvar and Farin whom Father ordered to stop him. They brought him back to us, still red with rage and with bruises already raising themselves on his face and arms. He stood before Father, gasping and muttering breathlessly, "My horse. He attacked my horse."

Father looked down at him. "So, my son," he said, "Th'art a fine archer and now I see you have proper courage in a real fight too. You are a warrior indeed! Come now to your mother and take food and drink after the battle." He smiled, and we all laughed with pleasure. I could not have been more proud of my brother.

20

Redhelm

After the sun had marked the mid-day, all gathered at the clear area in the centre of the settlement, where a long track of grass had been fenced off and marked at the corners with gay flags. This was the testing field and many warriors were making ready with lance-spears, heavy shields and many types and fashions of armour to compete one against the other. Some – fierce-looking men with no armour but a shield – wore cloaks and tunics of mixed woven colours. These were Welshmen, well known for their riding and fighting skill.

I was not alone in being beside myself with anticipation, and many gathered to watch, talking excitedly of which of the fighting men was likely to win the day and carry off the prize. But in watching that tournament, I received the knowledge that a warrior life bore much danger and cruelty as well as courage and repute. For the tests, blades and points had to be blunted, but that did not prevent injury. Any warrior knows the damage a heavy sword can do to flesh and bone, even with its edges dulled.

Despite the rules of the tests, tricks and covert assaults took place between combatants that shocked me. Early on in the mounted tests I saw one warrior, raggedly dressed with only a breastplate for armour, simply pulled off his horse from behind by his opponent. Some people laughed, but I felt angry for the poor man and went to my father with my complaint.

My father was with the Chief Wulfred, Lord Wulfirth and other men, watching from a raised platform at the end of the testing field. I climbed up and stood beside him, but had to pull at his sleeve before he noticed me. "What is it child," he said impatiently.

"Did you see that warrior pulled off his horse?" I said indignantly. "That was not just!"

Father laughed, "Daughter," he said, "Do you think warfare is just? These tests are not childsplay. They are to show a fighting man's caution as well as his strength and skill. No warrior will waste more blade or strength than is necessary to despatch an opponent. He needs to preserve his power for the next enemy. That man was fortunate to be pulled with a hand and not pushed with the tip of a blade."

He turned from me, but I stared at him, absorbing this new truth. Then he glanced at me again impatiently. "Do not watch if it frightens you, daughter. Go to see the stalls or minstrels."

"I am not frightened," I said, but he was no longer listening to me. I scrambled down from the platform and made my way through the crowd until I stood at the front of the fence. Although the rules of the tests ensured there were not a great many injuries, I saw blood shed and bones broken that day, and one young man taken off the field with the life gone out of him. It was terrible, but thrilling too, and I found myself carried along with the mood of the crowd, cheering and groaning as men triumphed or fell.

Torhelm entered the mounted tests and was unseated but uninjured early in the tournament. He left the field punching the air in his anger. As the competition progressed, fewer of the mounted warriors remained to ride another test. Of these, most were very strong and well experienced, as would be expected. A few younger riders stayed the field for a while but eventually only one of these remained to compete against the stronger men. This remaining young warrior wore a breastplate and helmet and rode a strong dappled-grey horse. His shield was painted in red with a green cross and border. This shield was of an unusual shape, being wide at the top and narrowing to a point at its lower edge. It caused much discussion among my brothers, who perceived that it afforded better protection and was less unwieldy on horseback than the usual round shields. Its shape also caused the cross which bisected it to be a better representation of the Christian cross, with its long tail. This young man, who was called Redhelm, had a wonderful way of deflecting the lance blows, catching them on the boss of his shield and twisting his body on his horse as he passed so that the lance would slide harmlessly to the side, whilst he directed his own weapon on the edge of his opponent's shield. Such tactics very often caused much stronger men to overbalance and become unseated, whereupon a great cheer went up from the spectators, for everyone likes to see the underdog triumph.

Soon, whenever it was Redhelm's turn to ride, the crowd of spectators became swollen and there were cheers and shouts of encouragement for the young warrior. Eventually he came against the champion lancer Brocmail, a powerful and skilled thegn in red, blue and gold which Archibald said were the colours of the new young king of Wessex. The crowd groaned like a single giant as Brocmail's lance caught Redhelm full on the centre of his shield and fairly lifted him off his horse. The young warrior fell heavily but sprang up quickly and made a low bow to his opponent who was wheeling his horse at the head of the field. All the cheers now were for the victor, but many young boys and children followed Redhelm as he left the field. Gytha and Aldyth went to find Torhelm and I joined them.

We found Torhelm recovered from the rage that had followed his defeat on the testing field, and surrounded by a small group of young men and women who admired him still for his rich gear and pleasant nature. Among them were my brothers, HestanandGodwine. Gytha and I sat down nearby, but Aldyth went without hesitation to Torhelm and asked him if she could fetch food or drink for him.

"A little cheese from your father's table, if you would," he said and then he looked over at me, "And Edith, would you fetch me a beaker of mead? There is a great thirst that comes upon a beaten man."

Everyone laughed, and I felt glad that he could overcome his defeat with lightheartedness. I was elated, too, that he had used my name, and I jumped up from my seat on the grass and went quickly to fulfil my charge.

I was returning with a beaker of mead when I passed a group of warriors who had just arrived and were unbuckling their equipment and resting their horses. One was a giant of a man, tall and powerfully built, with a plaited beard and long grizzled hair. There was something about his stance and the shape of his face that pulled at my mind, whether from memory or simply awe, I did not know. I turned my face towards him, my eyes large, and I fear I was not taking sufficient care of the brimming beaker I held between my hands. As I looked, some of the men saw me watching them and turned their eyes on me.

Now, my new dress was a good deal longer than my usual clothes, no doubt because my step-mother thought it wise to allow for my growth in the case of a costly garment. However, its length had caused me some difficulty that day and now became the source of my humiliation. As the ground rose slightly, my shoe lighted on the hem of my dress, tripping me, and I tumbled over in full view of my heroes, spilling mead into the ground. The men who had noticed me then broke into hearty laughter. I was bowed with shame as I retrieved the beaker and tried to stand up, but my foot was still fast under the hem of my dress and I simply tumbled over again. There was more laughter and by this time my face was hot as fire, with tears of misery rising to my eyes, which only shamed me more.

I sought to disentangle my shoe (whose leather fastening had somehow coupled itself to the underthreads of the hated dress) whilst at the same time fighting to control my tears; I knew that my lost dignity could not be recovered, for I laboured under the derision of the warriors, and this was as burdensome as any heavy rainstorm could have been to my efforts. As I struggled, a shadow fell upon me and I looked up to see someone crouching over me, his body shielding me from the view of the others who tormented me. He had on a warrior's breastplate and tunic, but looked no older than my brother Farin, for his face was soft and young. His hair, which was the colour of fox's fur, was shorn and tousled, and I perceived that he must have only just removed his headgear. His eyes were palest green like icy meltwater and bore an expression I could not read.

Any kind word would have made me weep, and so be further humiliated. But he simply said, "Keep still," and quickly dislodged my foot, straightening the puckered seam of the dress with a sharp pull. He lifted me to my feet and gathered the top of my dress up over my waist-belt, so that the skirt was shortened, making it easier for me to walk. "Now," he said, "take the beaker and get it refilled. Give care to your eyes and your task." He looked into my eyes with a direct stare, and I believe truly that he knew how I was feeling in my heart, for he gave my shoulders a tiny shake and said "You shall not weep."

The urge to cry fell away from me and I ran quickly back to the meadsman and waited my turn to have the beaker refilled. As I returned more carefully, having ensured that my dress was well bloused over my waist-belt, keeping the length of it away from my feet, I was joined by Archibald, who now had a impressive black eye – a trophy of that morning's fight with Jeneth Brown. I described to him the young warrior who had helped me.

"Did you say he had cropped red hair?" said he.

"Yes."

"Why Edith, that was Redhelm, from the testing field. It is Redhelm who has helped you!"

I gasped and turned to where I had last seen the young warrior, but Archibald said he had gone from Beornwine, for he had seen him go, riding on his dappled-grey horse and carrying his long red shield. Redhelm was gone, but I knew that I would never forget the steely kindness of the young warrior, his eyes of palest meltwater-green, and his words spoken in that light, stern voice *"Give care to your eyes and your task."* The memory of those words would often come to my mind over the years of my growing, when I felt my spirit stoop to grief or self-pity. So it was that the young red-haired warrior became as an image of courage to me long into my future.

21

Under a Canopy

As Archibald and I returned to Torhelm we saw that he was speaking closely to our brothers HestanandGodwine.

A glowing-faced Gytha joined us, "I introduced them to him," she said proudly, "and told him they were your brothers."

I approached Torhelm with the mead, glad to deliver it safely into his hands. He took it from me absently for he was questioning HestanandGodwine as to their experience with hunting and horsemanship.

"I am in need of a squire," he said, "but I am minded now to have two squires, for undoubtedly you work well together."

"We do, my Lord," said Godwine with a smile.

"And share each other's thoughts, on occasion," added Hestan in the manner of one who mourns.

Torhelm looked from one to the other. Indeed, I have said before that my brothers looked at their best that day in their embroidered blue and white tabards and red breeches. Torhelm, who was dark-haired, no doubt guessed the striking contrast such a pair of fair-haired squires would make with himself.

"We are to go with the Father to escort the harvest offerings to the Abbey tonight, my Lord," said Hestan.

"I too plan to join the escort," said Torhelm, "So we shall ride together!" He gave his wide charming smile, lifted the beaker of mead and drank it down in one draught, then strode away.

I was thrilled to think of my brothers being given the opportunity of squiring for such a fine and rich thegn. I could not contain my excitement but ran off to find someone to whom I could impart such news. To my great satisfaction I soon found my parents camped under a tree with my brothers Hereward, Alvar and Farin, and many of our household around them. They had raised up a sturdy canopy between two branches with, underneath, a trestle bearing much food and drink upon it, which made me realise that I was hungry again.

I ran immediately to Father, confident that my news was important enough to be taken straight to him. "HestanandGodwine are to squire for the Lord Torhelm," I said breathlessly. All stared at me in a most satisfactory manner. After a moment of silence, Elanor turned to my father and said in a quiet voice, "We could not expect them to stay always Finric. They have been mad to go questing for years."

I made to speak up in agreement, but Bebbe took me aside and gave me bread and soft cheese to eat. So I used my mouth for eating, rather than speaking, and instead followed the talk with my eyes and ears.

Elanor was looking into my father's face, the expression of which had turned to its easy anger. But he did not answer immediately, and I believe he accepted the truth of Elanor's words.

"They are my best warriors, and my best huntsmen," he said, "How am I to feed this great household without them?"

Hereward and Heath, the foremost farmers of our land, simply looked at him and Hereward's face flushed although he remained silent.

"You have two other fine huntsmen amongst your sons," said Elanor: then looking up at Archibald, who at that minute joined us, she smiled and corrected herself, "*Three* fine huntsmen and one of the best husbandmen in the country." With a gentle hand, she gestured towards Hereward.

Father opened his mouth as if to speak, but instead reached out and put his hand upon Hereward's shoulder, then took a draught of ale. "With HestanandGodwine gone I shall have to arm Alvar and Farin."

Elanor pulled Archibald towards her and began fussing over his bruised face, dabbing at it with a milk-soaked cloth. She continued talking to Father, "Farin is young, yet," she protested mildly, "Surely there are doughty bondsmen enough in our household to send if war comes near."

"Yes, but my own sons should be properly armed, and I have a mind to go to Einiog, for no better swords are made anywhere."

Farin, who was nearby and I could see was listening intently, spoke up urgently. "Father, if you are going to Einiog, take me!"

"Not you. It is meet that the elder sons accompany me. Hereward may come or not, as he wishes. And I shall take Alvar also, for he is next in age."

It happened that Alvar had sat down nearby to eat his bread and soft cheese, which he was mightily fond of. He looked up as his name was spoken, but scowled at the prospect of the journey to Einiog. Such a journey could be perilous, for it was well known that the Welsh did not always take kindly to travellers, even those with the means to purchase the highest quality goods that the skilled armourers of Einiog could produce. Alvar seemed as impressed as any of us by stories of questing and the fine appearance and manner of thegns, but I do not believe that real journeys with their dangers and discomforts held any attraction for him.

Farin could see Alvar's humour and cried, "But Father, Alvar would not wish to go, and he is not as strong as I. He takes cold more easily. I am hardy and the better hunter."

"The more reason for you to stay behind," rejoined Father.

I sighed. It was true that Farin was taller and broader than Alvar, even though, at fifteen winters, he was a year younger, but Father would keep to his belief in the rank of seniority, which had already created much discord in our family.

Father had heard me sigh, but only looked on me with a smile and said, "What, would you go to Einiog, Edith? Ride out with me and bring back swords for all your brothers?"

Everyone laughed, and no more was said of the journey to Einiog that day. But in truth, I would have loved to be taken by my father on that journey. I knew it could not happen that year, for I was his youngest child, but I expected some day to go to see the great Welsh armouries and witness the forging of swords. I longed for it.

At that time in my life, when I had not yet seen seven winters, the world of my imagination was as alive to me as the real world where I ate and slept and played. I knew that I was a girl child, and that girls did not seem generally to become fighting thegns. Yet I never conceived a future where I did not bear arms or ride to quest. Likewise, I had been told that I would never see a unicorn, for no such thing lived upon the earth. Yet I believed that, deep in thick forests, the shy creature dwelt, alive as myself.

Father fell to questioning Archibald about Lord Torhelm and his wish to take HestanandGodwine for squires. "He is a rich man," said Father, and I guessed he had been talking to Siric about the finely attired guest of his hostelry. "He would expect his squires to be well endowed with mounts and arms."

"So they are," said Elanor.

"Yes, but they will need better before they go. Any son of Finric Fly shall be seen well in the world. They shall have money enough, and clothes and arms."

Then, I was puzzled by Father's apparent change of mind from reluctance that the twins should leave, to this generous proposal to endow them with riches and new gear. Now, I know that my father saw his sons as reflections of himself so that if he was to let them go, he would do so with a view to his own status.

Before the morning of the Grain Rite I had been keen to see Fritha again, and had a great curiosity to see her meet with Hereward and observe again their fascination for each other. But the truth is that I had forgotten Fritha in the excitement of the day, full as it was with thegns and giants, feasting and marvellous sights. It is little wonder that matters of previous great interest to me had fallen to the background.

Hereward was not taking any great part in the family discussion of the planned journey to Einiog, and now I saw him stand and look across the field. Other eyes followed his, and I quickly scrambled up the tree behind us. It was a hazel and an easy climber, and I had a good start by clambering up my friend Heath, who was sitting leaning against it. Heath bore this with his usual good humour and I was soon sitting on one of the tree's lower branches with my eyes at the level of a man's. From there I followed Hereward's gaze across the field and past the booth where the holy man sat under his purple canopy at Chief Wulfred's booth.

Approaching him was a little group, moving slowly and awkwardly. It was Fritha Elfrith and her father with Fritha's mother seated between them in a little basket seat, which they carried between them, although Fritha's father had only one good hand and arm. His shield- arm, thin as a sapling, with a hand like nothing so much as a pale claw, was bound to his side, being quite useless. As I watched, they set down the basket-seat and supported the sick woman so that she might kneel before the Father Maldon. But, with a gesture for them to stay themselves, the holy man got up from his own seat and knelt before her, laying a blessing on her head and placing some sacred token in her hand. I felt a rush of warmth in my heart to see Father Maldon's kindness, and knew that I had been right to like him despite his sharp looks. He made some small prayer with the poor woman and then Fritha and her father again took up the seat bearing their dear one and carried her away.

Without a word, Hereward hurried off towards them. I leapt down from the tree, landing on Heath, who made some mild complaint that I did not heed.

"It's Fritha!" I shouted, "Mother, Fritha is come with her family, and they are blessed by the holy man!"

And I set off after Hereward.

As a family we met them, and without even the ceremony of "Gods Day" Hereward and Farin immediately relieved Fritha and Herin Elfrith of their burden, taking Fritha's mother up easily between them in her little seat. Elanor bent towards her. "Judith, are you well?"

"I am well, Elanor, I thank you." The reply was between a whisper and a murmur.

"But was it wise to come on this hot day? You are yet weak."

"I *would* come, for Fritha would not leave me, and I had such a wish to see the Rite myself!" Fritha's mother stopped and made a low cough. Her face had a moist look to it and was thinner than when I saw her last, but her cheeks were bright with a reddish flush, which I thought a sign of health.

Now my father spoke to Fritha's father. "Greetings to you Herin Elfrith. If it pleases you, bring your family to my canopy. There is more food and drink than we can eat and I would count it an honour for you to break bread with us."

Though a poor man, and small in stature, Herin made a noble bow, which my father returned as though they were equals. "Thank you, my Lord," said Herin, "The honour is mine."

I was struck dumb for a little time, partly from admiration at my own father's magnanimous words and kindly gestures, but also because this was the first (but not the last) time I heard him called 'My Lord'. Now he turned to Judith and, bending low, took her up out of her little seat into his arms as if she was a child, and carried her gently to our canopy, setting her down on some soft cushions that Bebbe quickly arranged there. We all followed behind and Elanor prepared platters of sweetmeats and savouries for our new guests, while Father fetched beakers of our own ale to Fritha's father.

Thus these poor neighbours of ours were treated as honoured guests. While I watched Elanor and Father making willing servants of themselves before them, I understood that, if the Elfrith family was raised up by such attention, then the Fly family increased its own nobility by showing kindness to those less favoured than themselves. Whatever the truth of it, for the second time that day, if for a different reason, I felt glad and proud to belong to my family.

Hereward set his horse's fleece-saddle on a fallen log nearby and offered it as a seat to Fritha, so that she might eat in comfort. He sat beside her on the grass, looking up at her as they talked softly to each other, neither of them touching any of the victuals that Elanor had brought. Thinking they did not care for the food, and my curiosity wanting an excuse to take me close to Fritha and Hereward, I carried a handful of honeycakes over to them. They made no notice of me at all, although I stood close by holding out the honeycakes towards them.

Fritha was asking after Hereward's wounded hands, "I hope the burns are healing now," she said. But, although he was looking at her face as she spoke, Hereward seemed not to have heard her. I thought that his mind was on something else that he wanted to speak of, but feared to do so. At least, that was how it seemed to me. Fritha said again, with a dip of her head and a little smile, "Your hands, do they heal well?"

Hereward held his palms out towards her and she took his hands in her own, examining the burn wounds, which, although still red, were healing well. Ignored, I took a bite of honeycake, and sat down to watch them, thinking there was something of fear in Hereward's countenance as he gazed at Fritha. But he seemed to take courage now that her eyes were no longer on his face. His lips moved; I think he said her name, although I could hear nothing of his voice save a slight whisper. She looked into his eyes; Hereward cleared his voice and there was so much love in his gaze that Fritha's face seemed bathed in the rosy glory of some invisible rising sun. I temporarily lost interest in my honeycake.

"Fritha," he murmured, "I am so happy to see you and be with you this day."

I thought Fritha flamed with beauty and graciousness. The plain saddle on which she sat might have been a throne and she a queen receiving courtiers. "I too am glad that we can be here together," she said.

Suddenly, there was a mighty shout from behind me and there were HestanandGodwine coming towards us with the great Torhelm between them, resplendent in his costly armour, and Archibald alongside them, running to keep up with their long strides. All thoughts of Hereward and Fritha's concerns were gone from my head as I saw my father rise from his seat and go to meet the newcomers.

Godwine stepped forward. "Father," he said, "May I present the Lord Torhelm." He turned to Torhelm, "My Lord, this is our father, the master Finric Fly." Father and Torhelm bowed deeply to each other, and Father said, "My Lord, you are well come. We have here only meat and poor foodstuffs and plain ale, but what we have is yours." He made a gesture for Torhelm to join our party under the canopy.

Torhelm supplied his ready smile and divested himself of breastplate and helmet, which he handed to Farin and Archibald, who were at his shoulder from the moment he arrived. "Indeed, sire," he said, "I have been fortunate enough to eat the meat of your household at Master Siric's table, and declare it to be of the first quality in the land." He turned then and winked at me, "As to your ale, I know it only by reputation, and am eager to become more closely acquainted with it." Everyone laughed at this, and I ran to fetch a beakerfull for him.

Soon Torhelm was seated at the centre of our party with a full plate before him and a brimming beaker of ale in his hand. He and Father spoke together for some time of travelling and combat and hunting. All of our household party (and many others, for Torhelm seemed always to have a small army of admirers following him about) stayed close, listening to these tales of adventure. Needless to say, I was there, drinking in every word, and whilst they were talking I saw Torhelm's expression turn from affable friendliness to sober respect as he heard of the battles Father had fought with the Lord Ulef in the Welsh and Mercian wars, and his valour in recent times in defence of Beornwine against raiders and other enemies.

It was only when I was forced to tear myself away from the group in order to empty my bladder that I saw Hereward and Fritha again, and remembered my earlier absorption with their concerns. I was coming back from behind a bush, much relieved, when I saw them walking a little distance away. They were close together, holding hands, and their eyes seemed locked in wondrous fascination at the sight of each other's faces. I thought they could not know of Torhelm's visit, and ran to them straight away to tell them of it.

"Hereward," I said, "The Lord Torhelm is come to speak with Father, for you know he is to have HestanandGodwine to squire for him!"

Hereward turned to me with the expression of calm pity that I have since seen often on the faces of those in the first throes of love when they look upon anyone but their beloved (I have seen a similar expression on the faces of simple madmen too – but it is well known that to be in love is to loosen the powers of reason for a spell).

"Yes Edith," he said, seemingly to humour me, "Is it not a fine thing for our brothers?"

I agreed with him, of course, but I could see that he had no real interest in anything but Fritha. Wanting to please them both, but not knowing what to say, I smiled at Fritha and took her hand. This made them both laugh lightly (I could not imagine why, but was beginning to accept they were both simple-minded in each other's company).

"It is good of you to leave such fine company in order to be with us, little sister," said Hereward, "And so, I think," he paused and looked at Fritha, who nodded, "Yes," he said, "You shall be the first to know: Fritha has pledged to marry me. We shall be betrothed today before the holy man, if our parents give their permission."

I could not pretend to be surprised, but was glad to hear of it, for I had never witnessed a betrothal. "But of course they will agree Hereward," I said, frowning, "Has not Father been talking to you of the Elfrith land? But perhaps Fritha's mother and Father will not agree."

"I think they will agree, little Edith," said Fritha, "but it is only meet that we should humbly ask their permission in a proper way, for we owe everything to our parents, do we not?"

I considered this question seriously, and decided it was largely true, so I nodded, continuing to hold Fritha's hand as we walked together to our canopy again. It seemed that I was, once again, to be bearing good news towards my family that day.

As we approached, we could see Elanor talking with Fritha's mother Judith. When they saw us, Judith struggled to her feet with Elanor taking her arm to help her. Slowly, they came to meet us, with Judith leaning heavily on Elanor's arm. Nobody else seemed to notice us, for everyone was listening to the great men talking of noble deeds. Now Fritha hurried forward, "Oh Mother!" she said, but she was smiling and it seemed nothing further needed to be said for both the mothers to know exactly what had transpired between Hereward and Fritha. Both were smiling, and yet both had tears in their eyes. They kissed Hereward and they kissed Fritha, entirely ignoring me, and then we saw that at last all the people under and around my father's canopy were watching.

We all returned to my father's canopy, making slow progress for the sake of Judith, who would not be carried. Herin Elfrith came out to meet his wife and daughter and Hereward formally asked for Fritha's hand in marriage. There was a stir among our party as people began to notice these events, and to see the sunrise faces of Hereward and Fritha. Then my father saw them, and stood to welcome us back, with all around him getting to their feet also. I had feared that Father would have lost interest in the Elfriths since the coming of great Torhelm, but it was not so, and he made a ceremony of receiving Hereward and Fritha together. Then Hereward fell to his knees before Father, with his head bowed but his back straight. "My Lord," he said, "I would take Fritha Elfrith to wife, if it is agreeable to you."

I held my breath then, for, despite his earlier kindness to Judith and Herin, I thought Father might not like Hereward and Fritha to marry, on account of the Elfriths being so much poorer than us. I need not have worried, for my father knew well that Hereward's marriage to Fritha would bring all the Elfrith land under his control, for Herin Elfrith could not work it himself and must give it over to our family, although he and his wife would never more want for food or shelter. More land meant more power, as Father knew, and he was well able to hire more bondsmen to our household.

Father's voice roared out with ale-fuelled volume, "So! I lose three of my sons in one day. Much of a blessing is this Grain Rite! Two of them off to squire for a great thegn, and now one to marry." He said it ruefully, but with good humour, staring at Fritha who blushed like a poppy. But Fritha's embarrassment seemed to touch Father's compassion and his expression melted from fierceness to benevolence. Hereward said, "I shall not be far, and the Elfrith land is not so great as ours. With Heath I can work both, provided we have enough bondsmen."

"And you shall have enough," said Father with a great smile, "I shall see to it that my son's household has everything it needs."

He turned then to Herin and they clasped sword-arms. "It is a good union, brother Elfrith," said Father. Everyone cheered and more ale was called for. It was agreed between Father and Herin, Elanor and Judith, that a great feast would take place at the second full moon from that day, and Hereward would then go to live with Fritha at the Elfrith household, at least for a little while. "That will give time for the making of a new house next to your own," said Father, "My son has much skill in the fair arranging of buildings, and my bondsmen will be at his service for the work."

Hereward's face was quiet with wonder at this rare display of praise and generosity, and I thought that, in simply escaping from a storm, I had played my part well in this new affection between Father and his eldest son.

Elanor spoke with Judith about the arranging of the feast, "There will be much preparation to do," she said with a smile, "And how I shall enjoy it!" She touched Judith lightly on the arm, "Do not trouble yourself with any of it, sister," she said, "Our household will supply all victuals needed, but I shall value your thoughts on what food we should serve, and who we might invite to the feast."

"You are most kind, sister," Judith replied, her voice soft and breathless, "I shall be happy with anything you arrange. I only hope to be well enough to see it all."

It seemed that, whilst I had been with Hereward and Fritha, Torhelm had settled an agreement with Father to take HestanandGodwine as squires. They were to ride together to the Holywell Abbey with the holy man the following day and then return to us before setting out with Torhelm to do business or battle beside him, as he required. This news thrilled me to my very heart. So it was true: my brothers were really to go questing with a noble thegn! I felt their luck, their wishes granted, almost as deeply as if I myself had been asked to squire for Torhelm. With the excitement of the day, the happy turn of events for Hereward and Fritha, and now this wonderful news of HestanandGodwine which touched the dream of my own heart, I was overcome with excitement. I skipped and jumped around, shrieking in my excitement and pestering the twins until Hestan said, "Be still Edith. Let us have some peace." His tone was more distracted than sharp, but his words had the effect of a slap and I surprised myself by bursting into tears, whereupon I was carried to my step-mother and rocked like a baby until I fell asleep.

But, in my dream, I rode beside my brother thegn – his hair fox red and his eyes meltwater-green. And we were travelling to quest.

22

Before the Holy Man

I woke only a little while later, feeling much refreshed. Elanor gave me some milk to drink and then pointed out a large group of people, congregating in the area before the holy man's canopy. "See, Edith," she said, "Here are all the youths and maidens who would be betrothed, all going to the holy man for blessing."

I jumped up, afraid that I had missed the betrothals, but Elanor reassured me it was not yet time. Then Hereward and Fritha, and also Heath and Bebbe were got ready for the ceremony. Fritha sat in front of her mother, who plaited sprigs of rosemary into her hair, while Elanor did the same for Hereward. I was sent off with Gytha and Aldyth to pick armfuls of flowers from around the edges of the field, where daisies, clover, buttercups and other such plants bloomed in profusion. Small bunches of these were put in Hereward and Fritha's hair, behind their ears and fixed into their garments at shoulder, belt, neck and seam. The same was done for Bebbe and Heath. A basket was filled with flowers and given to Fritha to hold. Then Father took his own seax from its scabbard at his waist, handed it to Hereward, and Elanor tied more flowers to its handle.

All this preparation was accompanied by much hilarity and good feeling towards the betrothal couples. Gleeful remarks were shouted to them by my brothers and other people of our household, although I did not understand many of these jokes and could not find anyone willing to explain them to me. Hereward and Fritha smiled and blushed under such mirth, but held fast mainly to each other's gaze and seemed to share a condition of simple bliss. I remember that I was happy in my heart to see them thus.

Then Hereward strode over to Heath and, the pair of them all bedecked in flowers, they clasped hands and laughed together. "I had not thought to be sharing this day with you in such a way, brother!" said Hereward.

"I am glad of it," answered Heath. They stood together – so handsome in the flourishing of their youth – and bowed towards Fritha and Bebbe who were waiting nearby blooming like two daughters of the Goddess Flora.

At last, Fritha and Hereward, Bebbe and Heath, began to move towards the gathering near the holy man's canopy. I ran alongside them with Gytha and Aldyth, throwing flowers at their feet. Soon all around the field was a circular procession of couples wanting betrothal blessings from the holy man. When the procession stopped, Chief Wulfred's youngest son, Alfred, stood with his chosen maid before the purple canopy. They took the first blessing from the holy man, and second were Hereward and Fritha.

I was aware, and understood, how my brother's place in the procession – second only to the son of Chief Wulfred himself - honoured my family, for it signified our high status in Beornwine. I wondered at it and was glad because I could remember our coming to that place - when we had nothing but ourselves and a tail of memory we would fain cast away. Seemingly out of nowhere, that memory touched me now, lightly but with intense pain, like a nettle burn. A shadow like the flap of a raven's wing fell over my soul, and my mind's eye was pierced by the memory of a stark white sun on a black background – the standard of the terrible Lord Orin. For that moment, in the midst of nobility and plenty, delight and celebration, I was lonely and cold amongst the happy throng.

With an effort, I threw off dark thoughts and gave my attention to the ceremony. Hereward and Fritha knelt side by side, heads bowed, before the holy man. He raised his hand over them and made an incantation in the magical Christian tongue. Then, at a word from him, they stood up and Hereward placed the seax in Fritha's basket. The Holy Father murmured something to them, whereupon they turned to each other and kissed. The cheer that greeted this sight came from all the Fly household and very many other onlookers, and it went on for a good time, signifying how my brother and his new maid were well-liked in Beornwine. This, I trow, had nothing to do with riches or high family, but was solely for the sake of Hereward and Fritha themselves, whose kindness and spirit brought forth love from everyone. They were well matched indeed.

We stayed and watched all the blessings – as many as twenty in all. Some of the couples, like Hereward and Fritha, were at the beginning of their union, others were well past beginning, for some of the maids showed great round bellies, and one carried her baby in her arms and had a double blessing from the holy man. Here we saw Mother Werberga casting flowers and sweet herbs over all the newly betrothed couples for a blessing. I greeted her joyfully and she seemed full glad to see me, and gave me her basket to hold while she twisted together some herb-sprigs in a tiny bunch and tied them on to a woven cord which she put around my neck.

"There, child," she said, "Here are herbs for a journey. May their scent strengthen you when you hunger and thirst."

Mother Werberga was indeed a surprising woman. I felt a blush come to my face, for she seemed to read my heart, but how could she know that I had notions of taking any journey, except the journey home at the end of the day? I thought well to question her, but she kissed me and hurried off to sprinkle her herbs over another couple. I tucked the herb-charm inside my dress to keep it safe.

When all the betrothals had been blessed we all walked back to our canopy, with Fritha and Bebbe casting flowers from their baskets to everyone around. I caught a little bunch of daisies that Fritha tossed to me, which I knew was a very lucky sign and would bring me a good husband. I was glad enough to have caught the bunch of daisies, although I cared little for the idea of a husband.

23

Hidden

More food and drink was consumed as the day faded to dusk, torches were lit and music played. Although my spirit still chirruped with excitation, my body was too weary even to stand. I curled up beneath a tree next to Archibald with Spin at our feet, and listened to a minstrel playing a ballad of love to Hereward and Fritha. The music passed so easily between my competing states of weariness and wakefulness that I knew I would not avoid sleep for very long. Yet I felt urgently within me that I should resist it, for there was something preying on my mind, a vital need that I must fulfil. My thoughts grasped the essence of that need, but the shape of it escaped me as I sank into dreams.

I awoke in my own bed at home. Bright spears of daylight penetrated the gloom of our shuttered house, but the still, breathing peacefulness all around assured me that my family slept late. The unnamed anxiety with which I had fought off sleep was now obvious and clear before my mind. I felt for the cord around my neck, and squeezed the little bunch of herbs which was still there, for Mother Werberga had tied it well. A sweet, astringent scent rose from the herbs, sharpening my wakefulness. I clad myself quietly and quickly in common-day dress, and lifted Spin into my arms to keep him quiet. Full of apprehension, I peeped into my brothers' sleeping loft. Hereward's place was empty, which hardly concerned me. I sought the presence of two others, but saw quickly that what I had feared had come to pass: HestanandGodwine were gone.

Struggling with the weight of Spin, but not daring to put him down for fear he would wake the others, I climbed down to the house. The house-dogs greeted me with quiet noses and I carefully opened the door, letting them out. I then drank a ladle-full of water and grabbed a handful of oatcakes which I folded into my dress. I was all haste but could take neither mount nor dog, for either would betray my purpose. I tied Spin to a tether-post where I was often want to leave him for short periods. He began to complain so I quietened him with the bribe of an oatcake, crumbled onto the ground to keep him busy.

Then I simply ran.

Sweat was on my brow as I reached my destination. And the field of Beornwine lay bright in the early morning sunshine, yet few people were about. I guessed that the last night's festivities lasted long after I had given in to sleep, and, like my own family, many people would not begin their day until long after their normal hour. I did not linger, but made straight for Siric's house. I knew every bed in the house was taken and that the stables would also be full, with many horses tethered outside. Among them I recognised HestanandGodwine's mounts, Willow and Archer. I muttered a prayer of thanks that the holy man had not yet set out to the Abbey with the harvest offering and its escort. I wondered if the twins slept inside the house near their new lord, but thought it more likely that they would have made a bed in the stables. Whichever was the case, I could not stay, for too many people knew me there and I did not wish to be seen.

It was my full intention to go with my brothers to the Abbey. I would answer my soul's need to travel with the escort, along with thegns, warriors and huntsmen: to be among that company. I knew that such an honour was not allowed to me, but I intended to take it anyway for myself. It was necessary for me to stay hidden, but I *would go*.

At the field where the Grain Rite had taken place, a few more people were beginning to stir. I saw that the carts loaded with harvest produce had all been left close together behind the holy man's canopy, which still remained from the day before, although no-one was under the sheet of rich purple cloth which was now damp with dew. The holy man himself, who had no servant but had come unescorted to the Grain Rite, was undoubtedly a guest at Chief Wulfred's house. Three young guards who had been left in charge of the carts had made themselves comfortable by dragging hay bales onto the grass and propping themselves against it. They all seemed deeply asleep but I saw that one of them was Jeneth Brown, his face swollen with bruises from the beating Archibald had given him and a livid bite-mark from my own teeth clear on his wrist. I stopped, fearing to wake him and be recognised. One of the other youths lifted a sleepy eyelid and saw me, but found this small child of no interest and settled himself back into slumber. There was an empty mead-jar lying on its side in the grass nearby and I guessed the senses of these young guards would not be very alert on this morning after all the revelry.

I recognised my family's cart nearby, piled high with hay, vegetables and fruits from our land together with a couple of smoked hams and other produce, as well as offerings from the Elfrith's and other neighbours, who had not their own carts. Meaning to remain as unseen as I could, I moved behind a group of tents set up near to the empty meadsman's stall. As I passed by the entrance to one of them, a man stumbled out of the low opening, and was suddenly face to face with me. I started with surprise and took a step backward. At the same moment I recognised him as the big warrior with the plaited beard: one of those who had laughed at me when I fell with the beaker of mead. He growled at me "What do you want boy?"

I was no coward, but there was something in the nature of his face that echoed in my memory, as it had the previous day. It discomforted me, but I found my voice. "Nothing, Sire," I whispered. Then, discovering a spark of inner satisfaction in being mistaken for a boy, I kindled my courage and spoke up, "I am only passing by."

He gave a grunt and a crooked smile, perhaps pleased to have been called "Sire", then seized me by the arm in a bruising grip. I gasped with the pain, but an inner sense told me not to cry out. He put his face close to mine and narrowed his eyes in a quizzical way. I could smell sour ale and something rotten on his breath. "Get me water," he ordered pushing me away with a final wrench to my arm that made me stagger. My instinct was to run far away, but I thought it would be better to bring the water and then flee as quickly as possible, rather than risk him coming to find me in anger if I did not do as he bade me. I ran to the well head and was glad to find a leather bucket half-full of water. I had no cup or beaker, so took the bucket itself, struggling along with some difficulty, for it was heavy and banged against my leg with every step. When I arrived back at the warrior's tent, he was sitting on the grass with his knees up and his big head in his hands. Another man crawled out of the tent, and noticed me. "What's this, Garth?" he said, "Some new servant of yours?"

The big man looked up, and, without a word, grabbed the bucket from me with both hands, drinking straight from it as easily as from a drinking cup. What water he did not swallow simply poured out over his face and beard. This was a curious sight which, foolishly, I watched for a moment instead of making my escape. In a flash his eye was on me, and he lowered the bucket to watch me more closely, as if he sought something in my face.

"Don't go away boy," he grunted, "I've not finished with you."

He raised the bucket again, and I guessed the previous night's drinking was hanging heavily on him. He was big, but I calculated that I was faster. I turned and darted off around the tent. A roar and the pounding of feet behind me told me he was following. Quickly, I ran behind the mead stall. I knew there were two sturdy ropes, stayed to the ground with strong pegs to keep it steady, and I knew they were hidden in the long summer grass. I took a chance and a leap, clearing the ropes by a small margin. I was rewarded by the sound of curses and a body falling heavily. This gave me time to reach the harvest carts. But Jeneth Brown was now awake and on his feet. His back was towards me, but he must have heard me running, because I saw him begin to turn around. Without a thought, I dived under the Holy Father's canopy and hid myself in a fold of damp purple cloth, from behind which I watched Brown peering about and then walking with stiff and painful movements towards a nearby tree, against which he began to relieve himself. A glance at the other guards told me they were still fast asleep and I stepped from behind the canopy and quickly eased myself between two of the nearby carts. Behind them was my own family's cart. In a minute I had climbed onto it and wriggled my way into the middle of a stook of sheaves. I lay there panting for breath and listening to my heart beating so loud and fast I thought Jeneth Brown or the dreadful Garth must hear it. I expected to be pounced on with a roar at any moment. By the time my heart had quietened itself, I knew I was safe.

The tied sheaves made for a prickly bed and I pulled my garment around me to protect myself from the sharp straws, realising that the oat cakes I had brought with me from home were gone – no doubt lost in my flight from Garth. However, I was not hungry, but had just begun to wonder whether I might be able to find a more comfortable hiding place when I heard voices and the sound of hooves over the ground. Peering between the sheaves, I saw a nearby cart being pulled away and oxen harnessed between the shafts. Soon there were sounds and movement all around me. HestanandGodwine came and, with Beron, our armed bondsman who was to keep charge of the cart, made ready our own ox in its shafts.

I held my breath for as long as I could and kept still until the cart began to move. I could not risk being discovered and taken home in disgrace. I wanted adventure, I was mad for it. The truth was, no thought passed my mind of the home and loved-ones I left behind. My being was focussed on a single object, to journey in the company of thegns. Beyond that, I had no aim. Neither motive nor reason, hunger nor thirst, weariness nor discomfort held significance for me. My will bade me go, and I *would* go, by whatever means or mode possible.

There were narrow gaps between the cart planks, which gave me a limited view, and from time to time as the day went on I glimpsed my brothers' horses near to the cart, and heard their voices and Torhelm's too, talking in jovial tones, although the creaking and buffeting of the cart prevented me catching the sense of their words. There was a halt at midday to let the animals eat, but I dared not move from my hiding place. We set off again, time passed to the jolting of the cart and my discomfort grew. First I began to feel hungry, and much regretted the oat cakes that had fallen from my dress. Soon, however, thirst took over from hunger, with nothing to be done to slake it. Now I remembered Mother Werberga's words. I felt for the cord at my throat and squeezed the little bunch of herbs tied to it, finding some comfort as their fresh scent filled my head.

Suddenly, there was a violent jolt and I was thrown against the side of the cart, with a great weight of produce threatening to squeeze the life out of me. I managed to suppress a yell, although my shoulder was sorely bruised where it struck against a wooden peg in the corner.

We stopped. Footsteps came close and there was muttering from Beron; then I heard Godwine's voice, not a hands-span from my head, "What is it?"

"The wheel's hit a rut. I trust to God the axle stays true."

"Lead on the ox slowly. I'll check the wheels."

We creaked; we swayed; we became upright. The press of compacted wheatsheaves against my side eased itself and shifted back into place. Something round and firm fell through the hay and banged against my head, then another. I bore the bruising silently. Soon, amid shouts that all was well, we resumed our steady pace and I was free to investigate what missiles had struck me. Imagine how I rejoiced to find that two large apples had fallen from a basket high above and now nestled in the hay next to me. Quickly I bit into one, thankful for its sharp and thirst-easing juice. I kept the other wrapped in a fold of my dress so that it could not roll away and, with my thirst temporarily relieved, if only a little, I managed to fall asleep, despite the motion of the cart and discomfort of my prickly bed.

At last the day ended and the travellers made camp, but there was no relief for me. I could not move from the cart without discovery, as Beron made his bed under it and spent a noisy night snoring, shuffling and mumbling so that I knew not whether he slept or woke. Furthermore, I was almost put to swoon by the stink of his farts. To make matters worse, it became needful for me to empty my bladder. The natural course would be to let my water out through the space between the planks underneath me. Indeed, I amused myself with the thought that to send a shower of piss upon Beron would be fair retribution for the venomous nature of his gasses. However, I was saved from this worst kind of discovery when Beron himself got up from under the cart and went off. Very soon I heard the sound of a watery stream hitting the base of a nearby tree, and I took the opportunity of relieving myself at the same time, only praying that Beron would make his bed in a different position when he returned and not notice the wet patch under the cart. Whether he did or not, I never knew, for, with my bladder relieved, I fell instantly asleep and did not wake again until the cart was being prepared to move in the early morning.

Thus began a second day of discomfort, thirst and hunger. Once the cart was under way, I was able to stretch my limbs, but my movements could only be minimal. Consider the pain of a child – used to running about freely through every waking hour – now constrained in a hard and prickly space for two days, without even being able to sit up. It was sorely hurtful to my spirit as well as my body. But that very spirit would not allow surrender and discovery. Wilfulness and determination kept me hidden, although I wept silent tears for my bodily distress. I early ate the second apple, conserving every drop of its juice, but it was little enough; my thirst grew. I eventually lay with Mother Werberga's herbs next to my face, inhaling their soothing scent, and pitching in and out of uneasy sleep.

At the dusk of that long day, I awoke to the jolt of the cart falling on to its stays as the ox was released from the shafts. The animals were led away, and there were sounds of men and women talking, words of greeting and invitations to rest, eat and drink. This caused me agonies of longing and resentment as, among many others, I heard the voices of the twins, Beron and the Lord Torhelm fading away, doubtless in the direction of comforts that were denied to me. My resentment was of course without reason, for my situation was entirely of my own making. Knowing this, I lay still, hoping the carts would be left alone long enough for me to make my escape and find water to drink. I was horrified, therefore, to realise that a number of willing hands had begun swiftly to unload the carts. Layer by layer, my hiding place was disappearing. I shut my eyes and tried to make myself small against the side of the cart, but night was still too far away to offer hope in darkness. As the next sheaf was lifted up, I was discovered.

24

Sacred Spring

"Hrmph!" said a surprised voice.

I opened my eyes, but did not move. A man wearing a plain woollen garment, with a wooden Christian cross hanging from a thong around his neck, was standing at the side of the cart, looking in at me. The man seemed neither fierce nor angry, only somewhat astonished to see a child lying there at the bottom of the cart instead of another sheaf of corn or basket of roots.

"What's this?" he said "Here is rich produce indeed, and very fresh!"

I thought there was a definite twinkle in his eye. Even so, it seemed prudent for me to make some movement, in case he was short-sighted or simple minded and really thought me to be a haunch of venison or large ham. I sat up and it was a relief to be able to move after so many hours.

"I am not produce," I said.

"Then you must be escort to the fine offerings upon this cart," said he.

I knew full well that only armed men of household or settlement were permitted to escort the harvest offering. There was no good reason for my presence, only the inexplicable urgency of my own will, which would seem like foolishness to others.

I hung my head. "I am not produce," I said, "And I am not an escort. I am Edith."

He gave a little bow, "Greetings Edith, you are well come to the Holywell Abbey. My name is Brother David."

Conscious of the indignity of my situation in contrast to his courtesy, tears of shame sprang into my eyes.

He looked down on me, and there was only kindness and pity in his eyes. No doubt I made a sorry sight, with straw in my hair and my dress all awry. He ceased teasing me and held out his hand, "Come child," he said, "You need food and drink, and then I shall take you to the Abbess Leoba to see what shall be done with you."

I told him that I had a burning thirst, and was taken straight to a stone basin through which ran a constant stream of pure water that poured from a rift in the rock. Brother David took a cup that lay upon the rim of the basin and filled it for me. I drank three full cups of water before I thanked him.

He nodded, "It is meet that an innocent child should drink first and so fully from the sacred spring upon arriving in our community."

I did not feel very innocent, knowing the errors of my ways, but as I looked at his face I saw limpid purity reflected there. Under the infinite kindness of those eyes, I felt my own faults washed down into the earth with the spring water.

He took my hand and we walked towards the space that was the settlement of the Holywell Abbey. Now I was regaining some of my self-assurance, and looked about me with great interest. The arrangement of the Abbey buildings was not unlike that of my own village of Beornwine. Here, instead of stone and wood, the perimeter boundary was a thick hedge - taller than a man - atop an earth bank, except in the north where the spring flowed and the natural cliff made for good defence. The dwellings and out-buildings were all made of wood, the bigger houses having many shutters open now to the summer air. There were two large hall-sized buildings - one bigger than the other - and two great barns which were stilted to protect grain from wet and vermin. To the north by the cliff face were three or four low thatched covers and I guessed that beneath these were storage pits such as the one my father had dug at home for the preservation of meat. All around the buildings were various neat gardens or yards, with low fences around them and I recognised many of the herbs and vegetables growing there, for we cultivated similar ones for our table at home. I saw men and women walking briskly between buildings, or tending plants or animals in the fenced yards. Those that we passed close by greeted Brother David by name with, I thought, friendly deference, and I guessed him well loved in that place.

All of the foremost Abbey dwellings carried Christian crosses over their doors. Brother David took me to one of these buildings from which most delicious smells of cooked food issued forth, as did the sound of many voices. Before entering, he washed his hands at a basin of water standing at the doorway. I was glad to see that others followed the same ritual as our own household and plunged my hands also into the water. He looked at me with a quizzical smile, but nodded as if he approved of my action. Inside the dwelling a multitude of people were eating at long candle-lit tables, with men occupying one side of the room, women and children the other. As to that, there was no barrier and little space between, and both men and women were moving freely between the two sides for purposes of conversation or the carrying of food and drink.

Shutters were open to the sky, but the late evening was drawing down and torches had been lit. By their light I could see wonderful patterned cloths hanging about the walls, and painted screens in different colours, some of them depicting figures of people, and some with the Christian cross represented upon them. Few people took any notice of us as we entered, for all were busy helping themselves from great dishes of meat, fish, cheese, bread and vegetables. Brother David led me straight to the head of the women's table, where sat a lady wearing a blue robe with a beaded chain strung across her shoulder-clasps from which hung a fine gold cross studied with gems.

"God's Eve, Brother David," said the lady, and I thought her voice like the music of minstrels' harps, so pure and resonant was the sound of it. She turned her eyes on me, and the compassion that I saw in them seemed to enter my heart, "And who is this visitor?"

I did not speak, but reached out and put my hand into hers.

"God's Eve, my Lady," answered Brother David, "This is Edith. She travelled with the harvest offering and needs our hospitality."

"She shall have it." The lady gave me a kind smile and, saying that she would see me again when I had eaten, put me in the care of a young woman who took me to the other end of the table, where many children were seated, all of them making as much noise as a flock of crows after a raiding hawk. The young woman, by force of good-natured authority, obliged them to make room for us on the bench and sat down with me beside her. I settled myself, feeling confused by the heat and noise of the place, and from being passed between three strangers in as many minutes.

The young woman spoke cheerfully, "My name is Enya, and you are Edith, I think?"

I nodded.

"Eat your fill," said she, "There is meat and fish aplenty, for we feast tonight to celebrate the coming of the harvest offering from all the farms and villages and settlements in the see of Holywell." She said this with some pride which I thought well justified, judging from the rich embellishments of this hall, and the great barns and storage-places I had seen outside. I might have been over-awed by all these wonders, but my body clamoured for the delicious food that was in easy reach, and I put away from me the admiration of splendour for as long as it took to fill my stomach. Before me on the table was a big joint of meat on a dish, and Enya cut a thick slice from it and encouraged me to eat, passing to me a hand of bread which she tore off the side of a fresh loaf. The meat was full flavoursome and tender. I dipped my bread into the gravy on the dish to make the most of its savour and ate until my stomach, offended at being half-starved for two days, was at last pacified.

Relieved from my hunger, I looked around me, trying to make sense of the loud and jovial world of souls in which I found myself. Sitting next to me was a fine-looking, large boy whom I deemed to be of about Archibald's size, and therefore nearly of an age, I guessed, to be sitting with the men. He had crisp nut-brown hair which tended to curl, brown eyes, a multitude of freckles over his face and arms, and a bright, vigorous look which appealed to me. I thought to engage him in a little talk, for I was full of questions about the Abbey and the people there. The boy, however, did not meet my eye, but concentrated on devouring a basin of blackberries that he held in the crook of his arm, as if his life depended on it. Most likely he thought I would have liked to share the berries (which I would) but had determined to keep them to himself. I abandoned my attempt to converse with the boy and turned away from him. I could see that, almost exactly opposite me at the far head of the table sat the Lady in the blue robe, and now that I had pause to think, I guessed her likely to be the Lady Abbess. In a loud voice, so that I might be heard over the din, I asked Enya if that was the case.

"Yes, indeed," said Enya heartily, "That is the Abbess of Holywell, our Lady Leoba, and at the head of the men's table is Abbot Tobias, and see Father Maldon on his right, who presided at the Beornwine Grain Rite." I recognised the white-haired priest with the sharp eyes, who had betrothed Hereward and Fritha. Now Enya's face softened, and she said "The Lady Leoba's name means *beloved one*, you know, and she is well named, for everybody loves her."

A voice at my left said, "That is true," and was emphasised by a bony elbow in my upper arm. I turned and the freckled boy was flashing an even-toothed, blackberry-stained smile at me. I glanced at the basin he had abandoned on the table and saw it was empty. It seemed that, having eaten, the boy was now prepared to be sociable. "I have more reason than most to love the Lady Leoba," he added, nodding and pausing with his eyebrows raised and his face charged with such significance that anyone would have been obliged to ask, "Why is that?" even had they no real interest in the answer. Despite some residual pique that he had failed to offer me any blackberries, my own curiosity and his friendly expression urged me to question him.

"Why," said he, "When I was found abandoned in the forest, she carried me to the Abbey with her own hands and had me brought up here with the same privileges as the other Abbey children."

"Why were you abandoned in the forest?" I said, "Did your mother and father not come to find you?"

The boy looked on me with some distain, "I have no mother or father except the Lady and Lord here at the Abbey. Who would need any other?"

I had to admit the enviable honour of being able to count an Abbess and Abbot as mother and father. Still, I could not wish for any other than my own father and step-mother. Often were the times that I had found myself temporarily lost in forest or on hillside, and they would come, or send my brothers to find me. Despite the boy's proud boast, I felt pity for the carelessness that had left him unprotected in the forest as a helpless baby. Perhaps, seeing both pity and envy in my face, he decided it was meet to further our acquaintance, for he held out his sword-hand and took mine, bowing his head and addressing me in a rather formal way.

"My name is Carau," he said, "What is your name and what brings you to join us at the Holywell Abbey?"

"My name is Edith Fly," I said, "I wanted to come with the escort to see the Abbey, so I hid in my father's cart under the harvest offerings."

Carau's brown eyes became round, "Where did you come from?"

"From Beornwine, but I think I must go home soon, as my step-mother and father and brothers will seek for me." This was the first time I had given due thought to those who would have missed me. More urgently, thinking of my brothers brought home to me how nearby two of those brothers must be, and how they would be sorely displeased to hear of my exploits. I feared I had brought shame on HestanandGodwine at the very time they wished to give good account of themselves to their Lord Torhelm. I glanced over to the men's side of the room, but could see little beyond those sitting at the end of the table. There was no sign of the twin golden heads of my brothers.

Carau had clearly decided not to show any admiration at this small child's adventures, "That is not such a brave thing to do," he said, "I am only ten winters, and yet I spent three nights alone in the forest last spring."

"That he did," agreed a voice over my head and I looked up to see Enya gazing in disapproval at Carau. "It caused much worry to the community and to the Lady Leoba, as you well know, you bad boy!"

I did not wish to offend either of these two new friends by admiring one's escapades or concurring with the other's disapprobation. I sought a neutral topic. "You look big for ten," I said. "My brother Archibald is twelve, but no taller than you, I think."

"I am big for my age," agreed Carau, nodding modestly.

"I am six," I volunteered.

"You look it," he said. Then he conceded, "That is young enough to be venturing away from home alone. Perhaps the Lady Leoba will permit you to stay and serve our community." Then he smiled, "I hope so."

I was gratified at this friendly gesture, but felt alarmed at his words. The monastic path, though probably interesting, held no attractions for me as a way of life. I wanted eventually to go questing. For the time being I was beginning to experience a yearning discomfort in the seat of my stomach, which squeezed more tightly every time I thought of home. I was a fool. What had I been thinking of? HestanandGodwine would certainly be angry with me, but they were my only hope of returning home. I was not ready to travel alone. I had never even been hunting and had little more chance of survival than had Carau when he was left alone in the forest as a baby. Kneeling up on the bench and craning my neck, I started earnestly to look for my brothers.

Seeing my agitation as restlessness, Enya took me by the shoulders and turned me towards her. "Well child," she said, "If you have finished eating, then I must take you back to the Lady Leoba, for she wished to see you after you had been fed."

I was about to protest that I needed to find my brothers and throw myself on their mercy so that they might take me home. I was prevented from speaking, however, because Enya, who had been casting her eyes over me in a critical way, now spat on a bit of cloth and began to rub it over my mouth and around my face to clean me of traces of food. Then she picked a few clinging fragments of straw from my dress and straightened it with a sharp tug or two. "There," she said, "You're as tidy as you can be. Come along." She held out her hand to me and I jumped off the bench and followed her up the long table, where we stood at the end of a line of women and children, all waiting to speak with the Lady Abbess.

When our turn came the Lady said in her beautiful voice, "Ah, Edith, I hope you have eaten well." I said that I had and she took my hand and gazed down at me as though I was the most interesting being she had ever seen, and not just the bedraggled naughty child which I was. "Now little one," she said, "Tell me what brings you here."

I hung my head and told her the ignominious nature of my coming there.

"Was your curiosity so great to see the Abbey?" she said.

I shook my head, "No, my Lady, I wanted to travel with the warrior guard."

It was the truth, but it made her smile. "So you have no wish to join our community."

"No, I want to go questing, but I know I am too young, and now I would like to go home, for my father and step-mother and Archibald will be afraid because I have been gone too long." I told her that Hestan and Godwine had come with the harvest offering and were to be squires to Torhelm. I said I thought they might be travelling home soon and would take me with them. The Lady Leoba turned and said something to Brother David who was standing beside her. He nodded and joined some other people grouped around a noble-looking man in a purple robe. This was the Abbot Tobias that Enya had told me of.

Brother David came back soon. "My Lady," he said, "I am told that a messenger was waiting here for Lord Torhelm's arrival with word that the land of his kinsman, Prince Cenred, is threatened by pirates. He did not wait, but has ridden to the south with his retinue. The bondsman Beron rides with them as messenger."

The Lady Leoba and Brother David and Enya all looked down at me. "So your brothers are not here to take you home child," said the Lady. "You will stay until the Beornwine people return home with their empty carts. Then you can travel with them."

25

At the Holywell Abbey

So began my stay at the Holywell Abbey and, although there was unease in my mind when I thought of home, the novelty of my surroundings came to the fore. I was put again into the care of Enya. Although she was brisk and kindly, I could see that she was not best pleased to be saddled with my company. Taking me by the hand, she hurried along the path between the cultivated fields and gardens in the direction of the largest building of the Abbey. This, as she told me, was the Abbey Church where she and all the other Abbey people went to prayer. I was much interested by this and glad to be taken along. Unlike the rich hall where we had eaten, the walls of the Church were lime-washed white and bare of embellishments except for a large wooden cross, carved with signs and runes, which hung behind a table that was covered with a white cloth. Many other people gathered there with us, standing quietly in lines facing the cross and table, until I began to feel hot with the press of bodies, so many were there. Then, by candle-light the Lord Tobias and Lady Leoba presided over the table which Enya whispered to me was called the altar. They led the congregation in marvellous chants and incantations all in the strange Latin tongue which is the language of the Christian church. Afterwards, as I followed Enya from the church into the cool summer evening which had become night while we were within, I asked her what was the meaning of the words they had spoken.

"It is the language of God," said she, "Only the higher priests and priestesses gain knowledge of the meaning of it, but we all learn to say the prayers, and that holds us greatly blessed." Her face was all soft wonderment and I thought that she was blessed indeed for she seemed to have cast off all the impatience she had carried before the church service. As for myself, I felt enchanted by the peace of this my first Christian church service, and, had I not already decided on a life of thegnly questing, I might certainly have considered becoming a high priestess, and learning the language of God.

"Now Edith," said Enya, "I shall take you to the women's dorter, where the unmarried women such as I live and sleep, as well as the orphaned children. There will be much to do on the morrow, with all the guests to look after. It is time to sleep." I did not argue with her for my day had been very long. I was light-headed with new experiences and sore with homesickness. Sleep would be a welcome refuge. She took me to a long dwelling house wherein were screened areas of differing sizes. Inside women and older children were setting down pallets, mattresses and blankets for sleeping. Enya peered into an area where some very young children and three or four babies were sleeping. A young woman was sitting there on a stool, feeding a tiny baby, which was sucking milk lustily from a thin leather bag. Enya whispered "All well?" and the young woman nodded, putting a finger to her lips.

"You can sleep with me tonight," said Enya and led me to a corner where there was a stool and wooden box next to a pallet covered in a straw filled mattress and a fleece. I crept onto it and curled up. Enya gently untied and removed my sandals, then covered me with a blanket. I watched as she loosened her clothes and removed the small wooden cross that hung from a strip of leather around her neck. Then she kissed the cross and laid it carefully upon the box. Suddenly, I wondered why there were so many orphaned children in this house. I opened my mouth to ask her. As always when I was curious, my impatience for an answer was pressing, but then I saw that Enya was praying, her palms together and her lips moving soundlessly. I knew I must not speak until she had finished. I began to find the flickering candlelight fatiguing, so I closed my eyes to wait.

When I opened my eyes, I could see the pale morning sky through the open shutter directly over my head. There was a warm space next to me on the bed and I knew I had slept all night next to Enya. I guessed that her movements in rising had woken me, and I glanced about me. Enya was gone but someone was standing over me, someone with a friendly smile and a freckled face.

"Ah," said Carau, "You are awake. Come quickly. It's time for Morning Prayers. Then I'm to take you with me until it's time to break fast, because Enya is to help with the guests."

I straightened my dress and pulled my fingers through my hair to tidy it, then quickly tied on my sandals and followed Carau, who was well ahead of me by now, out of the building. The sun was not yet up, although there was full daylight in the Abbey grounds. Carau, in a hurry, walked straight across a grassy field to the church. Following him, my feet and legs became soaked with dew and I knew it was very early. We were of the last to arrive at the church and we stayed at the back. I did not see the Lady Leoba or the Lord Tobias, and prayers were led by another priest, who presided at the altar. In the daylight that came through the open shutters I could see that all the priestly men and women were standing at the front of the church, nearer to the altar than everyone else. Carau and I, behind the rest, followed the adults in kneeling or standing or praying. As to that, Carau seemed to know the rules as well as any adult, intoning the prayers in full voice.

Now, I had never thought of romantic love for myself, and had been full of distain for my friend Aldyth's eagerness to think of her own marriage. Yet, when I heard Carau's voice reciting prayers in the perfect and mysterious Christian language, I thought it was the finest thing I had ever heard. My heart filled with admiration and with thankfulness that I was standing there beside him, among that congregation in the beautiful white church. I longed to be able to recite the incantations myself so that I might belong among them. For that one airy moment at the birth of the day, I wanted nothing else.

When the prayers were over we left the church and I followed Carau towards another long house, which he told me was the refectory. "This is where we all eat," he said. "Yesterday we feasted in the Chapter House because of all the guests who are here for the harvest offering. It is the only hall big enough to accommodate all of us together"

We did not enter the refectory, but walked around to the rear of the building where was an open-ended shelter of wattle and thatch with a great clay oven at the rear. I had never seen an oven so large, for it was four times the size of my step-mother's oven which yet baked bread daily for our whole household.

Carau could see that I was impressed. "Everything at the Holywell Abbey is of the finest," he boasted (since the Morning Prayer, my admiration of him outdazzled my judgement, and so any boasting on his part seemed only right and proper). He told me that his task was to prepare and light the fire for the oven, then when the oven was ready, to keep the flames low and steady to maintain the right heat. I knew that this was a skilled job, but Carau did not do it alone, for an adult brother of the Abbey was there before him, opening the oven and raking out ashes from the great feast-baking of the previous day. Carau told me quietly that this was Brother Carl.

"But do not speak to him just yet," he whispered, "He's bad-tempered in the mornings, and last night's wine will have made him worse than usual." He grinned at me secretively, and I let out a shriek of amusement which I immediately suppressed. It reminded me of the foolish giggling with which my friend Aldyth greeted even moderately amusing comments by my brother Farin. I had always despised this behaviour on her part, and it crossed my mind that romantic love does indeed deprive one of normal mental faculties, as I had guessed when observing Hereward and Fritha together. But all rational thought left me as I smiled up at Carau's golden freckles and tall frame, and I scampered after him as he set off to a fuel store nearby, where Brother Carl had sent him to fetch kindling for the fire.

Carau's skill with fire was as good as any adult's I had seen, and the oven was soon radiating a good heat. Meanwhile, the sun had climbed above the distant tree-tops to light up the buildings and grounds of the Abbey, and birds were singing their own noisy incantations to the day. Now more people arrived at the shelter in front of the oven, and began to mix and kneed dough for the bread. While he was working at feeding logs into the fire, or sprinkling water on top of the oven to keep it of a constant heat, Carau explained that these men and women, like Brother Carl and Sister Enya, were among the lay brothers and sisters of the Abbey who worked for the community but had no priestly authority.

"What about Brother David?" I asked, "He was helping to unload the carts, yet he seemed well known to the Lord and Lady, and spoke to them without being afraid."

Carau nodded, "The Lord and Lady know all of the Abbey brethren and sisterhood," he said, "But, you are right, Brother David is better known to them because he is a priestly scholar. Although he performs common tasks as all the Brothers must, he will be a Father soon."

"He was good to me."

"Brother David is full kindly," said Carau, "I like him well." He worked for a while, stoking the fire while I passed pieces of wood to him at his behest. When he was able to stand back for a while, waiting for the oven to heat, he said, "When I have lived twelve winters, I will be called 'Brother' too, and take the privileges of the Brotherhood. But that is not enough for me." I saw his face alight with ambition, and guessed that, like me, he had a passion to be a warrior and follow a life of questing. In the flicker of a bird's wing, I saw us riding together in plumed armour on matching steeds.

"What I want," he said, with his eyes on a distant time in the future, "Is to learn letters and scribing: to read the scriptures and become wise and good. I wish to become a Brother priest, like Brother David, and then a Father." He glanced at me, "I want one day to be Abbot of the Holywell Abbey."

I was violently disenchanted, my vision collapsing, as it seemed, around my ears. "But why?" I whispered, incredulous.

"The Lady Leoba and Lord Tobias are everything good and wise," he said, "They have saved me and nurtured me. I wish to repay them, to make them proud of me, so that they shan't regret bringing me in from the forest. Anyway, what could be better than to follow the life they live?"

I could only nod disingenuously. My imagination failed to see this jolly boy as a quiet priest such as those praying earnestly at the Abbey church that morning. I felt disappointed, but admired Carau no less for his dream of success which (to see it now in retrospect) was no more likely to be fulfilled than my own. As in most other walks of life, advancement in the Christian church was easier and more likely if one was from a prosperous family. As a destitute orphan living on charity, Carau's ambitions had little expectation of success. However, his self-belief, determination and love for those who succoured him shone so brightly, that I had no doubt he would succeed. Even so, my imagination, fertile though it was, baulked at the concept of marriage between an Abbot and a questing warrior. I decided regretfully that my first experience of romantic love, which had lasted for almost half of one morning, would have to be put away from me. Once the decision had been made, I felt more comfortable. Carau's figure and visage were, after all, more fitting to friendship than romance, particularly for me, a child of less than seven winters.

By the time the brown-crusted loaves were being removed from the oven on long wooden paddles, I was very hungry. We ate in the refectory with a group of other children, of which Carau was the eldest, giving him some authority. Adults were breaking their fast there also, most of them sitting quietly at the far end of the long table, well away from us children. It was not a big meal and several people came and went while Carau and I took our well-earned break from our early morning work. I was laughing at Carau mimicking Brother Carl's miserable expression, when a group of men entered the refectory.

The newcomers were warriors, and I could see they were just arrived, for they all wore riding cloaks and swords. As I watched them, I felt the smile shrivel on my face and a band of terror buckle my stomach so that the bread in my mouth became dust to me. At the head of the band of warriors was a giant of a man with long grizzled hair and a plaited beard. There could be no mistake: it was the dreadful Garth from whom I had fled at Beornwine only two days before.

I shrank against Carau, putting him between myself and Garth, who took no notice of me or any other of the children, but sauntered with his men to the far end of the table, where they were welcomed by one of the Brothers and served with bread, cold meat and cheese. Would he notice me? I expected it. Truly, all my instinct was to flee. Hurriedly, I rose from my seat on the bench, but my haste made me careless and I knocked my hand against a full beaker, which fell across the table, pouring a stream of milk into the lap of a girl opposite. With a shriek, she stood up abruptly, overturning the bench she had been sitting on, which toppled three other children onto the floor. I now found myself being yelled at by the girl and, with the whole refectory in degrees of curiosity and annoyance at the commotion thus unleashed by my clumsiness, suddenly every eye in the room was upon my face.

There was a roar that might have been the massive Garth coming to wreak revenge on me, or might have been devils of terror in my own head. I could not know which, for I ran blindly for the refectory entrance, emerged dazzled by the morning sun and was caught suddenly in flight, though my arms and legs still pumped helplessly, as in a nightmare of desperate pursuit. At last I stopped and looked up. I was caught by firm hands, clasped in thin but strong arms and gazed down upon by a face that expressed undisguised delight. The mist of terror cleared from my eyes and I found myself in the arms of my brother Archibald.

Only two cycles of day and night had passed since I saw him last, but I wept and smiled and clung to my brother as though half a lifetime had parted us. I knew then I was safe, for Archibald had been my saviour and my comfort for all of my short life. Reason might have told me that a boy of twelve winters, though doughty of heart and skilled with the bow, would fare badly in any fight with such a man as the warrior Garth. Nevertheless, all fear left me, and anyway, no massive enemy came upon us with fists and battle-axe. There was only the morning, fresh and innocent as the first of all days, and there behind Archibald stood my brother Hereward with Heath, laughing and clapping each other's shoulders with expressions of relief on their faces. I embraced them both, although I could not just yet release Archibald's hand. Hereward kissed me and I asked him, "Hereward, why are you not with Fritha? Where is she?"

Hereward frowned on me then, "Why, child, Fritha is at home along with your grieving family. We spent a whole day searching for you. Then Archibald said he was sure you would have been wild to follow the thegns and your brothers with the harvest offering, and wondered whether you had managed to do so. Father bade me ride here with Heath, and Archibald would not be left behind."

"Once the idea came to me, I knew I would find you," said Archibald.

I did not wonder at this, for it had ever been the case that he knew my mind. Now I was silly with happiness and relief, whilst still charged with the emotional vigour of my previous terror. I jumped up and down, trying to tell them all that had befallen me and everything I had done since the previous morning. But soon I saw that they were not attending to my words, but looking at me with solemn and serious faces. Now these three undoubtedly loved me well, and were most indulgent to my ways. I perceived that I must be in trouble, and now that their relief at finding me had subsided, I noticed the weariness of their movements and traces of exhaustion on their faces. Indeed, in much anxiety they had been searching for me all the previous day, and ridden hard all night. They had arrived only minutes before, leaving their horses with the stable-Brother at the Abbey gates. I felt shamed, and loath to make the excuse that I had to hide in the harvest cart to escape from Garth, for I had intended to do so anyway.

Recognising my disgrace, I hung my head and felt tears come to my eyes. At that moment a vision came to me of a young warrior with shorn red hair and eyes of melt-water green, and it seemed that I heard his voice, stern and light, "Give care to your eyes and your task. You shall not weep." It came to me that, of my own free will I had taken my first quest and it was therefore beholden to me to face the dangers and results of my own decisions. I had lived only six winters and a long summer, but I grew in those moments. I faced my brothers and listened with humility to their tale of my wrongdoings and my family's fears for me. But I did not weep then, nor on the next day when I arrived home and was beaten for my exploits. To my own mind, despite every obstacle, I had already set off on the road that would end and begin when I became a warrior.

There were farewells to make before I left the Holywell Abbey, and my brothers needed sleep. They presented themselves to the Lady Leoba and Lord Tobias; gave their respects to Father Maldon; made the acquaintance of Brother David and Sister Enya; and were introduced by me to Carau. At first, he and Archibald eyed each other like dogs from different packs, then Archibald blurted out, "Do y' hunt?" and they were chattering in no time about forest and moor, prey and weapons. Archibald's experience was greater with regard to arms, but Carau had survived alone in the forest when he had taken himself off from the Abbey community at times (and been punished on returning). He knew more of the habits of wild animals, and could fish from rivers with his bare hands.

While they talked, I listened, feeling comfortable in being disregarded for a while. I was full pleased that these two seemed friendly, but doubted Archibald would be interested in Carau's spiritual life and ambitions in the Abbey. In fact, when he spoke of it, Carau seemed to have Archibald's full attention. I felt proud of my brother's civility and never imagined that his apparent interest in Abbey life might be anything more than courtesy.

~ ~ ~ ~ ~

The boy is relieved to have found his sister. But the brightness in his eyes comes from another source. At the Holy Well he has found that a secret, searching aspect of his soul is unexpectedly at home. The fresh mystery of the place awakens in him a curiosity that is like a lost memory, and he listens eagerly to Carau's tale of Abbey life. Before he leaves, he takes a pebble from the holy spring. Notwithstanding another sacred oath, he makes a silent promise to return.

~ ~ ~ ~ ~

I was put into Enya's hands while my brothers slept, and she did not let me out of her sight. Indeed, she thought it meet to tie a length of rope from my wrist to her waist. This was a humiliation to me, but I bore it as a thegn might, and held my head high, except when I was trying to stifle my mirth at Carau, who followed behind Enya imitating the way her abundant hips swayed as she walked.

After a short sleep, my brothers ate and we left as the sun was at its height. I sat up in front of Archibald on Swift, as of old, looking back at the new friends I had met. Carau, Enya, Brother David and even the great Lord and Lady of the Holywell Abbey, came to bid us farewell. Before we left, the Lady Leoba spoke in her musical voice and said to me, "Be patient Edith; be happy." She kissed me and I felt a great love for her, although I did not understand her words or the sad smile she gave me with her "God's Speed."

When I arrived home, I saw on the faces of my father and step-mother the same expressions of glad relief followed by anger with which my brothers had discovered me at the Holywell Abbey. After an initial celebration at our arrival (and some tears from my family and our people), everyone was sent from the house, and Father beat me, although his hand upon my rear quarters did little more than sting. When he had finished he left me quickly, without looking at me, but making a strange choking sound, and I thought there were tears on his face. Elanor, who had stayed in the house with us, ran to him. I felt that Father needed more comfort than I did and for the first time I felt deeply shamed by the thoughtlessness of my behaviour. Indeed, no thegn would purposely cause distress to those he loves.

That Grain Rite, in the summer of my seventh year, was indeed a time of great change for my family. Apart from the loss of HestanandGodwine, Hereward had become a man, and made his oath to Fritha. His place in our family was forever changed, although he would live near enough for us to see him every day. As for me, my exploits had stripped me of my 'baby' status in the family. Their attitude to me was altered, and mine to myself.

Some three days after my own return, our armed bondsman Beron rode home with a message from HestanandGodwine. Lord Torhelm was needed to aid his southern bondsman, whose lands were suffering from frequent raids by enemies coming from the sea. The twins, of course, were pledged to serve Lord Torhelm and could not be spared. So we would have no ceremony of safe-passage, or formal celebration for their squiring. My bright brothers were gone and we knew not when they might return.

26

The Commonplace Book

In the days that followed my return from the Holywell Abbey, I wanted to atone for the hurt I had caused to my family. I stayed close to the house and close to my step-mother, trying to help in the daily duties that occupied her for the good of our family. After having met Carau and so many other orphans at the Hollywell Abbey, I felt full grateful to have such a home where I was loved, and I wished to show myself of use. But I fear I was more under Elanor's feet than a help to her hands. However, she never did chide me, but patiently showed me the tasks of bakery and dairy in which I had formerly shown little interest. In truth, it was only a short time before I felt constrained and impatient with such household matters, yet I endured them as a punishment more fitting than the mild beating my father had given me.

"You should be out of doors, Edith," said Elanor one morning when we were in the dairy with Bebbe. I had been churning, and looked up to see them laughing roundly at my sighs of which I had been unaware.

"No Mother, I must help. Do let me help," I said.

"Well then, as a change from churning, let Bebbe show you how to form the new butter with the pats."

Indeed, it was enjoyable to shape the cool creamy butter into rounds with the wooden paddles. Whilst I worked, a memory came to me of my visit to Mother Werberga with Archibald. It seemed many ages ago, for so many things had occurred since. But I still kept by my bed the dried remains of the travel-herbs she had given to me at the Grain Rite, remembering how they had sustained me through hunger and thirst on my painful journey hidden in the cart. Suddenly, my conscience accepted this as a fair reason to run out in the free air, for it was meet that Mother Werberga should be thanked and that I should take to her those things she had requested on my last visit. *"Bring fresh butter and wheat-flour"* she had said, and here under my hands was the very finest new butter, which I had helped to make.

Elanor agreed straight away to my request, but said I was not to travel alone, "It is beyond Beornwine," she said, "And too far for a child of your years to travel alone."

I looked hard at her then, but saw no acknowledgement on her face of the journey I had undertaken very recently without any proper escort. Bebbe prepared a bowl of fresh butter and a bag of wheat-flour while I fetched Bracken and released Spin, who was tied in the yard, for he was not allowed to follow me into the dairy. Meanwhile, Elanor sallied out to enlist my brother Farin as my escort.

Now, I liked and respected my brother Farin, for he was a fine huntsman – skilled with bow and spear - and a brave rider. Yet he was not known for patience, least of all with his little sister. Even so, he agreed readily to ride with me, (it happened that there was a new bondswoman of Siric's household that he had met at the Grain Rite, and he was eager to see her again). Elanor gave him messages to deliver at Beornwine and charged him to bring back a flagon of wine from Siric's house.

We did not go soon, for Farin had to make himself ready. When I went to look for him in the house, I found him alone, dressed in the fine tunic and cloak he had worn to the Grain Rite. He had Elanor's polished copper mirror in his hand and was so engrossed that he did not notice me. He was practising diverse expressions in the mirror; smiling, turning away and glancing winningly at himself, pouting his lips and tossing his head. I crept away, stuffing my hand into my mouth so as not to give myself away by laughing.

Soon, we were off. It lifted my heart to be riding away from my guilt and shame at last, with my handsome brother riding proudly ahead, my dog running alongside and gifts in a basket before me. We stopped at Hereward's house to greet the folk there, then rode on down to Beornwine. Farin had no wish to go further with me, and I rode on alone, with Spin beside me, to the little house among the trees by the river where Mother Werberga lived.

She was sitting outside on a stool, in front of her small fire, as the last time I had visited with my brother Archibald, and she rose with a smile as I approached on Bracken, just as if she was expecting me. Spin ran straight up to her, sniffed her hand and lay down quietly at her feet as if she was an old friend.

"So, Edith," she said, "You have brought your dog to meet me."

"This is Spin," said I, proud as I was of him.

"And what a fine animal he is!" she said, and I glowed with pleasure, for I loved to hear my dog being praised. I slipped down from Bracken's back, careful of the loaded basked I carried.

"I have come to thank you," I said, "And to bring what you asked for."

"What thanks?" she asked.

I told her about my exploits and how the travel-herbs had sustained me through heat and hunger on my journey. "But I am ashamed," I said, "because my family thought me lost, and I caused them much sadness because I did not think of how they would fear for me."

"You must tell me everything," she said, "But first, show me what you have brought and take some refreshment with me."

I unloaded the basket there in the sunshine, onto a board next to the door of her house, with Spin waving his tail beside me and nosing too closely at the food. I growled at him "Get away!" and he sloped off, lying down with a great sigh, and accusing me of injustice with his eyes. Mother Werberga exclaimed with joy at the butter and flour, and the new cheese and cooked haunch of meat that Elanor had sent.

"The butter should be kept cool," I advised with the authority of my new dairy-wisdom.

She carried all the produce into her house and I followed her inside. In the gloom there I saw just a simple room with a swept-earth floor. To one side was a bed platform with fleeces and woven blankets folded neatly upon it. There was also a sturdy-looking chest and a raised board with earthenware beakers, jars, bowls and pestles of varying sizes upon it. Above, a small wooden cage hung from the roof. Into this she stowed the butter, cheese and meat.

"It will be safe here from hungry creatures such as your dog." She touched Spin gently (for he had been swift enough to get up and follow us into the house) and he gave her hand a quick lick of friendship, despite his disappointment that all the food was now beyond his reach. She took a piece of hard biscuit from a covered jar, and gave it to him. After devouring it with the relish of a starved wolf, he circled with joy at her feet until I sent him off again.

Taking two beakers, she went outside again and ladled into them some herbal brew that had been simmering on the fire. We sat together in the sunshine with our drinks while Spin took water from a large bowl at the woodland side of the yard. "I always keep that full," said Mother Werberga, "And have many visitors from the woods, who would rather drink here than go down to the river." She told me that badgers, foxes and even hares had taken water there without fear. "And many a mother deer has brought her young one to me."

"And a unicorn? Have you seen a unicorn?" I blurted it out without thought, and she turned to me with a questioning glance.

"Few have seen the unicorn," she said, "For that is a creature who lives between our world and the other one. If one of us happens close to the edge when the unicorn is stepping over, we might see him, or so I have been told."

"So you never have seen a unicorn." My disappointment was great, for if this wise one, trusted by all manner of creatures, had never set eyes on a unicorn, what chance was there for me?

She took my hand in her palm, which was smooth and brown. "Edith, we cannot strive to see a unicorn, nor any of the blessed ones. They will come to us if they will." She got up from her stool and smiled down at me. "Now, child, we have work to do. For we shall use the fine butter you brought to make a special food for you to take back to your family today. It will help atone for the worry you have caused them."

Behind her house was a small oven of clay and stone. She brought a burning stick from her fire, and I helped to bring firewood to fuel the oven, which we tended while I told her all of my adventures, and admitted the shame and the pride that had come to me through my wilfulness. "It was as if my body was an oven," said I, taking inspiration from the task before me, "Seeing the thegns and warriors at the Grain Rite, and all the carts ready to go off to the Holywell Abbey was like a flame and I became more and more heated until I just had to go!"

Mother Werberga laughed and nodded, "I saw it in you," she said.

"I thought it strange when you gave me travelling-herbs, for it seemed you must have guessed what was in my mind."

"I did guess it, Edith, for I saw it in you that first time you came here with your young brother. I saw the roaming spirit in you, and I see it still."

I stopped then and stared into her eyes, which were warm and dark. She only smiled and went to push another stick into the oven, but I could not move. This was some truth that I had to grasp. It was a truth I knew at the heart of me but which had been covered over by the disgrace that I had allowed was deserved, because of the anger and anxiety I had brought to my family during my absence. Mother Werberga came and crouched again beside me where we could see the fire glow through the oven entrance. I told her how I had loved the Lady Leoba, and how well loved she was by all the Abbey people.

Mother Werberga nodded, "She is indeed beloved, and a wise one also. Did she say anything to you?"

I looked across at her in surprise, "Do you know the lady?" I asked.

"I know her indeed, for we are of the same family."

This astounded me, for I could not see any immediate connection between the noble lady in her costly robes, presiding over the prosperous Abbey, and this old woman living in a hut in the woods. Mother Werberga saw the surprise in me (indeed, I never could hide any thoughts or feelings from that wise one, for she had a great gift of seeing).

She laughed lightly, "Oh yes, child, I know the Lady Leoba. She visits me here and I go once every year to the Holywell to take the waters. It is not so far, although the road begins to seem longer now that my old bones stiffen in the cold seasons."

There was much that I wanted to say to satisfy my curiosity, but all seemed presumptuous or bad mannered. She saw my discomfort and gave me a kind touch on my arm, saying again, "Did she say anything to you?"

I found my voice.

"When she bade me farewell, she told me to be patient and to be happy."

"Ah!" Mother Werberga nodded, "And what do you think she meant by that?"

"Only for me to be a good girl and be quiet and still and do the work that I should. That is patience, I suppose." As I spoke, I was holding another stick ready to put it into the oven fire, and I broke it sharply into two pieces across my knee. This stung both my hands and my knee, but expressed the frustration I felt at the household duties I had been trying to learn with Elanor lately, and at my failure to do them patiently.

Mother Werberga went to the oven and tested the heat with her hand. She seemed satisfied and put a large stone over the entrance to keep in the heat. "Now," she said, "we prepare the mixture."

I followed her back to the house and watched as she unlocked the small chest. I was most surprised to see what she brought out of it and laid upon the board outside; it was a leather-bound book. Here was another, most unexpected aspect of Mother Warburga's character – that she had the power of reading. She brought the book out to the board outside and bade me help her collect from the house everything she needed. This included the wheat flour and butter that I had brought, some light brown powder in a jar, a linen bag of oatmeal, some dried berries and a bowl and spoon for mixing. She let me taste the berries, which were currants, dried with their seeds removed, and they were delicious.

"Do not eat too many, child," she warned me, "We shall be needing them."

Then she opened the book, turning the pages until she found what she was looking for. Of course, none of the marks set upon that page meant anything to me, but I was greatly curious as to their meaning. "Is it a holy book, Mother?" I asked.

She looked up and smiled, "No, child, not holy, for these are only my own writings, to help me remember the way of growing plants, making foods and brews that should be familiar to me, but which are easily forgotten, especially if I make them only rarely, as in the case of these sweet biscuits we shall make today."

"But how precious that is, and you have written it yourself!" I cried and reached out my hand to the book, but stopped myself, for I knew she might not want childish hands upon it. She did not hesitate, but passed the book into my hands with open generosity that warmed my heart and satisfied the stomach of my curiosity, for to be allowed to handle any book was wonderful to me. I knew that I could not understand it, but I sat down with the book open upon my lap and turned the pages, pouring over the strange marks and symbols upon them. I knew their great power, for if I could only understand what was written there, then I too would be able to make healing brews and fine foods. I looked up at her, my eyes shining, "It is magical!" I cried.

"Everything on the earth is magical," she said, "But we do not always realise that truth. This Commonplace Book of mine is plain and dull compared with a petal unfurling from the bud, or a spear of wheat grown tall from the seed. It is only the novelty of the book that makes it seem special to you."

"Are they all recipes that you have written here?" I asked.

"There are other writings, which are personal to me. They would not be of interest to anyone else and shall go to my grave with me."

"But others might learn from your writings, Mother," I said, "For you are a wise one."

A shadow seemed to pass over her face then, "But this is where distortion begins," she said. "Wisdom cannot be set and fired like a pot, but should alter as the seasons alter a tree. That is why I fear for the truth written down in holy books. I fear that the purity of wisdom at the heart of them will be lost as human understanding alters. It is better to find our own wisdom in the world we live in than to follow blindly what has been written down by some stranger from another time."

I hardly listened to her, so excited was I to realise the power in reading and writing. But she took my hand and held it hard until I dragged my eyes away from the mysterious, magical writings to look at her face.

"If I can, I shall burn this book before I die," she said. "The Lady Leoba knows my wishes in this respect, and now you know also. Keep my book a secret in your heart, and let it burn when I am gone." I was still puzzled as to why Mother Werberga should want to destroy such wisdom and such a precious book, which I would fain own myself, whether or not I could read the markings there. But I nodded seriously to her, for she wanted the comfort of my agreement; and she seemed satisfied.

Now she cut a large piece of butter, put it into the bowl and set me to beat it with the spoon until it became soft and white, as I had done oft-times when helping Elanor to make honey-cakes. Then she took a hand-full of the light brown powder and put it into the bowl.

"What is this, Mother?" I asked.

"Taste it," she bade me.

I took a little onto my tongue and my mouth lit up with an earthy sweetness, purer and denser than honey.

She smiled to see my face which must have been round with wonder. "It is a root that I discovered in the lee of yon hill," she said, "I found it to be full sweet, so I dried some and ground it to this powder. Now I have grown some from seed and it is in my garden. I hope it has set a good root and will be ready for harvest in the spring."

Now, under her direction, I stirred the powder into the butter, together with the flour, oatmeal and currents, as she poured them in. The mass became stiff and difficult to stir, so she took the bowl from me and mixed it through with her strong hands. Then she pressed the mixture onto a large, flat, earthenware bread-platter and we took it to the oven. She tested the oven's heat by putting her hand close to its clay roof. "Come," she said, and I felt the heat also. "Do you notice that it is less hot than is needed for bread-baking?" she said, and I nodded. We rolled away the oven door-stone with a sturdy stick and she placed the platter inside the oven, on the flat stones either side of the fire. Then we replaced the door-stone and waited, replenishing our beakers with herb-brew from a flagon that had been cooling in the shade, for it was hot near the oven, yet we could not leave it for the care of tending the precious biscuit cooking within. Quite soon, a wondrous sweet scent came stealing lightly from the oven. Mother Werberga rose and moved the door-stone.

"This is not like a bread or risen mixture," she said, "No harm will come from opening the oven during the cooking." She peered inside, then closed the door-stone. "A little longer," she muttered, and with a piece of fine charcoal made some marks upon the page of her book that bore the words for the biscuit recipe.

The sun was circling to the west as I reluctantly took my leave of Mother Werberga. It had been a day I would not forget, for in her company I had taken in new ideas about truth and wisdom, and begun to understand that what she called the 'roaming spirit' in me might not be a matter for shame after all.

More than this - with Mother Werberga I had made the most wondrous food that I had ever tasted. After the biscuit was finished cooking, she had cut it into round shapes and put each one carefully to cool in the food-cage within her house. Then she had gathered together the left-over scraps of biscuit from between the circle-shapes, taken one to taste herself, and given the rest to me to feast upon. And as I sit here now, so many years later, writing these words by ink-quill and guttering candle-light, my very mouth waters at the memory of it, for nothing so rich and crisp and sweet has ever favoured my pallet and stomach more, nor pleased my mind so, since I tasted that wondrous food for the first time.

When the biscuit-rounds had cooled, she took only one for herself. The others she wrapped carefully in a piece of clean cheese-cloth, and stowed them in my basket for me to take home to my family. She placed a sheaf of different herbs from her garden above them "Give these to Elanor," she said, "These are the herbs in the brew we drank today. It is a new mixture I have been trying, and a good one, I think."

"It was indeed most refreshing, Mother," I said, wanting to please her. I went then to fetch Bracken, who was tethered underneath a shady tree nearby, but before I reached him I turned again and ran to Mother Werberga, flinging my arms around her waist and burying my face in her skirt. "Thank you Mother," I cried into her garment, "This has been the best of days. I do love you so!"

She disentangled me after a moment, holding me by my shoulders, and there was a sweet, soft light on her face. "Bless you, child," she said, kissing me on my forehead.

I mounted Bracken and called to Spin, while Mother Werberga handed the basket up to me. I thanked her again and said, "You have given me so many gifts this day that I fear I cannot repay them."

"Do not fear that, Edith," she said. "There is no debt owed on your part." I doubted her words, but I have come to learn since then that no gift has more value than the love of a child, freely given.

153

I turned Bracken's head and he trotted on to the narrow road nearby, eager for his own stable, no doubt. To the east lay Beornwine and the Fly-Elfrith lands of my home. The river flowed north-west from there, past Mother Werberga's house and on to the sea. I stopped Bracken for a moment and looked down the way along the river to the north. It was easily passable, I thought, by a girl with a pony and a dog. I felt the same pull of longing for the unknown road that had overwhelmed me on the day after the Grain Rite, but I knew now that I was not ready for any such adventure. I would need to learn hunting and the use of weapons, and also to improve my horsemanship before I was properly prepared for the journeying that Mother Werberga obviously believed was a right and proper life for me. I looked back and saw her watching me calmly, not showing either curiosity or anxiety. I waved, giving a little shout and urging Bracken to canter away so as to give a fine impression of the questing girl I hoped to become. Unfortunately, he spied a succulent clump of dandelion leaves nearby and stopped to munch them in a leisurely fashion despite my urging and beating his sides with my heels. I looked back to Mother Werberga, but she had retreated to her house and had not (or so I thought) witnessed my humiliation by my own disobedient pony.

At Beornwine I sought out Farin, who was supposed to be my escort for the day, but he was billing and cooing with his love - a pretty girl with smooth brown hair. He was not ready to take charge of his little sister and, with a sharp gesture of the hand, he warned me off.

I wandered away, leading Bracken. It might have been a good opportunity to find Gytha and Aldyth and regale them with my adventures at the Holywell Abbey, but I dismissed that idea. It suited me better to sit alone quietly for a while, for there was something pressing on my mind.

I soon found a suitable place where there were plentiful dandelions for Bracken to munch. I settled myself with my back against a comfortable tree and Spin, irritatingly, fussing around almost in my lap. "Be off!" I told him. But that dog was reading my mind as easily as Mother Werberga could read a recipe in her Commonplace Book. "Be off!" I cried again, "There's nothing for you here."

At last he slunk away and lay down with a great sigh only a little way distant, where he continued to watch me, his head resting disconsolately on his feet. I took my basket upon my lap and carefully unwrapped the parcel of biscuits – only to look upon them, you understand, and think of the pleasure it would give my family to eat them; and how they would praise me for making them (for I had done most of the mixing, after all). How surprised I was, therefore, to find that a kind of absent relish had come upon me, and I had eaten one of the biscuits without thinking.

"No more," I said to myself, avoiding Spin's eyes as I took up another biscuit (somewhat over-brown at its edge, and not fit to present to my family). This was closely followed down my throat by another, defective because of a rather uneven shape. I was sorting through the remaining biscuits, noticing many imperfections that would render them suitable for eating only by me, when I was shocked out of my gluttonous enthralment - and the shame and sickness that would have resulted - by the appearance of my brother at last, with the girl clinging to his arm.

I quickly wrapped up the remaining biscuits and made ready to ride home, whilst Farin kissed his girl and promised to see her again on the morrow. It seemed to me most probable that there would be another betrothal in the family full soon, until I recollected that this girl was unlike the one I had seen him with not an hour before, for she had been smooth-haired and slender as a young sapling, whereas this one was short and curly-haired, with a rosy countenance and bulky breasts.

"Who was that girl, Farin?" I asked when we were out of earshot.

"That was Mythwyn," he replied.

"And who was the one I saw you with before?"

"Ah," he said, "Now that was Rhoathwar, or was it Ethel?"

I fear my mouth drooped open a little as I stared at him, but he bestowed on me his best dazzling smile and I inferred that romantic love was not always of a steadfast nature, such as Hereward's for Fritha. Still, I was glad that Farin seemed to be in a high good mood, so I laughed with him and readily agreed to keep it from Elanor that he had not escorted me all the way to Mother Werberga.

27

The Lady Cwena

My illegitimate venture to the Holywell Abbey had far-reaching consequences which no-one could have guessed at the time. The most immediate change it made to my life was that Brother David became a regular visitor to my father's household. His first visit was a few days after the full moon following my own return from the Holywell Abbey. When I saw who it was climbing down from his shaggy-coated pony, I fairly flew into his arms. He laughed and carried me to Elanor who was hurrying from the house, wiping the flour from her hands that she might greet our revered guest. He told us that the Lady Leoba had especially charged him to enquire as to my safe arrival at the lap of my family. He also brought word that a message had been received at the Abbey from the Lord Torhelm. Brother David assured us that the news was good, but said he was charged to deliver it directly to Father.

"My husband is hunting today," said Elanor, "But Edith and I would be full pleased to serve you with meat and drink while you wait for his return."

"I thank you, Lady," said Brother David with his kind smile which made me feel that he was offering us rest and comfort, rather than accepting them from us. I ran to fetch bread and ale and water for him, while Elanor directed Alvar to put up screens and a bed at the end of the loft that we kept for visitors now that three of my brothers had left home.

That evening, with full formality and before the whole household, Brother David delivered the message from Lord Torhelm. Unrolling a sheet of fine parchment, he cleared his throat and read clearly, with due ceremony, what was written thereon:

"To my Lord Abbot and the Lady of the Holywell Abbey,
"The Lord Torhelm - he of the ancient royal line of Cuthwulf – sends his humble greetings to your persons and household.
"He asks that it be known in your house and abroad, as you may choose, that the Lord Torhelm has in these last days ridden with his

brother the Prince Cenred to a great victory over the northern pirate raiders. For the present time, he remains at his brother's eastern stronghold, there to oversee the building of mighty new defences in that region.

"*If it please thee, the Lord Torhelm requests that a message be taken to the Fly household, north of Beornwine, to send his regrets that neither himself nor his squires will be able to attend the wedding feast of the Lord Finric Fly's eldest son. He hopes that Lord Finric will accept the gifts here sent withal as a mark of the wedding and of his satisfaction with his new squires, Hestan Fly and Godwine Fly, both of whom did honour to themselves and their Lord in the recent wars.*"

At this, all our people let out a great cheer, for all were glad indeed that HestanandGodwine had lived safe through and fought nobly, bringing credit to our family.

At the mention of '*gifts*' I looked with curiosity at the long, sack-wrapped bundle Brother David had brought with him and which now lay on the table before him. On opening, this proved to contain a sword, heavy and true, in a rich scabbard set with gems. Beside was a purse of gold coins. All this was marvellous to us, for, although it is meet that a thegn gives return for a squire from a good family, yet this was more than any one of us might have expected. I heard Father speak of it later to Hereward, saying that doubtless Torhelm was richer than we knew, and his brother had most likely given him reward for riding so readily to his assistance with a good retinue and two new squires well skilled with bow and spear.

It was on the day of Hereward and Fritha's wedding feast that my father was given a great honour. During the feast Chief Wulfred (attended by Lord Wulfirth and all the rest of his family) made a speech acknowledging Father as Provider and Defender of the Beornwine lands. "As a mark of his status," said the Chief, "I hereby consign to the Lord Finric all the lands that lie between the Fly and Elfrith fields, and those lands shall be called Flytun."

During the Chief's speech, and the cheers that followed, I saw a strong light in my father's eyes. It was not simple gratification, but acceptance of a deserved tribute. I felt it reflect on myself and all of our family. I was glad of it, and grateful too, for I never forgot how we came to that country and how these people took us willingly to their hearts.

Thus, despite the loss of Hereward, Hestan and Godwine from our household, our family's status and prosperity was bettered greatly in those days. Following Hereward and Fritha's wedding, a band of bondsmen went from our household to work on the Elfrith land, ploughing and planting areas that had not been touched for years. They also built a new house, dry and airy with a stone fire-pit and smoke funnel for Hereward and Fritha and the Elfriths. Three of Father's bondsmen and their wives went to live there also and small houses were set up for them in the Elfrith homeyard, and a stable also and outbuildings. Much of this was made possible through Torhelm's generous gift of gold, and so Father was also able to hire new bondsmen to our household, and make houses to accommodate them.

And so, by the time a year's wheel had turned and another harvest-time come, many changes had happened in the place that now bore my father's name. Within that same year, what Carau had predicted also came to be: Brother David became Father David. Very soon he was engaged to teach book-learning to the Lord Wulfirth's youngest son. He came to live at the Lord's Hall at Ufer Hill, and, as well as teaching the boy, performed holy rites there and at Beornwine whenever they were needed, for at that time Father David was the only holy man living in our country. He travelled home to the Holywell Abbey regularly and, on his way back to Ufer Hall, would often visit our house to talk with Father and Elanor and - he said in jest - to check the condition of his 'harvest produce' by which he meant me, referring to how we met when he found me in the cart.

At the Beornwine Grain Rite that following year I followed my father, along with all my family, to be presented to Father Maldon who had come again from the Holywell Abbey to bless our Rite. Father stopped before him and presented himself:

"Finric Fly, my wife Elanor and my sons and daughter and bondspeople," said Father, stooping to kiss the rich hem of the holy man's cloak.

"Blessings on your house," said the Holy Father, in a dull tone. He had been blessing people since the early morn, and I guessed it was exhausting work. But then he started a little, as if he had dozed off to sleep for a second. "Fly?" said he. "Ah, yes, I recollect. I have a message for you my Lord. The Lady Abbess Leoba requests that your daughter Edith shall visit her at the Holywell Abbey."

I caught my breath and stared at Father, for he had earnestly forbidden me to go anywhere beyond the bounds of Beornwine, on pain of being confined to house for a whole moon cycle – which I could not have born. Father was doing some staring himself, and I saw his expression change from surprise to gratification as he obviously considered it an honour for his daughter to be particularly invited by the Abbess of Holywell. He bowed, "Yes, Father," he said, "She shall be ready."

"Let her come with your harvest offering, and return with your guard," said Father Maldon, shooting a sharply amused glance in my direction to remind me of my mode of travelling the previous year.

And so I rode my pony alongside the mounts of my brothers Alvar and Farin, who guarded our harvest cart that year. I was as proud as ever I have been to travel thus among armed guards and huscarles alongside the rich offerings of Flytun. And it became the pattern of each year's harvest, that I would travel with the offering to the Holywell Abbey to visit with the Lady Leoba. There I would be reunited with Enya and Carau, be feasted and generally have a wonderful few days before returning again with the empty cart to our home.

At that time, Elanor's acquaintance with Lord Wulfirth's wife, the Lady Cwena, became closer. At the Grain Rite the previous year they had talked together in a courteous way. The lady had admired the dress that Elanor made for me (which had caused me such humiliation but brought me before my hero Redhelm). Not long afterwards, Elanor made a smaller version of the same dress and sent it to Cwena as a gift for little Lewitha, who was about two winters younger than me. Cwena rode over herself to thank Elanor, and thus began their friendship.

I well remember the occasion of that first visit. Cwena was a beautiful lady, with Saxon-pale hair worn in braids. Her dress and hair ribbons were of fine smooth blue cloth, which folk said was costly silk, and she was shod in leathen shoon, soft, shining and pointed about the toe. Whilst sitting with Elanor she stretched out her legs so that her feet showed under her long dress. Then she turned her feet at the ankle and everyone followed her gaze to the fine-stitched footwear.

"What lovely shoon," said Elanor.

Cwena nodded and flashed her a glance, "Indeed," she said, "My husband sent for them by the Eastern Merchants. They are the same pattern as a pair worn by the Queen herself."

All were speechless to hear this, and I wondered that she wore such rich dress on an ordinary day. But I came to understand that the Lady Cwena had few occasions on which to enjoy wearing her finery, and so she donned her best to visit Elanor who might be plain in comparison, yet was the highest lady in that country, with the exception of Wulfirth's step-mother, Mordeth, who was deaf and old enough to be Cwena's grandmother.

The Lady Cwena had travelled far from her own home to marry the Lord Wulfirth, and was oft-times lonely for her family. It is my belief that Elanor became as an elder sister to Cwena, who was the younger by some ten years, and oft times the lady's caparisoned horse would be seen in our stable yard, and her servant taking his ale and talking with our men nearby.

Though young, the Lady Cwena had a stiff way about her. When I ran to greet her on that first visit, she bowed her head gravely and said "God's day, Edith," in such a formal manner that I was shy, and did not hug her as I would other friends, but bowed in my turn and gave her "God's day," in reply. I thought it strange that she never brought her children with her, but left them in the care of servants. Later, Elanor told me that Cwena's manner was learned at court where she was brought up. "All is formal there," she said, "And no court lady has the care of her own children." Elanor said it was difficult to change such ways, but that I must try to be natural with her, for she was a lonely lady who needed kindness.

The next time Cwena visited I remembered Elanor's words, and gathered a bunch of late honeysuckle, clover and daisies, together with a spray of rosehips, and brought them to the lady. She did not smile, but looked greatly surprised, then nodded earnestly as she thanked me. I wanted to tell her that they were for kindness, which she needed, but I was old enough now to be embarrassed by my own truth. Besides, in the Lady Cwena's presence, I was always infected by her own awkward reserve, so that I became reserved also. Still, with my heart full of compassion for the lady, I stayed beside her and as her attention seemed all on the flowers, I thought to speak of them.

"The rosehips are from a bush in the copse," I said. "See they are such a bright red? I found the honeysuckle nearby, and I am glad, for they look well, do they not my lady?" Then I could think of nothing else to say and looked again to the lady's face. I was surprised to see a tear running fast down her cheek and, without thinking, I caught it on my finger. "Do not cry Cwena, my lady," I said earnestly, "I had not meant to displease you."

She smiled then, and it was lovely to see her beautiful face graced in that way. "Nay, Edith," she said, "I am not displeased. The flowers are full beautiful and I could not want a sweeter gift."

I smiled back then, relieved that I had not offended her, "Yes," I agreed, "The honeysuckle does smell sweet, and the clover too."

Cwena looked at Elanor and they smiled together. Feeling I had done my part in extending hospitality to our guest, I ran off to play catch with Spin.

After that, the lady Cwena began to greet me with greater warmth, and always with a smile. She would bring me little gifts such as a ribbon for my dress or hair, a cake cooked by her servant and – once - a little silver brooch in the shape of a feather. This I loved so much that I kept it safe in the box by my loft bed, to wear for May Day, Yule and other important celebrations.

Although the lady Cwena was strange, I began to count her a friend to me, as she was to Elanor. Indeed, she was full generous to my step-mother, bringing her gifts, and staying for long hours talking with her under the oak, or in a screened corner of the house if it rained.

On one day, late in the following spring when the new oak leaves were unfurling on the branch, the pair of them were sitting talking and drinking beakers of sweet herb-draught when Rob of Dale, the travelling merchant, rode into our yard. We children ran to him, much excited at his arrival, and he distributed a handful of coloured ribbon-stubs and some sweet nuts, which we gathered gleefully. Then his eyes lit upon the two ladies sitting under the oak. He dismounted and, taking his harp, bowed low before them. As was his custom, without any word of greeting, he began to sing, accompanying himself upon his harp.

I have told before of the attractions of Rob of Dale. He was a young man, with soft large eyes and brown hair worn in ringlets, and his voice was as full and lucid as a blackbird's. He told marvellous songs and stories, and played wondrous music upon his harp, which I loved.

Now our people gathered near as he sang '*Bring a Briar Rose*' and '*Under the Moon.*' When he had finished, he turned to the ladies and bowed again. Cwena's eyes shone and she clapped her hands like a girl. Elanor smiled to see her friend so happy.

"Oh, but I love music so!" Cwena told her, "When I was at court, we had music every day, for the King had bards and minstrels to sing and play every evening, and often in the daytime too."

Next, Rob brought a little table and upon it displayed all the fine things he had brought. Among the ribbons, strings of beads and other trinkets was a painted box which Cwena was very taken with. "I shall buy it," she said. "It is just the size for my gloves." From a little bag at her side she took a gold coin and held it out to Rob, saying in her cold, sweet voice, "This is in payment for the box, but also for your singing."

Gallantly, Rob knelt before her on one knee with his head bowed low, and held out his hat for her coin. When she had dropped it in, he took it and, with his flashing eyes full on her face, placed the coin inside his shirt, next to his heart. At this, she and Elanor both laughed, and Cwena's face was flushed.

"Go to the house now," Elanor told him, "Bebbe will give you bread and ale. Methinks you will be asked to sing again too, for you cannot disappoint all these children."

With another bow before the ladies, Rob picked up his goods and set off to the house, with a trail of bondspeople and children behind him. I scampered after them, hoping to hear Rob tell a story of the unicorn, which he had done before, and I thought him full knowledgeable about those faery creatures.

It was not a very long time afterwards that I heard Elanor telling Father that the Lord Wulfirth had hired a bard to live at Ufer Hall. Elanor was busy setting a meal on the table and we were all sitting waiting to eat. "The bard is not young," she said, "But the Lady Cwena speaks well of his skill with the harp and lyre. She is taking lessons on the lyre and will learn to play herself."

Father nodded, "Music is a fine thing," he said. "Perhaps you might learn to play also. Then you can delight me as much with tunes as you do with these pies." And he took a huge bite from the venison pie that she had just set before him.

Everyone laughed and Elanor assured him that she had no time for learning the lyre or any other musical instrument.

"That is good," said Father, "I would worry that the pies might suffer."

It is true that, oft times after Cwena had been visiting, Elanor would hurry to complete household tasks with a guilty look, but Father said she should not concern herself. It was meet that she should have a friend of high rank, and there were bondswomen enough about our household to fulfil most tasks.

But Elanor's friendship with Cwena brought trouble to our house, and danger too, although it seemed innocent enough at the beginning.

One morning, although I was supposed to be helping in the dairy, I had borrowed Archibald's full-sized wooden sword and was practising with it (or 'playing', as everyone else called it) near to the oak where Elanor and Cwena were sitting alone, talking and eating sweetmeats from the Ufer Hall kitchen. I took little notice of their words, for their conversations were generally of clothes and women's lying-in and household arrangements, which held no interest for me. But now their voices dropped to low, urgent tones. This, of course, raised my curiosity and I moved a little closer to them that I might hear better, although I continued with my sword-practice. I was behind them and, anyway, they were too engrossed to notice me.

Elanor was saying, "But, Cwena, you must not speak so of your husband, even to me. No-one should hear such words."

"I must speak, Elanor. But for you there is no-one I can turn to. Hear me, my friend, do."

Elanor nodded, but put a finger to her lips, and Cwena continued more quietly. Still, I heard a good amount of it.

"I do not know how I shall endure it," she said. "I may as well end my life, if this is all I shall have to look forward to in the future. He is often from home by day, at the hunt or about the land, and at night he has no speech but of animals and crops and fighting. He employs our bard for my sake, but has no love of music himself and cannot sing the simplest tune." Her voice caught; her face creased, and she surrendered to tears, covering her face in a fine embroidered kerchief that I thought too good for such use.

Elanor looked greatly troubled, but stroked Cwena's hair, talking to her all the while, "My dear, the Lord Wulfirth has the care of much land and many people. Needs must take him from you a good deal of the time, as my husband is from me. We must be thankful that they are not often away for long periods of time, for the country is peaceful just now."

Cwena looked up. Her eyes were red and her voice angry, "I would he was from me for always!" and her face was in her kerchief again.

I put my sword tip to the ground and remained still. This was shocking but also exceeding interesting; I resolved to give it my full attention.

"Hush," Elanor stroked her hair again, "Hush, Cwena. I would not have you say such words. Are you so very miserable?"

The answer was a nod and a stifled sob.

"You are young," murmured Elanor, "You have not yet learned that the love we bear our husbands must alter as time passes. It is quieter, the passion less intense."

"I have no love for him! I hate him! He repels me!"

This shocked Elanor and she looked around her, clearly fearful that Cwena's words had been overheard. In the blink of an eye I had turned from them and was slaying an invisible dragon - yet I was too close for Elanor's liking.

163

"Edith!" she called sharply, "Have you finished your task in the dairy?"

I shook my head.

"Then go, child. I cannot have you playing worthless games when you could be usefully employed. Go now!"

I slumped off, glum of face, trailing Archibald's wooden sword behind me and reflecting that *"such games"* would not seem so *"worthless"* to Elanor should she ever need me to save her from a real dragon.

It was not more than another moon cycle from that day when I awoke at night from a deep sleep to the sound of galloping hooves in our homeyard. In a minute Father and many bondsmen were outside with torches and weapons. I pushed open the roof-shutter by my bed and saw that the Lord Wulfirth was in our yard, mounted upon his horse. Father approached with his torch, then Elanor was beside them, a shawl pulled over her shoulders, her face yellow and grey in the torchlight. The Lord Wulfirth bent and grasped Elanor's arm quite roughly and they spoke to each other in earnest tones, but I could hear nothing. Then Father mounted his own horse and rode off with Wulfirth.

Elanor entered the house again and I heard her voice below, talking with Bebbe and some of the other women. I dared not join them although I was full of curiosity and some alarm. I slept fitfully until the flash of our house torches and the clatter of hooves woke me again, and I looked out to see Father come home with the other riders. The Lord Wulfirth had someone upon his horse with him. Her arms were tied with rope about her waist and her head and face were covered with a cloth, yet I saw beneath her robe a small foot shod in leathen shoon, soft and pointed about the toe, and I knew it was the Lady Cwena.

I crept downstairs and, finding the house in uproar, was able to hide myself behind Father's high wooden chair and observe what I could of events. There was the sound of horses leaving our homeyard, then Father came into the house with his men. Elanor served him with a cordial from a pot that was warming on the fire. I could smell the honey and wine as it bubbled into the cup. Father held the cup, but did not drink. "Now I shall hear the truth," he said, in a loud, clear voice that was the nearest to anger I had ever heard him use to Elanor. "Tell me, wife, what know you of this affair?"

Elanor spoke in a low voice that was choked with tears, "Only that Cwena was unhappy. I did what I could to bid her be steady, but she is young and wilful."

"Wulfirth believes that you conspired with her to arrange this elopement with Rob of Dale. He would have you brought to trial over it. I had to draw my sword, and set my men to stand against his before he calmed his rage."

In my hidingplace I gasped, and the spirit of terror galloped into my head. Was there to be war between us and Wulfirth?

Elanor was weeping, but trying to speak through her tears, "No!" she sobbed, "I have seen nothing of Rob since he came in the spring. Cwena admired his singing, and he was gallant but most respectful. I never expected any such thing of him."

"You can expect nothing of him now," said Father roughly, "For Wulfirth ran him through the throat with a sword, and had his harp broken about his head. If he lives, he will never sing again."

Elanor shrieked, and so did I, for Father's words were so terrible. He heard me and came to fetch me from behind the chair. He was not rough with me, but only put me in Elanor's arms, and we clung together, weeping.

"Edith, child, I would you were less curious," he said, "These are not matters for a child."

I hardly made sense of his words, for my cheerful, kindly Rob of Dale had become a terrible, broken image in my head, his music drowned in blood. I screamed again at the thought of it, and Elanor quietened her own sobs to hold me close and stroke me gently until my shivering lessened.

Then she turned her face, streaked with tears, to Father. "But what will happen to Cwena?" she asked in a whisper.

He sighed, sat down and took a long draught of wine cordial from his cup, "Do not look so fearful wife," he said. "I do not think the Lord Wulfirth will do any great harm to his lady, although he has the right. Such great ladies come with ways too fine for their own good, but they come with protection also. Her connections with the King will likely save her. Besides, Wulfirth loves her, even now." Father looked thoughtful, and spoke very softly to Elanor so that no-one but she (and I, sitting in her lap) could have heard. "The man was keening and weeping like a child after he had recovered her and we were riding home. I was beside him, and I heard. No, I do not believe she will come to any harm." Father then looked into my eyes and put a comforting hand to my face, wiping away my tears with his thumb. "You are young, daughter," he said, "But as you have chosen to hear all this, then let it be as a lesson to you. Remember that a woman should always keep faithful to her husband, happy or not."

Any ill feeling between my father and the Lord Wulfirth was mended full soon, and they were riding to hunt together again before the autumn. But I gave much thought to these matters: It was a long time before I recovered from my grief for Rob of Dale, but I came eventually to think of the Lady Cwena's fate as darker even than his. She was kept at Ufer Hall under the watch of armed guards. I saw her sometimes when I went with Elanor to sit with her in the hall or court – for, although she never visited us again, except under the guard of her husband - after a time she was allowed to receive visits from her friend. I believe she did speak with Elanor when they were alone together. However, to me she seemed always cold and pale, reverted to her former stiff manner (which no amount of wild flowers could soften) and remained completely silent until I had run off to see the horses or play with little Lewitha, the lady's daughter.

It seemed wrong to me that the Lady Cwena should be kept captive by a husband she did not love. This fearful law that thus restrained women of high rank did not apply to more lowly people. I knew this because I had seen women of our own household change their husbands on occasion, when they were not happy with their union. I began to think that to be of a high family could bring not only wealth and pride, but also rare troubles not visited on less noble folk.

28

A Love for Alvar

With work, festivals and the sacred round of seasons, our lives passed and I grew to a child of ten winters. These years had seen changes in our family.

Fritha's mother lived only long enough to see her first new-born grandchild, a boy with a sweet disposition and a smile like my father's. They called him Eldric and I loved him well. I would often ride or run over to Hereward and Fritha's house to play with him and his little sister Hylda (named for our mother) who was born within the same year. Thus their family grew despite the loss of Fritha's dear mother not a year after their wedding.

Another welcome addition to our household came with the birth of Bebbe and Heath's son Pepin, who was born soon after Hylda.

I continued to visit Mother Werberga twice or more in every moon cycle. We were great friends and she showed me secrets of baking, brewing and herb-growing, and taught me gentle ways with wild animals so that they would feed from my hand.

Archibald was now a man of sixteen winters. As a farmer he was hard-working and conscientious. As a huntsman he was well respected by all, being an outstanding horseman and surpassing even Farin in his ability to shoot a true arrow from a galloping horse. I missed Archibald as a playmate, but loved him no less for that; Archibald was my hero, the one I looked to most for guidance and the example I most wished to follow.

In was in the summer after little Hylda was born that our family was increased again, not by a birth, but by another marriage.

Alice was the orphaned daughter of the Chief Wulfred's sister, and some days after she came to Beornwine, all of our family was invited to a feast of welcome for the girl. Whilst not greatly pretty, she was friendly, tall and buxom with splendid chestnut-coloured hair and strong arms that lifted me like a baby when we were introduced. She told me that she was greatly fond of children and talked with me alone for a little while. I told her about my dog, Spin, and found out that she shared my partiality for honeycake. I could not help liking her well, for she laughed a lot and was kind to me. Both Father and Elanor seemed well pleased with her also.

As we were riding home afterwards, Father said in a loud voice (on account of the several beakers of mead he had drunk), "Wulfred is looking for a husband for the young lady Alice and I put it to him that she would make a good wife for Farin. Marriage would steady him and it would be a fine union for our family."

It happened that Farin had given little attention to Alice or any of us that evening, for he was busy making eyes at the various pretty young women in the company. Hearing Father's words now, he looked up quickly with an expression of shock on his face (I suspected that the powerfully-built Alice was not his type). Before Farin could say a word, however, another voice spoke:

"But I am the elder to Farin. Should not I marry next, Father?"

The speaker was Alvar.

Alvar had remained a strange one over the years. He liked young women well enough, and many of them seemed to like him at first, but none stayed in his company for long. I wondered if he might be a cruel lover, for I did not forget his former rough treatment of me when he found me alone in the wood.

Father glanced at Alvar now with his usual measure of discomfiture, for he seemed never to understand Alvar any more than I did. But he cleared his throat and said, "You are right my son. If the lady would wish it and the Chief Wulfred agree, then it might be so."

I doubted the lady Alice would want to marry Alvar. I think my father doubted it too, and he spoke no more that night of a union between Chief Wulfred's family and our own. However, future events proved surprising, and I witnessed the beginning myself.

One morning I was foraging at the banks of the river Beornwine, between our lands and the village, seeking a moisture-loving plant that Mother Werberga had asked me to bring to her. I was deep in dreams of questing when I heard Alice's merry voice. Along with hers was another which I did not recognise: a man's voice in a warm, cheerful tone that matched Alice's own. Imagine my surprise when I looked up to see that the voice belonged to my brother Alvar. He and Alice were sitting in a sheltered spot where the river bends, shielding them from the view of anyone looking from Beornwine. I stepped back quickly and made to walk away, yet to hear Alvar's voice with this new, blithe expression was wonderful to me and I stayed to listen for a while. After a certain kind of silence, I heard Alice speak:

"Alvar," she murmured "Love, do not pinch me in that way."

"I shall," he said in something like his usual manner.

"No. You shall not." She did not raise her voice, but the next moment I heard Alvar give a sharp squeal, quickly suppressed, and then Alice again, quite gently, "You *shall* not."

There was a little groan and then a long space of muffled movement and soft whispering.

I thought it past time that I was gone from there and I walked away as stealthily as I could.

It was only a matter of two or perhaps three days afterwards that Alvar and Alice came into my father's house together. Our evening meal was about to begin and most of our household was present. Alvar entered the house and stood, hand in hand with Alice, just inside the doorway. And the expression of clear happiness upon his face made my brother almost unrecognisable to me.

"Father," he said, "I have brought the lady Alice to join with us at our family meal."

Alice added in her merry, direct way, "And I would seek to join your family always."

The expression of utter shock on my father's face was replaced in a second by astonished delight. He stood up and strode over to where they stood, kissing Alice's hand and clasping Alvar to his heart in a way I had never seen before. Elanor also hurried to the couple and kissed them both. I was not far behind her, for I felt very lucky that the charming Alice was to be my sister. Indeed, I would have been ready to love any woman who could effect the transformation of Alvar into the pleasant and affable man who stood smiling among his family. At last I found myself looking directly into his eyes without fear and, indeed, I saw nothing but kindness there.

The alteration in Alvar seemed to me nothing less than a deed of wondrous magic and I spoke of it to Mother Werberga the next time I went to visit her.

"Human love is indeed a magical thing, Edith," she told me.

"Yes, but surely it has not always such an effect!" I exclaimed. "My brother Hereward loves Fritha well, yet he has not changed because of her."

"Are you sure?" Mother Werberga smiled and continued to shred herbs for the pot, letting me ponder that question.

"Well, he seems stronger, perhaps, and talks to Father more like a friend than a son, now that he has his own household and his own wife and children."

"Is Hereward not altered then - by his love for Fritha?"

"Perhaps he *is* in some measure," I agreed, "But Alvar is a different person. When he comes into the house, or I see him in the homeyard, I hardly recognise him. What could have caused such a change?"

She nodded, "It is true that some people do not become completely themselves until they have found someone who loves them truly and whom they love also in equal measure. Alvar is one of those who has been lost, perhaps since your mother Hylda died."

I shivered and moved closer to Mother Werberga. She held me to her, for she knew of the black terror that could strike me when my mother's death was spoken of. Yet in her company I was rarely afraid and I was so entranced by the notion of Alvar's happiness that the horror of old memories hardly touched me this time.

"Alvar can be cruel," I said, "But Alice is strong."

Mother Werberga looked at me questioningly. "Have you been spying?" she asked.

"No, but I almost came upon them by accident," and I told her what I had heard by the river.

She chuckled, "It is as well that Alice has physical strength to surpass your brother. She will save him from the darker reaches of his nature and, in turn, he will respect as well as love her."

And so it came to pass that the lady Alice's union with Alvar was arranged with satisfaction between the Chief Wulfred and my father. Alvar had little strength of arms or skill at husbandry - for his talents lay in marvellous carving and beautiful carpentry. However, Alice had a fair fortune of her own, and Chief Wulfred gifted more land to our family to mark the marriage. So they were able to set up a fine house not far from us, with its own homeyard and outbuildings, and a number of loyal bondspeople chosen from our own household. I believe that all our family, including Alvar himself, were happily astonished by the turn of events that saw Alice become a member of our family, and her pleasant nature raised all of our spirits in an enduring way.

I was living contentedly – secure in my home and family; happy with my dreams of questing, of finding the unicorn; yet still deep in my safe childhood – when I heard the word again.

It was the Beornwine Grain Rite in the summer following my tenth winter, and I was having a good day. The weather was fine; Redhelm was there (I had watched him unseat one of the King's champions and nearly made myself sick with cheering); the Holy Father had brought special greetings to me from the Lady Abbess Leoba, who was expecting me the next day; Alvar and Alice were to be betrothed and I was to walk with them in the procession and carry Alice's basket of flowers. I was happy. In fact, I was almost beside myself with joy.

Why is it that at such bright times a sudden intimation of darkness can come to us? So it had happened with me before, and so it was with me on that happy day.

I had forgotten myself; all my attention was on my blissful brother Alvar and his beautiful new love. They were at the head of the procession and there was the sound of much merry laughter and many good wishes called out to them from the crowd. All at once, amid the prattle and calls of the people, I heard – quite clearly - a voice saying *"She carries the witch-blood."*

I stopped moving, my eyes – unseeing - on the basket of flowers I was holding. My body was shaking; I was discovered; someone had found out the evil in me and was telling everybody. I waited for cries of derision; I waited to be cast out of my happy childhood and sent back to my lonely terror in the secret hidingplace from where I had watched my mother being slain.

There was a soft commotion around me and Alice was there, stooping to look me in the eyes. "What is it Edith?" she was saying kindly, "Are you ill, little one?" I shook my head and she took my hand and I walked with her and Alvar straight up to the Holy Father. After a few steps, I took courage to look around me and into the crowd. I saw kind faces and merry faces and indifferent faces, but none that accused me, or sought my downfall. That word had perhaps not been directed at me; perhaps it had not been used unkindly, for I knew 'witch' meant 'wise-one' yet I could not hear it without being afraid. I soon found myself recovered, and was then angry that I had allowed the terror to enter me again. Strong at last, I smiled at Alice and stepped back, for it was time for her union with Alvar to be blessed by the Holy Father. I watched, the warm day settling its own blessing on my shoulders once more, and I was ready to hand the basket of flowers to Alice when the time came.

Thus, I lived a happy life: and thus, on occasion, I suffered times of dark terror. In such a way we are often alone in our existence, yet then we are rescued and come back to the sweet life of the earth. I was born with no physical fear; wounds did not trouble me. My only dread was that fear itself would come upon me again. And come it did, though it were only rarely – visiting me in nightmare dreams, or in words spoken innocently by a stranger. In my darkest times I feared there was evil in me, and I feared that the terror would come, shaking its finger and telling me that it was so.

29

A True Warrior's Purppose

During all the changes in our family and fortune, my father looked well to the government of his land and household. He came to understand the importance of well-managed farmland and did not fail to consult Hereward and Heath on matters of agriculture or animal husbandry. Father's power and wealth grew, and his friendship with the Lord Wulfirth became a close bond, more so now that they were connected by marriage through Alvar's union with Alice.

The Wulfirths had made one of their journeys to the Royal Court so that the Lady Cwena might meet with her family. I was in our homeyard one after-noon, when I heard the notes of a sounding-horn across the fields. I ran to our watch-hill and saw the Wulfirths returning – the Lord and Lady ahead on their caparisoned horses, with their guards about them, flags flying and horns sounding. It was odd that they should come to Flytun before going on to their home at Ufer Hall, but all well-come was made to them by Elanor, and soon the Lord and Lady were taking cordial and meats before the fire, for it was a cold day. I myself brought them a platter of honey cakes, and they spoke kindly to me. They seemed full happy, despite their long journey, and I saw them exchanging glances and smiling together. I thought them the happiest I had seen them in each other's company since the terrible time of Lady Cwena's elopement with Rob of Dale.

Soon Father came in from the hunt and hurried in to our house to greet them.

"My Lord!" said Father, "You are returned!" He bent to kiss the hand of Lady Cwena, murmuring, "My Lady." Then he turned quickly to the Lord Wulfirth again. "I hope there is not bad news?"

Cwena laughed in her reserved way, "No bad news Finric, but my husband would not wait to tell you what news we bring. He insisted we come straight to his friend even before going to our own home!"

"And you must stay here this night, Lady," urged Elanor, "for you will be tired from travelling, and you have far to go yet. Travel on in the morning, do, and take your rest and food with us! Your men and horses will be well provided for also."

"You are most kind, Elanor," replied Cwena.

"I thank thee," added Wulfirth. "And I am in no mind to travel on, for I wish to stay and celebrate with my brother." And he stood and clapped my father in a close embrace. Then he stood back from him and they smiled upon one another with the genial camaraderie of brother warriors and hunting partners - which they were.

But Father's forehead creased in a puzzled frown. "What is it, Lord? What is this news you bring?"

The Lord Wulfirth turned to his pack which he had laid on a board nearby. From it he took a scroll, sealed with wax and a red, blue and gold ribbon. He put the scroll into Father's hands and Father stared at it. "It is the Royal seal," said Wulfirth, proudly. He slid his hand-knife under the seal and unrolled the parchment. Peering from behind my father's elbow, I could see rows of black-inked lettering, together with some capitals in red and gold. Lord Wulfirth cleared his throat and read from the scroll:

"By Order and Command of the Royal Court and by the word of the great and noble King Arthur, let it be known that Finric Fly, Warrior, Provider and Defender of Beornwine, is hereby named a King's Thegn under the Order and Governance of the Lord Wulfirth of Ufer."

Wulfirth stopped, his cheeks flushed and a great smile on his face. Father was also flushed with shock and pleasure. "How can this be?" he said.

The Lady Cwena spoke up, "By the commendation of my husband," she said, smiling.

"Indeed," said Wulfirth. "I did commend you to the King as one who has faithfully and nobly served our land. He was glad to grant my request."

There was much celebration in our house that night, with ale and mead in abundance and our household swollen by our Lord and Lady and their guard, as well as Siric's family who came from Beornwine. My father was much gratified by this new honour. It was only in later years I understood that any King or Lord would want to secure the loyalty of men with power and influence such as my father.

Father kept the scroll locked away in the heavy chest that was kept in the room he shared with Elanor. When I was older, she told me that he often took the scroll from the chest, unrolled the parchment and gazed upon the seal and the lettering, even though he could read not even a word of it.

Along with the conferring of the title of King's Thegn, Father was granted more lands under the gift of the Lord Wulfirth. Our household increased again with bondspeople to work the land, but all this brought with it greater responsibilities. Over time, Father came to lead our hunt no more than twice a fourt'night and spent more of his time making sure of provisions and security for our extended household and those of his sons. While such wise efforts increased his prosperity and status, my father's countenance became gradually more stern and morose. Previously, his somewhat stormy nature had shown sunny flashes of mirth and celebration. But Father's new conscientiousness cast gloom on our household and I only saw brightness on his face on the hunt days, except at times of great family rejoicing, such as when first Alice and then Bebbe blessed our family with new children. Then, Father could be seen smiling once more as he joyfully ordered feasting and celebration for the whole household.

Such a time of rare celebration began early one winter morning when, after an absence of more than four years, my brothers HestanandGodwine rode into our homeyard.

The twins had sent some few written messages in the time since they had ridden off with the Lord Torhelm, and we knew that their time had been spent serving with Torhelm's kinsman, Cenred, who was a great Prince given rule over much of the Anglish lands. Travelling now with Torhelm and his retinue into the Middle lands of Wessex, my brothers had found themselves less than a day's ride from Beornwine, and asked leave to visit their family. Now it happened that Torhelm had taken a fancy to a young woman of the hostelry near his camp and it suited him to break his journey there. He gave HestanandGodwine three days' leave of absence. Were it not for the Lord Torhelm's lust for the young woman, he might well have joined my brothers on their family visit for, as we knew, Torhelm was an affable thegn.

I was at Beornwine visiting Gytha and Aldyth when I heard the news, and rode home as quickly as my pony Bracken could gallop. I slowed him as we came into the homeyard and saw there two men of identical appearance dressed in costly and fine-looking warrier garb with light armour. They had evidently just arrived, for they were untying spears and shields from their horses' harness and giving orders to our stable-men as to the care of the beasts. Of course it was HestanandGodwine, for on their faces one still bore brightness and one shadow in equal measure. Yet they were changed, so I felt awkward and did not run to them - for these were men of experience and, it seemed, far above the brothers I had known. I came slowly to the stables, saw to Bracken and greeted Willow and Archer, the fine horses that Father had gifted to my brothers when they left us. Then I entered the house by the little rear door, so that I might observe the newcomers quietly until I was ready to be seen.

Thus it was that I happened upon Godwine washing behind a screen. He was undressed to the waist and I saw a great scar crossing the powerful muscles over his left shoulder. I watched as he dried himself and put on a fine shirt and tabard. Then he took up his sword in its scabbard, making it ready to belt it around his waist. But then he hesitated, and I guessed his thoughts - that he was at home, and could leave off weapons for a spell. It was then I stepped towards him.

"Edith!" he cried holding out his arms with a look of delight that gratified me and helped me put away my shyness. Still I did not run to him, but walked slowly forward and put my hand on the sword that was in his hands.

"Shall I wear it for you, little one?" he asked gently. I nodded and the next minute he had strapped it on, lifted me in his arms and was striding into the main house, where the table was being set with food and drink for the travellers.

"Look what I have found!" he said, holding me up like a prize. With Godwine's joviality all my solemn awe departed from me, to be replaced by excitation. I jumped from his arms to greet Hestan and assailed them both with questions, information and victuals in excessive measure until Elanor scolded me to be still.

My brothers stayed with us for three nights - long enough for a feast of welcome to be prepared, and long enough for them to tour the Fly holdings, so that, with Father as their guide, they might view the expansion of our lands and meet their sisters-in-law and the children. It was now we learned of a further growth in our family that I had not thought of. Both Hestan and Godwine had been married, only days before their present journey.

"That was why we did not send word to you," said Hestan, "And why we so much wanted to make this visit, so that we could bring the news ourselves."

"I hope that you may come again soon," said Elanor, taking each of them by the hand, "And bring your brides with you. Then indeed there shall be celebration!"

They told us that, following victory in the lengthy wars where they had fought with Torhelm for his kinsman the Prince Cenred, they were rewarded with bounty and marriage to two ladies of the Prince's household.

Father was greatly pleased by this news, and that evening many cups were raised in tribute to the twins and their brides. But I wondered in my heart whether these unions were love-matched. It was the first time I had heard of a woman being given as wife in reward for a man's loyalty to another man. I knew, of course, that Alvar's marriage to Alice had been arranged between Father and the Chief Wulfred. But Alice and Alvar had loved each other before any arrangement was seriously thought of; everyone knew that. I did not like the notion that a woman's life might be handed over at the inclination of the men of her family. I did not like that notion. It reminded me of the tragic and silent Lady Cwena, and made me feel cold.

But then I looked again at my handsome brothers, golden and noble as they accepted the tributes of their family, and I did not think the twins' new brides would lament their union. I hoped they did not.

The next morning Father was wearing the half-angry and half-pained look that often followed a night of ale and celebration. Yet he solemnly called all my brothers to join him, including Hereward and Alvar who had spent the feast night at our house. They walked together away from the house in the direction of the pond. I saw Elanor's eyes follow them, and this made me curious, for she always knew Father's wishes and intentions. I hurried to catch them up. When Father saw me, he looked as if he would send me away, but then he gave a little resigned nod. I knew I could stay. At last, they stopped and stood in circle, with me at the outside. I thought I saw on Father's face a struggle between duty and painful emotion, such as the time when he brought news to one of our bondswomen that her husband had died of fever on a journey. It made me anxious, even though I knew all the people I loved were safe.

Father turned to HestanandGodwine, speaking in a low voice: "My sons, it is meet that I should ask, and that all your brothers should know, whether you heard any word in your travels?" He finished with a note of question in his voice. I had no inkling of his meaning, but all my brothers had sombre understanding written over their faces. What was this? All eyes were on HestanandGodwine, who glanced at each other.

Then Hestan spoke, "At the Prince Cenred's household some have known of a Mercian Lord whose standard is black with a white sun upon

177

it, but none have seen him in some years. And none knew if he went by the name of Orin."

At the sound of that name, terror struck me; the sky turned black and the ground beneath my feet would not support me.

The next moment I opened fearful eyes. I had fallen to the ground, but Archibald was supporting me in his arms, all concern and kindness, and my entire attention clung to his face, for only there did my deliverance lie.

"I should not have allowed her to stay." It was Father, crouching beside me. "Forgive me child, I should have sent you away. It is not meet you should be made to remember such things."

"But I do remember!" I cried, "It is in my head, Father. I must remember, whether I wish it or not."

He took me up in his arms then, and with his big strides carried me back to the house. There he delivered me into the arms of Elanor and thus made comfort for himself, if not for me.

~ ~ ~ ~ ~

Archibald has grown and, although still young, is as much a man as many twice his age. He has many wants and cares, not least a steadfast concern for the little sister whose life he saved. Unlike any other of her family, Archibald knows that Edith's ambition of riding to quest is as real as any boy's. He sees trouble ahead for her because of it. When she fell and he ran to support her, he looked into her eyes and saw the terror there. He knows how to save her and will not hesitate to do so, even though there is little chance of any quest of hers being fulfilled.

~ ~ ~ ~ ~

It was later that Archibald sought me out, to assure himself of my recovery and to bring me a little bowl of fresh wild strawberries that he had found and gathered expressly to bring me cheer. Not quite recovered from my attack of the terrors, I was sitting wrapped in a cloak under the oak with Spin for company and I took the bowl of berries onto my lap with full gratitude, although I could not eat them. I was glad and grateful to see my brother, for I had a question to ask and trusted nobody but him to answer me honestly.

After considering me gravely with his knowing eyes he said, "What is it?"

"Why," I asked, "am I so struck down by the terrors? You suffered as much by our mother's death as I did. How should I loose my wits and you stand tall?"

"You are young, sister," he said.

"I am older than you were when you carried me to safety. You did not quake then."

"You were my only care. I had to cast all else from my mind. I had no time to suffer until later."

"You suffer now at those memories. All our brothers do also."

He nodded.

"Then it is true," I said roughly, "I am a coward. For all bear it bravely but me." It was the worst fault any thegn could carry, and I rose to my feet, scattering strawberries, wanting to walk away from my shame. But he stopped me, a strong hand on my arm.

"No, Edith," he said, and by his voice I knew that he shared my pain. "Listen to me, sister," His other hand was on my shoulder and he stared earnestly into my eyes. "Do you not know what gives me courage?"

I shook my head disconsolately.

"It is the knowledge that I shall ride to quest," he said, "And that my quest shall be to avenge our mother's death. I have had the terror also, and the same fear of cowardice. I took my trouble to Father, and he gave me this weapon against horror and dread:"

Archibald paused, with the attitude of one who is about to present a valuable gift. Slowly, he said, "Father reminded me that my quest is no childish boy's adventure, but a solemn vow – a true warrior's purpose. That purpose is like a sword to me, and my anger keeps it sharp. No terror can withstand it."

He looked into my eyes, "Such a purpose can be yours also. Will you take it?"

Archibald was sixteen – almost a man – and yet he stood before his child sister and he offered me this salvation against terror. I went on my knees, straight-backed before him with my head bowed. Had anyone been watching, they would have seen a kind brother indulging his little sister in one of her games. Like a King accepting a thegn's loyal vow, he placed his hand on one of my shoulders and then on the other, but I swear to you that I felt the weight of a sword lying there. Then my eyes were open, blazing into his, and I believed truly that this was no game to him, but that he honoured my acceptance of quest, as truly as if I had been a man, and not a simple girl-child of ten winters.

I stood up again with new hope and a sudden return of my usual appetite for food. I glanced at where the bowl of strawberries had fallen, but there was to be seen only an empty bowl and my guilty-looking dog, licking his lips and slinking away from behind the oak tree.

30

Secret Blood

It had always been so in our house. At one point during every moon cycle – usually at waning or dark moon – Elanor would take to her room and remain there quietly for a few days. This had always been known in the house as 'Mother's moon-time,' and I had never doubted the naturalness of it. She did not shun me, but I would be required to knock at the door of her room before I was admitted to see her.

One day I simply asked her, "Why do you stay here Mother, at this moon-time?"

"It is my moon-course, Edith, when I bleed as grown maidens bleed, before they bear children."

For a moment I could not speak, though my eyes were wide and my head full of questions.

She smiled, "Do not look so frightened child!" she said, "I am not hurt: only a little tired. These few days give me rest and quietness, which is much needed."

"But why do you need rest and quietness? Why do maidens bleed?" I had never heard of such a thing, and could not keep the shock out of my voice.

"It is when my moon-blood flows that I know no child is planted in me by your father's seed. I do not expect it, for it never was so with me."

Suddenly, a great sadness came over me and that sadness was made of many parts: I loved Elanor truly, and most truly did she merit such love. Yet I felt keenly for a moment that I was not her own child. I had lost my true mother, and Elanor had never brought any child of her own to birth. I did not know whether I loved Elanor as much as I would have loved my own mother, had she lived. I did not know whether Elanor loved me as much as she would have loved a child of her own, had there been one. Such musings deepened my sadness, and tears rose to my eyes.

"Do not weep Mother!" I cried foolishly, for it was I who wept, "You do not need a child! You do not need a child because you have me and Archibald and all my other brothers. We love you. I love you."

181

Elanor reached out and took me into her arms, for I was sobbing. A voice in my head told me that this was no way for a future warrior to behave, but I would not listen. I was disturbed to learn of this strange suffering of maidens; I was grieved by my darling Elanor's sadness. I *would* weep and behave childishly because life was tragic, and I needed comfort.

After that time, I did notice women sometimes speaking in low voices of their "moon-course" or "moon-blood" as if it were a secret. It explained why Bebbe or some of the bondswomen were pale or unwell for a few days. I never heard a man speak of it, although any married man, such as my father, must have known of it.

"It is one of the female mysteries," Elanor said, "like child-bearing. Men wonder at it, but they rarely speak of it." She would now often talk to me privately of the moon-courses. "It is nothing to fear," she said, "All grown maidens have it, and women too, when they are not carrying a child in their belly, or breast-feeding." Once she showed me the bowl that she used to catch the blood, and explained how she wore a thick woollen sling between her legs, hooked on to a little cloth belt under her clothes, to catch the flow if she had to leave her room during her moon-course. "It is well that you understand all this now," she told me, "For when your own time comes you will know there is no reason for fear. And becoming a woman is cause for celebration, when a girl's father and the grown women in her family bring her gifts."

The notion of receiving gifts was encouraging, but I was not greatly pleased to hear that the humiliation of becoming a woman would be deepened by the discomfort and inconvenience of the moon-blood. But what Elanor said was true; when, the time did eventually come for my own moon-courses to begin, I had much knowledge and no fear of it.

31

Father Rides to Einiog

Hestan and Godwine were gone all too quickly, and our life returned to its normal round of days. When they had ridden away I felt - despite my new life-purpose - some of the melancholy that always struck me in the days following the Grain Rite or Yule Solstice celebration. As for Father, his gloominess returned with a deeper quality. On the first huntsday following the twins' departure, he did not order matters with his usual relish, but set Farin to lead the hunt, and spent the day chopping wood. Although Father did soon return to hunting, his sorrow seemed rarely to lift. I thought that he was often on the edge of wrath and, although the days were long gone that he would raise a hand to son or bondsman, all approached him but warily. There seemed a grieving dissatisfaction and angry longing in his manner.

My step-mother Elanor was of a gentle nature, and did not speak readily of her worries, but I understood the depth of her concern for Father's mood when she spoke to him one evening. I had passed my eleventh winter at that time, and we were approaching springtime. Father had led the hunt that day, and it had gone well, so there was more of lightness in his step and voice than usual. Elanor brought a hot wine posset to him and then sat beside him as the bondswomen cleared the table of our evening meal. "Finric," she said, "You have not spoken for some time about your plan to travel to the Welshlands to have arms made for your sons."

Father looked at her in some wonderment, but did not speak at once.

"Since Hestan and Godwine visited," Elanor continued, "I have thought much of this. Farin and Archibald keep your old sword bright between them, but Farin is past twenty now, and perhaps should bear his own sword."

I knew well that Elanor was a peaceful creature and had no wish to see the boys go off to war or quest, so I listened with the same puzzled attention as Father.

"Although Hereward and Alvar are less skilled with spear and bow as their brothers," said she, "It is meet perhaps that they also should bear a sword for festivals and feasts." She added, "They are married men now and, as sons of yours, should carry such a mark of your family's honour. Do you not think so?" Elanor spoke tentatively, but she was a wise one and knew that speaking of Father's status would please him. More than that, she had put to him the notion of a journey – a quest not without danger, for it was a long way to Einiog in the Welshlands where the best arms were made.

"That is true, my love," said Father and I saw a glow of eagerness light up his face, "I have been meaning to arm the boys properly for these years, but since HestanandGodwine left, with the ordering of our lands and people, there has been little time for such quests."

"You should go, Finric," and Elanor turned her face full to him and put her hand gently to his arm, "You will be back before the harvest. Hereward can manage the household along with his own. Archibald is young, but well able to lead the hunt, as you have said many times, and we have skilled and faithful bondsmen enough to cope until you return."

"Yes," said Father, "It is time also that I looked to our weapon store. I know well that we need more arrow-heads, bows and spears, for who is to say how much longer this time of peace will last?"

Elanor nodded and smiled, but her face paled a little in the firelight and I knew she feared my father's absence, even while she encouraged him to go. He put an arm around her, "Yet, I'm loath to leave you my love," he said softly. They kissed, and I felt the cold breath of exclusion that anyone can experience in the presence of lovers who have eyes only for each other. But I happened to have Bebbe's latest baby on my lap, and held the little one to me for warmth and comfort, so I did not mind.

So it was that my father took the journey to Einiog to fetch weapons for his household. After some discussion and wise words from Elanor, he agreed that Hereward could not be spared from the land; Alvar was unsuited for such a journey and Archibald was too young. Eventually Father decided to take with him Farin and Heath and six strong bondsmen tested in hunting and weaponry. Among them was to be Beron, who had guarded the cart on my covert trip to the Holywell Abbey and travelled with HestanandGodwine on their first quest with the Lord Torhelm, bringing back messages from them to our household. Beron was our principle armed bondsman in whom we all trusted.

I knew that Archibald must have been yearning to go with them, but he held his peace, as any true thegn would do, and vowed to do his part in guarding Father's household until his return.

Before he went, Father set up a tower on the watch-hill to the north of our home. He ordered a regular armed watch there, day and night, and another to guard the home yard itself. I think this eased the anxiety he felt at leaving us, as did the sight of Hereward, Alvar and Archibald standing with their spears and knives before a goodly force of loyal bondspeople to bid him farewell. Archibald, at seventeen, was taller then than Hereward and as broad as Heath. Father knew he would be an able hunt leader, and fight any raiders courageously. Father must have left with an easy heart, for few households could be better protected in those days.

It seemed to me a full long time that they were gone, while early spring unfurled, blossomed, became summer and turned from green to gold.

It was towards harvest time and there had been several days of sunshine following soft rain; the grain was fat on the stem and we expected a good harvest. The Lord Wulfirth and his family were away from home, visiting the Lady Cwena's brother in the south. Father David rode over from Ufer Hall to see us, and to sample the cider that our brewerwomen were preparing, which was known to be of excellent quality, our orchard being in a sheltered, sunny position that made for unusual sweetness in the fruit. Elanor invited him to stay with us until the Wulfirths returned. That made me glad, for I always felt safe and full of hope in Father David's presence.

I spent a whole day with Archibald, riding the bounds of Flytun to check that all crops were ready for harvest. While we rode, he spoke to me of his hopes for a life of questing. He was taking instruction in reading and writing from Elanor.

"Godwine advised me to do so," he said, "For all squires are literate these days, and he said that he might find a place for me if I learn to write."

Archibald was, of course, as fine a huntsman as any of our household and thus most skilled with the bow and spear. Latterly, having taken advice from Hestan and Godwine, he had been practising the movements of swordplay with his wooden sword. "It is of little use until I get a real sword of my own to practise with," he said, "But it is meet to be familiar with the movements." He glanced at me, knowing I would understand his problem. I nodded in sympathy, for indeed I wanted a sword for myself also.

And I was glad to be riding with my brother Archibald, sharing his hopes and dreams, as we awaited the return of our people from the armouries of Einiog. Thus, I was a happy child with the harvest-time coming on and my heart singing in anticipation of a new Grain Rite, as the sun ripened a harvest fit to welcome a father's return.

There were no clouds on the morning my father rode home. The first I knew of it was when a shout went up from Worik, who was keeping the watch. "RIDERS" he cried in his clear, massive voice, and then "'TIS THE LORD FINRIC, RIDING HOME!" and I was running, with all my family and household about me and Spin at my feet (still swift enough, although he was beginning to age), to the high land where the watch tower stood.

It was a fine sight that greeted us. Below was a group of horsemen with two carts alongside. As we came to the top of the hill, they caught sight of us. Several of them waved, and the horsemen broke into a canter. One was carrying a spear staff with a long coloured flag fixed to the top. This flew out behind them as they galloped towards us. I have rarely seen a sight that thrilled me more.

I could see there were four new men riding in my father's company, and many eyes turned upon them now. "Welshmen," said Worik. All were good-looking men on fine horses. Their tunics were of cloth woven in patterns of mixed brown and blue and red. All of them rode with their feet thrust into loops of leather which hung one each side over the horses' shoulders, and now I could see that Farin and Heath had adopted similar additions to their horses harness. The benefits of this innovation became obvious as they approached, for with their feet in the loops, Farin and Heath raised themselves, waving their spears, and looked to me like gods of war, seeming almost to stand on their horses' backs. When they reached us and dismounted, I threw myself at Heath, for I loved him well and had missed his kindly and tolerant ways with me. He stooped .and clasped me in his arms, saying that I had grown and that he hoped I had been good, and all the kinds of things that loved-ones say to children who have been absent from their lives for a while. I began chattering in my usual way, telling him of Alice's new baby girl, and a tree struck by lightening, and a new well found on Hereward's land. Soon, though, I paused and stopped as I examined his face. He set me down, turning to greet his wife Bebbe and their three little children. It was then I noticed a wide scar, healed but fiery red, on Heath's jawbone and I saw also that Farin was carrying a weakness in one arm, and that Father was limping.

Now some of our bondspeople's faces changed from joyful welcome to bitter sorrow, and I realised that, although the retinue was somewhat larger than when they had left, there was no sign of two of the bondsmen who had ridden out in Father's company. One was Jeugh, a man I knew little, only that he was tall and a good huntsman. The other was well known to me, for Beron, our chief armed bondsman, had belonged to our household for longer than I could remember. I looked quickly from one face to another, realising suddenly that I could not see him, and now his wife Magba was keening fearfully, her eyes wild and wet as she clutched her baby girl in her arms while her little son clung, wailing, to her skirts. Soon we heard that Father's band had been forced often to fight in the time they had been away and that Beron and Jeugh had fallen. Many were the questions put to our people, and they might have been kept for hours on the watch-tower hill, had Elanor not raised her voice in protest. Although she was a sweet soul, my step-mother had always exerted quiet authority in our household; this particularly so since Father had been away. Now she lifted her hand and said, "There shall be no more speech until all our beloved travellers are fed and rested. Let us go back to the house!"

So all returned to the homeyard, where a table was set up out of doors so that all our people could see the home-comers and hear them talk as they ate and drank their fill. Father David made a short prayer of thanks for Father's safe return and another in tribute to the lost men. But there was no rest for the travellers until many stories had been told of the road and of battle and valour and woe. Before the meal, Father set a double armed-guard, both at the watch-tower and about the homeyard itself. "I should have gone a year or more ago," he said to Elanor. "If you had not urged me to go, it might have been too late."

Because the Lord Wulfirth kept a good force of men, we had always felt fairly defended. But Father told us that now much of the country beyond Beornwine to the Welshlands was become hostile, with warlike bands roaming, destroying farms and stealing goods. Their small party had been forced to battle within two days of leaving us.

"When Hestan and Godwine were here, they told me of new perils in the country," said Father, "But I was too full of my pride in them and in myself to take full notice of their warnings." He put a hand to his forehead in a gesture of chagrin, "I have been over-concerned with domestic matters these past years. It is my fault that we were so ill prepared and unpractised in the arts of war."

Listening to my father then, I felt disturbed to hear him thus berating himself. Indeed, the tones of self-abasement in his voice were new to me.

187

However, I have learned much in the long years since that day; I know now that, while we live, we go on learning forever to the end. Father had grown in wisdom and humility in those few moon-cycles since he left us. He was, indeed, growing to deserve the honoured status that he already held in our community. Now he glanced at Elanor, "I must speak with the Lord Wulfirth full soon. We have been at peace too long."

It was at that first battle that our two bondsmen had been killed.

"We were ambushed," said Father.

They had been riding through peaceful country with occasional villages where they were greeted kindly by the inhabitants. On the second day they had stopped to eat a midday meal in an open spot that seemed far from any danger. Suddenly, they heard the wing-rush of arrows and Jeugh fell screaming with an arrow through his neck. The attack was coming from a small copse nearby. For a moment everyone was stilled in shock, looking at the injured man with blood spurting from his wound. Then Father was on his feet, sword in hand. Farin had Father's old sword, and Heath ran to fetch spears and bows from the cart. That was when an arrow hit his jaw, scraping to the bone but glancing off. Now the assailants came forward, well armed, and protected by their shields.

"Our shields were still with the horses," said Father. "That was foolish." He shook his head in a grimace of self-disgust, yet I respected him more for admitting his fault.

A howling group of raiders made for the cart, throwing spears and brandishing swords, for they wanted both to prevent Heath collecting the arms and to steal our weapons for themselves. Father leapt to Heath's aid, with Farin and Beron close behind him. Other bondsmen were taken on by the remaining raiders. Our people fought bravely, though they were ill-armed with only hunting knives and short spears. That was when Beron was killed, facing three raiders without flinching and delivering a mortal blow to one of them who was about to strike Farin. This had left Beron himself undefended and he fell to an enemy weapon. Father, Farin and Heath were set upon and all took injury.

The turning point was when a raider's sword shivered Father's own weapon from his hand and then hacked a vicious blow at his leg. It was a dire wound, yet it kindled my father's potent anger.

"That was when I felt the battle-power come to me," he said quietly, "And my rage lent me both skill and strength that I did not deserve."

"Aye," said Heath, in an awed tone, "And the Lord Finric was like to be Odin himself come to save us, for he took a spear in each hand and ran at the raiders with a great roar."

"I lost one spear in a man's head," said Father, "And pitched the second straight through the shield of another, pinning it through his breast."

Then Farin spoke up, his face alight with memory, "I saw terror come upon the other raiders then," he said, "But I was afraid, for Father was now without arms or shield, except for his seax knife. I was injured, but everyone else ran to his aid. Heath here took up Father's sword under the noses of the villains and put it in his hand. Then they were running, with our people on their tails, though their numbers were more than twice ours."

It was a victory, but it left Father's party weakened and grieving. Apart from the two dead, most of our men carried injuries, some of them serious.

"We needed to get help and shelter to deal with our wounds," said Father. "By good fortune we were only a short ride from a goodly farm-holding where we had exchanged a hind for bread and wine that very morn. We tied up our hurts as best we could and got ourselves thither. They took us in and a herb-woman sewed up our wounds and dressed them well." Father glanced at his injured leg and moved it stiffly. "It was necessary for us to fight but once more before we reached Einiog, and twice on our journey home, but never were we caught unprepared again."

There was a look of weighty nobility in my father's face and he seemed to wear hurt and fatigue and travel-dirt as a man twenty years his junior. I knew then that my father was born to be a warrior and leader of fighting men. What I saw was evident to all around, and Archibald, who was sitting close to Father, slipped from his seat onto his knees in an impulsive gesture of tribute. Father looked on him warmly.

"I have a fine sword for you boy," he said, "And a shield also. When next I ride out, you shall come."

I knew that he did not mean any hunting trip, and for me a sudden darkness fell, although the sun was still bright as I saw my dearest brother pass from his boyhood and become a man in the eyes of our community. The child in me felt the loss of my oldest playfellow, but I knew what his heart longed for - to ride out as warriors do, for he had an honourable quest to follow. So I made no sound or movement, only watching silently and, though only a child of eleven winters, I made there my first adult action, crushing the desire to disturb Archibald's happiness with childish jelousy or envy.

All noble acts have their reward and mine came very soon. For after Father turned to speak to Hereward, Archibald's first smile was for me, in a glance that any thegn might give a brother warrior who shared the dearest wish of his heart.

At last, the brightness of homecoming began to fade from the travellers' faces and a great weariness seemed to fall upon them, especially the ones who were wounded. Father's eyes closed for a moment and Elanor stood, saying to him "There shall be no more talk until you are rested. All wounds must be attended to now. Then our most welcome Lord and his sons and loyal people who are home at last, shall sleep."

Father got up from his seat, forcing the weariness from his body as he stood straight, and all were silent as they waited for him to speak. "The Lady Elanor is right," he said, "We need to have our wounds tended and we need to rest. Accommodation and a proper welcome must be made for the new men who have ridden home with me and who I would fain keep in my household, for they are loyal and doughty warriors, who fought valiantly."

A murmur of approbation circled the crowd and the Welshmen bowed their heads modestly. Then Father raised his voice, "But first I say this," he said, "Before any celebration can take place for our return, we shall give prayers and laments for those who were lost. Both were valuable and faithful people to me, and can never be replaced. I shall make provision for their families. Neither wife nor child shall suffer want through their loss. Today we rest because we must. Tomorrow we shall mourn." He turned to Father David. "Father, will you prepare meet prayers and lamentation for our dead? I would fain give them proper rites, for there was little time when they were buried, and their spirits need to be released from the earth into freedom."

"It shall be done, my Lord," said Father David.

Then great bowls of boiled herb-water were brought into the house, where beds were made for the travellers. Those who were uninjured washed themselves, then lay down and were asleep in moments. Though the work of the house continued around them, nothing disturbed the sleepers. Even when Spin walked over Heath's chest before I could stop him, and licked his face (for Heath was an old friend to Spin) he stirred not.

The wounded counted six, including Father, Farin and Heath. They were tended by those of our people who were wise in healing, including Elanor of course, and Bebbe, who tended her husband first. I was wide-eyed with curiosity to see the wounds, and followed Elanor closely until she said "Edith, you may stay if you can be useful and do my bidding. Otherwise, go outside and be not under my feet."

"Oh, let me help Mother!" I entreated her. So she gave me a bowl of water to hold while she uncovered Father's leg wound, which was bound closely in cloths that were matted and stained. Elanor scooped up handfuls of water onto the cloths and the water ran back into the bowl all dark with old blood. I held the bowl carefully so that no drop should fall on the bed beneath and make Father uncomfortable. When the cloths were well soaked and had become soft with the water, Elanor carefully unwound them from Father's leg, dropping the cloths into the bowl. At last, the wound was exposed. Across the thick flesh of Father's calf I saw a long gash, criss-crossed with dark stitches. At the top of the wound the flesh was red and puffy, with a little yellow ooze crusting amongst the congealed blood at its edges. I stared; old memories beating at my composure, but my courage kept them at bay.

"Now Edith," said Elanor, "Take this bowl away and bring a fresh one with wormwood and nettle-herb water. Ask the women in charge for the right one." I lifted the bowl carefully, glancing quickly at my father's face. There I stopped, for his eyes were full on me, his face displaying such an expression of love and kindness that I could not move. He smiled in a most gentle and reassuring way. I smiled back at him, yet did not forget myself, but looked to my task as I carried that bloody bowl away and fetched a fresh one as I was bid, without spilling a drop.

When I returned with the fresh bowl, Elanor was smiling and talking gently with Father. I could see that certain lines of concern were gone from her face and, in my turn, I felt reassured. Now she took fresh cloths and cleaned the wound of the old blood and puss. "This has been well tended," she said.

"Aye, for the herb-woman who stitched it was a wise one indeed," said Father. "Her son, who was chief in that village, told me it was great luck that put us in her hands."

Elanor nodded. "'Tis true. The stitching is good work, and there is only a little infection, despite the size of the wound. It will be healed soon, for now you can rest and take good food and be made well."

The next day was fine again and all our people gathered in the home yard to honour the passing of our men Beron and Jeugh. Father David put up a table before the door to our house and spread a fine white cloth upon it. There he set the large Christian cross that was kept for holy services such as these, with a candle either side of it. Beron's wife Magba and Jeugh's wife Sharn were brought with their children to the front, while everyone else stood behind. Father David stood at the table and bowed his head. All did likewise and there was silence among us, all but Magba's baby daughter – a sunny child – who cooed softly as Father David began the lamentation for the dead. Father then made a short speech, telling of the bravery of our lost men. When he spoke of Beron, he named him 'Freebold' for the first time, thus honouring his bravery and giving freedom and title to his children, for Beron had served our family well, and died saving Farin's life.

"We buried them with their spears and shields, as befits any warrior," he said, "And with Christian crosses over their eyes. Now they are mourned by those who honoured and loved them, let their souls be free to ride with the holy ones, by the love of Christ."

Father David then made a loud "Amen", which all followed. Afterwards there was a feast, but I ate little, for the thought of Beron lying dead in the ground far from his home robbed me of my appetite. I took my dog and walked all the day with my memories of this strong and doughty man: seeing him guarding the cart where I hid on my adventure to the Holywell Abbey; riding off with Father to hunt and serve in battle; galloping into our homeyard with news of HestanandGodwine; giving farewell to his wife and little children the last time ever I saw him.

I remembered that Beron had saved the life of my dear brother Farin, and that his family would always bear the title 'Freebold' bestowed by my father. I knew that my sorrow for Beron would always stand alongside great pride in his courage. It was then that I thought of the others I had lost many years before: my sweet brother Harald - who died on the battlefield avenging my mother's murder – and Eldred, quiet and kind and strong, who had killed two of Orin's men in the same battle, mended Father's wound before dying of his own injuries, and now lay far away in a quiet forest clearing under the green mound we raised over his body. These two also deserved to be remembered with pride beside the grief.

At last, as Spin and I came to the river above Beornwine, I sat on the bank and thought of my mother, whose death brought terror and despair into my head. I faced the blackness now and saw that her courage in the face of torture was the greatest of all, for she had neither wept nor screamed, nor shown any fear at the point of death, so that her watching child should not be destroyed by what she witnessed.

Thus the loss of poor Beron helped me to bear those earlier losses and taught me that death has no power in the face of courage, and love is not drowned in grief when we can honour those we have lost.

That evening, I sat by the fireside among our crowded household, listening to the new Welsh bondsmen singing ancient tales in their beautiful voices. Soon, I slept, and when I awoke the room was still full of our people talking softly, though many slept and the fire glowed warmly in embers.

I slipped away then to Magba's house, and found Farin there, his eyes swollen with tears and Beron's little son sleeping in his arms. I went straight to Magba and she held me close for a long while. Then, as the night wore on, she made a brew of mulled milk and cider for us all to share. I did not sleep again that night, nor yet did Magba or Farin, for we all kept watch through the darkness.

With the dawn, Magba rose and we followed her out of the little house. Farin had the sleeping boy in his arms and Magba was carrying her baby girl. There in the open circle of our homeyard, we saw the morning star like a great lamp in the clear sky, and the soul of our beloved Beron sailed free at last into the heavens.

Because of the tribute he made to the dead, Father did not distribute gifts until the third day after his return. Then the wonderful new swords were displayed – one each for all my brothers – all in fine scabbards of wool-lined leather. Archibald's was a fine double-edged sword of medium weight, with a layered pommel, simple cross-guard and leather-covered grip: an excellent sword for a young warrior.

There was a new household knife for Elanor, its handle beautifully wrought in silver, with a fine leather scabbard and chain to hang it from her belt. She was mightily pleased with it.

Then Father turned to me, "I have a gift for you too, daughter," he said with a smile, handing me something wrapped in a cloth. I was much surprised, as I had not expected anything and I quickly unwrapped the gift. It was a household knife, smaller and plainer than Elanor's, but with a good blade of my hand's length, exactly in the shape of a seax. With it was a looped leather scabbard decorated with red and green circles. No other gift could have as much surprised and pleased me and I threw my arms around my father to thank him. As soon as I could, I took myself away to a quiet spot with only Spin as company, and drew the blade from the scabbard. I sat there for some time just looking at the shape of it, knowing it was a symbol of freedom to me just as Father's own Seax was to him. I was quite aware that he had not intended the gift to mean any such thing, but only as a pretty and useful possession. I wore it every day from then on, and was taught the care and use of it by Elanor. It was my first blade.

32

A Most Noble Virtue

The new danger abroad from warlike bands and raiders was taken with full seriousness by our father. He ordered that all men of fighting age in our household should be taught the use of weapons as a precaution, and he undertook their instruction himself, for there was no better or more experienced warrior anywhere. He set aside a rough, sloping field as a training-ground, and many of our men soon became well skilled with the bow, slingshot, spear and shield. The Lord Wulfirth came to talk with Father about armed men and defences. Pales were cut and raised in a continuous barrier around our homeyard and near land, with a gateway upon which was set a constant watch. A similar ring of pales was set about our watch-tower to the north. Although the work of the farm had to continue, my home began to look like a fortress, and my father strode about with the weight of years lifted off his brow. He did not neglect our wealth of land, but charged Hereward to hire land-wise bondsmen at the Grain Rite, so that the land would be worked as usual while our men were being trained to fight.

Archibald was eager to bid Farin and Heath show him what sword actions they had learned at Einiog. They showed him gladly and all three practised daily, along with the young Welshmen, Grant, Davy, Gladwyn and Ina. It was heavy exercise. I kept them company, as did many of the young of our household, none of us ever tiring of watching the swing and thrust and parry movements, and practising them ourselves with what wooden swords and sticks we had. One day, Heath offered his sword to Alun, a big boy of about thirteen winters who had been watching avidly. Alun took the hilt in both hands and raised the great iron sword into the air, although his teeth were clenched and his arms shaking with the weight of it.

"Me too!" I cried, "Oh please let me try, Heath. Let me hold it!"

They all laughed. Even Archibald, flushed with exertion and pride, stood with the men, threw his head back and laughed down at me.

At that moment, and for the first time, I recognised the full force of the difference between us. What I understood was deeply profound and filled me with a sense of loss darker than my grief for Beron. Archibald and the others were laughing, not because of my small stature and few years which ill-fitted me to wield such a heavy sword. Their laughter had a finer edge to it that cut me deeply:

They laughed not because I was a child, but because I was a girl.

And all the acts and deeds and dreams I held to be the best and most desirable in life were denied to me. They would always be denied to me. I knew it then as I stood before my brother Archibald and the others, and that knowledge was like the earth falling away from me, leaving nowhere for me to be.

Something of this brutal disillusionment must have shown on my face, for Heath ceased laughing and looked at me kindly. "Well so you shall try," he said, "Go on Alun, let little Edith take the sword."

So Alun stood the sword before me with its tip on the ground and leaned the hilt towards me. I took it, my hands gripping the plaited leather binding. I struggled and heaved, but I could do no more than lift the tip of that sword a finger's breadth from the ground. It was the final humiliation. Heath took it off me and demonstrated a perfect low swing (an excellent movement for honing strength, accuracy and control). I should have stayed to observe and learn; I heard in my head the voice of the young knight, Redhelm, *Give care to your eyes and your task.* Yet, this time, it neither braced nor comforted me. I turned and ran for the house, so that none should see my shame any more.

There in the doorway was Elanor. She had been watching all that transpired. What she garnered from my expression, I do not know, but she held me to her for a moment as if it was she who was in need of comfort. Then she said softly, "It is not for a Christian girl to learn the lore of arms, Edith. We are not as the heathens, who have their women warriors."

"Then I wish I was a heathen!" I cried, my face working as I tried to control my tears. But it was useless; the tears would come, and I sobbed into her shoulder.

That, I think, was the last time Elanor carried me. Despite the weight of my growing body, she gathered me up and brought me inside to her especial place near the hearth. By the wall there was a fine big chair with wooden arms that Hereward had made for her, and upon it were many soft, patterned and embroidered cushions that she had sewn herself. Here she sat with me on her lap, rocking me until the worst of my sobs had calmed.

"Beloved one," she said, "You must listen to me now, knowing how precious you are to me. Dearest, you must never say such a thing again. Never say that you wish to be heathen. Such words are bad for you. Bad for all of us."

Now Elanor was one for whom the phrase 'loving kindness' was surely made. I know that she would never have said one particular word that struck fear into my soul. But I know she was thinking that a girl with such sinful desires could be named a witch. I know it now, and I knew it then.

So I clung to Elanor – a baby for the last time because I would soon be too heavy for her to lift – and she stroked my hair to calm me while we sat quietly together, not heeding the clatter and shouts, bumps and laughter of the men's world outside. At last, the fire was in need of replenishing. Elanor stirred, looked down into my eyes and smiled. "There *is* something that a Christian girl can accomplish with honour," she said. "It is a most noble virtue, which every thegn should possess. How would you like to learn reading?"

I sprang up, feeling my eyes widen as Elanor's face reflected my own delight.

"Yes please!" I cried, "Oh yes my darling Mother!" and I flung my arms around her. She was still for a moment, and if in her stillness she was thinking of that other mother who had given me birth, then I did not know it.

"We will not concern your father with this," she said, "But keep it a secret between us, and have your lessons when we are alone. When the Grain Rite is over, and you have returned from Holywell, we shall begin."

So it was agreed, and I did not even tell Archibald. I kept it from him because I needed something to balance the betrayal I had felt as he stood with the men and laughed at my femaleness, as if I was some strange creature of another world, and not a human girl with as much love of adventure as he. Had he forgotten our talk under the oak tree of only a few moons ago, when I accepted my true thegn's quest? I could not believe it, but was too offended at the very thought to challenge him.

Whilst nothing could mar my love for Archibald, the incident did mark the beginning of a change in our friendship. For he was a man, tall and strong as almost any other in our household. Father trusted him as hunter and farmer. Should there be a war and our family called upon to serve, he would go. He practised his reading, but was far more often seen performing swordplay - swing and thrust and parry – until the sword was like an extension of his own arm, so skilled was he at wielding it.

But if Archibald had his swordsmanship, I would soon have another skill well recognised as a thegnly attribute. I would be able to read – and better than he.

33

The Testings

The Grain Rite that year was only a moon cycle after Father's return from Einiog. The harvest was in early and the feast preparations in our household were made with the usual excitement and bustle. I was past eleven winters now and not considered a child, so I was called upon to spend time at the dairy or baking ovens and I soon tired of it. So I began to rise from my bed before cock-crow and ride away to Beornwine or to Mother Werberga, so as to keep away from chores for the day. I also often took food and drink and rode to a little open glade I had found on the forest-road to Ufer Hall. There I would practise archery and also try out the sword-movements I had seen my brothers practising. I only had the wooden sword Archibald had given up to me now he had his own true sword, but in fact the wooden one was well made and heavy enough for a girl of my age. I would practise hard for long hours, then sit under a tree to rest and eat before practising again. My arm ached, yet I did not mind for I knew I was improving my swordsmanship. But it was long before I would show myself with my sword anywhere near home, for I had no wish to be laughed at again.

Of course, Elanor soon noticed that I was regularly taking myself away from the household. When I returned one day, brown from the sunshine, my sword-arm aching satisfactorily, she came out to me as I was letting Bracken out into the paddock.

"You were missed today Edith," she said in a quiet tone that yet gave me a stab of guilt.

"I am sorry," I said, shame-faced, "I have been tired of working and wanted to be out in the summer air." (It was something Elanor often urged me to do – to be out in the summer air – and I thought to strengthen my defence by using her own words against her.)

"Well, we would all like to join you Edith, and so we shall at the Grain Rite when all is prepared for the feast. There would be nothing for anybody if we played all day as you do. Now please put your sword away and call your father to supper. He is with the boys at the whetstone."

When Elanor referred to 'the boys' she meant my two unmarried brothers, Farin and Archibald. Both were really men, as Archibald was past nineteen, and Farin twenty-two winters - and a tested warrior after the journey to Einiog. I was happy to join them at the small thatched cabin where the whetstone was housed, and where Father was training them to sharpen blades. Everyone who owned a blade carried a small whetstone at their belts; indeed I had one myself to sharpen the little houseknife that Father had given me. But for a perfect sword-edge or if there were many weapons to sharpen, a full-sized whetstone was needed. We had a good one – massively heavy, thick and long, rounded slightly at the edges. It was smooth-looking but very hard and slightly rough to the touch. As I approached I could hear the regular rasping, ringing sound that my father's sword made when he was sharpening it. Father demanded that swords were kept blunt for practise, to prevent cutting injuries. But he kept his own blade true at all times.

I saw him standing in front of the stone, which was raised up on a sturdy tree-stump so that he could use it standing up. No-one moved as I entered and we all watched as Father bent with smooth, regular movements across it, sweeping the edge of his sword along its whole length as he moved, then turning the sword around and treating the other edge in the same way. Then he stepped back, holding the hilt whilst balancing the flat of the blade on the stone. He motioned with his head and Farin tested the edge carefully with his finger, gasping softly as it drew blood. Archibald stroked his thumb lightly from the middle of the blade to the edge, and raised his head in a half-nod, whilst Farin nursed his cut finger in his mouth.

"If y' can learn the method on this stone, ye'll get the feel of whetting," said Father. "No matter how deft and quick any swordsman might be, he'll not win through without a true blade."

All were silent as Father raised his sword and, with one movement, settled it into the scabbard which he was wearing at his waist.

I judged it time to speak. "Father," I said, "Elanor calls us to supper."

They all turned as though seeing me there for the first time.

"Very good, child," Father said, but at the same time, both boys spoke:

"Father ..." said Farin.

"We wanted to ask ..." said Archibald.

Father turned and glanced from Farin to Archibald, frowning. They looked nervously at each other, then back to Father again.

Farin cleared his throat and raised his head. "Father," he said "I want … We both want to ask your leave to compete in the hand-to-hand testings at the Grain Rite."

"No." said Father immediately, but he did not move, only frowning from one to the other of them.

"You went to the testings yourself at a young age, you told us," Archibald said quickly. "Is there any way to practise real hand-to-hand combat except at the testings?"

Ignoring the question, Father said, "Enter the archery tests; that is your gift. I wage you will win as you won last year."

"But a warrior must be skilled with the sword also – as you are Father!"

Father did not answer, but looked at Farin, "You are still injured in the arm. It would be foolish to fight in the tests with that weakness."

"But in a real battle I would have to fight with a wound!" said Farin, "Indeed, I have done so! I want to show what I can do!"

"It is true that you had to fight with a wound on the Einiog road. You have no more need to be tested. Your valour is well known. No Lord would allow a valuable warrior to fight injured in a common test! It would dishonour me to allow it."

This was rare praise and explanation on my father's part, but we all knew he would brook no further argument without quickening his temper. I knew Farin would love to enter the tests as a known warrior and be pointed to and praised like some of the renowned warriors who would be there. But he stood back now and I saw his shield hand go to the injury at his opposite shoulder.

Father turned to me and said, "So, your mother calls us, Edith. We must eat!" He ducked under the roof of the cabin and set off across the home yard, still limping heavily from his own wound.

But Archibald hurried after him. "What of me, Father? I have practised daily with my new sword. I can wield it easily now. Blades have to be blunt for the tests, so I cannot be badly injured, and I am strong." He stopped. Father had slowed his own pace, and I saw he was in pain from his leg. Archibald stood before him. "Father," he said, "I am ready."

I thought Father would raise his voice in anger now, but the opposite happened. His shoulders sagged and he said, "Then fight, boy; enter for the hand-to-hand if you must." He turned from Archibald and limped slowly to the house, with Farin beside him. I walked with the two wounded warriors, not understanding my father's sudden attitude of sadness, but wishing to comfort him – although I did not know how. We all left his youngest son, triumphant and ignored, standing alone in the yard.

I could not watch.

My anticipation of that Grain Rite had been marred by the knowledge that Archibald was to fight in the hand-to-hand tests. The day was cool and windy, whipping random rain-drops into my face, and I felt the elements were in accord with my mood, which was disturbed and turbulent. Even seeing that my hero Redhelm had arrived did nothing to calm my apprehension. The truth is that, ever since he had saved my life when I was small child, Archibald had carried my own security more surely even than my father or step-mother. Despite my new-found courage, it was difficult for me to contemplate injury or danger to my brother. It was all very fine for us to talk together of living the life of a fighting thegn, and I respected him for entering the tests, but when I saw the reality of him being hurt in battle – even a controlled one such as these – I could not bear it.

When I saw Archibald hurt and on the ground in the first hand-to-hand test, my head filled with rage and my heart with darkness. Although he rose again to beat his opponent, I had not the courage to watch the later rounds. Hereward's little daughter, Hylda, was begging to be taken to watch the giant, so I went with her and we laughed and shrieked with the other children. After a while we saw Hylda's brother Eldric coming to join us, along with Heath and his own young son, Pepin. Taking no notice of the giant, the six-year-old Eldric ran to meet us. "Edith," he said, his little face all red with excitement, "Archibald has won his round and is drawn next against Halbert!"

I felt a rush of pride that my brother had come so far in the testings to be drawn against the famous thegn, Halbert, but the pride fell away in a moment and I was left in terror for my brother.

Heath was standing beside me and must have seen the fear in my face. He put his arm around me and said, "He cannot be badly hurt, Edith, for you know the swords are blunt."

I leant into the arm of my old friend for a moment. But it was not possible for me to be comforted. I had watched the tests at every Beornwine Grain Rite for five years. Nearly every year someone was killed and, although the blunted swords they used could not easily cut, yet I had seen arms slashed to the bone by the pure weight of a blunt sword; I had seen bones broken and blood spilt, and I was afraid for my brother whose face already was bruised and his leg bloodied from the earlier testing rounds.

I looked back towards the testing ground and could see Archibald re-strapping his breast-plate for the hand-to-hand against Halbert. Then, with a frown on his face, he looked up and all around until he caught sight of me. His face cleared then as he strode over, calling to me. "Edith, you will be there to see this fight, will you not?" Reaching me he took my hand, saying earnestly, "Remember what we are to each other, sister! Seeing you here supporting me will give me courage."

"She cannot, Archibald," said Heath, "You must understand. She is afraid."

And to hear those words – spoken kindly by Heath – suddenly released their truth from its power over me. "No," I said, "I *shall* watch you. Of course I shall."

Archibald smiled his rare, wide smile, and I saw his face flooded with relief. I realised then that to be reminded of his valour as a little child would strengthen him in the tests. My brother needed me, and that need had more command over me than any fear. I watched as he prepared, strapping on his iron helmet, weighing the blunted sword in his hand, tightening the strap of his shield. As he entered the field I cheered and smiled, seeing his eyes on me. And only then, as he turned away from me, did I raise my own eyes to look at his opponent - Halbert, the great thegn who had ridden in the mounted huscarle of the King himself. Then my heart quailed, for Halbert was a tall and mighty warrior, much greater in weight than Archibald, and far greater in the experience of all the arts of warfare.

~ ~ ~ ~ ~

Archibald stands in the testing ground, a borrowed shield in his hand, for his own was broken in an earlier contest. His muscles and bones have been put under a strain he has never known before, but his mind sails over these hurts; all his attention is on the one who approaches. His opponent is both tall and broad: a warrior at the height of adult vigour and skill. Such skill has learned not to disregard a weak-looking challenger, especially one with such quiet watchfulness in eye and body. The thegn does not pause but, with a roar echoed by the crowd, throws his weight behind his shield and onto the boy. The crowd has seen such an action before today; they expect Archibald to have the breath knocked out of him. But there is a scramble and the boy stands again, even before the thegn regains his own feet. Hardly even panting, Archibald raises his sword and brings it down with speed and force onto the thegn's shield, allowing the sword's own weight to find its way. The shield splits and sunders, but Halbert is on his feet. Not waiting to recover full balance, he uses the great power of his sword arm and his own weight against the boy's shield and then, with a swift backward action that belies the weight of his sword, knocks Archibald's own weapon out of his hand. And the crowd is crying: "Halbert! Halbert!" This great thegn has not let them down, nor given any lie to his fame for valour and fairness. He sheathes his sword and goes to the boy, clapping him on the shoulder and speaking a few words into his ear.

Archibald is beaten, and out of the test, but he has given a good account of himself, and is glowing now with the rare praise bestowed on him by his last mighty rival. "A worthy adversary, boy." The thegn had said to him, "Much rather would I have you fighting for me and not against!"

~ ~ ~ ~ ~

34

The Magic of Letters

I loved my reading lessons and couldn't get enough of them. Elanor would take me up to her room when the early work of the morning was over and the men had left the house. At the beginning she taught me from her book of Roman writing, which she said was used by holy people all over the world. At first she would not let me touch it, but I was so in awe of the book with its fine cover, big pages and splendid lettering that she relented, allowing me to turn the pages myself; verily, I was most careful and reverential in handling those pages. What marvels I learned from them of the world and of the Holy Christ! But what was almost more marvellous was how the letters themselves transformed from meaningless patterns into words of wisdom and legend as thrilling as any bard's tale – just as if someone was standing before me, speaking.

I learned so quickly and so well that Elanor taught me to scribe also, by making marks with a piece of hard clay onto a flat stone or piece of wood. As to that, Elanor admitted little prowess in the skill of scribing; I learned as much from copying the shapes in the book, then practising sentences of my own, as I did from her. But it was Elanor's sweet encouragement and praise that spurred me on to do better; such was her kindness.

Elanor then decided that I should learn Anglish also, from the plain, smaller book. This I loved, and it seemed more magical still, because the words spelled out into our own tongue. When I learned to write Anglish, I could take meaning from my own head and put it into letters which Elanor could read.

The gift of letters has always been like magic to me and although I have now owned this skill for a long lifetime, I never tire of the wonder of it. To know that I can speak to another person by the agency of letters upon a stone or piece of parchment is a marvel. The first true message I ever wrote was '*Mother, I love you*' which I scribed upon a small, flat piece of wood and handed to Elanor. She was full pleased and kissed me, saying softly "Thank you Edith. What sweet words!" That was delightful, and more so because the house was full of people at the time, yet the message was secret between us. Elanor took the piece of wood and kept it ever after in her oak chest.

Elanor agreed that I could tell Mother Werberga about my new lessons, and I was quick to do so. She was very interested and always ready to hear about my progression in reading and scribing. There came a time when I knew that I had the ability to attempt to read what was in her Commonplace book, although I did not have the opportunity. However, one day, at Elanor's request, I asked her for the best method of preparing a certain mix of herbs for assisting sleep. "Go and get my book, Edith," she said. When I had brought the book into the light, Mother Werberga was not to be seen and I guessed she had gone to the midden to empty her bladder. I found myself sitting with the book on my lap, knowing that I could open it and most likely read anything inside. I did not, for I knew Mother Werberga considered it private to her. Soon, she returned to me and saw by examining my face that I had not opened the book. I told her so anyway, "I did not look at it Mother," I said, with some pride in my own self-control.

"Thank you Edith," she said. "You do not disappoint me. Reading is a noble virtue, but knowing when to refrain from using one's powers is nobler still."

I flushed with something that I hope was better than pride and then she rewarded me by showing me the page where was written the recipe for the sleep draught. Thus I saw Mother Werberga's own script of hand. It was strange and spiked, but not difficult to read. I read the recipe aloud so that I would remember it to tell Elanor. After that day she often allowed me to read a recipe and to copy it for my own use and Elanor's, but I never did look in that book or turn any page there without Mother Werberga's consent. I knew there was wisdom and mystery on those pages that I would fain know, yet I could not. For I loved and respected that old woman and felt it a great honour to be trusted by such as her – and to deserve that trust.

So in my delight at learning this new craft, the year's wheel turned easily for me, and as I passed my twelfth winter, Elanor thought it right to tell Father of our reading and scribing lessons. Indeed, I was so full of the wonder of my new skills that I could ill contain it between myself, Elanor and Mother Werberga. Besides, Elanor did not like to keep secrets from Father for too long. She of course chose a good time to tell him, when they were alone together, and, surprisingly, he never objected - only sometimes laughing a little at his 'learned daughter' which seemed a matter of ridicule to him, as opposed to his pride in his literate sons. I did not care; it was a relief to be able to talk about my new skill to anyone who would listen. Soon Father hit on the idea of having me read from the scriptures to the whole household on the sabbath, and I was proud to do so, especially when Father David was at our house, for he praised me much for my skills.

My brothers also took some pride in my achievement. Most notably, at Alice's suggestion, Alvar prepared for me narrow tablets of close-grained wood for me to write upon. He worked on them in his spare time, cutting thin sheets from a log with his finest saw, and then smoothing them with plane and sand. Verily, I have never seen finer work even to this day, although I am now fortunate to have plentiful parchment and velum at my disposal on which to make my writings. Next to my own seax houseknife, those tablets were the best present I could have wished for; I valued them most highly and, unlike the fine presents Alvar crafted for me when I was a child, I felt he had given them to me to please me, not to gain praise for his own skill.

It was through my lessons in scribing that I first came to write a story in letters. It was an old one I had heard told many times by travelling bards and by members of our own household on winter nights when all were gathered about the fireplace.

The story was about Roburt, a young man who, because his father was a slave, was refused permission to fight for his Lord, whose name was Elfestan. Yet Roburt was brave and true. Still, he was left behind to work in the fields when the other men rode away to battle. While Roburt was asleep that night, the god Odin came and told him that if he followed him at once without a light, he would become a renowned warrior. Immediately, without fear, Roburt got up and followed the great war god into the dark. Meanwhile, Elfestan's army was hard-pressed by the enemy, many of his followers being killed. In a dream Odin appeared to him and said that a great champion would come and save his army. But first, Elfestan was to take two great spears and a costly silver-covered horn into a place deep in the forest and leave them there. Elfestan did as he was bid by the god. The next day, Elfestan's army was becoming overpowered by the enemy when the sound of a great horn was heard over the clash of battle. All looked up to see the god Odin himself storming into the battle with a huge spear in each hand and lightening flashing from his wild hair. He struck a thunderbolt from his spears into the heart of the enemy warriors, whereupon they took flight. All of Elfestan's army fell down in thanks to the god. But when the Lord

Elfestan looked up again, it was not Odin but Roburt who stood there with the horn hanging across his body and the two spears in his hand. A voice said, "This is the champion of Elfestan's army," and paid tribute to him. After that, Roburt always fought at the right hand of the Lord Elfestan, and became the greatest warrior his country had ever known.

This was a popular story with us, and I scribed it onto four of the wooden tablets that Alvar had given me. I made the story as if it was told by a boy who had followed Elfestan's army, and seen everything that happened. When I had finished, I was much pleased with myself, and took the tablets to Archibald, who was in the house at the time.

I have said already that Archibald was not as skilled at reading as myself. He bade me read the story to him and when I had done so he said that the whole household should hear it. So that night, after supper, I took the tablets to Father.

"Father," I said, a little fearfully, "I have made the story of Roburt and Elfestan in my letters."

Now, the story of Roburt and Elfestan was a great favourite with Father, who was a renowned warrior himself. "Let us have it," he said, and all listened while I read. Afterwards everyone marvelled at the story and made much of me for it, and I was called upon to read it again twice more. I was never more proud than when Father came to me and took away the tablets to the chest in his room, saying they should not be washed off to be written upon again, but kept with my letterings upon them, although he did not himself have the skill to read them.

That night I woke as I often did when Father and Elanor came to bed, for their bed was close to mine in the loft. I heard them speaking in low voices on the other side of the partition. Eventually, it was only Elanor's soft voice I could hear and soon I realised that she was reading the Roburt and Elfestan story to Father from the tablets. It filled me with wondrous sweet happiness to know that my work had pleased my father so. I have had many audiences for my stories since that day, and much admiration for them, but none that pleased me so much as my father's silence while he listened to the words that I had written.

35

I Come to Ufer Hall

As well as writing my own stories, I continued to read the Holy Scriptures in both Roman and Anglish until I knew almost all by heart. I had set myself the task of comparing the two holy texts, chapter for chapter. The Anglish text was, of course, a translation from the Latin that I did not think always accurate. I would make my own versions of the passages I disputed, although I had few materials for writing. Simple ink mixed of burnt stone-dust and vinegar was easily enough come by, but there was little in the way of parchment or velum – only stiff, ill-preserved animal skin. I favoured the beautiful, smooth wooden tablets that Alvar made for me, but they were long in the preparation, whilst I could cover both sides with writing in an hour. However, this want was fulfilled when one day Father rode home from the Holywell Abbey with many rolls of parchment which he had purchased from a merchant there, and from that day he willingly provided me with more whenever I asked. This must have cost him dear, yet my father had become a prosperous man and he was proud of my scribing ability, so it pleased him to help me.

I had almost completed my comparison and translations of the texts, and Elanor declared my work to be finer than anything she could produce. She resolved to show it all to Father David. But she also had something else in mind, and it happened that I overheard her conversation with him on the matter.

I was aloft one morning, quietly at my work, when I heard Father David arrive. I intended to go down to greet him just as soon as I finished the line I was translating, but I stopped my work as I heard my name mentioned.

"Edith loves her letters, but I have taught her all I know," Elanor was saying. "She has little interest in household tasks although, as to that, she is proficient in them all. Those are her honey cakes you are eating. They are as good as any I bake."

I heard a grunt that was Father David's full-mouthed approbation.

"As you well know," Elanor continued, "Edith has a restless spirit. But I have found her much quietened by learning. Until she marries I am mindful to keep her occupied in that way."

"That is wise," replied Father David, "And I see why you wish to keep bright her passion for learning."

"Can you advise me?"

There was silence for a short while, and I guessed Father David was consuming more honey cake, but perhaps he was thinking. His next words surprised and pleased me.

"The Lord Wulfirth has charged me to educate his daughter, the young Lady Lewitha, at the Holy Scriptures, but the girl has little zeal for her letters. It occurs to me that the Lord and Lady might agree to another young lady joining the lessons. Edith would be company for young Lewitha, and steady her, perhaps."

The notion of my being a steadying influence was a novel one, but this did not occur to me. I was thrilled to think of having the learned Father David as a tutor, and that my lessons might take place at the great Hall on Ufer Hill. I could not stay at my task any longer. In my excitement I ran along our loft and down the ladder in a minute and threw myself into Father David's arms notwithstanding the beaker of ale at his side and the honeycake travelling as it was to his mouth.

"Stay child!" he cried, "You are becoming too much of a weight for me!" but he laughed genially, made room for me on his chair and offered me half of his honeycake. He looked down at me quizzically. "What age are you now Edith?" he asked (with his mouth full).

"I am past thirteen winters now," I said, wriggling out of the chair, for I was too excited to keep still for long, although I did not feel I should bring up the subject of the conversation I had overheard between him and Elanor.

Father David shook his head, with a smile, "Ah, speak not of winters," he said, "for a young, happy one such as you should rather count your age in summers."

"Well then, I am passing my thirteenth summer," and I smiled back at him.

"How are your reading and scribing skills progressing? Elanor tells me you are a fine scholar."

I ran to fetch the scrolls I had been working on with my translation of the Roman Holy Text into the Anglish. Father David began to read, and I saw his smile fade into thoughtfulness. When he looked up, there was an expression on his face that was much like the way the Lord Wulfirth looked at my father – as if he faced someone of equal status. He questioned me about some of my word choices and nodded at my replies. Then he looked up at Elanor who had been standing behind me, watching and looking at my writings over my shoulders. "Yes," he said, "She is certainly ready to learn more. She is more than ready." He turned to me, "Edith," he said, "Would you like.to come and read the texts at Ufer Hall; would you like to study with me and learn more?"

I do not know how I answered him, for I remember none of my actions but only my emotions at that moment. It is enough to say that I could only have been more pleased if I had been told that I was to ride off that morning and become squire to a renowned thegn.

The first time I came to Ufer Hall to my lessons, Elanor insisted on riding with me, even though I knew the way very well and could probably have ridden there much more quickly alone (Elanor was a nervous horsewoman). In fact, it was some time since either of us had been to Ufer Hall. Since Father's journey to Einiog and the fortifications and defences he had been working on since, Elanor had been kept busy running our growing household. As for me, my interest in the scribing arts kept me much more at home than I ever had been in my life. When I did go abroad, it was to my married brothers' houses – or to Beornwine, where lived my cousins, Gytha and Aldyth. Although I despised the girls' lack of interest in following a warrior's life, yet they had proved recently to be avid listeners to the stories I invented. This increased my fondness for them and, indeed, they had always been kind to me, especially Gytha.

The truth was that, previously, I had been glad of a reason to be too busy to visit Ufer Hall, and I believe Elanor felt the same way. The Lord Wulfirth had at first suspected her of being complicit in his wife's elopement and, although that seemed long forgotten by him, she had never since been comfortable alone with the Lady Cwena. As for me, I had always been expected to play with the little Lady Lewitha on these visits: but I found her imperious and rude. I would have preferred to be with her brother Osred, the Wulfirths' second son, who was much more friendly and affable. We never saw the elder son, Kyneth, who had been sent to the King's Court some six years past, when he was twelve.

Now I was perfectly willing to tolerate young Lewitha if it meant I could study with Father David, and I set out for Ufer Hall that day with a happy heart. When we arrived in the courtyard of the Hall, I was quite surprised to see the Lady Cwena come out to meet us with Father David, the young Lady Lewitha and a bondsman with a sword in a decorated scabbard at his side. The two ladies were dressed in what looked like festival clothes, and I was a little conscious of my own plain riding dress, though it was freshly washed. Elanor also was wearing ordinary clothes, and I guessed she might have wished she had worn something finer. I jumped down from my pony and the Lady's armed bondsman (who himself was dressed more finely than I) helped Elanor down from her horse. In her own cool way, Cwena seemed glad to see us; she came straight away and kissed Elanor and then me, not seeming to mind our common dress.

"Elanor," she said, "Sister, I am so glad to see you and Edith. It is long since we were together, and I am full glad our girls are to take lessons together with Father David."

It was a pretty speech, and I warmed to her, for to call Elanor 'sister' was a kindness and an honour.

"Come," she said, "Let us go and take some cordial and you shall tell me news from your home and from Beornwine." She turned to Father David. "I leave the girls in your care," she said, and guided Elanor towards the main house. The armed bondsman followed at a respectful distance. I remembered then that the Lady Cwena still lived under the constraints imposed by her husband. Although it was full six years since her thwarted elopement with Rob of Dale, yet she was never seen outside the gates of Ufer Hall without her husband and, even inside them, was under constant guard. The bondsman in his fine dress and ceremonial scabbard was no ornament to the Lady's status; he was there not only as her protector, but also as her keeper. I guessed this was humiliating for her, but she did not seem to feel it, and smiled almost happily to Elanor. Truly, it had been some time since she had seen her. To a Lady who did little in the way of cooking or sewing, and was not allowed to ride abroad, Elanor's visit must have seemed like a festival day.

Then young Lewitha, who was some two winters younger than I, turned to me. "What is that you are wearing?" she asked, her little nose wrinkled up in a sneer.

Now, I had no real care for clothes, although I was happy enough to wear finery at the right time. However, I had already noted the contrast between the Wulfirth's clothes and those of myself and Elanor. I looked down at my plain white sleeve-dress and brown tunic. "We wore plain clothes to ride in because it looked to rain," I said lamely, keeping a hold on my temper. I would have been happy to box the girl's ears for her insolence, but I knew my precious new lessons with Father David depended on her. I had no intention of being sent home in disgrace on my first day.

"I suppose a common girl such as you *will* wear such things," was her reply.

211

I felt the rage in me gather at my throat and flood my face with an angry blush, but I did not speak, and Father David came to my rescue.

"Do not speak so, young lady!" he said to her, "Your mother and father would have you behave like the young noble-woman you are. That means to treat all visitors with respect and kindness!" Father David clearly shared none of my fear of offending Lewitha. He shook his finger in her face, "The Lady Edith is no common girl, for her father is first in this country, after your own father's family. She is also a great scholar – far greater than you will ever be – I wage!"

To her credit, Lewitha did look shamefaced at this scolding, although she did not apologise, only took my hand and said, in a complete contrast to her former tone, "I am glad you are here anyway, for we can play together after our lessons! I shall take you to my room and show you all my dolls, and you can dress my hair."

My heart sank only a little at the prospect of having to pay for my lessons by playing with Lewitha; I had given up dolls long ago with the demise of poor Bertha, who had never recovered from her ducking in the pond. But nothing could dim my eagerness to see the scrolls and texts belonging to Lord Wulfirth. Until now, the only books I had ever seen were Elanor's, which I worked from at home, and a very few pages of Mother Werberga's commonplace book.

So I looked down at Lewitha and squeezed her hand, "Yes," I said with what I hope looked to be a kindly smile, "Of course, and I hope you will enjoy our lessons also."

Father David led us into an airy room behind the chapel where he lived, which was built on to the Hall. There we sat on a cloth-covered bench before a long table, upon which were already laid a plain-covered book, a slate tablet and writing chalks and inks.

"Your first lesson will be in reading," he said, removing the ink to a board nearby. I watched as he scribed *LEWITHA* on the tablet. "You see!" he said, smiling, "This is your own name – Lewitha."

The girl looked at the tablet, then at Father David's face. He was beaming – and I knew he felt the magic of letters just as I did. She looked at me and then down at the letters again, a smile beginning to form on her lips. "I want to do that," she said.

Father David put a piece of chalk in her hand and set the tablet before her. At the same time he pushed the large, plain-covered book in my direction. I turned to the first page: *The Traveller,* and immediately was lost in a wondrous tale I had never heard of before.

Thus began my lessons.

I would travel on horseback to Ufer Hall twelve or more days in every thirty, unless the weather was very foul. Sometimes Elanor would accompany me and make her visit to the Lady Cwena. I would read while Father David taught Lewitha her lessons. This was not always easy, and I was rarely left in peace; for all her first enthusiasm at writing her own name, the young Lady soon lost interest and I would be called upon to coax her into staying at the work for a little longer. I had little patience for teaching, yet tolerated her slowness as best I could, knowing that, if not for her, I should never have the opportunity of reading the great stories of holy and valiant men in the many texts the Lord Wulfirth and Lady Cwena owned. Often, I would read aloud to Lewitha, but she was never a great scholar, preferring to play and ride and dress her hair than to learn reading and scribing. Even so, she did make some slight progress at her lessons.

After an hour or so, Father David would say, "Enough," and Lewitha would jump up straight away and pull me out into the inner courtyard at the centre of the Hall buildings, or to her room if it rained. Often, to my relief, she was called away to her mother or nurse. I was glad then to watch Lord Wulfirth's armed men training at battle-action and weapon practise.

In that courtyard, I renewed my acquaintance with Lewitha's brother, Osred, who was a little younger than I. He was a friendly boy who was soon to be sent south, as his elder brother Kyneth had been, to be educated at the household of one of his mother's kinsmen. He was looking forward to the experience.

"There will be other boys there but none shall better me at sword-play!" He gave a swipe with his sword over my head, but I did not flinch although I heard the song of it as it passed.

"Ha!" he said, "You are brave!"

I told him that I was as much interested in the warrior arts as he.

"Indeed? Then you may use my spare sword and I can teach you!"

He marched off, leaving me in the yard, feeling a little bemused. Soon he returned with a sword only a little smaller than his own.

"My brother Kyneth sent me his boy-sword when he took his full-sized one. You can use my old one."

My heart was beating hard as I took the hilt to my hand and lifted the sword. It was heavy but boy-sized; I found I could wield it. Over that summer and autumn before he left for the south, Osred taught me the skills of swing and thrust and parry when I was free from studying and playing with Lewitha, and nobody bothered to stop us. I saw the Lady

Cwena watching us once, but she only gazed in her sad way and walked on.

Therefore, I was a happy girl in those days, hardly knowing whether I was more eager to go to Ufer Hall for the joys of its library or of its armoury.

I could never ask Osred if I might keep the sword; such weapons, even child-sized ones, were costly possessions of the family, and I knew it was not his to give. But it was through Osred that I first developed the skills of my sword-arm, and I believe I never really lost them afterwards.

It was at Ufer Hall that an incident happened which was not of any import either then or later – yet it marked a change in my life.

I had ridden over there one autumn day, but there was no lesson because Father David had been called to an old servant of the household who was dying. We were not permitted to use any of the texts or books without Father David being present, so Lewitha and I were free. There was no chance of weapon-practise, for Osred was nowhere to be seen; he had ridden out that day with Lord Wulfirth's hunt, and taken his sword with him.

Lewitha told me of a litter of new puppies born the previous day to her father's best hound bitch. "Let us go and see them," she said.

I was willing enough to look at the little newborns and we walked across the inner courtyard to the stables where the dogs were housed. A young bondsman of about my own age was coming out of the stable as we entered. He held the door for us and bowed his head as Lewitha passed through, ignoring him in her usual imperious manner. As I followed her in, the bondsman caught my eye. What happened I can hardly describe; he did not smile, but his glance – direct and compelling – seemed locked to mine for a long second. I felt myself blush with an odd sensation of both weakness and power. The next moment he was gone, but I could hardly concentrate on the young pups snuggling together so prettily as their mother nursed them. Lewitha passed one of the little creatures to me and I held its tiny, helpless body and stroked its soft brown fur to quieten it, but all I could think of was the bondsman's eyes. Was this love? I was past thirteen winters and, accordingly to Gytha and Aldyth, well old enough to be in love. Perhaps this was it. I was surprised and not a little confused. The only time I had previously suspected myself of feeling romantic love was as a little child when I had first met the boy Carau at the Holywell Abbey. My feelings for him had changed very quickly into simple friendship. And, after all, Carau had been clever and brave –deserving of admiration. Why should this wondrous sensation –

far stronger and more exhilarating than friendship – thrill through me at the glance of a stable boy I knew nothing of?

Whatever brought on this fascination, it was very short-lived. Father David soon arrived back at the chapel-house and summoned us to our lessons. As we walked back across the courtyard, I saw the young bondsman again. He was carrying a stook of hay into the stable, and did not notice us. I stared at him as I walked. He was going about his business with his mouth half open and his shoulders stooped, which made him look stupid, and his hair resembled nothing so much as a clod of rotten thatch. I concluded that he was less appealing from a distance, and could not find anything to like about his face or his figure or his stance. I found myself, surprisingly, not to be in love after all.

It seemed a very strange episode, but it was the beginning of a new period in my life, when boys not very much older than me seemed much more interesting than previously. Indeed, before long I was used to receiving such glances as the young stable-boy had given to me, and I became particular as to which ones I would return. I seemed to be in love every day – sometimes every hour – with a different lad. However, after that first time in the Ufer Hall stables, I was always careful not to show my feelings, because they were generally very fleeting. Eventually, I realized that it was really only my body having these passing fancies, and I allowed them for they were pleasurable enough, and the boys often beautiful. However, in my mind and soul I held to the true creature I knew myself to be – a scholar who planned a warrior life, with a true quest-vow I could not relinquish.

36

Yule

"Make yourself useful Edith, please!" Elanor's voice was sharp. She had caught me with my wooden sword, which I was about to take outside for battle-practice. "You wished not to help with making cakes for the Yule festival," she said crossly, "So I must make them myself. Now you shall run to Beornwine with this cheese and honey for Siric. That will be better exercise for a great girl of your age than playing with toys!" She held out a basket to me with unusual insistence.

It always filled me with rage to have my precious wooden practice-sword referred to as a 'toy' and I flared with sudden fury. "You never let me do anything I like!" I shrieked, casting my sword into a corner and snatching up the basket before stamping out of the house without giving Elanor time to point out the injustice of my words.

I had been feeling out of sorts all morning: too unsettled for study, too lazy to work, irritated with everyone who crossed my path. Now, fuelled by rage, I half-ran all the way to Beornwine, most of which was uphill – notwithstanding the weight of the laden basket. Accordingly, my ire was spent in action, and I came up to Siric's hostelry in a better mood – indeed much regretting my words and angry thoughts against Elanor and a little anxious as to the condition of my sword which I had thrown down with such violence. In my calmer state of mind I was glad enough at the prospect of talking with Gytha and Aydith, whom I had not seen for a fort'night. Although the girls had little interest in study and none in following the thegnly life, still they at least admired men who practised the warrior arts and thus we had some interests in common.

The chief bondswoman in the hostelry thanked me for the honey and cheese in the basket, "Master Siric will be glad to have this in time for Yule," she said, "for his kinsman Fulben is expected here   for the festival, with all his family." Then she raised her voice, calling, "Gytha! Aldyth! Your cousin is here to see you."

"Oh, Edith!" Aldyth's voice came from the back of the house, "Do come and see the new dress Gytha has made!"

With little curiosity, I wandered down the long house to the family sleeping quarters at the end, where Gytha and Aldyth had their own room. I saw Gytha standing on a low box wearing a long robe dyed russet-red and fastened at the shoulders with metal clips. Underneath she wore sleeves of green with woven cuff-clasps. Aldyth was sitting on the floor below, pinning the dress hem to the level of Gytha's heels.

"What do you think?" asked Gytha, not troubling to greet me.

I put my head on one side, interested despite myself, because Gytha, now buxom and womanly at almost sixteen winters, really looked well in the dress. Its colour gave an extra glow to her normally rosy cheeks and her brown hair was combed and shining, plaited loosely and tied with a red ribbon.

"The dress looks well," I said, smiling to please her, "The colour suits you, but Aldyth is making the hem too long. You will trail it through the mud and it will likely trip you too."

"Oh she shall not trail it in the mud," said Aldyth, "For it is for the Yule festival when Bencarad comes, and she shall hold up the hem like a lady."

"Who is Bencarad?" I asked, looking curiously at Gytha, whose face and throat had suddenly flushed to a red deeper than the dress she wore. She glanced at me shyly and opened her mouth, but Aldyth spoke first:

"He is younger son to our father's kinsman Fulben, from Bramleah, east of Holywell, and he comes to live with us for a time!"

"Fulben and all his family are coming," said Gytha softly, "And Bencarad is to stay on afterwards, for Father needs ..."

"...Father needs another man in the house now," interrupted Aldyth, who paused for a second to give me a look as one who would impart a great secret, "and Gytha has had her first moon-course, so she needs a husband!"

I looked again at Gytha, who seemed both pleased and embarrassed, but she gently rebuked Aldyth. "He might not like me, sister," she said.

"And you might not like him," I added, receiving a look of incredulity from my friends, both of whom had been yearning to marry for as long as I had known them.

"It will be me next!" Aldyth squealed, pushing out her breasts, which were small enough not to be noticed at all.

When I returned home, I gathered a little bunch of briar-rosehips, all stripped of their thorns and tied with an ivy-vine, to give to Elanor. True to her gentle nature, she did not mention my fierce mood of that morning, only kissing me for thanks, before putting the rosehips in a little jar and placing them on the supper table. "I've put your sword in your room, dear one," she said. "It is not damaged."

I ran to her and hugged her for her kindness in caring for my sword, even though she did not approve of my using it.

I took little notice of the table-talk that evening, for my thoughts were turning slowly around the words and preoccupations of my two cousins, and something else that had been occupying my mind these last weeks. After supper, I took a candle and went up to my little room aloft. There I pulled off my tunic-dress and under-sleeves. I looked down at my breasts and saw what I had suspected for some little time: they were puffy and swelling out of proportion with the growth of the rest of my body. And lately they had been tingling and aching like a healing bruise. I was still small and slight – and only just passing my fourteenth winter. But I knew full well that the growth of my woman's body had begun.

Around that time, there had been talk of my brother Farin being betrothed to a young woman who was with child. But the day after my errand to Beornwine, another girl came to our step-mother with a baby in her arms, claiming that Farin was the father of her child also. Farin disputed this, although with little vehemence, and no-one was convinced enough to deny the girl, knowing Farin's reputation. Father did not like either of these young women, for he wanted girls of higher status for his sons. Farin himself seemed unable to choose between the two girls, and I suspected there were others he liked more. Father questioned him with only our closest family present.

"Is it true that you have lain with both these women?" he asked with some fierceness.

Farin cast his eyes up, as if recollecting with difficulty, "The one - yes. The other - no. Or, I do not think so," he said, "She is ill-favoured of face, and that child looks nothing like me."

I saw Father's mouth twitch, but he retained his grave bearing, although his eyes shone a little. "Do you admit that you *might* have lain with her – but can't remember? How is it possible that you would not remember such a thing?"

Farin shrugged his shoulders and made a gesture of appeal, "How should I remember them all?"

At this point Elanor took me by the shoulders and hurried me out of the house. "It is not meet that a young lady should be listening to such talk," she murmured, shutting me outside, but re-entering herself. I was a good deal put out, for Farin's misdeeds were most interesting.

I was not told how the exchange ended, but Father decided that Farin should be parted from the temptations of Beornwine. He resolved that, when the Yule celebrations were over, he would send him east to HestanandGodwine at the household of the Lord Torhelm. This was no punishment for Farin, who had been wanting to travel again ever since his return from the Welshlands with Father. Archibald begged to go with him - to bring back messages, he said – but I knew he was wild to take a long journey, having missed the expedition to Einiog.

At first, Father refused leave for Archibald to go. "With Farin gone, I cannot spare such another hunter and warrior," Father told him.

"But Father," argued Archibald, "I have no real experience of battle. If the Lord Torhelm will let me ride with his men for even a little time, I will learn much, and come back better skilled."

Of course, Father had many bondmen whom he had now trained to fight, as well as the Welsh warriors, those who had travelled back from Einiog with him. These four had settled happily with us (two of them having married with bondswomen of our household) and were great huntsmen and - in need - doughty defenders of our land. So Archibald's absence would not cause dire loss in our defences. Also, Father must have had in mind Archibald's sworn quest to seek and take revenge on our mother's slayer. This quest was more deeply forged in him than in any other of my brothers, as Father knew, for Archibald, like me, had witnessed our mother's torment.

And so Father did relent and give his permission for Archibald to accompany Farin to the east, but he was to return within three moons, and to this Archibald agreed. I was glad for him, but knew those three moons would be slow and lonely for me, for never had I been apart from my dearest brother for such a long time.

As for the young women, Mythwyn and Inegard, who had made their complaints of Farin, Father took them to our household, where they could work and care for their infants. In the following Spring, Mythwyn was to give birth to a rosy-faced girl with Farin's wide green eyes. Everyone called her May, for she was born at the time of the blossoming hawthorn, and brought as much joy as that early flower of spring, such was the sweetness of the child's nature. After May was weaned, Elanor brought the child and her mother into the house. Mythwyn became a valued house-servant and May as much a beloved child of the family as myself.

That Yuletime, before Archibald and Farin went away, stands important in my memory, it being the last winter of my true childhood.

In the winter months, there was time and necessity for building, maintenance and the protection of our home against the worst of the weather. Father had been speaking for some time of having a threshold built, such as the fine one at Ufer Hall. This was an addition built on to the entrance of the house, like another room with its own walls and roof which had to be passed through before entering the main door. Its most important function was to protect the house from the worst of the cold and weather, which would diminish the house warmth whenever the door was opened. Hereward, who was well skilled in building and carpentry, had made a small one for his own house and was now engaged in erecting a larger one for our main house. He had the idea of setting up a pair of benches along the two walls, so that people could sit and take off their muddy footwear and outer clothes before entering the house. He set to work, and all my brothers helped in the building. Father did little of the work himself, but took great interest in its progress and made many suggestions, which Hereward did not usually deign to follow.

"When will the threshold be finished?" was Father's oft-heard query. He wanted it ready by Yule, when Siric and his kin from Bramleah were to come over from Beornwine for a feast. Elanor was also very eager for her home to be improved by the fine new threshold, but her encouragement took the form of gentle praise and a good supply of spiced ale and honey cake for the workers.

Yule was a festival that I always enjoyed, when the sacred log was carried in to the house and brought to flame in celebration of the sun's heat and light returning after the darkest season of the year. It was a time of feasting and of gifts. Father David told me of the great Mass that was always made at Holywell Abbey for the Christ on that day, for He was born at the Winter Solstice end, when light began to return to the earth.

With the talk of Farin and Archibald going away, I lost my own sluggish mood and set to work making Yule gifts for my family. For my brothers and their families, I made sweet biscuit (using Mother Werburga's special recipe and the sweet powder she generously gave to me). To each of my brothers' children I gave one of Alvar's fine writing tablets bearing their name in my best Anglish script, so that they should grow up knowing the shape of their name in writing.

Elanor saw me scribing the children's names in bright red and green paint. "Edith, what a fine gift!" she said with a smile. Would you make such a one for your father also?"

I stopped and looked at her questioningly. "But he thinks little of scribing," I said, "And would not thank me for a gift of lettering that he cannot read."

She looked again at my work, the letters glistening with wet paint, and a still and quiet smile was on her lips. Then she turned her eyes to me. "I think it would please him greatly to see his own name written out," she said, "Perhaps on a tablet that we can hang on his chair."

We heard the voices of Hereward and Alvar outside and went to greet them. Hereward had brought along a good-sized log of dressed and weathered oak. "Here you are Mother," he said for greeting, "'Tis the lintel for your threshold. I've been working on it at home. We'll have it up by tomorrow perhaps and, if the dry weather holds, Heath will finish the thatching in another day."

Elanor clapped her hands and went to examine the lintel more closely. It was then I had a notion of a fitting Yule present for both Elanor and Father. Soon, when Elanor was back in the house, I spoke to Hereward and Alvar about my idea.

"Let me write Father's and Elanor's names across the lintel," I said, "I'll make the letters large and broad, then Alvar might carve the shape of them into the wood."

Both Hereward and Alvar readily agreed to this, the lintel was taken to Alvar's house and I spent an evening there, carefully marking out the lettering. Alvar began carving straight away and, by Yule's eve, it was ready. Then Archibald and Farin begged Father to join them on a last hunt before their journey. By pretending that Farin's horse was lame, they contrived not to return until after dark when the lintel was up and the thatching done. Likewise, I made sure that Elanor was not outside when the lintel went up, so neither she nor Father saw it properly before the next morning. Indeed, Elanor was full busy in the house with Bebbe and many more bondswomen and myself, all preparing for the Yule feast.

The next morning dawned bright, and I could not wait, but called Father and Elanor from their beds full early. "Happy Yule!" I cried. "It's time for gifts!"

They both grumbled a little at my childish excitement, but were surprised to find Archibald and Farin also up before them. The house and threshold doors were open and Hereward, Heath and Alvar were all gathered with their families outside the house. Taking a hand of each, I pulled Father and Elanor along.

"Wait child," said Father. "Am I not to be allowed to spend a little time looking at the inside of my own new threshold?"

"Oh, but you must see the outside first!" I insisted.

They smiled indulgently for, after all, was it not Yule's morn, when children were expected to be excited? They followed me outside.

And there, in beautifully shaped and carved lettering across the fine oak lintel of his new threshold was written the names of my father - honoured and respected in his adopted land - and of his lady, who was loved by all, and who loved his children as if they were her own.

Elanor put her hands to her mouth in a kind of shocked delight, and tears sprang to her eyes. Then she took my father's hand and read slowly.

FINRIC FLY AND ELANOR FLY OF BEORNWINE

The wooden walls of our house and its thatched roofing always had to be replaced and repaired every few years. It would be the same with the threshold. But I knew that strong oak lintel would last for many a long age, and that folk in unknown future years would see my letters drawn with love into the shape of my father's and step-mother's names.

It was a happy moment for me and for my brothers, especially Alvar and Hereward, when Father's eye's lit up with gladness and pride to see his name upon his house. I knew then this was indeed the best Yule gift any of us could have given him. Of such is the magic of letters. Father even went so far – within a few moons following Yule – to learn to scribe his own name as it appeared at the entrance to his own house: FINRIC FLY OF BEORNWINE.

I dressed myself for the Yule feast in my best dress. This had been new for the previous Yule, but was now a little short and tight. I had never given much care to clothes, but this was an important feast, so I combed and plaited my hair, then fastened the shoulders of my dress with my silver clasps, and hung my string of coloured beads between them. Then I took my feather-shaped brooch and pinned it to the neckline. I looked into Elanor's copper mirror to check that the shoulders of my dress looked straight. As I glanced at the reflection of my face, I saw that my cheeks and lips looked round and full; my eyes large and lustrous. It was a surprise to me to find myself as pretty as my cousins, and I spent a little time smiling and cooing winsomely in that mirror and then laughing at myself. I put it away quickly as I heard Elanor's step on the stairway. "Edith!" she called, "Are you ready child? Our guests will be here full soon."

"Yes Mother." I stepped out of her room where I had gone to dress.

"Let me see you." She turned me around to check my dress and made a small adjustment to one of the shoulder-clasps. She tweaked at one of my plaits and then stood back and frowned a little. "You look very well dear," she said, pulling at the front of my dress, "But I should have prepared a new garment for you. You have grown so, and this one fits you ill. Let me try one of my own dresses on you."

I'd had enough of dresses and looks. I wriggled out of her grasp. "Oh Mother," I said irritably, "It matters not." And I ran down to the house before she could have any more ideas about changing my clothes.

We had decorated the house with greenery – ivies and hollies and mistletoe with their black and red and white berries. The house was almost as bright as day with the number of torches and candles all about the walls and boards, although there were pails of water aplenty and two boys charged with the duty of ensuring that nothing caught alight that should not. There were boards set with many dishes and platters, bowls of apples, nuts and dried berries, jars containing branches of red hips and haws and, overall, the scent of roasting meat, sweet cakes and spices. All looked like a fairyland; even Father's sword, hanging with other weapons on the wall, was decorated with greenery, its hilt shining like gold in the firelight.

Siric's kinfolk had arrived from Bramleah only two days before and I had not yet set eyes on any of them. I was quite eager to see Gytha with her suitor, but I felt a little shy of all the strangers. Shyness was not a usual state for me, but I felt not quite myself in my festival clothes and with my changing face and body which I was not yet accustomed to. So I did not rush out of the house when Heath brought word that Siric was entering our gateway. Father went out to greet the guests with my brothers, but I stayed with Elanor and the other girls and women in the house.

They took longer than we expected to enter the house, for Father kept them outside, admiring the new threshold with its carven lintel. At last, Elanor went out to them. "Welcome to you all!" she cried, "Finric, bring our guests in, do, for there is food and spiced ale and cider to be had. Bring them in while the food is hot!"

There was another delay while the inside of the threshold was admired, but then our guests entered the house and there were cries of admiration at the sight of all the lights and decorations. Most of the folk from Siric's household had come, as well as about ten strangers, whom I guessed to be Siric's kinsman Fulben and his family. I watched for my cousins, and they soon came in, all dressed in their best. Gytha did indeed look well in her long dress, which she had obviously held well away from the mud on her journey from Beornwine. Three or four young men were amongst the guests and I soon guessed which was the eagerly expected Bencarad; one young man stayed near to Gytha and gave her his eye many times, speaking now softly, now laughing with her. For her part, in his company Gytha seemed to bloom like a rose in the sun. Indeed I was very impressed by the transformation. She certainly looked to be the most comely young woman in our company that eve, although I had never thought her to be of more than ordinary beauty before.

I called Aldyth to me, offering her a plate of honeycakes. "So that is Bencarad," I said. "He seems well pleased with Gytha, and she with him."

"No," said Aldyth, somewhat sullenly, as she helped herself to three cakes, "That is his brother Ham. They speak with no-one but each other. Everyone knows she was supposed to be for Bencarad, but she likes Ham best."

"And he likes her too," I observed, taking a cake for myself. "She's beautiful enough, the God knows."

"I don't consider that she is so very beautiful," said Aldyth. "She never has been thought beautiful. I am the pretty one."

"You look well enough Aldyth," I said, for she looked to burst into tears, which would have been embarrassing.

Just then another of the new young men came over to us. He looked to be about sixteen or seventeen winters and was tall and well-made, with curling yellow hair and a friendly expression. "So you are Edith," he told me, "They say you make the most tasty cakes in the country."

"These are made with Mother Werberga's recipe," I said, offering the platter of cakes. "She told me what to do."

"So, you are modest as well as being a good cook," he said.

I laughed, "I like to cook because I like to eat. The best way of having what I want is to make it myself."

He seemed amazed by the notion. He slapped his forehead and grinned in a very stupid way – which yet made me laugh – and said, "So that is how I can get all the honey cakes I want. You shall teach me how to make them and I shall cook and eat day and night until I am too fat to squeeze out of Siric's door. Then you will have to visit me because I'll not be able to come and learn any more recipes from you."

He smiled and flashed his eyes at me in a manner that made me suddenly aware of my changing body. I blushed and laughed at him, and the laugh came out of me sounding like the silly squeals I had heard from Gytha and Aldyth when they sought to make young men think themselves cleverer than they really were. I stopped – more embarrassed by myself than I had been by any of his words. "Well, you will have to help yourself now," I said, putting down the platter of cakes and turning away, "For I am needed to help serve the other guests."

He stood away from me and made a great bow, which caused me to blush and laugh again (although this time I was careful to keep my voice low). I saw that other folk around us were smiling and laughing too (except for Aldyth, who liked it not that I was attracting more notice than herself). I went out into the yard to offer a honeycake to Spin (who had been banished from the house for the evening). There I stayed for a while, stroking my old dog and cooling my face in the winter air. I knew Bencarad was no more important to me than any of the other handsome lads that might charm me for a day. I reminded myself once again that such temporary attractions could not touch my true heart's self, which sought only the life of a questing warrior. Yet, thinking again of Bencarad's comical behaviour and ready wit, I smiled to myself. I was glad that he was coming to live at Beornwine but, in truth, I cared not whether he or his brother Ham was to marry Gytha.

Giving Spin the last morsel of honeycake, I straightened my rather tight festival-dress and returned to the house.

37

Changes

"Edith, Edith!"

I was hidden in my little room, away from any work that I might be asked to do, and deeply absorbed in writing a story. My hero was receiving rich bounty from his King, whose life he had saved from a fierce dragon. I was in no mood to be disturbed.

"Edith! Where are you?" Now I recognised it as the voice of my nephew, Eldric Hereson, and it penetrated my concentration without displeasure, for I was full fond of the little boy. I put down my brush-pen and stood up, submitting to the interruption. Yet the world of fantasy held me, and my eyes went back to the line I had just written: *"I name you Thegn of Honour," said the King, and everyone bowed in tribute to the young hero.*

There was the patter of swift hands and feet on the loft-stair, then across the boards. I flicked back the curtain-barrier to my room and Eldric flung himself into my arms, as if we had been parted for a year, rather than the two days since I walked over to play with him and little Hylda, while Fritha tended her new baby girl.

"Edith!" He was panting from haste, and I hugged him and smiled at his red-faced excitement, while he found his breath.

"What is it child?" I said.

"Archibald; He is back!"

"Where?" I did not wait, but was at the stair-head in a moment. I had not heard any horse-hooves in the yard.

"He has ridden straight to Ufer Hall with messages. Maybe he will be here soon."

The news had, of course, reached Elanor before me and downstairs the house was bustling with activity. When she saw me, Elanor smiled, "This news will make you happy, dear one," she said.

Truthfully, I had found little to please me that winter when Archibald was away and the weather bitter cold and dull. Even lessons at Ufer Hall were interrupted by heavy snow falls and, lately, by a fever illness suffered by Father David, which worried me greatly. Now I felt the sweet lightness of good news, and I hugged Elanor happily. "I could wish he had come straight home to see us before going to Ufer Hall," I said.

"But I am glad he goes there first," she answered with a smile, "For afterwards he will be able to rest here at home with no other duties. And it gives us time to prepare, for we will feast this night for your brother's return." She scanned our empty table as if it was already loaded with festival fare. "There is a mature cheese I have been saving, and a cask of good ale. Bebbe is firing the oven now; you have time to make some of your honey-cakes if you wish."

I was soon measuring out wheat-flour, yeast, honey and pig fat. I had to manage without eggs or butter, for the hens had not yet begun the spring laying, nor had the cows come to calve; my honeycakes would be plain, but tasty enough. Our household was short of fresh food, as was always the case at the end of winter, but we had plenty of grain and flour put by from a good harvest, and there was still a store of wrinkled apples and very few dried plums for flavouring meat and sweets, kept for just such an occasion as this. I took a couple of plums from the store and broke up the firm, sticky flesh, scattering it into the mixture.

The word soon reached the households of Hereward and Alvar, and they arrived with their families so that they might greet Archibald on his return. At last, as my honeycakes cooled, there came the sound of hooves and calls of welcome from the yard, and I dashed outside. There a young man in travelling gear was sliding down from old Swift's back. It was Archibald, being greeted by Father and Heath and my brothers, with little Eldric jumping up and down for joy. For a moment I felt shy, for here was another brother grown to a man while I waited at home. But his eyes sought me and his arms went out to me, and it was my own dear Archibald whom I loved more than any other being in the world. I hugged him and then he stood back, saying, "But, Edith, you seem to have grown a woman in these few moons!"

I blushed in awkwardness and some little annoyance while everyone measured me with their eyes, but I could not deny I had grown and I could not let my embarrassment mar my dear brother's homecoming. So I just said, "Elanor is preparing a feast for you, and I have made plum honeycakes."

"Hurrah!" cheered Archibald, making everyone laugh at him and turn their attention from me. The next moment Elanor was with us, kissing him as the dear son he was to her.

"I am later than I would have been, Mother," he said, "For I was charged with messages for Ufer Hall, and I thought to deliver them first, so that I can now rest easy with my family."

"You were right to do so," said Father. "And the messages were important?"

"Indeed," said Archibald, "For I made a new friend at Prince Cenred's Hall. I met him at prayer in the chapel and we often rode or ate and drank together, although he was not in Cenred's fighting huscarle, but there to help with the ordering of men and land and buildings, after being brought up at the King's court."

"But this new friend of yours sends messages to Wulfirth," said Father, "Is he connected with Ufer Hall? What is he: some farming holy-man?"

"More than that; he has proved himself a brave warrior. Indeed, he has ridden with the King's own huscarle. But his talents and fancy turn to the government of farmland and building." Archibald looked to Hereward, our foremost landsman, who nodded and smiled.

"But who is he?" asked Elanor, "What was it that took you to Ufer Hall before coming to your family?"

Archibald's smile broadened, "He is Kyneth, eldest son of the Lord Wulfirth and Lady Cwena, and he bade me send word that he is coming home to Ufer Hall before the end of the summer."

"Kyneth!" said Father. "So, the young Lord is to visit his family."

"He comes to stay, for the King has granted him lands past the borders of Lord Wulfirth's own. He brings grain for planting and bondsmen skilled in farming and hunting. He will be our new neighbour."

Archibald slept out the rest of the daylight time, taking only a little food and drink before retiring to the loft, for he had been riding for three days in bad weather with little rest. Yet he rose up fresh before the evening, dressing himself in his old festival clothes with a fine new buckle at his waist. "It was a leaving present from HestanandGodwine," he said.

There were presents also for all our family, buckles and brooches for the men and a finely worked headcloth for Elanor, sent by Hestan's wife Mathilda. "She is well known for her embroidery skills," said Archibald. To my humiliation, my gift was a doll – a stupid-looking thing with a badly painted face, dressed up like a lady.

"Thanks," I muttered, and was surprised when everyone burst into gales of laughter.

"Oh, child! Your face!" laughed Elanor: and I realised that my lip was curled and my nose wrinkled in disgust at my childish gift. I began to smile, and then joined in the laughter.

"You can give the doll to Hylda," smiled Archibald, "For I have another gift for you which I think you will like better."

"Another gift? Where is it?" I scanned the room keenly.

"For that you will have to wait, because I do not have it here. It is coming later."

I was intrigued, but Archibald would not be persuaded to speak any more of my mysterious gift, and I had to content myself with the mixed pleasure of anticipation.

While everyone ate and drank, Archibald told us of his adventures. He and Farin had been welcomed with pleasure by HestanandGodwine and Lord Torhelm, who presented them to his brother, Prince Cenred. He and Farin were entered into Torhelm's mounted huscarle company and rode in several defensive battles against pirates and other raiders.

"We always outnumbered them but once," said Archibald, "When a few of us were riding the bounds of Prince Cenred's hall-grounds, some twenty unmounted raiders attacked. They made to put their spears to our horses tendons. Two of our number fell with their horses under them and were set upon and killed. I was fortunate in being a little distance away. I could not risk arrow or spear, for our own men were too much among the raiders, so I dismounted with my sword and shield, and entered the fight. Although we were outnumbered, our men were the stronger and braver – and better trained also. Those raiders who were not slain soon fled, and we let them run."

It was a tale of valour and victory, yet Archibald's voice had quietened with his last words, and his eyes looked down, unseeing, at the table before him.

Father, who was sitting next to Archibald, grasped his shield arm and looked into his eyes. "So you have taken a man's life," he said. It was not a question, and the look they shared was not one of triumph, which I might have expected, but seemed to admit some heavy understanding beyond my comprehension.

"We made prayers on our return," said Archibald, "For our own men slain, and for the dead of our enemies."

Silently, Heath raised his beaker of ale, and all the warriors around the table did the same. They drank, then Elanor also took up her beaker and said, "Welcome home to Archibald!" That broke the silence which had seemed to exclude me from my brother, and there was laughter and celebration around the table again.

229

So my brother Archibald returned home with the experience of real fighting, and with a look to his eyes that told me he would not stay long. He had always intended riding to quest – the one quest all our family knew of, although it was not spoken of in those days. It seemed almost as though the avenging of our mother's murder was a tale, like the legends of warrior-gods, for telling at the hearth-side of a winter night. Yet it could not be told, for the quest had yet to be fulfilled. It seemed to me in those days that only Archibald and I remembered that, and even we two hardly ever spoke of it. For me, it was a dark remembrance, knowing that - in the eyes of others - my femaleness would make it impossible for me to fulfil it, and knowing it would take Archibald away from me, perhaps forever.

If Father had been reluctant to let Archibald go with Farin to the Lord Torhelm's lands in the south, he now seemed to accept his youngest son's true role as warrior. He rode with him the next day to Ufer Hall and Father settled it with Lord Wulfirth that Archibald was to be taken into his household to help guard the land, ride to war when needed and learn from the experienced warriors in the Lord's mounted huscarle. It is traditional that sons are sent away from home for such purposes and thus Father arranged it with the Lord Wulfirth, for they were good friends, and almost equal now in wealth.

"Edith!" This time it was Elanor's voice calling me, a catch of impatience in her voice, and I knew I was to perform some tedious duty, called from my little room where I lay in a dark reverie, feeling heavy and tired. It was perhaps a fort'night after Archibald's return and he was away at Ufer Hall for the day, although - as usual - he would likely return that evening to eat and sleep with us. I did not answer Elanor's call, but wondered to myself why it was that the sound of my name, "Edith" was so weighty to me, like a burden of duty, a burden of what I *was*, a growing maiden whose childish ideas of a warrior life were no longer tolerated. In turn, this put me in mind of what I was *not* and of the contrast when Archibald's name was spoken, the sound of it seeming to ring with joy, with pride and the promise of adventure and renown.

"Edith!" She called me again, and I stamped disconsolately down the ladder-stair to help prepare meat for the evening meal. I did not join in with the bondswomen's chatter as we worked, for my mood was black.

I felt no better even after the evening meal, sitting around the table with all our household about me and meat in my belly. Archibald watched me during the meal, his eyes mild with sympathy, for – as always – he seemed to know my mood. Afterwards he called me aside and we went to sit in the threshold, where he spoke quietly and cheerfully of his activities that day in Lord Wulfirth's huscarle company.

"This is good for me, Edith," he said, "For I am learning much from the other huscarles. Many of them have as much warrior experience as our own father, and have ridden with Lord Wulfirth since before he was a King's thegn."

I did not speak, knowing his quest to ride away, which could not allow him to stay long in this country.

"But, I will be home every night, except if I am on duty."

"*A warrior is always on duty*," I said miserably. It was a saying we had used in our games when we were children.

Archibald looked on me with soft eyes. It was not always necessary for us to speak. He knew that I envied his life but that my love for him could not well support envy. I knew his heart, his strength and skill, and his vow to ride to quest. It would half break my heart to see him go, yet he must go and – unlike me - he *could* go, with everyone's help and everyone's blessing. I was glad of this for his sake, yet I resented it deeply for my own. I looked hard into his eyes with my resentment and envy, my hurt and my love.

A little frown of puzzlement creased his fair brow, and he asked with his eyes but not with words, *What troubles you sister?*

His gentleness was too much for me. "What of your quest?" I hissed, my voice threaded with venom. "Why do you stay? You should go; you are skilled and strong enough now. It is past time. What keeps you?"

He blinked once, as though I had struck him - so bitter were my words. Then tears sprang to my eyes, for I hated my temper, especially when it hurt those I loved – and I loved none more than my dear brother and saviour Archibald.

"I stay for you Edith," he said simply. "I fear to leave you, for you are unhappy. In a year or two Father and Elanor will likely have you marry. Perhaps then I shall go and fulfil the vow I made for the memory of our mother."

I stared at him; to me it was clear he had forgotten my own vow, which he himself had witnessed. He had forgotten it, or disregarded it as a childish game.

Just then, Elanor came into the threshold with a beaker of cordial for each of us. She had overheard Archibald's last words and she smiled saying, "Edith is indeed likely to marry, for she is growing to be a pretty young woman, as everyone knows!"

This was too much for me. In a passion, I leapt up from the bench, disturbing Spin who had been snoozing at my feet. "I shall never marry!" I shrieked, rage and humiliation battling for primacy in my breast, and I ran from the house, ashamed of the tears that would not be stopped.

At that moment I hated Archibald and Elanor, Father, Hereward, Fritha, Heath, Bebbe, Alvar and Alice. Indeed, I hated everyone that I loved. As I raged from the house, every creature I saw was a subject of my resentment. Little Rose, Alice and Alvar's daughter, was standing in the yard with her thumb in her mouth, watching the chickens. She smiled sweetly when she saw me, and raised her arms to be lifted up, but I fled from her – even Spin, who trotted after me with a concerned expression on his doggy face, incurred my anger. I glared at him, crying through my tears, "Be off, you foolish dog! I do not want you."

I sought solitude and ran for the wood, with Spin still following at a wary distance. The day was growing to dusk and I was near to the hazel trees, the scene of my disturbing and painful encounter with Alvar so many years before. This was a place I usually avoided when alone, but now I went there purposely, for the being I hated most at that moment was my own self, and I wished neither comfort nor peacefulness for myself. Yet I did find both comfort and peacefulness there, for in my careless speed I tripped on the great root of a hazel tree, fell to the ground - grazing both my hands - and burst into sorrowful, passionate sobs that lasted for what seemed a long time, shaking the devilish ire from out of me, while Spin, sensing it safe to approach now, licked the tears from my face and healed my hurt hands with his kisses.

Soon, a great peacefulness came over my body, and I took my dog onto my lap, there under the trees, and wept again for my harsh words and thoughts. I kissed his muzzle and stroked his yellow-and-black fur which was now quite clouded with grey. This reminder that my pet was growing old brought forth a fresh set of tears, for I did not think I could bear to live without both Archibald and Spin – one to a world of valour and adventure that was denied to me – the other to the realm of death.

Nobody reproached me for my outburst, nor drew any attention to me as I crept back in to the house and up the ladder stair to my room, not wanting to be seen with my eyes so swollen from weeping. Elanor soon came, bringing me a drink. She did not question me, but kissed me and tucked the bed-cloths around me as if I was a little child. As she left me I managed to say, "God's night," to her without bursting into tears again. She answered me, "God's night, dear one." And I wetted my pillow with a few more tears before I fell asleep, wondering how I deserved such love from my family when I treated them so ill.

I slept deeply, but then woke in the night with the belly-ache. The shutter above my head was half open and a bright waning moon gave light to the loft. I got up, for the pain in my belly denied me any sleep, although I was too ashamed of my behaviour the previous evening to call Elanor or disturb anyone. Spin awoke, but I quietened him and he lay down again. I tiptoed out of my room, past Archibald, who was the only sleeper in the main loft area, and down the stairs. There was a little light in the main house from the fire embers and I began to walk up and down the length of the house room, trying not to disturb those of our household people who were sleeping there. The walking gave me some ease, and at last – exhausted - I climbed the stair again and lay in my bed, curled up around my painful belly.

I awoke late, needing to use the piss-pot in my room. After I had used it, I was curious to see that the liquid in it was dark. On closer inspection, I saw that it was half blood. It only shocked me for a minute, because I soon realised what had happened. I looked at the shift I had worn in bed and saw brown blood-stains on it also. Feeling rather weak, with my belly still aching a little, I put on my plain day-dress and went to find Elanor. She was busy, as always of a morning, preparing the household breakfast along with some of our bondswomen. She was kneading bread dough, but she looked up at me with a kind expression that recognised my eyes were still swollen from my weeping the previous night.

"Did you sleep well, dear one?" she asked.

Suddenly, I felt shy – there among the adult women with whom I now stood as equal, although none but me knew it. I glanced up, but the bondswomen were taking no notice of me. I put my lips to Elanor's ear and said softly, "Mother, I think my moon-course has come."

To this day, I remember Elanor's expression as she received this news. Can you imagine a loving face suffused with mixed pleasure and sadness, excitation and regret and sympathy? Such expression did my mother's face carry in those minutes.

"Are you sure?" she said, keeping her voice low.

I nodded; "There is blood," I said.

"Come with me." She turned to Mythwyn, "Can you finish kneading this bread? It is nearly done."

With a glance of curiosity at me, Mythwyn nodded and took Elanor's place at the table. Elanor went up the ladder-stair with me following. She took me into her own room, where she closed the door, pushing the big chest against it. "None shall come in," she said with a smile. I was grateful, for it was my father's room also and I did not want him to come in just then – nor, indeed, did I want any other man or woman near us just then.

Elanor examined me and confirmed that my moon-blood was indeed flowing. She showed me a little wooden bowl, similar to the one she used for her own moon-blood. "I have kept this ready for you for some time," she said. "You can use it in your room while you rest or work at your letters."

"But I don't have to stay in my room for the whole time, do I?" I asked, "I am tired today, but I cannot be kept inside for days on end!"

She smiled, "No, indeed, Edith, nobody could ever try to keep you from what you wish to do!" Then she showed me a woven belt with tapes and hooks, which she fitted around my waist, next to the skin. She took a thick pad of raw wool and showed me how to wear it between my legs, hooked to the belt-tapes. "This will catch the blood while you are away from your room," she said.

She helped me to find a way to sit comfortably over the bowl and then she fetched food and drink and our spindle-whorls from the house. There we stayed together for the rest of the morning, spinning and talking. I felt tranquil and safe in Elanor's company, though my belly still hurt a little from time to time. She talked to me of adult things – of men and love – and of the power of women. I could not help blushing to hear some of it, although I would have been blind, deaf and stupid not to be aware already of mating between men and women. When the midday came, she brought bread and meat for us on a platter, and upon it was a little pot with a few white forest-floor flowers.

"Bebbe went to gather them for you," said Elanor, "They are the first of the year, I think, so cold has it been."

I smiled and then frowned, "Why does Bebbe fetch flowers for me?" I said. And then, without Elanor answering me, I knew. All the women in the house – probably every woman in our whole household by now – and all the men too, most likely – knew of my flowing moon-blood. I blushed again, and felt the humiliation of this wholly personal matter being the talking-fodder of everyone.

"Why must other people know?" I mumbled.

"It is no matter for shame, but for celebration," said Elanor, "For it marks your womanhood."

I nodded, for she seemed so proud and I could not tell her how this put another great obstacle between me and my quest, for I knew she would be angry at such a notion, counting it childish. So I put aside my loneliness and humiliation and allowed her to draw me gently in to the world of women, which I did not want, yet which had its appeal, nevertheless.

As evening came on, I washed and dressed myself, and Elanor combed my hair and plaited a white ribbon into it. We went down into the house together and Bebbe was there with the other household women. They all smiled at me and, beginning to enjoy the attention, I smiled back, kissed Bebbe and thanked her for the flowers. Then Elanor and I wrapped warm cloaks around us and she led me out of the house. We walked all around the homeyard and then out of the guarded gate and through meadow and wood until it was time to return for supper. This was my first walk as a woman.

When we returned, Hereward and Fritha, Alvar and Alice had arrived, come from their own households for the evening. My marriage-sisters greeted me as though I were a visiting princess, and presented me with gifts. Fritha gave me a pair of woven cuffs and Alice brought a spindle-whorl, carved over with leaf-pattern, in which I recognised Alvar's work. I was admiring these things and thanking Fritha and Alice for their kindness when I noticed someone sitting in Elanor's chair against the wall, close to the hearth. With a cry of joy I ran forward, for it was Mother Werberga. I was surprised to see her, because her visits were very rare.

"Mother," I cried, "It is good to see you! Are you well?"

"I am, child. And how does this day find you?"

I nodded and said in a loud whisper, close to her ear, for her hearing was not always very good, "I am well, but my moon-course has come."

She nodded and, of course, she already knew. It seemed the world knew. She pushed into my hand a tight-bound little bunch of herbs. Their scent was sharply familiar to me and I looked at her in surprise, but she only returned my look calmly. "It is my gift for your womanhood, Edith," she said.

Everyone gathered for supper, which had been prepared as for a small feast, with a haunch of venison and a honeycake, despite the late spring season. Father had me sit next to him and, although to my relief little was said, he raised his beaker to me, calling out "To my daughter, Edith, the morning-star of our family!"

Everyone raised their beakers and drank to me, but I flushed with pleasure at my father's words, for always since my childhood was I surprised and thrilled when he spoke praise or fond words to me.

When he had drunk, I fetched the mead-jar to refill his beaker. "Thank you daughter," he said, "And now I have something for you." On the table before me he placed something wrapped in a bit of white cloth. I unfolded the cloth and saw there a golden brooch of cruciform shape, set with a clear crystal. Now, I have never cared very much for ornaments, yet I knew such a beautiful thing was of great value. I stared at it in astonishment, wondering what I had done to deserve such a gift. Elanor hurried to my side and pinned the brooch at the neckline of my dress. At last I found my voice and thanked my father who smiled and kissed me. Then Elanor presented me with an ivory comb with a beautifully carved handle. I gave her my bewildered thanks and she laughed.

"Do not look so surprised, Edith," she said, "It is meet that you should receive gifts. They are for your womanhood and we hope they will give you pleasure also."

"Indeed," I said earnestly, "They do give me pleasure. Thank you!"

I did not sit up much longer that evening, for I was still exhausted and overwhelmed by my painful night and strange day. By the light of a candle I went up to bed, and Elanor found me there a little time later, arranging my new gifts on the little chest that contained my books and writing materials. I lay down then and she put the covers over me, stroked the hair back from my forehead and kissed me. "God's night, sweet one," she said, as she had been saying to me nightly since we came into each other's lives. She left the candle burning and, although I was full tired, I did not blow it out for some time, but lay thinking about my day and looking at my new possessions. And I knew myself to be a richer girl, although I had lost my childhood.

But I woke from time to time throughout the night, with the scent of Mother Werberga's herbs in my nostrils; and I wondered at it, for it was the same scent that had kept me company when I had hid myself in a cart and got taken, without leave, to the Holywell Abbey when I was a small child. It was the scent of travel-herbs – a gift for a journey.

38

Kyneth

So my brother Archibald became a man, and I a woman, at the same time. I enjoyed the extra respect that was afforded me by my new status. As for my desire for quest – I never lost it. If the gifts from my father and the women of my family – welcome as they were – had seemed to tie me into a new, feminine life, Mother Werberga's herbs carried me back to my vow of quest. I pondered that she may have given me travel-herbs as a symbol of my new life-journey as a woman. Yet, to me, they afforded hope that my dreams were not lost. I begged from Elanor a scrap of fine wool to make a pouch, and sewed the herbs into it. I wore them always around my neck, pressing the pouch to release their scent whenever it seemed that life would hold me and keep me captive in an existence that I wanted no part in. Yet, I could not ignore the real changes that were happening to me; I began to learn about the way my body responded to the moon-times. It seemed that I had a cycle, part of which carried me through a time of excitation, when I might feel agitated with joy or melancholy or rage, this would be followed by calm and fatigue, when my blood flowed, after which my energy would gradually rise and I would feel lively, powerful and inspired.

I was determined now that I would keep my body strong and active, by duty to my quest vow, and it was at this time that I began seriously to practise archery. At Ufer Hall I had seen the Lady Cwena and her women with their bows and arrows, firing at target-shields. When I told Elanor of this, she decided that archery was not, after all, an unwomanly pursuit, so she began to tolerate my bow-practise. This was a relief to me, as I could practise on our own testing-ground when the men were not using it, and I became fairly well skilled with the bow and arrow. When they saw this, the men showed some respect for my skill, with Father himself taking some pride in my prowess. One day I took up a javelin that someone had carelessly left on the ground. I threw it and it landed near and sideways-on, but I practiced and nobody stopped me. Before too long, I could aim a javelin and throw it true. Soon, whenever I rode out, I carried bow, arrow and a couple of javelins with me.

It was at about that time I started hunting, and this is how it came about: I was heading home one evening, late, and had come to the little rise between the wood and the ride down to Father's tun. In the dusk I saw a swift movement out of the corner of my eye. I looked towards it, but there was nothing; I turned my head away and there it was again, a darting, fleeting progress through the summer grass that stopped, then sped acrossways, then stopped again. I notched an arrow to my bow, then stayed my own movements and waited. Another dart of speed and I had the pattern of it in my head and the knowledge of a pair of long brown ears, just above the grass tops. But I had to sense where it would next rest. With my bow taut and a quick prayer sent up to the hunter goddess, I freed my arrow. It flew and the hare dashed to meet it, falling with a squeal as the arrow pierced its leg and pinned it to the ground. I ran, and found its leg broken and bleeding. It attacked me with claws and teeth as I tried to put my hand to it. I had been taught to break the neck of a chicken for the pot, and I tried the same method on the hare. It only squealed the louder, twisting in my hands and scratching and biting all the more. If it had not been pinned through the leg by my arrow buried deep in the ground, it would have been away, broken leg notwithstanding. As desperate as my prey, I took the animal between my hands all slippery with blood, and – upon my third attempt - broke its neck over my knee. And there I sat in the grass, panting for breath as though I had run a fast mile, and all messed with my own and the hare's blood. It was then I saw the row of teats along the creature's belly.

I took her back to the wood and buried her there. I could not take her home, for, although it was a fine feat to shoot an arrow into a running hare, everybody knew that a mother hare with suckling young should never be killed. Thus my first successful hunt was no matter for celebration, but for secret shame, and I wore long sleeves until the wound marks of her teeth and claws on my arms had healed. From then on I made sure to know a mother hare from any other, but I did not cease to hunt and, after a little time, took home my first legitimate kill, a young hind. This caused great amaze in my household, and Father gave out peals of laughter at my lucky strike. When I brought home my second and then my third kill, Father did not laugh so hard, only saying:

"Well, daughter, I deem it time that you rode to the hunt with me and your brothers!"

He laughed as though such an event would be a matter for mockery, but I was ready mounted when they next rode to hunt and, beyond a dark glance at me, Father did not raise his voice against it. I shot a hind from horseback that time, although the arrows of others also found the same mark, whilst still more landed in the ground around her; no-one could be sure that my shot had been true. It was not long, however, before my skill with the bow was witnessed by Father himself, and I saw a flash of pride in his eye, although he maintained hunting was no work for a woman.

I happened to be passing through the threshold one day when I heard Father speak to Elanor about this. They were standing together quietly with their backs to the door, facing the warmth of the fire; and the silence throbbed between them so that I knew they had paused between two sides of an argument. Elanor's face in the amber firelight looked troubled and Father took her hand "We can at least be sure that she can protect herself when she rides out," he said. "It is no bad thing for a woman to have such skill."

I stood still in the shadows, surprised and glad to find an unexpected ally in my father.

Meanwhile, the stories I made in my mind and in my growing store of writings held all the valour and adventure I could desire for the time being. In them, I rode with courageous warriors, fought dragons and conversed with magical unicorns and holy people. Often, around the fire of an evening – in the house or out of doors, I would be asked for a story, and then I would fetch one of my parchment rolls and read what was written there to the assembled household. Thus I shared my stories with other people, and thus those stories came to be more real.

For the time being, it was enough.

The seasons changed, the harvest came in and I took my annual journey to Holywell Abbey as a woman for the first time.

Some days after my return from Holywell, I took the benefit of a fine day and rode out to Mother Werberga's house, returning with a basket of special herbs and a recipe – for I wished to bring a healing mixture to Father David; who continued to suffered badly with fever once or twice in every two moons. I came home in the early after-noon, riding slowly to keep pace with Spin who had come along with me, gambolling like a pup at first, but tiring after the run, for Spin was an old dog now.

We were some distance away from the bounds of our homeyard when I saw riders ahead of me. They were three, with one riderless horse beside, and they were being admitted through the guard-gate into our home yard.

This was the scene as I passed through the gate myself only a few minutes later:

Elanor was in the homeyard, greeting a lady who was being helped from her mount by two young men, dressed as warriors. One of them was Archibald. The other, a little shorter and slighter than my brother, had his back to me, but I thought not of him in that moment, for I saw immediately that the lady was Cwena, her face all alight with pride and happiness. I stared in surprise, for this was the first time I had seen the Lady riding out without the escort of her husband since that terrible night half my life-time before, when she had been brought back from her elopement with Rob of Dale against her will.

Now the Lady put her hand on the young man's shoulder and stepped lightly down from her horse. "God's day Elanor," I heard her say, "Here is my eldest son Kyneth, come from the King's court to make his home again in this country."

Elanor put out her hands to the young man in her sweet gesture of welcome and he turned towards her. I saw hair of rich brown, sun-bleached where it curled at his shoulders to the same light colour as the Lady Cwena's; I saw also a close-cut beard, straight brow and delicate features which were yet large enough to be manly. His eyes were wide and grey-green, and they lit up now with kindness and respect as he took Elanor's hand.

"How glad I am to meet you, my Lady," he said. "It is long I have wanted to know you, for my friend has spoken much of your kindness and beauty." He half-gestured to Archibald as he spoke, and my brother's face reflected the genial openness of the other man. I could see they were close and happy in each other's company.

Did I feel jealous of this friendship? The truth is that no such thought crossed my mind. My only instinct was to join this circle of warm cordiality that I saw before me. My wish passed through the air like a benign javelin, and all four of them caught sight of me as one.

"God's day, Archibald!" I called, jumping down from Bracken, and handing him over to old Worik and another bondsman, who had the charge of our visitors' horses. Then, turning quickly to the Lady Cwena, I said, "God's day, my Lady."

"Edith!" The Lady Cwena turned her happy face towards me and her son followed her glance.

I think it is true that Kyneth's eyes widened as we looked at one another, and then he gave one of the friendliest smiles it has been my life's pleasure ever to experience. "Edith?" he said, "Then you are Archibald's warrior-sister!"

I answered him with smiles while other people spoke; I know not what they said, but I can tell you that I esteemed him without reservation from that one moment, for the look in his eyes honoured me as a woman, while his words acknowledged my true quest. My eyes shone from Kyneth to Archibald and back again, knowing that my brother must have spoken about my quest with respect, and therefore dignified me in the eyes of his friend.

"And now sister," said Archibald, "it is time for you to receive the gift I promised you, for Kyneth has brought it with him from the household of the Lord Torhelm."

I looked about me with wonderment and curiosity, while Archibald took my hand and brought me to Worik, who was holding one of the mounts that our visitors had brought with them. It was a young mare, who moved restlessly while Worik stroked her and offered a handful of oats to quieten her. This was the riderless horse I had noticed when I viewed them approaching our bounds. Immediately I guessed that this was Archibald's gift to me, and I gasped and put my hands to my mouth, feeling my face flush with shocked delight. For she was beautiful – a good-sized bay, strong in back and leg, with the sweetest face and bright, dark eyes.

"She is three years old," muttered Archibald beside me, "And trained to carry arms. Yet have a care when you approach her – she is spirited and wary of strangers."

I hardly heard him as I walked up to my horse, standing quietly and letting her notice me, while I breathed in the scent of her. All was quiet as I stepped forward and bowed my head, putting my face close to hers, as I had seen Archibald do a hundred times with nervous horses. I closed my eyes and felt her breath, warm and damp, against my chest.

"Here, little one," old Worik said to me, "Take some of this for her." He poured a few oats into my hand and I held them to her mouth. She nibbled them gently from my hand, and I took the bridle from Worik, and led her around the homeyard before bringing her back to where Archibald and the others were watching. Then I gave her up to Worik, and turned to my brother, wrapping my arms around him and holding him tightly, for I could not find words properly to express my gratitude. He held me for a moment and then said, "What name will you give her?"

"Dancer," I said, without a thought.

"Ha! An excellent name, for she is light on her feet and never seems to tire!" The speaker was Kyneth, and I went to him now and, although I felt shy, held out my hand to him:

"Thank you for bringing her," I said simply.

Kyneth grasped my hand in a comradely way, then bowed his head as if he might kiss it; he did not do so and I know not whether I was glad or not. I kept my head bowed to hide my blushes and saw that his hands were broad with strong, long, chiselled fingers – a builder's hands, a dreamer's hands. Then he looked up at me with his eyes twinkling, "It is my guess you will be riding her by this day's end."

"If she will have me."

"She will have you, for I saw the patience in you when you approached her. I have watched over her in these months since your brother left the Lord Torhelm's lands. Archibald particularly wanted her trained as a warrior horse and I saw to it. She is spirited, but not nervous of noise or alarms. Any warrior would be glad of such a horse."

Now Elanor spoke up:

"What a fine gift from your brother, Edith! And now, let us make our guests well-come, and not keep them standing here." She turned to Cwena, "Would you come in to our house, Lady?"

"I would, my sister," said Cwena sweetly, "But the day is set fair; let us sit under your oak tree and enjoy the air."

It was a happy hour as we all sat taking spiced cordial in the sunshine until my father rode in from the hunt with Farin and Heath. Archibald went at once with Kyneth to present his friend to Father. Then Father's big chair was brought outside and he sat there, questioning Kyneth about his fighting skill. He nodded approvingly as the young man spoke with full modesty of his battle experience among Prince Cenred's coastal guard in the south, and I felt as proud and glad of my father's approval as if Kyneth had been my own son or lover.

"That is a fine new threshold you have there," said Kyneth, nodding towards the house. Father immediately took him to see it, pointing out the inscription across the entrance with some pride. They disappeared inside for some minutes and when they reimmerged Father's eyes were alight with interest.

"So," he was saying, "You built the King's new long-hall."

"Only part of it," replied Kyneth, shaking his head modestly, "I made a design for the Queen's private chapel there and - by fortune - the Queen favoured it, so I oversaw the building of it. Later the King sent me to Prince Cenred and I made a hall for the prince and another for the Lord

Torhelm. It was there I met Archibald and learned what true horsemanship is."

He exchanged a friendly glance with Archibald and thus turned the talk from himself.

But Father was not minded to yet change the subject, although horsemanship and war would generally be his choice. "I want to extend my house," he said. "It is no longer big enough for the size of our household, and my wife would like a private room to sit quietly away from the household."

"I can help you," said Kyneth enthusiastically. "And my guess is that your present stone base would support a further level above your present loft, should you wish it."

"So you plan to stay living close to your family now?" questioned Elanor gently.

"Indeed," Kyneth smiled towards his mother. "When the King granted me a tun in recognition of my work, I asked that it be in this country, near to my father's lands. It will be good to be close to my family once more. Also the land yields rich harvests as well as having plentiful stone, so I may build a strong hall for myself."

Father fetched beakers and a cask of ale, and Elanor ordered food to be prepared. Soon afterwards, the Lord Wulfirth rode up with Lewitha and Osred, who had himself recently returned from his uncle's household in the west to join his father's huscarle. In a short time, members of our family also began to arrive - Hereward and Fritha, Alvar and Alice with the children, and then Siric came from Beornwine, with, Gytha and Ham and Aldyth. All were, of course, curious to see the Lord and Lady's eldest son, who had not been in these lands since he was a boy. All brought foods with them from their own households, and an unplanned feast was made.

Archibald brought Kyneth to meet Hereward. "This is my eldest brother," said Archibald. "It is he that built our threshold and many of the houses and stores on our lands, and he manages all the Fly farmlands under our father."

Kyneth clasped sword-hands with Hereward. "I am glad to meet you sir," he said. "I hope you will advise me about preparing land for planting when the time comes, for it is long since I lived in this country."

"I should be glad to," said Hereward in his mild way, "What kind of land have you?"

"I know not, only that there is much of it, with some small settlements but no large household or village. I have not ridden there yet, for I only arrived yesterday evening. I doubt I'll be ready to begin ploughing for a year yet."

"Your success with crops will depend much on the lie of the land."

"Would you have time to ride with me and give me counsel on this?"

"Indeed, it would be a pleasure. I begin to plough in a fort'night, as the moon wanes. Until then, I have time."

They grasped hands again and lifted their beakers of ale together. I was glad to see a flush of pleasure on Hereward's face, for Kyneth seemed both to need and to value his counsel. Thus Hereward's land-skills had been appreciated more by a stranger in a few minutes than his own father ever had done.

Everyone liked Kyneth.

My horse was fast and light of foot. As the moons passed, we became used to each other and I felt we were of the same mind. She had needed little training on my part; indeed any training seemed to be two-sided. If I urged her too strongly to do something she was willing to do anyway, such as a quick turn or challenging jump, she would simply stop until I ceased my urging. I found soon that she would respond with the lightest touch to any direction. I loved her and would rarely let any other have the care of her. Almost my first thought on waking was to go to her stable or paddock to feed or groom her, and we would go for a gallop every morning, whatever the weather. Conscious of her warrior-horse status, I usually carried my bow, arrows, javelins and a large shield, borrowed from my father's store, when I rode her. People became used to seeing me thus and I heard myself called a 'warrior-maiden' – in tones of voice that were only half-jest.

And yes, in those days I awoke happy every morning. Indeed, life was like a pleasant dream where my story-writing and my new horse met in a reality where I was free for a time. No-one called me to work at the oven or dairy, and the only tasks given me were to carry messages, generally long-distance to Ufer Hall, as both Father and Elanor seemed to have much to communicate with the Lord Wulfirth and Lady Cwena. As to that, the messages were generally trivial, but I never complained, for such errands gave me more time with my horse and allowed me to see Archibald.

At Ufer Hall I always visited Father David, who continued in ill health and was not able to teach me any more. In the winter months I feared greatly for him, but every day he still struggled from his little chamber beside the chapel to preside over the holy service at daybreak and evening. When I visited him, he would allow me to fetch one of the sacred texts and I would read to him. He would lie back on his bed, listening with his eyes closed but with an intent expression on his face.

"Thank you child," he said one day when I had finished. "I know the holy words well enough, and yet I still seek for understanding."

"Let me come and read to you every day, Father," I said.

"Thank you Edith, but you have your life to live. I do not want you spending your days with an old man."

Tears sprang to my eyes. "But, Father, I said, "You know how I love to read, for you have taught me so well."

"Yes, yes." He paused, for speaking made him breathless. "Do come to see me, Edith. Light this dim room with your brightness."

"I will." I took the holy book back to the room between the chapel and the house where all the precious texts were kept. There I wrapped it in a soft cloth and stowed it with the others in a chest. I brought the key back to Father David, who remained the custodian of the library. I sat with him and took his hand. It was as warm as ever: a kind hand.

"They are sending a new priest," he said softly. "He will read to me every day and help me conduct services." He opened his eyes and looked brightly at me.

"That is good," I said.

"Indeed. So I shall not need you to read for me. But come, Edith. Do come."

"You know I shall."

"But now, go. I wish to rest and there are others here who want to see you more than I. Be off with you."

The sweetness of Father David's smile belied his harsh words as he released me. I kissed his hand and walked out into the light. Dancer was ready for me in the stables and she called out as she recognised my footfall. I almost skipped across the yard, feeling the life and strength in my limbs, which contrasted sadly with poor Father David's ill-health. And yet I could not deny the happiness that coursed through me in the bloom of my health and youth and freedom. In minutes I was on my horse's back and we were out of the Ufer Hall courtyard and speeding across open countryside.

39

A Builder and a Dreamer

I pulled up my horse at the top of a rise just between the outskirts of Wulfirth's worth and the boundary of Kyneth's new tun. This was marked at present only by an area of cleared land, now grazed by sheep to prevent any autumn re-growth. No ploughing was planned until the following spring, but Kyneth was well ahead with his preparation. Not a league ahead of me a group of figures were busy setting great posts into holes that marked the rectangular framework of the hall, with a great fire-pit dug at its centre. Others were lifting stones on pallets and setting them down on a flat area of ground in front of the hall. I could see how the work had progressed even in the two days since I last came there.

He was there; I knew him immediately, even from this distance, and at that moment he raised his head and waved in my direction. I nudged Dancer gently with my knee, we set off again at a steady canter and were soon at the site. Kyneth walked to greet me and he petted Dancer as I dismounted.

"I have brought the axe you wanted from Father," I said, passing it to him.

He took it, examining it with satisfaction. "It is good of you to bring it."

And we smiled and smiled at each other.

"The work is coming on well," I said.

"Come and see."

We walked the area of the house and stone-laid earth, which would form a large area free of mud next to the house. I was surprised and impressed by the size of it. Kyneth was rosy-faced with pleasure as he pointed out the length and straightness of the posts.

"The forest here has yielded the finest timber ever I saw," he said. "There's everything I need for beams, staves, posts and tie-beams and flexible branches for weaving neat walls. I think there's enough good timber here for a whole town."

I smiled and nodded and made what agreeable comment I could manage. Building material was not a subject to which I had ever in my life given any thought before, yet - attached as it was to Kyneth's enthusiasm - it seemed to me now as rare and amazing an object of attention as a wooden spoon is to a little baby.

"What do you think?" He was looking closely at my face.

I studied the site again. I had not seen anything so big anywhere except for the great Church at the Holywell Abbey.

"It is like to be the grandest house in the region," I said.

"The grandest ..." He hesitated, searching my face uncertainly, "Do you think so?"

"For certain it will be a work to be proud of." Then I looked him honestly in the eyes, saying, "I only wonder if it is meet that your house should be finer than your own father's hall."

As clearly as the sky displays the elements, so Kyneth's face carried the signs of emotion. It was one of the things I liked about him. Now I saw at once how my words struck home. He grasped my shoulder with one hand and put the other to his head. "I am a fool," he said.

I smiled, "You are no fool. It's natural you wish to do your best according to your talents."

"But not so as to demean my father's dwelling, nor indeed that of your own father."

Together we turned and looked silently towards the beginnings of Kyneth's new tun. Although the house was barely begun and the farmland raw and unploughed, I saw in my imagination a prosperous and comely dwelling, where grew a fine family and powerful household; I heard horses hooves upon the stone-flagged yard; and smelled the scent of many harvests safely gathered.

"It would be wrong to cease this or reduce it in any way," I said, almost to myself.

He did not speak, only nodding in agreement as he gazed at the site as if he also saw before him the scene that had opened up in my own mind's eye.

And then a solution entered my mind. I turned to him. "Let this be a pattern for an even finer dwelling built for your father on his land! You said he wants changes to his hall. Why not build a new one for him? You say there is plenty of timber in the forest."

He looked at me, then said slowly, "Of course. You are right." His eyes widened, "I shall speak of it to him this night! The same shall be done for your father; he also wants changes to his house."

Kyneth's face was flushed with pleasure. Most men might be expected to feel daunted by the responsibility of setting up three fine new halls, but such tasks were like food and drink to Kyneth, and the planning of them the very lifeblood of his soul.

"Edith, what a friend you are!" he said, taking my hand in both of his, "What would I do without your wise counsel!"

It was my turn to flush now, for I had never been called wise counsellor before and I imagined my friends and family laughing at such a notion. Besides, I thought the idea that Kyneth might build his father's house was so obvious that anyone might have thought of it in a moment. But I did not voice my opinion, preferring to bask in the warmth of Kyneth's smile. He looked as happy as though I had given him some precious gift and I could not but be gratified to have caused his gladness.

Soon the sun reached its high point of the day and the workers rested. Meat and bread, ale and water were brought out and I was invited to eat with Kyneth and his men. I had made plum cakes that morning, which I now shared with them. All were most respectful to me, compared with my own household folk, who had known me most of my life and still often treated me as if I was a little child. Kyneth's men, however, followed his own manner with me, so I felt every one of my fifteen winters.

It had become a custom when I visited Kyneth for us to ride to the rise which made a good viewing point for the building work. When we had eaten, he called for his own horse and mine to be brought to us, and we rode together. "Are you still satisfied with your mount?" he said as we walked our horses side by side.

"Indeed. As much as ever. She improves every day."

"As you do also," he said.

"Well," I answered him, "I do practise archery and javelin-throwing. Yesterday I hit target from horseback at a canter for eight out of ten attempts."

I looked at his face and he was smiling. Then I knew that the 'improvement' he spoke of had nothing to do with my warrior-skills. I blushed and smiled in return.

"But truly," he said seriously, "You are more skilled than many of the youths of your age in my father's huscarle."

"And how much better should I learn if only I could be trained with them as a brother warrior!"

"That is impossible."

"I know," I said darkly.

But he continued, "That is impossible because you would be always with them, and I could not enjoy your company and be advised so wisely by you and ensure I keep up with my horsemanship so that you cannot always beat me in a race!"

I laughed, "As to that, it is your fault for training my horse so well before you brought her to me!"

"And you are a scholar also," he went on, "Better than any I know. As to your cooking skills, I have not tasted a better plum cake, even at the King's court."

He had stopped laughing and was looking on me with a gentle, almost puzzled smile. "I think, Edith, you could be anything you wished: A warrior-maiden; a scholar of scripture in a Holy Abbey; the wife of a great household. I wonder which you would choose?"

This was a fine pleasure for me: to be praised thus by my friend and to be talking of my hopes for the future without the restraints of social custom. I smiled happily under Kyneth's admiration. Indeed, if at that moment a magical unicorn had appeared to grant me one wish, I could not desire to be anywhere else in the world: not even riding to quest.

Laughing, I said, "Perhaps I would be a wife and a warrior too!"

"Why not!" he cried, "Come, I'll race you to the top of the rise!"

My horse was encumbered with the arms and shield I always carried when riding her; Kyneth rode free. Yet I beat him in the race, and had an arrow notched to my bow before he arrived. Yet I could not bring myself to point it at him, even in jest, and I slackened my bow and put away my arrow. He rode hard at me, pulling up his horse close next to Dancer. Then, he simply reached out and, gathered me into his arms, pulling me from my horse on to his. I knew then that his arms were strong, but I did not resist him anyway, and we spent a long time kissing, even though it was a little awkward with the two of us sitting on his horse in that manner, and with me still wearing the quiver of arrows at my back. When he whispered, "I love you, Edith," I felt supremely happy, even despite the crick in my neck. It was impossible for me not to love Kyneth. And so I did love him. How could I help myself?

After that, my first thought on waking every morning was not my horse, but Kyneth. And I slept ill at nights, preferring to lie awake and re-live the words he spoke to me and the feelings in my body as he kissed and held me. Long nights thus I lay awake in bliss, thinking of him. Nor did I feel tired in the day time. My strength was greater, my bow-aim truer. Now I saw him daily. Oftentimes he would be riding into our homeyard before I was out of my bed; and as I stepped down from the loft-ladder into the house, there he would be, taking a breakfast drink of milk-and-ale and talking to Father and Elanor. And I would go immediately to him, giving "God's Day" to everyone and receiving smiles from everyone in return. I would stand close to him, and without a thought slip my hand into his.

Sometimes, he would have Archibald with him. Now my brother was tall, handsome and full modest. Indeed, for all my life I had considered him the paragon of male beauty and nobility. Yet it was the sight of Kyneth that made my heart leap: his brown-faced sweetness and slim figure; features that were masculine but delicate; a smile that took my strength away from me; the sturdy hands of a builder and a dreamer.

40

.

A Token from Redhelm

For the Grain Rite the following year, after I had passed my sixteenth winter, Elanor made a new dress for me of costly woven linen, and I let her plait ribbons into my hair. I left my shield and weapons at home and played the lady. Kyneth laughed with delight when he saw me, but I was keen as ever to see the tests and he watched with me as Archibald took part in the mounted tests for the first time. My hero, Redhelm, was there, but Archibald was not drawn against him. My brother was unfortunate to be drawn in the first round against a huge warrior, who knocked him off his horse in the first gallop. It was clear that he was not badly hurt, but Kyneth murmured, "I think his horse turned a hoof."

Archibald smiled ruefully as he walked over to us afterwards.

"Bad luck, brother," said Kyneth.

"I should have been ready for him," said Archibald. "I knew what I was up against, but he caught me out of balance." He looked worried. "Would I could try again! I would not make it so easy for him another time."

I shared my brother's worry. The test was not simply a game, but practice for real war. Had this been a true battle, Archibald would likely have been killed. My feelings must have been displayed on my face, for he smiled, "Don't fear, Edith," he said. "This has taught me to be more wary of these heavy men."

"Had you thought of training up a new horse?" asked Kyneth. "Yours is getting to be old for a battle-charger. A younger one would increase your own power in mounted battle."

"No," answered Archibald, "Swift knows my every thought. That is rich recompense for any slight loss of speed or strength. Besides, he is yet a mighty horse – stronger than many."

His words were delivered lightly and seemed full wise, but I knew Archibald's loyalty for his horse. Indeed I shared it, for Swift had carried us both to safety when we were little children. "Swift is one of the best chargers in my father's stable!" I cried, rather shocked to hear any suggestion of weakness in my brother's mount, whom I loved as much as Dancer and Spin.

"He is indeed a fine charger," said Kyneth.

And we turned to watch the combatants in the next round of tests.

Redhelm was drawn in the next round and my heart beat with excitement as he rode up to the testing-ground. He seemed never to change, although it was now the tenth Grain Rite since I first saw and was inspired by him. He was as youthful as ever – clean-shaven and slight, with the bright crop of red hair, revealed when he removed his helm. He could not have been more than twenty-six winters, yet his prowess at the mounted test seemed to strengthen year-on-year. He no longer rode the big, dappled-grey horse of former years, but a striking black mare, tall and powerful as a stallion.

"That big horse must be a great asset to that warrior," said Kyneth, "For it will make up for his own small stature, if only he can control it well enough."

"That's Redhelm," said Archibald, "His horsemanship is second to none. He is likely to do well in the tests."

"Yes!" said I eagerly, "He is a great warrior!"

Archibald smiled, "Redhelm was kind once to Edith when she was a child. He is her hero. But it is true, his battle prowess is well known."

Kyneth glanced at me and I saw a trace of anxiety or jealousy in his face. But he could not mistake that I had given my woman's love to any but he. He must have seen this clearly in my face, for his troubled expression passed away and we smiled at each other.

"Where is he from?" he said.

"We know not," said Archibald. "He comes often to our Grain Rite, sometimes with a group of Welsh huscarle, but I suspect he is not beholden to any Lord, for he usually rides here alone."

"And have you not asked him where his country is?" asked Kyneth, looking at me, "I thought you would know more than this about your hero!"

I shook my head silently, looking towards Redhelm, as he checked his weapons before the next round.

Despite being the daughter of a King's Thegn - one of the foremost men in that country - and despite spending most of that Grain Rite on the arm of Kyneth, who was heir to the chief Lord of the region, I felt unworthy of approaching Redhelm. No-one seemed to know him well, and he exchanged no more than a word or two even with warriors with whom he had fought in the wars.

We watched as Redhelm won round after round in the tests with ease, using the same method of balance and shield-work that he was well known for and which no other man seemed able to master. He was only well-matched by the big, heavy warriors, such as Halbert, whose quickness and agility almost matched his own; then, he would sometimes be overpowered by sheer weight.

But this year he was at his best and he did indeed come against Halbert after they had despatched all other contenders between them. Halbert had already won the sword-tests, for no-one could match his prowess with the great blade. On horseback, however, he was better matched with Redhelm; although Halbert was quick and flexible, his weight meant that he needed a heavier horse and this could affect his speed in the horseback spear-tests. But as they rode towards each other, it did not seem possible that Redhelm could remain seated. He did not flinch or feint, but rode steadily towards Halbert. There was a clash and Redhelm's shield split and shattered under Halbert's spear. But at the moment of impact, Redhelm's horse shied sidewards and suddenly Halbert's flank was exposed to Redhelm's spear. Seeing the danger, Halbert raised his shield to protect himself, but this put him out of balance. Redhelm took the advantage and lunged with his spear towards his opponent's shield. Halbert fell, held to his horse, but ended on his feet on the ground, his horse fiercely stamping its foot and standing between its master and his enemy. No real battle would be over in such a case, but by the rules of the test an unseated rider was deemed vanquished. Hundreds of watchers leapt up, cheering wildly for Redhelm, who quickly dismounted to clasp sword-arms with the great warrior he had overcome, who stood a head taller than he.

As Redhelm jumped to the ground, I noticed that a buckle fell from his horse's harness. I grabbed the hems of my dress to keep it away from my feet and ran onto the testing-ground, picking up the buckle and running with it up to Redhelm. Panting, I held it out to him. "It is yours," I gasped, "You dropped it from your horse." My face was red, but not with exertion.

Redhelm pulled the helm from his head and shook his hair. He did not smile, but stared at me with his melt-water eyes. Then he took the buckle. "I thank thee," he said in the light, stern voice that I remembered. I stood, looking brightly at him, remembering how he rescued a little girl from humiliation: *Give care to your eyes and your task. You shall not weep.* But there was no recognition in his eyes. And why should he remember that scrawny, distressed child in the well-dressed young woman before him?

He bowed his head and moved away to his horse, but perhaps he had seen disappointment in my face, for he turned again to me. Though fully grown, I was still very young – and I dare say I looked it.

"It is a valuable buckle," he said. "I am glad to have it back."

I stared at him, holding my breath, for this was a long speech to treasure in my memory.

His mouth twitched into something like a smile. "So you have been watching the tests?"

"Yes! And I always watch you. I think you are ..." I heard myself sounding like a silly child and I stopped.

"Then perhaps this might interest you." He was holding something out in his hand and I took it from him.

"It is only the broken tip of this spear I have used today," he said, adding, "It is no proper payment for the buckle."

I gasped with delight – a fragment from the winning spear! What a treasure! He only bowed again and led his horse towards the platform from where he would receive his prize of a bag of silver from the Lord Wulfirth. I ran back to Kyneth and Archibald.

"Look what he gave me!" I cried, showing them the small shard of broken-off steel. I think they were not very impressed, but I wrapped it carefully in a bit of muslin and carried it home that evening, where I sewed it into my pouch of journey-herbs that Mother Werberga had given me. I have worn them always on a cord around my neck: a pouch of journey-herbs and the tip of a warrior-spear given me by my hero Redhelm. The herbs became powder years ago, and the pouch has been repaired and reinforced many times, but as I raise it to my face now, still it retains a faint scent of herbs amid the iron, and reminds me that my life-journey is not over yet: not yet.

That after-noon, I followed my cousin, Gytha, at her marriage-blessing to her husband Ham. I carried the flower-basket and watched as they knelt and then kissed each other before the Holy Father. Gytha looked most happy and beautiful, all decked in flowers and with her belly well rounded with her first child. By my side was Aldyth. She was happy enough to see her sister married to Ham, for she hoped that Bencarad would now be for her. In fact, Aldyth's hopes were not to bear fruit, for Bencarad left Beornwine straight after seeing his brother married, not even waiting until the next morning. I guessed he would be missed, and not just by Aldyth, for he had been a friendly and cheerful presence at Siric's house.

After the ceremony, I went to Kyneth, who had been watching and was waiting for me. He circled my shoulders with his arm. "You are more beautiful than any bride here today," he whispered into my ear. I did not answer him, but only smiled. We walked around the edges of the field, not seeing any of the stalls or hearing the minstrels, only finding an affinity with the other lovers we saw sitting on the grass or disappearing into the trees. It is a time I remember most happily, for we exchanged words of love and thought not of any thing but only of each other.

"I never in all my travels met with a girl like you," he said. "None ever so beautiful; none ever with a fraction of your courage and action. But I knew at the moment I first saw you, riding into your homeyard that day when I was visiting with my mother and Archibald..." He looked at me, "I knew then ..."

"And I never truly cared for any man outside my family," I replied. "When I saw you first, it seemed that I already knew you – that I'd known you always."

He kissed me and held me, although we were often in the full view of his family and mine. As to that, all looked upon us with smiles only, and all seemed to think it meet that I should be loved by the Lord Wulfirth's heir, and that his love should be returned by the daughter of Finric Fly, the King's Thegn.

41

Enemies

I rose up early on the day following the Grain Rite, for I was to ride as usual to the Holywell Abbey. This year, however, I was not to be the only woman travelling with our harvest guard. It had been decided that a group of young educated women from our country should travel to the Holywell Abbey, there to stay and be schooled by the holy women at the Abbey until two moons had passed. As usual, I was looking forward to the journey, and to be seeing the Lady Leoba and Carau and Enya again, but now I only felt an aching longing in my stomach because I would not be seeing Kyneth for so long. Two moons seemed like two life-times to us, but he could not come with me, for the building and preparation for his hall and tun was moving on apace and he would not leave it.

Archibald was made captain of the guard travelling with the Beornwine harvest offering this year. From my father's household also rode our Welsh bondsman Davy and young Eldric, Hereward's eldest son, who was now nine winters and very excited to be allowed to escort the harvest offering with his kinsman and hero, Archibald. This was no speedy journey, for the loaded carts could not travel quickly. I rode Dancer and wore my normal journey-clothes, carrying my bow, javelins and arrows as was my custom. None but one of the other girls was armed; she was Ethela, the daughter of Eben Freeborne, Lord Wulfirth's mounted huscarle captain, and she carried bow and arrows. I did not know her very well, for her mother had died when she was an infant and she had been brought up with her kins-people near the Holywell Abbey, only visiting her father two or three times in a year. But Archibald had met her since his time with Eben in the mounted huscarle, and I had heard him speaking well of her. I rode up to her and made greeting. She was a little older than me - so I guessed - riding well and with confidence even though her horse was nowhere near as good as mine.

"Do you shoot from horseback?" I asked.

"I can. I have been practising," she replied, smiling in a modest, friendly way.

"Could you hit that tree at a canter?" I pointed to a nearby willow that grew on the riverside.

"I might," she laughed, "But I fear the risk to Master Siric's cart and its escort too."

It was true that Siric's cart and its sleepy driver, drowsing between a cured pork haunch and a basket of apples, were nearer to the tree than would make a distant shot absolutely safe.

"You'd wake him, at least," said I, "and save him from falling into the river."

We laughed together as we watched the well-fed guard flopping from side to side on the cart.

I calculated that, with my proficiency, I could send an arrow easily to the centre of the tree trunk without any danger to the man. I was longing to put my horse to a canter and show off my skills to Ethela, for there was something in her serene friendliness that made me want to impress her. Yet her very modesty made me ashamed of my own conceit, so I curbed my urge to action, and cast about in my mind for another subject for talk.

"Have you been to the Holywell Abbey before?" I asked.

"Indeed!" her eyes shone, "I have travelled there many times and prayed with the Lady Leoba."

"Oh! You know the Lady Leoba!"

"Yes, she has been a wonderful spiritual guide to me. I love her well."

I was a little taken aback with envy that this girl was so well acquainted with my beloved Lady.

"I also met her at the Holywell Abbey," I said quickly. "I have been going there since I was a little child. I love her too."

I did not mention the illegitimate nature of my journey to the Abbey on that first occasion, but I guessed that Ethela had heard of it, for she smiled and nodded.

"She speaks of you often. Indeed, everyone knows of Edith the warrior maiden."

Her words poured a salve of flattery over my envy but gave me pause to realise that I had not taken the time to pray much on my visits to the Abbey as she had done. The truth was that I loved reading and scribing for its own sake, not so much to grow in the spiritual wisdom that I found on the pages of the holy texts.

Such self-scrutiny discomforted me a little, but I loved being called 'Warrior Maiden' and decided that I liked Ethela very much.

"You must be very learned in the spiritual life," I said.

"Oh no, I have so very much to learn. I think it will be a lifetime before I have even a tiny amount of the Lady Leoba's wisdom."

As I watched her face, I knew it was not so; I knew myself to be in the presence of a good soul that I could never aspire to: one whose wisdom was already great. I consoled myself with the thought that at least I had much more skill at the warrior arts than she, and that I was loved by Kyneth.

Just then, Archibald rode his horse alongside ours.

"So, you have met each other!" he said.

Archibald was the other side of Ethela and, as we turned towards him, I saw them look at each other. In that moment, I forgot about comparing myself with Ethela. Indeed, I forgot everything in the sudden knowledge that my brother was in love.

"Yes, your sister has been full kind and courteous to me," answered Ethela, smiling.

This was a strange pass for me. Consider that, despite my infrequent resentment or temper against my most beloved brother, I had always been confident I was the foremost care of his life. Now, suddenly, I saw my place in his heart inhabited by another. The shock was too intense for jealousy or any other base emotion. I knew it must show on my face, and I looked down quickly, pretending to pluck a fly out of my horse's mane. It would be selfish to expect Archibald not to have a love such as my own with Kyneth: and truly I wished only happiness for my brother. In a moment I had composed my face as best I could and was about to return Ethela's friendly words with some of my own, when an arrow flashed past my ear and landed in the dirt at my horse's feet.

Immediately, I knew we were being raided. This was the reason for the harvest guard – not just an honourable pilgrimage for warriors, but to protect the sacred offering from marauding enemies that might prevent the valuable foodstuffs from reaching their proper destination.

Before these thoughts could even pass into my mind, all three of us had sped our horses away; no-one with warrior training remains within range of an enemy shooting from above. I circled my horse at a safe distance and saw the raider quite clearly at the top of a tree near the edge of the wood beside us. I knew he would not be alone, and I looked to Archiballd for orders.

"Edith! Ethela! Stay here!" he called, wheeling Swift and galloping to join our guard who were already engaging the raiders with swords and spears. I watched, all my instincts clamouring to join the fight, but my training compelling me to follow orders.

Then in utter horror, I saw my little nephew Eldric Hereson charging forward with a small knife in his hand. He was aiming for a raider who had come around behind the greater force of our guard, spear and shield in hand. Seeing Eldric making for him, he turned with a dreadful scowl and took aim at the child with his spear. For the first time then I experienced how the gods of war lend time to the brave. I found my mind watching coldly while my body raged into action. Before he had time to thrust his spear forward, I had charged up to him on my horse; at the same moment, Eldric ducked under the enemy's shield arm and stabbed his knife into the man's leg. Roaring with pain and rage, the man stabbed forward with his spear, but before he could touch the boy, I struck down from above with the edge of my shield, breaking his sword-arm. He screamed and bared his teeth at me, clutching at his injured arm. In rage and disgust, I thrust a javelin deep into his face; he fell, scrabbling at the javelin shaft with his hand, while blood burst from his face in a crimson fountain. I watched in horror as he burbled his last breath, but more enemies now appeared close by and my first care was for little Eldric. I dragged the boy onto my horse and put a short gallop's distance between us and the scene of battle. By now Archibald and the guard had despatched the other raiders and made short work of these that were left, chasing most of them away into the forest. All then gathered in relief and celebration, for none of our people was injured.

"I doubt they will be back," said Archibald, "No matter how hungry they are. And may they tell their friends that this harvest offering is not worth stealing – too great is the price they will pay!"

Everyone cheered, and soon afterwards Archibald ordered a halt so that we might eat and drink and tell tales of the fight, as is the custom.

I found myself not to be hungry, and went to empty my bladder and then to check on my horse, brushing the splashes of dried blood from her coat. Archibald came to me then. He put a hand on my shoulder, but I could not look him in the face.

"Ethela and Eldric have told us of your fight with the raider," he said.

"Eldric promises to be a fierce warrior!" I said, flashing a smile at him.

"He will live to give credit to the Fly family name, thanks to his warrior aunt," Archibald answered quietly.

I looked at him then, and I believe he could see between us my appalled memory of the raider, dying at my hand.

"Edith," he said gently, "Death is part of battle."

"I did not need to kill him." I almost whispered it, such a terrible confession did it seem.

"It was battle fever," he said. "Oft-times it saves us from dying at the hand of a wounded enemy who will come back to kill us if we spare him. Do not mourn the presence of battle fever in your blood. It is given by the gods to keep us alive."

I shook my head, feeling miserable. This was beyond any expectation of mine. I had always thought my first kill would be a matter for pride and celebration. Archibald did not touch me but stood close and, when finally I found the courage to meet his eyes, I saw there a look of the deepest understanding, and I knew suddenly that he also suffered in this way.

"Tomorrow we shall be at the Holywell Abbey," he said. "Before we take rest or food there, you and I shall go to the waters and make prayers for dead enemies. There the God of compassion shall give you peace."

I felt the burden of my guilt fall away from me, and was able to reason with myself that I had needed full speed and force to save Eldric. A softer heart may have spared my enemy, but could not have saved my beloved nephew.

Archibald and I walked back together to our people and I told him I was glad that he loved Ethela. It was my gift to him in return for the deep understanding he had extended to me in my guilt. And as he accepted my blessing with a happy smile, I realised that it was true: I was glad that he had found a love worthy of him.

"Will you marry?" I asked, thinking I knew the answer.

But a shadow fell over his face. "I cannot, Edith. Not soon in any case. I have a quest to follow, as you know. And I must leave soon to take it up. For if I do not, then you will. I am a man, and stronger than you will ever be. I must find Orin and kill him, so that I can release you from our quest. Then you can marry and be happy, and so will I."

He ended with a smile, but I frowned, for there seemed to be some misunderstanding between us.

"No …" I began, but had no chance to finish what I would say, for Eldric was running towards me, his face bright with excitation.

"Edith, here you are!" he cried, throwing himself into my arms. I held him tightly for a moment, feeling Archibald's arms around us also, and for the first time the reality of the danger Eldric had been in crossed my mind. I imagined the horror of having to give Hereward and Fritha the news of their son's death, and tears came into my eyes. But I released my grasp and he took my hand and Archibald's, looking between us with delight.

"They are calling me warrior-boy, as Archibald was called when he was my age!"

"And you are like him," I said, "For I have never seen a braver deed than when you attacked that raider on your own."

"It was brave indeed," said Archibald, "But a warrior needs first to learn skills so that his bravery will not be wasted. One of those skills is to know when to act and when to follow orders to wait." He looked severely at Eldric and the boy's smile faded. Archibald continued, "You put yourself and Edith in danger."

Now I felt sorry for Eldric, who was hanging his head in shame, but Archibald crouched down, looking up into the boy's face.

"This is your first battle-lesson," he said, "I know you will learn it well, so that your wisdom and skills will some day match your bravery, and you shall become a renowned warrior."

"I will," said Eldric, with a serious expression much older than his years, "I will learn it well."

"Good lad!"

Archibald stood and we joined the others, but I took the earliest opportunity to whisper to Eldric, "We fought that enemy together, did we not? You stung him well with your knife!" And I was rewarded with a grateful smile from my favourite little boy which, in turn, lightened the burden of guilt that was my own first battle lesson.

42

Love Before All

As Archibald had promised, we prayed together at the sacred spring as soon as we arrived. I took a cup-full of the fresh, cold water to drink. Then I put my feet into the stream and poured cup after cup of the water over my head and body, feeling it truly washing away the worst of my guilt, and my prayers for the soul of my dead enemy were taken into the forgiving earth along with the holy stream.

As I rose up from the stream, there was my old friend Enya hurrying towards me with a thick, dry cloth to wrap around me. I cried out with pleasure to see her, and allowed her to laugh and scold and chatter as she dried me and brought me to the house which was to be the quarters of the Women's School.

"Here you will sleep and study all the holy works," she said, her eyes shining as she showed me a spacious dorter with pallets all laid with cloths and sheepskins for sleeping.

"Will you be here with me, Enya?" I asked.

"Me? What foolishness! I am not for holy study, for never could I read or scribe if I looked at the scrolls forever!" she said. "And who do you think would order the children's house if I was to spend my time with you?"

"Is the children's house full?"

She nodded, and her voice dropped, "Fuller than ever since a summer fever-sickness brought death to many birthing mothers in the villages around here. I have five new babies now to my care."

"Will they live?"

"Two weakling ones are with nursing mothers. The others are fed with sheep's milk. By God's help may they all live." She made the sign of the cross over her body.

"You should be with them now," I urged, "I cannot keep you just because I am a little wet."

"I shall not leave you until I am happy you are dry and will not turn to fever," she said firmly, stripping off my wet dress and rubbing my body with a coarse cloth to dry it.

"You are kind," I said, wincing at the rough treatment of my skin.

She took a fresh dry dress and pulled it on me. "I know not why you wish to take the part of a man and fight enemies," she said, her face close to mine as she tugged at the shoulder-fastenings of my dress, tying them tight and firm "But I would have done all I could to save that child, as you did, and I honour you for it." She stood back to check that I looked respectable in a way so like that first time I came to Holywell that I laughed out loud.

"There, do not laugh," she said, but smiled in her turn. "I always think of you as my own charge since ever you came here with your naughty ways."

I could have reminded her that now I was a grown woman and a scholar, no matter what she thought of my warrior activities, but I simply stood and smiled at her, for it was good to find myself loved and cared for so far from home.

Archibald stayed only long enough to sleep and to pray at the Abbey Church . The next day he was away, with Eldric and many of the guard who came there with us. He came to bid farewell to me and Ethela.

"I do not believe those raiders will be any trouble to us," he said, "But other folk should be warned that foodfare, goods and life might be in danger on the road to Holywell. I must return with speed."

I hugged and kissed him, and thanked him for being my blessed brother.

He smiled at this, "And I thank you too, sister," he said, "For being the dear sister of my heart, but also for saving the life of our beloved nephew. None in our family will forget it; all will bless you."

The terrible guilt I had felt for causing the death of the raider had left me with a new modesty that could not bear this praise. I simply said, "Take my love and blessings to Elanor and Father and everyone."

Archibald then made his farewells to the Lady Leoba, Lord Tobias and other folk of the Holywell Abbey, who were assembled near the gates.

"There is one among us who would ride with you to Ufer Hall," Lord Tobias said, "For he has been called there by Father David and is much needed, I believe."

"Oh, Father David is our dear friend," said Archibald, glancing at me. "I heard that a Brother was to go and be helper to him. Let him ride with us, and well-come!"

Then I saw a tall, curly-haired young priest, hurrying from the church with a travel-bag over his shoulder. "Forgive me!" he called in a cheerful voice, "I was making a last prayer in the church, and did not know it was already time to leave."

"Carau!" cried Archibald with a big grin, "So it is you, brother, who is to travel with us. Why did you not tell me?"

"We were speaking of other things last evening, brother," said Carau, clasping sword-hands with Archibald.

I was close beside them, and I heard Archibald say in a low voice, "You let me speak only of my own concerns. I am shamed now that I did not even ask to hear yours."

"Non-sense. I knew we would have many days in each other's company, as we are now. You will hear enough of my affairs to make you tired full soon!" He laughed, then turned to me, saying, "Edith! There has been no time to talk with you, but I trust I shall see you at Ufer Hall when you return home?"

"Indeed, I hope it will be so!" I said, delighted to see my friend again and to know it was he who was to give his hands and his heart to the care of my beloved Father David. We spoke a few more words together and then he mounted the old pony that had been lent to him from the Abbey stable for the journey.

I turned again to Archibald, for everyone was mounting horses and harnessing oxen to the carts; it was time for final leave-taking. I did not see my brother at first, and then I noticed him talking earnestly with Ethela. Again, I saw between them the look of devotion I had noticed before. But I stilled the leap of jealousy in my stomach, and it was replaced by the consolation of knowing my brother was loved by one whom I was already beginning to esteem.

"It's been a bitter blow to him, but he's taken it well," said Enya next to me as we watched the procession set out.

"Of whom do you speak, Enya?" I asked curiously.

"Of Carau," she said. "He was a wayward child, yet he's turned out well enough. This last deed of his makes me proud: full proud. Yet I weep for him."

I reflected that Carau had been the first infant under Enya's care when she was a young woman. She was like a mother to him.

"He will only be a brace of days ride away, I said. "You will see him again often."

"You mistake me," she said. "I would have been glad to see him go to his heart's quest, but he has lost the chance, and I doubt another will come."

Her words stilled me, as did the tears in her eyes, now I could see they were not for herself. "And what is his heart's quest?" I asked softly.

"There is a plan to set up a new Abbey in some far-off place," she said, gesturing aimlessly at the sky. "Carau was to be made Father and to lead the mission. Now someone else will be chosen and they shall leave without him."

"He has gone to Father David instead," I said bleakly.

"It was his own choice. He told me that his Lord Christ put love before all things, and that he would follow the same road."

A gentle hand touched Enya's arm. It was the Lady Leoba standing beside us.

"Do not mourn for him. He has made his choice, and it is a good one. There will be another time for Brother Carau. He has a long life ahead of him."

I watched as the column of carts and its escort of riders moved down the road. At last I was able to pick out a curly-headed figure on a pony, and I knew I was watching one who had set up an example to me. I reflected that Brother Carau had put the care of another over a longed-for and honourable quest. But my heart quailed to think I might be required to do the same.

43

In the Company of Women

I enjoyed the passage of two moons at the Holywell Abbey when I stayed chiefly in the company of women, finding them to be as far advanced in philosophical wisdom as any men I had known. The foremost Lady of the company was, of course, the Lady Leoba. We girls all loved her and I believe every one of us was jealous of the time she spent with another. As for her, she was fair with all of us, although I sometimes felt she had a particular fondness for myself and also for Ethela. Oft-times she would call the pair of us to take bread or cordial with her during a rest time, and we would talk together – or, at least, I would listen while they talked. In those times, I felt my earlier instinct about Ethela to be confirmed – she was a truly good soul with unusual wisdom and grace. I understood why the Lady Leoba might want Ethela beside her, but never why she chose me also. The experience made me grow in humility, and I came to think of Ethela as a true sister.

What did we speak of in those hours? Of the nature of the old gods and of the Christ and Mother Christ, and how we might find the best of the old in the truth of the new; Of the sanctity of the soul and its place in our worldly lives; Of the miracle that is life and growth; Of the rules of conduct and kindness. Under the Lady Leoba's kindly counsel, I learned to at least try to have more gentleness and patience, even when my body craved action. This one lesson proved valuable in my later life, for passion restrained can charge the force of wisdom, and guide an arrow or sword-hand true.

I hardly rode my horse or weighed a javelin in my hand during the whole of this time: so exhilarating and compelling was the questing spirit for wisdom and grace among those women. In addition, I was in love. While much of the daytime was taken up with tasks and discussion and prayer, my nights were restless with longing for Kyneth. I was not alone in this hunger, because many of the young women in our school were in a similar state. One girl wore green willow withes around her head for a sweetheart lost in battle, and all we love-lorn girls looked on her with awe and sympathy. She was called Rhian - a dark-haired beauty of the Lady Cwena's kin, who had been brought up at the King's court and arrived at Ufer Hall only days before our Grain Rite. Although the willow proved her to be in mourning, she had several dresses of costly form which made my own clothes look dull. One rainy evening when we were sitting spinning and talking after our food, Ethela asked her gently how long she had been wearing the willow.

"For almost a year," answered Rhian. "Soon I am to leave it off, but I think my mourning shall never end. That is why I have been sent here, for I shall refuse to marry any other but he," and easy tears slipped from her eyes and down her pretty cheeks.

"Shall you become a holy scholar then, and never more think of men?" said Enid, a wide-eyed and rather stupid girl from Chief Wulfred's household.

The Lady Leoba looked up from her work, "There are other occupations, besides scholarship, for a solitary woman," she said. "And Abbey life does not exclude marriage, as you all know." She smiled, for she herself was married to Tobias, who was Abbot as she was Abbess of the Holywell Abbey, although they had no children of their own.

"But there are many unmarried women and men here," said Enid.

"True. All willing to work for our community are welcome here. Not all are scholars, by any means, but there are many mouths to feed and children to care for."

"I cannot do such servants' work," said Rhian, shuddering a little. "And I cannot study, for it bores me and, besides, I can think of nothing but Breyan." Her mouth quivered and more tears wetted her face.

I stared at her, for it was surely a heavy discourtesy to speak so ill of the scholarly work taught by the Lady Leoba and her holy women. Moreover, the tasks of preparing food and caring for children, which she called 'servants' work, were respected occupations in my own household at home, always under the supervision of Elanor, whom everybody honoured. I knew it was the same at the homes of most of the girls there and, indeed, for the Lady Leoba herself. Despite her high responsibilities at the Abbey, she could be seen oft-times stirring a pot of food with a child on her hip. I did not think the burden of grief excused Rhian's ill-mannered words.

"How can you be bored?" I said in a loud voice, "How *can* you be bored in such company?" I gestured to the Lady Leoba, knowing this was a challenge that the girl could not meet. But she met my look with a tragic and imperious one of her own, while her lips trembled and the tears flowed.

"I meant no such thing," she whimpered, "Only that my grief allows no thought but he!"

This resulted in a flock of girls crowding around her in clucking sympathy, offering their hand-cloths to wipe her face and shooting annoyed glances in my direction.

Neither the Lady nor Ethela moved from their seats, but continued calmly to spin, while I tried to curb the urge to fling my spindle at Rhian's pretty head.

"Her life at court has not been as ours, no doubt," murmured Ethela, glancing at me.

A spell of peacefulness and wonderment had been cast over me by the women's school, and I had been calm, studying well, and patient in my longing for Kyneth. Now the spell was broken. I wanted only to fetch my horse and ride full-pelt, day and night, back to my own love, fighting anyone who would stop me. My hand tightened over my spindle and I stood, measuring the distance between my throwing arm and the despicable Rhian.

But in that company I could not allow myself to give in to violence. I glanced at my two honoured companions; I took a long, shuddering breath; I sat down and re-balanced my spindle.

Thus, when the other girls had finished fussing round their queen of tragedy and came back to their seats, I was able to meet Rhian's eyes with real sympathy. After all, she could not help her ignorance. I only pitied her future life, with no occupation, no love of wisdom and no husband or children to love her. I need not have wasted my pity, for the next day Ethela and I saw Rhian stumble whilst walking near to a good-looking young huscarle. She fell gracefully onto a clean patch of grass and he rushed to assist her. She gave him a wan smile and thanked him with her large, lovely eyes. When we passed him a moment later, he was staring after her with his hand on his heart.

Ethela glanced at me, "All young men had better beware when Rhian returns to court!" she said, and we laughed our way back to the House of Learning.

We had been at the Women's School for twenty-eight nights and the full moon was come around again when an unexpected addition to our company arrived. I was with a group one morning, discussing an ancient text called *Redlaf's Story*, only because it had been gifted to the Abbey by a king's thegn of that name. He had cut the text carelessly in order to have it bound into costly book-covers to show his wealth and generosity. Thus, the meaning was only discovered with difficulty. Further, it was written in a language near-like Anglish, but difficult to understand in meaning. In fact, I had been awake most of the night in the study-room, by candlelight painstakingly translating a few sparse sentences.

"It reads *The god of life* – or it might be *The god of bread – punished men who put poison on their staves.* But it might not be *poison*, but *remedies.* The markings are so similar, I had to guess much of it."

"Is there any good to come from such translation?" said one of the other girls. "I have heard that all old texts and stories should be destroyed, and only Christian gospels remain. What use have we Christians for the lies told of old gods?"

I was taken aback to hear my hard work thus maligned, but Ethela spoke up:

"We have learned here that there is wisdom in all the works of earth and of human endeavour," she said. "If any can find truth in these old stories, it will be such a gifted scholar as Edith, who works hard to uncover the secrets within."

Ethela was well loved among the girls and heads nodded in agreement. No-one spoke any words against her and she bent to the text, querying one of the markings with me. I was instantly engrossed in the work, for that particular tale was new to me and I was keen to use the gist of it in a story of my own. Therefore I took no notice when someone else entered the study room. It was Ethela who looked up and said, "Well-come, Mother."

"I thank thee," said a familiar voice, and I looked up to see Mother Werberga standing before me.

"Mother!" I ran and threw my arms around my old friend. I was taller now than she, and her back and limbs seemed to have become narrow and thin since I held her last. I was surprised to find tears in my eyes at this visitor from home and I made much fuss of her, bringing her food and cordials that I had made myself, and basking in the sun of her praise as she commended them.

"Who brought you?" I asked, "Has another cart come from Beornwine?"

"I need no cart to bring me along this old road that I have been travelling all my life," she answered.

"But were you not guarded? Can you have walked all this way?"

"What guard does an old woman need? I can still walk well enough, although I am slower than you. The nights were warm and I had my cloak."

I heard footsteps hurrying towards the house and then the outer door opened and the Lady Leoba was there, her arms around Mother Werberga as mine had been. Then she stood back, taking her hands and gazing into her eyes.

"God's day to you daughter," said the old woman.

"God's day. You are well-come: so well-come! I am glad indeed to see you. Have you eaten? Have you rested?"

"Yes. Young Edith has fed me in queenly fashion and I want no rest now I have seen you."

"Then, come. Let us talk together."

They went together out of doors. I would have liked to go with them, but I was not invited and I returned to my work. The sun was well down when I left the house, and saw them walking slowly around the yards and gardens of the Abbey with their heads close together, deep in conversation.

Later, when we all sat around the hearth together in the evening, I was able to speak with Mother Werberga again.

"Are you well, child?" she asked, taking my hand in hers.

"I am."

"I heard of your valiant action when you saved the life of the boy Eldric Hereson."

I only nodded, ashamed to show any pride.

"Did that experience change your mind about a life of questing?"

Nobody had asked that of me before and I had learned in my time at the Abbey to search my mind before answering an important question. I gazed into the eyes of this one who had always seemed able to read my mind. She nodded thoughtfully, although I had not spoken.

"And has anyone else caused you to change your mind?"

I understood her meaning. She was speaking of Kyneth. I smiled, saying, "Have you seen him?"

"He was at my house only days ago. He had heard I was to travel hither, and begged me to bring a token to you." She put her hand into a fold of her dress and pulled out a small cloth bag, tied about the top with twine. Opening it, she took out a flat white stone, smooth and polished. It was the size of a large man's thumb nail and it had a hole drilled through the top so that it might be threaded with a cord and worn around the neck. I took the stone in my hand and it glowed, milky and iridescent, in the candlelight.

"It is a moonstone," she said. If you sleep with it close beside you at the full moon, you will dream of your true love.

I laughed, delighted. "I dream of him every night anyway!"

She looked at me in a way I could not read. "I think you love this man well," she said.

I nodded. "I do. And he is the only man I could be happy with. For he loves me just as I am, and he understands my quest."

"I wonder if that is true."

"It is!" I flushed in the face of her doubt. "I know he will ride with me as a brother warrior and marry me as a lover." I had never actually voiced these thoughts before, not even to Kyneth himself, and I flushed deeper as I admitted them.

She nodded, saying gently, "Be happy, child. But do not expect too much of him. His gifts are not great in the warrior arts. I think there is another path for him."

"No!" I stood, suddenly fearful in a way I did not fully understand. "No, his path is with me and mine with him. We love each other. How can it be otherwise?"

She only nodded again, her old, dear face all kindness in the firelight.

Soon, I went to my bed, opening the shutter beside me so that the night air might cool my hot face. Beside me on my pillow, glowing in the light of the full moon rising in the east, was the moonstone that Mother Werberga had brought from my one true love.

In my dream, the unicorn was beside me on the road. I felt full of happiness and energy and I moved swiftly, my bow in my hand. In the distance, a figure appeared on the road ahead, walking towards me. The unicorn spoke, "This is the one you told me of?"

"Yes," I said, "He is my one true love." And I started to run.

I have said that Ethela had become as a sister to me. The resentment I felt at Archibald's love for her was mostly gone, for I wanted it gone. Yet neither of us spoke much of him, and not at all of their love for each other. Still, his name passed between us on most days and I believe I made sure to let her know that I would accept her gladly as a marriage-sister.

The school drew to its end. I awoke on our last full day there, satisfied with all the learning and praying and studying and felt I was leaving the Holywell Abbey a wiser and more scholarly girl than when I arrived. I had learned to be still and control the passions that might lead me into inapt violence. But I did not forget my quick action that saved the life of my nephew. I was shriven of the guilt that had befallen me at the killing, and I now came to allow myself satisfaction that my skill and swiftness had prevailed in my first test. Waking into that new day, I

271

looked for the last time around the dim sleeping-house, and was filled at once with happiness and relief that the long period of reflection and study was over. Two moons seems a short enough time now that I reach the end of my days, but to that active girl of sixteen winters, it seemed a long age. I thought of my horse, Dancer, whom I had not ridden for such a long time that she likely judged I had no more use for her; I thought of my true love, and wondered if he ever thought of me. Pressing the moonstone that I now wore on a cord around my neck, I hugged myself in the pleasurable belief that he did still think of me as I thought of him. Had he heard of my fight with the raider? Would he be proud of my courage and of my scholarly work at the Abbey? And what of my family? How I longed to see them and bask in the love that I always received from everyone in that household, which had certainly not been the case at Holywell. It was sure that not all the other girls and women at the School had much affection for me, but I knew that the Lady Leoba loved me and Enya loved me and so did my heart-sister, Ethela. I looked down now at her, and saw she was just beginning to wake. "Come, sister," I said, "Do not sleep through break-fast on our last day here!"

She smiled at me and gave me, "God's Day, sister." Then she knelt on her bed, closing her eyes in prayer, with her hand on a small wooden cross that Archibald had given her, which she wore always.

I followed her example, as I always did, although I had no holy cross on the cord about my neck – only a glowing moonstone, and a pouch containing the broken tip of a winning spear and some sharp-scented herbs for a journey.

The School made the last of its prayers together, led by our own beloved Lady Leoba. After thanksgiving for our time together, Leoba raised her hands for silence.

"Daughters!" she said "I thank you all for your contribution to this first Holywell Women's School. I thought it meet that the women of our land should be learned in the arts of reading and scribing and philosophy. I believed women would blossom under the learning of the holy scripts. You have proved me right, and I thank you."

She paused, her face radiant with pleasure, before she spoke again:

"There are two here who deserve especial praise." Her eyes scanned the room and seemed to light on me. I glanced beside me and behind me, then back to the Lady, unbelieving that she could be singling me out. She smiled warmly, "Yes, Edith," she said, then looked again around the assembly, "Edith Fly's translation work has added notably to the enlightenment of the Holywell library. Edith, come here; I have a gift for you."

Thus, to my discomfiture, I came to the front of the room before all my sisters and received what the Lady held out to me.

It is a book of prayers in a plain, wooden cover, which I have yet covered again many times over the years in cured skins to protect it from rain and the buffeting of travelling and of being read constantly. My travelling being over for the present, I have made for it a cloth cover embroidered in purple and gold threads and tied around with a silken cord: I am not well skilled in embroidery, yet my work is lovingly done and the book lies here on the table before me, as I write.

I was overcome with surprise at the richness of the gift and the honour, but all were clapping their hands together to show their approval and, as I blushed and made my way back to my seat under the smiles of my sisters, I reflected that I was better liked than I had believed – or, at least – better liked now that I had been honoured.

Leoba now raised her hands again. "There is another here who deserves especial honour. It is my task to tell you all that your sister Ethela Freeborne has voiced her desire to go with the mission to set up a new Abbey in the north. I could have chosen no better soul to go with the men, for her humility, wisdom, kindness and courage are rare, as are her strength and horsemanship. All will be needed for such a quest. Ethela, come!"

I think my mouth was open with shock and distress, for Ethela had spoken none of this to me. She cast me a guilty glance before going to stand before Leoba. The Lady took her by the shoulders and turned her to face the gathered women.

"I give you my much beloved daughter," said the Lady. She did not address us, for her eyes were raised to the cross that had been painted above the lintel of the house. All the women clapped again, but I was weeping too much to think of anything but that I was losing my heart-sister, and that Archibald was losing her also. I left the room and went weeping to the stable, where I consoled myself on the shoulder of my darling Dancer. Soon, I guessed the reason for Ethela's decision: Archibald had told her he would not marry her because he was determined to leave for his quest: She was not skilled enough in the warrior arts to ride with him; she had therefore chosen the holy life and would go far away from her home and all those who loved her. The knowledge of this did not ease me and I felt again the old curse laid upon my family by my mother's violent death. I sobbed again into Dancer's warm coat.

Ethela found me there and dried my tears on the hem of her dress, as a mother will do for her child. "You are the first sister of my heart," I said in an accusing tone which really meant, *How can you go?* But I knew the answer.

"Edith," she said. "We are both grown women and this time at the Abbey has guided us upon our life-path. Do not blame me for choosing a way that would not be your choice."

"Oh!" I cried bitterly, "I could never choose the holy life. That, I have always known."

She nodded gently, "And I shall miss you sorely, my sister. Who will make me smile as you do, and who shall wake me at day-break and urge me to action?" She smiled as she spoke, and I returned a watery smile as best I could.

"But what of Archibald?" I said. "I know you love him. Of course you must love him!" And I raised my eyes to her in sudden shock, for the notion than anyone might not love Archibald once he had given his love had never before occurred to me. "He loves you! I know he does!"

Ethela nodded again, "It is true." She sighed. "And yet our pathways do not run alongside each other at present. So it must be."

I peered through tear-blurred eyes and, although the stable light was dim, I saw sadness and pain on my sister's face. I recollected that her decision was not divided from Archibald's own vow to begin his quest. How could I speak to her accusingly thus? What would the Lady Leoba think of her honoured scholar were she to hear me? I reached out my arms to Ethela.

"Oh, sister, I am shamed. Forgive me."

And she put her arms around me.

The following morning, I watched Ethela ride away with the mission, my own bow and quiver of arrows over her shoulder. "You will need to be well armed," I had said. "This bow will serve you well." She had thanked me, and turned her face to the north. She had many companions: strong, armed holy men who were skilled in defence, and four of their wives. They took with them all that might be needed to make a new holy dwelling-place: sacks of grain and building tools and cooking pots and some few precious holy texts.

I was myself to lead the Beornwine women back to our own country, although three mounted huscarle had been sent from the Lord Wulfirth to escort us. I harnessed Dancer and stowed my javelins and shield at her side. She stamped her foot and nuzzled at me in a distracting way that yet made me laugh. "Yes, my sweetheart!" I said, "We are riding again this day!" And Dancer skipped and shied with excitement. I weighed Ethela's bow in my hand. It was lighter than I was used to, but would serve me well enough for a short journey when neither hunting nor battle were likely. I would get a new one for myself as soon as I could.

I went to make my last farewell to the Lady Leoba, and she brought me to her own quarters so that we could talk privately.

"I thank you, my beloved Lady," I said, "This time at the School I shall always remember."

She looked at me quizzically, taking in my travelling gear and the quiver-belt already slung about my shoulders, her glance finally resting in my hair that I had plaited with a red ribbon. At this, I blushed, and she laughed gently.

"You are eager to meet with your lover once more?"

"We are going to ride to quest together."

"It is indeed a blessing for two who love each other to find a shared quest." The smile faded from her face and she gazed at me earnestly. "You are a very fine scholar, Edith. Indeed I would have asked you to come and work beside me at Holywell, had I believed that was right for you. You are a proven warrior also. But you are a young woman and I do not think your way is yet set. Perhaps you will marry Kyneth Wulfson. He is a man who likely deserves such a woman as you might become."

I guessed she had spoken with Mother Werberga of me and Kyneth. But I'd had my fill of discussion of my future. I wanted to see no further ahead than a swift ride home and the sight of my beloved Kyneth. Leoba embraced me, gave me a sealed letter for Mother Werberga and another for Father David, and we walked out into the day that would take me home by its end, for we would travel quickly, having no slow carts or oxen in our company and all riding on horseback.

44

Kyneth's Tun

Eager to reach our journey's end, we stayed only a little time with Mother Werberga. I only dismounted to embrace her and deliver Leoba's letter.

She looked at my face and touched the red ribbon at my brow. "Do not wait, child," she said. "But come to see me soon, and we will take a cordial together."

"I shall indeed!" I said, feeling guilty but grateful to be released from my guest-duty, which obliged me to stay and drink with her.

She noticed the moonstone on the cord around my neck, and she smiled and held it in her dry old hand for a moment. "Go to him," she said. "Be happy."

I felt much discomforted to think that my desire was emblazoned upon my face so clearly, especially as I was leading the guard on our journey back to Beornwine. But I kissed my old friend again and mounted Dancer. My horse was as fresh as if she was just out of the stable; the day's journey seemed not to have touched her at all. When she saw the pasture-field before the gates of Beornwine, she seemed to know my heart as well as Mother Werberga had, and I was hard-pressed to hold her back from a wild gallop.

They all met us there on the pasture-field. Even the old Chief Wulfred was there, carried in a seat, for he was old and much infirm. His wife Mordeth, little better than he in health, sat beside him, and I felt the honour that they had bestowed upon us, to take the trouble to meet us outside the gates. But they seemed to enjoy the occasion, and I hurried first to where they sat, taking their hands which were reached out to me in well-come. The Lord Wulfirth and Lady Cwena were there beside, with their family and household; and next to them were Father, Elanor, Hereward and Fritha, Alvar and Alice and all their children. I did not see Archibald, and I guessed he was on duty, as I did not believe he would leave for his quest without bidding me farewell. I saw Siric; I saw Aldyth and Gytha with a baby in her arms; I saw nearly everyone I knew from Beornwine, even our old adversary Jeneth Brown stood in the crowd, his arm around a young woman, although he scowled in his usual way when he caught my eye.

And I saw Kyneth, there among his family, but I could not approach him. His absence from me had endowed him with a radiance in my mind that no human man could easily wear, and now his slim figure and honest face seemed no more than commonly beautiful to me. His smile was one of welcome and friendliness, but I could do no more than smile awkwardly and nod in his direction when I dismounted. After all, I did not wish to throw myself into his arms and be stared at by all the company. Unaccountably, I felt tired and disappointed.

Elanor hurried to me with smiles and kisses, whereupon tears sprang into my eyes and I almost fell as I put my arms around her. "Where is Archibald," I said, "Is he on duty?"

"Archibald is indeed on duty," she said, "And now, my dear child, you are tired from your journey. Come now to Siric's house and rest."

I let her lead me into the house, not looking around me at anyone. Some of them may have been disappointed, but there were other young women to welcome home, not least the beautiful Rhian who had now left off her willow withies. I sobbed for a minute or two on Elanor's breast, and then dried my eyes. She was looking at me in kindly puzzlement. "What is it, dear one?" she said.

"I do not know – only that everyone expects me to do one thing or another," I said. "But I do not wish to decide at all. Might I not just be home and happy and ordinary for a little while."

"Well, of course," she smiled brightly. "That is all I wish of you for the present." She wiped the last traces of tears from my face with the hem of her dress. "A little feast has been prepared for you and the other young women, here at Beornwine. But if you wish to go straight home, then so you shall."

"A feast?" I asked, snuffling into a hand-cloth and wondering if my nose was very red.

"Yes. Roasted meats and cakes, and the Ufer Hall minstrel is to play."

I began to feel a little hungry and to have other concerns also. "But I am in my travel-clothes," I complained.

"Feast-robes have been brought for all of you, and I have here a new dress that I have been making for you in these moons while you were away at the Abbey. Will you not see it?"

It was a good feast. With Elanor's help, I was wearing a dress of the finest wool, dyed yellow and embroidered with blue, and she had re-plaited the red ribbon in my hair. I tucked under my dress the stained pouch with the spear-tip and herbs, but I wore the moonstone prominently in the middle of a string of beads across my shoulders. My eyes were recovered from my bout of weeping, and I felt quite queenly in my new dress.

A few speeches were made by the kins-people of the young women who had been away at the School. I was made much of for my scholarly work and also for the story of my battle-fight.

One of my sweetest memories of the feast that evening was when little Eldric Hereson led his parents by the hand to see me. Both Hereward and Fritha had tears in their eyes as they thanked me for the life of their son. But I could not take too much gratitude. "Our boy is like to be a great warrior!" I said, turning their attention to their son, which was easily done - as is the case with any parents. "I hope he has been practising with the bow whilst I have been away?"

"I have!" he said. "Come and see me now, Edith. Come! Let me show you!"

But it was decided that the day was coming dark and there were too many people about for anyone to be safely shooting arrows nearby. So I promised to watch him at his archery one day very soon, and he contented himself with playing a game of chase with his friends.

At first I had avoided coming close to Kyneth, and it had been easy, for all my family wanted to speak with me, and then there was the feasting and speeches and story-telling. But at last I found my eyes seeking for him, and he immediately came to me. His eyes were large in the firelight as he took my hand. At once - at the simple touch of his hand - all my disappointment and discomfiture left me. The veil of ordinariness that seemed to have descended upon him at my return lifted once more and I saw his true nobility and beauty. I remembered how he was honoured and respected, how he was loved by my own brother Archibald even before I knew him; I remembered his gifts of vision and creation, the reports of his valour in battle; his quiet dignity: And the knowledge that he was sitting before me with my hand in his, looking with such love and pain into my eyes, was hardly to be born.

"Do you not love me anymore Edith?" he said softly. "Now that you are such an honoured lady, do you not want your old Kyneth?" There was not any tone of blame in his voice, only a little rueful smile on his face. And I could only wonder how it was that this first young man in our country, whom any woman would take to her heart in an instant, could love me, little Edith Fly, who was chased away from her early home by those who thought her very life an evil deed. However it had come about, this good and noble man loved me and, though I did not deserve him, I could not purposely cause him any pain. I caught hold of his hand with both of mine and poured kisses and tears upon it.

"I do, I do!" I cried. "Forgive me dearest. I was tired and bewildered when I returned, so strange and long has been our time apart."

His own eyes shone with unshed tears for a moment, but then he pulled me to my feet, for the minstrel was playing *Under the Moon,* a lively tune for lovers, and we danced hand-in-hand with many other young folk and old. Afterwards, we found a good seat together against the side of Siric's house and I went and brought meat and cakes and ale for him, and we sat together again.

He told me of his work whilst I had been away. "It is all complete now," he said. "The tun is ready, ploughed and set for an autumn planting, and the house is built. Will you come and see it tomorrow? Or will you be too wearied after today's ride?"

"I long to see your house finished!" I cried, "And I am not wearied! It was lack of action that wearied me at the Holywell Abbey. I should be glad of another good ride tomorrow, and so will Dancer. I want to visit Father David first, and I have a letter for him from my Lady. Shall I come to you at our normal time?"

"Let us travel together. I shall spend this night with my family here at my grandfather's house. I could come to your father's house at day-break and we can see Father David at Ufer Hall and then ride on to my tun together."

"Yes, let us travel together." I agreed happily. He kissed me then, very gently, as though he feared my lips might reject the touch of his own. And I think you might guess that there was no such rejection in me, but that I kissed him back, and thus we stayed in each other's arms for a full long time, until the night was old and the fires burned low and my family took me out of his arms and home to my own bed.

As I gazed the next morning on Kyneth's tun, I found it hard to believe so much work had been done in the space of a couple of moons. Where the flat stone base had been, there rose a fine long hall of large proportions with many shutters in its sides and a good-sized threshold facing the direction of the rising sun. There were stables, a great oven, a forge and other out-buildings with, between them, the stone-set homeyard. I noticed cooking smoke beginning to darken the new thatch of the house roof and, as Kyneth viewed the scene, he nodded with satisfaction.

"It is as I ordered," he said. "My people have made a well-come for us." He turned to me and I was overcome by the brilliance of his glance. "Come!" he said, "Let us race!"

He set his horse to gallop, and I too gave Dancer the signal to run. But it was my desire to arrive at Kyneth's house after him, and Dancer knew my mind. Thus it was that her hooves rattled onto the stones of the fine new homeyard only after Kyneth's own horse was already at rest there. And thus it was that, by the time I arrived, Kyneth had already dismounted and was standing ready to help me jump down from my horse. Now, I had never needed help in jumping from a horse since I was an infant, and Kyneth knew this well. Yet I found it easy now to allow his strong hands and arms to take my weight, and we laughed into each other's faces as he set me on my feet for the first time on that stone yard.

Several bonds-people - some of whom I knew from the Wulfirth and Wulfred households - were waiting in the yard, arrested in their work at our arrival.

"Well-come Lord Kyneth and Lady Edith!" one of them called, and came forward to take our horses. This was a big, deep-voiced man in the dress of a huscarle, but with earth-soil on his hands. "We have been planting this morning, Lord," he said. "By my reckoning, we should have an early harvest of kale and leeks after the winter, for that sloping field faces the sun and will be sheltered from the coldest winds."

"This is Heron Freeman," said Kyneth to me. "He is of my father's huscarle, but has a love of husbandry. He has been as eager to see the new tun turned to good use as I myself, And I have known him full partial to a dish of spring kale with new butter!"

He gave Heron Freeman a friendly slap on the shoulder and everyone laughed together. I could see that they all thought well of Kyneth, for their eyes followed him with the loyal warmth that cannot be forced or bought from any servant, slave or bondsman, but only earned by respect and kindness. Kyneth then brought me to a stone well-head, set near to the house. "We have had great luck with the well," he said. "It has yielded abundantly all through these dry summer weeks, and promises to serve both household and land in the future."

He pulled up a bucket and brought me a cup of pure, cold water to drink, then he brought me into the house. We entered through the threshold, which was full spacious and airy, big enough to hold a small feast within. From there, we came into the house. Shutters were open to the light and I saw a long hall room with a great fire-place in the centre with a Hereward-funnel above it, to carry the smoke away from the living and sleeping areas up to the roof. There was a further funnelled fire-place near the far end, with a table-board set up nearby laid with hot cooked meat, roots and leeks for our dinner. All sat around the table on logs, for no proper benches were yet made, and we made a merry meal of it, like a group of friends at a picnic, for Kyneth never held with the ways of rank and ceremony.

I spent the rest of the day in that company, giving praise to all that Kyneth had made. There were separate sleeping-chambers above the house, with space for storage in a further loft area. Beyond the food preparation area in the house was another chamber with shutters to bring in plenty of light.

"I thought this like to be a chapel," said Kyneth, "And perhaps a study area."

"It is as large and fine as the one at the Women's School!" I declared. "And better than the one at your father's house."

"I am glad it pleases you," he smiled, "For I made it with you in my mind."

45

With the Huscarle

"Will Archibald be here this eve?" I asked, "I long to see him." We were on our way back to Ufer Hall, from where I would ride on to Flytun.

Kyneth moved his horse nearer to me and touched my arm. "He has gone," he said

I knew at once that he meant Archibald was gone to quest, and I was immediately astonished and hurt, both at Archibald leaving without waiting to see me, and at Kyneth never mentioning anything about it to me, though we had spent the whole day together. I stared at him, my face stiff with anger. "Why did you not tell me?" I said.

"I feared to spoil the happiness of this day, so I waited. I meant to tell you now."

"You meant to tell me now?" I echoed. "But had I not asked, would you have told me? Would anyone have told me what is evidently known to every soul at Ufer and Beornwine except Archibald's sister?"

"I would," said Kyneth calmly. "This is the time I chose to tell you. Had you asked me earlier, I would have spoken to you of him, but you did not ask." His plain, honest way of answering me disarmed the challenge of my rage, but could not soothe my hurt.

"I did not ask because I was told he was on duty," I said, my voice rough with the effort of keeping back tears.

"It is so; he is on duty. It was at my father's order that he rode away." Kyneth put his hand into his tunic and took out a small, folded parchment, tied with cord. "He charged me with this to give to you." He held it out to me and I took it out of his hand.

Archibald was a fair enough scholar, but I could see at once that his scribing-hand was much finer than formerly. I judged he had been studying, perhaps with Ethela, since his time at Ufer Hall, although he had not spoken to me of this. This was another aspect to my brother's life that I had known nothing of, and bitterness pressed my heart, but only lightly, for I had learned at least some humility in my time at Holywell.

Now I was eager to read his message. I straightened out the stiff parchment.

Edith, my dear sister. I am writing this as I get ready to leave for the east. I spoke to my Lord Wulfirth of my quest, and he – my most generous Lord – speeds me in my own search by making it his also. He gives me good companions, arms and leave to stay away until my quest is fulfilled. I am to return with news for him of the Mercian state of arms and defense.

Edith, sister of my heart, I ride now for our mother, and for you. I hope to return in time for your wedding. If I do not, then remember I will be with you in spirit on that happy day.

If there is any weakness in my resolve, it is to face you as I depart. So I make my farewell by these written words and leave with you, by their shape, the love of your faithful brother

Archibald

"So he has gone." I spoke really to myself, but Kyneth answered me.

"He spoke to me of it, for we are like brothers." He looked as though he might be afraid that I would retort with anger, but my feelings were too deep and manifold for any speech.

"He opened his heart to me on this subject because he knew of my love for you." Kyneth continued, "He knew he could trust me thus. He is afraid that, if he does not take this action, then you will ride away without help or guard. He cannot support his fear for you, and so he has gone."

I nodded, for it was the easiest thing in the world for me to understand – that Archibald would act to protect me. Now Kyneth leaned forward on his horse, so that he was looking up into my eyes.

"By this, Archibald releases you from your own quest vow," Kyneth's eyes were soft and beautiful as he spoke, "If that is your wish, Edith."

Can anyone be released from such a vow by the will of another? No, that can never be. I knew it then, but, looking into Kyneth's eyes and once again feeling my own unworthiness in the face of this fine and noble man, I was overcome. I could not answer him with my true mind. I only said:

"I should not be without help or guard if I rode with you," and I managed a wan smile, for Kyneth looked so happy; I could not pain him.

"And we ride well together, do we not?" He smiled. "Come, dearest, I shall return with you now to your father's house."

We galloped our horses a while, and I did not let Kyneth win the race. Then, cheered by action, we rode side by side and he told me of his plans for the Lord Wulfirth's new hall. "It shall be twice the size that it is now," he said, "with a raised floor of wooden planks, and a private chamber for my mother, as well as a separate chapel. It will be as you advised, finer than my own house, and when it is built, I shall make another for your father."

"What great plans you have!" I exclaimed.

He slowed his horse and took my hand, "I had many plans for my future," he said. "Now I want only to spend the rest of my life beside you." This was a signal for a kiss, and for a great surge of happiness within me, for what could he mean but that he *would* ride to quest with me? It seemed certain, yet neither of us spoke of it directly; I simply leaned over for his kiss. Indeed, Kyneth and I were becoming quite skilled in kissing on horseback.

In time, we resumed our journey and Kyneth spoke again of his building plans.

"You will have much work to do," I said.

"By my reckoning, all shall be ready by next summer's Grain Rite. My father has given me leave from military service to give my attention to it."

I nodded thoughtfully, "But you will want to spend some time at warrior-training," I advised. "I myself feel a weakness in my throwing arm through lack of practice for these two moons when I did nothing but study and scribe, and I fear my skill at archery has suffered also. I am stiff now from only two days' riding. I need to return to my practice or I will lose my skill, and I think you will find the same, should you neglect it through your work."

"We can train together every day if it pleases you," he said, his eyes so tender that I felt he would do anything at my bidding. Indeed, his words cheered me greatly.

"It does please me!" and I gave him my best smile.

"Then come to me at Ufer Hall in the mornings. We can train together with the huscarle before I begin work."

I paused, gazing at his face to discover the truth of his words, for it was one of my dearest wishes to take real training with a band of warriors. "With the huscarle?" I asked softly.

"Yes, I shall charge Eben Freeborne to make a plan of training for you, and we shall ride together every day, for I shall come to your father's house in the mornings and bring you home also."

Eben Freeborne, Ethela's father, was Lord Wulfirth's mounted huscarle captain, who had many battle-honours. "I know Eben Freeborne's daughter," I said, "I think he will be sorry that she left this country with the Abbey mission to make a holy house in the north."

Kyneth nodded, "But she shall be well guarded, I believe."

I reflected that Ethela had ridden away to more adventure than was allowed to me, but that she carried in her blood some of the valour of her father Eben.

Thus it was that I accepted Archibald had left on his quest. And thus it was I went to bed that night the happiest of women. For Kyneth loved me indeed, and Kyneth planned for us to train in the warrior arts together. And why should he do this unless he believed – as I did – that we would ride to quest together when his work at Ufer and Flytun was finished?

It was as my true love had promised. Every morning if it did not rain – and sometimes when it did – he would come to our house at sunrise. Oft-times I was ready for him, and would meet him on the road. We would kiss and then ride together to Ufer Hall, often galloping our horses side by side; we took a pride in our skill and I thought there were no two warriors in the world who rode so much in accord, except for my brothers HestanandGodwine.

The Lord Wulfirth's huscarle was a great force of an hundred or more men. At times of war, this number would be swollen by my own father's warrior bondsmen and many more from Beornwine. Wulfirth took a care to train all other men in his household and that of his father, Chief Wulfred, as well as any other of suitable age from all the lands under his order, so that they would be a fighting force to be reckoned with whenever they were needed. I was used to seeing training going on at the Ufer Hall fields at any time of year.

I had never myself been into the training fields and it was a thrill to me when Kyneth led me in there for the first time. A band of about twenty men were marching with their spears; shields painted in vivid colours; and bags full of heavy stones, which could be valuable weapons in their own right, fired from leathern slings. Some of the men called out in a friendly and respectful way to Kyneth, who returned their greeting cordially. I recognised several youths from Beornwine and, among them, my old adversary, Jeneth Brown, who was grown tall and heavy of limb. I nodded to him, but he only stared darkly, not choosing to scowl at me as he was used to when my connections were less powerful. He seemed to have kept a resentment for my family far stronger than was deserved by a boyish fight long ago.

Instructing a group of riders at the far side of the field was a strong-looking man in battle-dress, mounted on a dappled grey charger.

"That is Eben Freeborne," said Kyneth. "Come, I'll bring you to him."

I felt discomfited, but Eben Freeborn was full kindly, bowing his head quickly and then clasping my sword-arm as no-one had ever done since my child-games with my brother Archibald. I felt both honoured and unworthy of such a tribute.

"I've heard of your valiant actions on the road to Holywell, Lady," he said. "It will be a privilege to have you at my order."

I flushed and felt still more unworthy, knowing my success at saving my nephew had more of instinct and luck to it than valour. But I had no time to be either modest or conceited, for he ordered Kyneth and me to arm ourselves and join the other riders straight away.

I spent most of that day in riding to form and learning how to avoid taking off my own comrades' heads whilst attacking enemies with the sword from horseback. It was a wonderful day for me and, although my arm ached from wielding my borrowed sword, I rode home a perfectly happy girl.

Eben Freeborne was a fine man, full wise in all warrior arts. He was of average height but broad of shoulder and arm and a fine example to all the men under his orders, carrying arms at all times and dressing always ready for battle in a thick leathern breast-plate. He wore his hair shorn at the shoulder with a wide fringe over his forehead so that his eyes should have a clear view. Many of the huscarle copied this style and it was a mark of their respect for him that they did so. He was fierce and strict, but I never knew him cruel in act or word. He was most kind to me, making sure to guard me from the roughest of the huscarle in the practise tests. But he soon understood that I had no wish to be treated differently, although I had not the strength of a big man. Still he kept me beside him and thus I had the fortune of learning tricks and arts of mounted fighting from a renowned warrior and great teacher. I saw in him some of the patience of his daughter, although he had the skill and valour of a great fighting captain. I came to see how it might be to have a father who encouraged and respected me in my ambitions. And yet I did not envy Ethela; I did not envy any woman, for I thought none could be so happy or as fortunate as I.

Many times I kept to the training for the whole day. I had much to learn, for fighting alongside others was far unlike the simple, individual practises of sword-play, spear-action and archery. There were complex moves to learn, all governed by the various notes of the sounding-horn, which was like learning a new language in itself. I loved it.

Often, Kyneth was not able to join me for the training, for he had the responsibilities of his work. But when I had finished, I always went to find him and he would show me how the new hall was progressing. Then he would nearly always ride home with me. It was the best time of the day for me, and I believed for him also, for we loved each other. I truly believe that this was the happiest and most carefree time of my life. But that time could not last for very long, because however long and stubbornly I turned my face away from thoughts of my future, yet that future rode towards me on fast galloping hooves, and I could not hide or run from it.

I loved my training, going at it as a hungry dog to his dinner – as if I could never get enough. I believe I learned quickly and my arms-master, Eben Freeborne, seemed satisfied with my progress at arms, both on foot and mounted. After a time, he agreed to allow me to compete in a test with some of the younger boys. For some time we had been practicing swordsmanship, and I loved my borrowed sword that Eben had chosen for me from the Ufer Hall arms-store. I did well in the tests, for most of the boys I was set against were younger than I.

"It is not right," I complained to Eben after easily despatching five boys from the test with a simple balance of sword and shield – not even cracking a shield but simply knocking most of them over.

He nodded slowly, "You are far more skilled than the others," he agreed.

"Then put me against men of my own age. Already I have killed a man in battle. Is it fair I should be set against boys? How shall I improve my skills if I never work hard to overcome an opponent? "

He nodded again, then looked me straight in the eyes. "I cannot, Lady," he said. "You are too precious to the Lord Kyneth."

"But Kyneth *wants* me to train! How can we ride together to quest if I am not as able as he? I might be called upon to save his life!"

Eben looked down at his feet, then up at me and then down again. He cleared his throat. "You are most able, Lady Edith, but I cannot put to you test against one who might injure you. I cannot."

I threw my hands up in frustration and made some wordless cry that may have expressed my feelings. But now my master gave me a steely look that shamed me.

"Forgive me Sir," I said, immediately bowing, with my sheathed sword across my hands in the gesture of submission we had been taught, knowing that a warrior's first lesson was to follow orders and submit to the greater wisdom of his master. But I resolved to speak to Kyneth about the subject. He had not come yet to training, and the day was closing, so I mounted Dancer and went to meet him at the site of the new hall. He must have seen me ride into the courtyard, because there he was, striding towards me as I dismounted.

"Edith! Dear one, come and see; it is finished!"

The new Ufer Hall stood next to the old, but was half again as big, with a threshold the size of the Chief's house at Beornwine. Around the outside walls, bands of iron were nailed between the posts. Kyneth pointed out that this was a style of strengthening buildings from attack which he had seen at the King's court and the houses of other great Lords. "It was a costly business," he said, "But Father wanted it."

Inside, the house-base was raised with plank-flooring, with a great fire-pit lined with stone in the centre. Turf-filled wooden benches lined the walls and a wide stair led up to a high loft.

The Lady Cwena was there, directing the setting up of the great table-board which was in the process of being moved from the old hall. She looked up in an agitated way as we entered and I concluded it was not the best time for a visitor to appear in her new home, but she straightened her skirt and approached me with her hands out in formal welcome.

"God's-day, Edith" she said in the cold way she often used, and her eyes swept down my body, taking in my riding-gear. I felt myself blush and was only glad that I had left my bow and weapons outside. It was a mistake thus to walk into the new house as I had into the one Kyneth had made for himself.

"Forgive me, my Lady," I said, "I did not know you were here."

"And why should I not be in my own house?" she asked in a way that made me squirm.

"I urged Edith to come Mother," said Kyneth, "For she has been much interested in my building work ever since I began the work at the tun."

She turned her cold glance on Kyneth. "It is not for you to urge Edith to enter my house without my leave."

I was more than surprised to hear the Lady Cwena speaking thus to her own son who had constructed this magnificent house for her. I felt my eyes stretching in astonishment and could only cast my gaze at the floor.

"Perhaps she might return at a more fitting time," Kyneth murmured.

"She *might* return, should she be invited." The Lady Cwena's voice was bitter, and at once I pitied her, knowing that her formal manners did not allow such discourtesy and that she would regret it before she saw me again. Now she turned to two bondsmen who had carried in a large carved chest and were setting it down against the wall. "Not there, fools!" she screamed.

Kyneth took my arm and brought me outside. He raised his hand to his forehead and closed his eyes for a moment. I put my hand gently on his arm. "It is a magnificent hall," I said.

He gave me a grateful smile. "All that is needed now is for the old hall to be dismantled. Some of the old timbers are in good condition and can be re-used for grain-stores or other out-buildings. Then, next spring, I shall work on your father's new house.

We fetched our horses and took our well-known road back to Flytun. I knew it was not a time to speak to him about Eben's refusal to put me to test, so I did not speak, but went through in my mind the sword-actions we had been practising that day. After a little while, Kyneth spoke:

"My mother sometimes finds the responsibilities of the household a trial. She is more often very quiet, but is sometimes driven to anger for mysterious reasons." He shook his head in bewilderment. "I think it would be good for her to ride out more often, but she rarely does so, unless Father be with her."

I nodded, but could not answer him. He seemed not to know of his father's old direction that Cwena should not ride beyond the Ufer courtyard without his own escort or order. I wondered, not for the first time, whether Kyneth knew of his mother's elopement and the terrible night of her return, which was a dreadful childhood memory for me. Kyneth was already living at the King's Court at that time. I closed my eyes against the horrible vision of my poor Rob of Dale with his throat cut and his harp broken about his head.

"I have hopes that you might be friends and visit with each other after we are wed."

At first, I did not think I had heard him properly. I shook my head and said, "I did not hear you Kyn."

"After we are wed – I hope you and Mother might be friends, and visit with each other."

I smiled and nodded, but now I could not mistake him. Some deep pit opened inside me. It touched on the uncertainties that had been itching at my mind lately, losing me sleep, and it allowed me to see what they were. I loved Kyneth and wanted to marry him, but it had been my belief that he would ride to quest with me after we were wed. Now I could no longer remember when he had agreed to that. I had been happy when he proposed that we should have warrior training together, but the truth was that he rarely joined the training himself. I had told myself that his work did not allow him the time, and that anyway he was already a trained warrior. But the advice I gave him about practice was not a whim of my own; it was well known that a warrior needed to practise regularly with sword and bow, javelin and shield if he were not to lose his skill. Even my father still practised every day when he was not hunting: there being no finer training for battle than hunting. Kyneth never hunted.

I had put it from my mind, but now I remembered the concern of Mother Werberga and my Lady Leoba. I had believed that I could have Kyneth and also fulfil my ambition to ride to quest. Was it possible that I might have to choose? I rode close to him and took his hand. Straight away he raised my hand to his lips.

"I would not be an ordinary kind of wife," I said.

"You are never ordinary," he answered me, "But you are the only wife I would ever want."

"I am more of a warrior than a wife."

"What do I care? I respect and admire you for what you are. You can ride to visit my mother in full armour with a pack of war-dogs at your feet if you wish it – although I doubt even they would protect you from her wrath if you caught her on a bad day!" He laughed and yet I could not answer him, for it seemed he did not think my interest in arms and pride at my skill with the bow was anything more than a hobby, and I reflected that his mother did indeed practise archery herself. He looked into my eyes, no doubt noticing my pensive expression. "I love you," he said, kissing my hand again, "Do you think my love has bounds or conditions Edith?"

He leaned towards me for a kiss, which we had learned to do easily as we rode, our horses keeping pace, step for step, with each other. But even as I kissed him, I had the terrible, disloyal fear that my own love for Kyneth might itself be conditional.

46

Jeneth Brown

After that talk with Kyneth, I somehow never mentioned to him the subject of my being allowed to enter proper warrior tests with youths of my own age. It felt wrong and somehow humiliating to have to ask him and, when we were alone, I could not find the words. Yet the words would spring clear to my head when I was far from him, or when there were others with us whom I did not wish to hear me. So I did not speak, and I was not allowed to have any part in the testings, in which I saw men triumph whom I reckoned I could beat. However, it happened that I was to be put to a test, one unplanned and more dangerous than any watched over by my master of arms at the Ufer Hall training-grounds.

The weather came in cold and wet. It seemed more like late winter than early autumn and it rained so hard that leaves were torn from the trees before they were ready, and crops for spring harvest could not be planted in the heavy soil. One morning, when a three-day rain had ceased for a spell, hating to miss my warrior-training, I took Dancer out on the road to Ufer. We had only gone a few paces beyond our guard-gate when I had to turn her home, for she was up to the hocks in mud and I guessed Eben would not train any horse in such conditions. Besides, Dancer was likely to be exhausted before we arrived. I put her into the paddock that had rails laid across one corner so that the horses could stand without their feet in mud. But I was disconsolate and wanted exercise; I put on some old boots, wrapped straws around my legs to keep out the worst of the mud, and set out to walk to Mother Werberga with a gift of fire-wood on my back.

I had gone beyond Flytun and was passing a small wood to the south of Hereward and Fritha's land when I felt a great blow to my head and fell heavily to the ground.

It was only a moment or two that I lay stunned and, even before I could will my body to move, I knew I had been attacked: someone had hurled a stone at me. I remembered Eben Freeborne's counsel, similar to my own father's words of advice to his sons: *Never believe an enemy will cease attacking once they have begun. Act immediately.* I was alone, stunned and hampered by the pack of fire-wood on my back, yet instinct or training bade me move myself. I scrambled to my knees, crouching with the firewood at my back to afford some protection while I unhooked the straps that bound it to my back. Another big stone clipped my ear, but I was free. I tried to look around, but I was half blinded by blood pouring over my face from a scalp-wound. I dashed the blood from my eyes and saw that my enemy was one man alone, and I knew him immediately. It was Jeneth Brown and he was striding towards me on his long legs, hurling great stones with a sling-shot from the leathern bag at his waist. For a moment I thought that he had mistaken me for some foreign raider, and I called out to him:

"Jeneth Brown, I am Edith Fly. Do you not know me?"

There was plain hatred in his face as he answered me. "I know thee, bitch! I know thee for a woman who thinks herself a warrior." He sneered. "But see how you fare now without your vicious father and cowardly brothers to run to. See how you fare now – filthy witch."

His insults for my family did not touch me – they were so laughably untrue. The word *witch* might have threatened me with old fears, but I knew enough not to give mind to the taunts of enemies. It was clear to me that Jeneth Brown intended to kill me. He was attacking me deliberately, and must know he would be punished severely if I lived to report it to Father or Kyneth. I guessed he had seen me walking alone and followed me. I did not waste time cursing myself for coming out without horse or dog or any arms save my old household knife. I ran.

I ran like a hare, acrossways and back, losing my boots in moments and glad of it, for they hampered my progress. I used hands as well as feet to help me move through the wet, heavy ground, stopping and then taking off again in a different direction to confuse my enemy. I did not run away from Brown, but towards him, guessing he would be faster than me over any ground: therefore I would have somehow to fight him if I was to survive. He was slinging stones at a steady rate, most of them missing me, for he did not seem to realise at first that I was moving towards him, and therefore his aim was not true. Then I heard him cry out in rage and saw him coming to meet me, a rock in one hand and the other fumbling at the knife in his belt. None of my training thus far had prepared me for hand-to-hand combat in these circumstances; I knew only to make use of whatever I could, and I made sure that my own little knife was in my hand, with the staying-cord secure around my wrist. Thus, I came to face my enemy.

As we closed upon each other, his foot slid into a mass of wet leaves and he stumbled and slipped, dropping his weapons. With my crouching gait – arms and legs still working to speed me over the muddy ground – I reached him before he righted himself. Taking up the stone he had dropped and, putting my full weight behind it, I struck him on the side of the head. He gave out a groan and fell to the ground with me on top of him. He must have been stunned, but he rolled himself on top of me, got his two big hands around my neck and began to squeeze the life out of me. I was shocked and appalled by his strength, but I gave no regret to my diminishing existence, only resolving to use what life I had left to kill Jeneth Brown. I could not move for his weight upon me; his grip was agonising and stifling, yet my little knife was still in my hand; with what strength I had left, I thrust it upward. Immediately the terrible pressure around my neck was released, but I kept my grip, pushing the knife further inward. Brown squealed and twisted round, making me loose hold of my knife. It was up to the hilt in his side but still attached to my wrist by the staying-cord. I gripped my other hand to my wrist and wrenched it out of him.

"Ahgh! Bitch!" he cried, clutching one hand to his wound while he swiped at my head with his other fist.

I backed away, gasping for breath but still looking for an opportunity to disable him. His knife was lost in the mud and we were both alike covered in mud. There was blood running from his head and from the wound in his side. I also was again half blinded by the blood over the side of my face. But I took the handle of my knife again in my hand and held it before me. Its blade shone red – tip to hilt – with Jeneth Brown's blood. I saw him gazing at it in horror and disgust as if it were a hornet that he feared would sting him again, and I raised it towards him, letting him see the edge and point of the blade. He gave a cry of revulsion; then he turned and stumbled away.

I did not follow him.

I know not how much time it took me to reach the house of my brother Hereward. I was shivering, my head wound was causing me pain and my injured throat would hardly allow enough air to pass for me to breathe. When I was a little distance away, I saw Fritha out in her homeyard, drawing water from the well. She saw me and stopped. I tried to call out, but could manage no more than a croak from my swollen throat. I sat down, exhausted, but she did not come to me, so I stood again and staggered on. She was staring and it occurred to me that I was a fearsome-looking prospect of mud and blood, stumbling towards her without greeting. Then someone was beside her: it was Eldric. I heard him cry out:

"Mother, it is Edith! It is Edith!"

Then they were running to me, calling for help, and I was soon in the hands of friends, being carried to Fritha's warm hearth.

When the worst of the mud was got off me, it was found that I had many bruises and cuts from Jeneth Brown's stones. The original wound to my scalp was the most troublesome and Mother Werberga was brought to sew it up and heal my bruised throat with spells and poultices.

It was more than a day before word was got to Kyneth of my encounter with Jeneth Brown. Before that my father went out hunting on foot with Hereward, Heath, Alvar and a band of our armed bondsmen. They took dogs and they were hunting a man, although there was little trail to follow, for more heavy rain had erased all marks of blood or footprints. Even so, it was not long before the dogs found Brown lying in a thicket of undergrowth. He was already dead, and his body was taken back to Beornwine. The wound I dealt him must have been more serious than it looked and, besides, he'd had no-one to care for him, for he could not return home after attacking me. I did not like to think of him dying alone, cold and comfortless, yet how could I regret my actions? I myself would have been dead had I not fought him with all my strength and will.

The Chief Wulfred himself came to question me about the killing of Jeneth Brown, for it was a grave matter when one member of our community caused the death of another. He spoke to me kindly and gently and I answered him as best I could in croaks and whispers. He looked at my throat and my other wounds and examined my little house knife.

"They call you warrior-maiden, Edith Fly," he said, "And rightly so, it seems. I remember when your father brought his family to us when you were a tiny thing; even then you would have joined him and your brothers who helped us to rout the raiders on that first day."

"Yet, I did not seek this battle with Brown, Sir," I croaked earnestly.

"Indeed not, indeed not," he said, patting me on the head as though I was still that little girl he spoke of. Even his gentle pat hurt my injured head, but I tried not to wince, for the old Chief meant it kindly.

Mother Werberga watched over me for some days, not allowing me to be taken home or moved from Fritha's hearth, and fiercely forbidding Kyneth or anyone to talk with me for more than a few moments. My spirit was slow to mend the dark wound that came in the knowledge I had taken another human life. Indeed, such scars never fade. My physical hurts, however, quickly began to recover. At last, when Mother Werberga had watched me make a goodly breakfast one morning of bacon with eggs and oatcakes, she said:

"You are lucky, child: you have not taken any fever even though this head wound was deep and dirty."

"There is no luck in it," I said, in a voice that was almost normal. "It is your care that has saved me."

She smiled and shook her head gently, "It bodes well for your future that your body can withstand such injuries."

"Good!" I laughed. "Does that mean I can go home now and ride my horse again?"

My own father brought my horse to me so that I could ride home. The weather had come round dry and windy, so the ground was hard enough for horses to make good way. Father came alone, bringing Dancer at the side of his own steed. Before we left Fritha's house, father turned to me,

"I have something for you, daughter," he said. In his hand was something wrapped in a piece of lambs-fleece. I took it from him and unwrapped it. It was a knife; a full-sized seax-knife in a good sheep-skin scabbard.

"If my daughter is not safe to walk abroad alone, even in my own lands, then she needs a weapon to defend herself," he muttered, and then looked into my eyes. "I know you can use it as well as any man."

I thanked him briefly, but my heart was more full than I could ever express to him. It was not the knife itself – although I was full glad to have such a good one – it was the meaning behind the gift. A seax-blade had meant freedom to me since I was a child, knowing such a blade was the sign and symbol of freemanship as given to my father by his own Lord.

We rode home together. I still felt stupidly weak but glad and proud to be riding beside my father, his sole companion on that short journey. And I could not shake off the notion that he had conferred on me the status of a freeman, although in my heart, I knew it was not so.

47

The Old Chief

Because my father's tun was only a short distance from Beornwine, news naturally reached us there sooner than Ufer Hall. Indeed, Ufer messengers very often stopped at our house on their way, unless they were in the greatest haste, for, although my father was of lower rank than the Lord Wulfirth, yet they called each other 'brother', and what was joy or sadness for the Wulfirth's house was the same for ours.

Thus it was that a messenger came to our gates one morning in the early spring. Our household was breakfasting and Kyneth was with us, but I had finished eating and returned to my room to fetch my weapons. Away from the clatter and babble of breakfast, I heard through my open shutter the sound of horse's hooves. There had been a fort'night without rain and someone was taking advantage of the firm ground and galloping at speed. I peered out of my shutter and saw a rider in the colours of the Chief Wulfred, making for our gate. In moments I was out of my room and down the stair:

"Messenger!" I called as I headed out of the door, closely followed by most of our household.

It was Orworth, an armed bondsman of Chief Wulfred's household, whom I knew from huscarle training. He did not dismount, but called grimly over my head to my father who was close behind me:

"The Chief has taken a fever. He looks close to death. I have to fetch the Lord Wulfirth."

Kyneth called out, "Orworth! Tell my father I shall go now to Beornwine. I'll see him there!"

"Yes, Lord."

Elanor said, "Has Mother Werberga been called?"

"Yes, Lady," answered Orworth. "She has been with him this night. It is she who sends me now. I cannot wait." He turned his horse to make away, but my father shouted:

"Stop! My daughter's horse runs faster than any in this country. Let her take your message."

"If she passes me, Lord, that is all to the good," Orworth called over his shoulder, "There is no more message than this – that Wulfirth must come in all haste."

He was gone, but someone was already fetching and harnessing my horse. Quickly I embraced Kyneth. His face was pale, for I knew he loved his grandfather, the old Chief, well. He grasped my hand, "Come to me at Beornwine," he said.

"I'll be there by noon."

Dancer loved to run and it was not often I gave her full leave to gallop headlong, for fear she might fall and seriously injure herself. But this day I put such concerns away and Dancer sped along joyfully. It was not long before I overtook Orworth, who waved as I passed. Long before the time I would usually arrive, we galloped through the gates of the Ufer Hall courtyard.

I delivered my message and the Lord Wulfirth was on his horse and about to leave with a band of his mounted huscarle by the time Orworth arrived. Wulfirth questioned him shortly, bade both of us take refreshment and stable our horses, and was gone.

I did not wait long, only making sure that Dancer was rested, fed and watered before riding back to Beornwine. Orworth rode with me, much concerned for his Lord. We did not stop long at Flytun, where we found most of my family already gone. As we approached Beornwine it was almost like a feast-day, so many people were arriving there from the surrounding farms and tuns as the news spread. Enquiring quickly, we were told that the Chief still lived, but that he was failing.

I got down at Siric's house where my horse was taken by the stable-keeper. "All the stable space has gone, Lady," he said, knowing me and Dancer well, "I'll tether her outside with some good hay to eat."

"Thanks," I said, "She will need water too. I have ridden her hard already this morning." I slapped my horse lightly on the shoulder and entered the house. Aldyth was there, busily serving hot draughts and ale to the many travellers; I rolled up my sleeves and helped her.

"What is the Chief's fever?" I asked, standing next to her at the board, pouring beakers of ale.

"I know not," she said, "but it struck quickly, for I saw him yesterday. I was fetching water from the well and he stopped and spoke to me kindly, as he always does." Her voice caught and we met each other's eyes sadly. The Chief seemed to have been old for all of our lives, yet he was always a kindly man, like a grand-father to us.

"He will rally," I said, without conviction.

"I think not."

"Mother Werberga is with him, is she not? She knows powerful herb mixtures. They cured Eldric of the wet fever when he was an infant."

"But she herself is not hopeful. I heard her say so when I went to the Chief's house with a jar of mead for Lady Mordeth just before you arrived."

We were both silent and still for a moment, but then Alice and Alvar came into the house, and I went to them, embracing Alice, who was much distressed, for she was full fond of her kinsman Chief Wulfred. I had found a seat for her and brought her a small beaker of cordial when I heard my name called out amid the throng in Siric's house.

"Edith. Lady Edith Fly!" It was Orworth, my travelling companion of that morning, who had entered the house and was looking about for me. I went to him at once, with everyone's eyes on me.

"You are wanted," he said. I went with him and he led me quickly to the Chief's house.

Although I had lived in that country for most of my life and spent a good deal of time within the walls of Beornwine, I had very rarely been within Chief Wulfred's house. He held the highest name in our district, yet his house was old-fashioned, with its wall of stone curved against the outer wall of the village. Servants' and other out-houses were built nearby for his bonds-people, but the house had nothing of the fineness of his elder son's seat at Ufer Hall, or, indeed that of his younger son, Alfred, who lived in his wife's country to the far west. It seemed a rather poor living-place, except for the fine painted threshold and the standard bearing his colours of red and green which stood outside the door. It was well known that the house had been there for many life-times, with only the roof and upper walls being changed as wood and thatch rotted down. Wulfred himself had been born there and was said to be most fond of the old place. However, the fact was that everything within the walls of Beornwine belonged to the Chief and the use of any of the houses, wells and stables was at his bidding. It was his benign kindness that gave a sense of freedom to everyone there, but his authority was protected by loyal huscarle and by his powerful son. He and his wife Mordeth made all celebrations in Siric's house, which was spacious and laid out for guests; they rarely invited large parties to the old house. I had only been in there a few times, when I was a child and Elanor had a mind to take me with her when she had been visiting old Mordeth.

Now Orworth quickly ushered me within. The threshold door was low, almost touching my head, and Orworth himself had to bow low to come inside. The sun had been shining brightly outside, and the inside of the Chief's house was so dim that at first I could see nothing. Someone took me by the arm and I heard The Chief Wulfred's voice say weakly, "Ah, it is Edith, the beautiful warrior-maiden."

The one next to me put his arm around me, and I knew it was Kyneth. "Come," he whispered, "He wants to see you."

My eyes were clearing swiftly now. Some light came from the open door, and a small shutter in the wall was also open. More light came from two torches thrust into iron stands near to a low bed where I could see the Chief Wulfirth lying, looking shrunken and pale without his purple robe. Kyneth brought me to the bed-side and there we knelt so that the Chief could see us without having to exert himself. Thus, close, I could see his body quaking with shivers and his face wet with sweat. I noticed now for the first time that Mother Werberga was there beside him. Now she held before his nose a shallow dish of smoking herbs; I was close enough to smell their pungent astringency. It seemed to revive the Chief and he looked at me.

"My grand-son loves you," he said. "That is well. It was a good day that brought Finric Fly and his family to us." He stopped, looking above our heads. Perhaps he sought for my father, who was there in that crowded throng within the dim house, but I think Wulfred's poor old eyes could not see him, and he looked again at me. "I remember you on that day; you wanted to follow the warriors into battle." He gave a little, straight smile but then closed his eyes as a fresh bout of shivering struck him and a new film of sweat covered his face, running into the creases of his skin and dripping into the bed-cloths and sleeping-shift he wore. Mother Werberga brought the smoke-dish towards him, but he shook his head and instead she gently wiped his forehead and face with her own dress-hem.

He did not speak any more to me and he soon raised a weak hand to the Lord Wulfirth, who came to him, and so we moved away from the bed-side to give room to others.

I stayed in that dim and airless place for all that long after-noon and evening and into the night. For most of the time I sat on the floor beside Kyneth, who sometimes quietly stole kisses from me and other favours too that stayed secret easily in the dark, although we were surrounded by other people. I do not believe that either of us felt any disrespect for the Chief Wulfred in taking our joy in each other thus, as he lay dying. Bright, living things need to remember that they have a duty to the gods of life, and to hold to that duty even at the most solemn times. Little children know this well, for they will be active no matter how many customs bid them be still. Kyneth and I had a need to remind ourselves that we had a right to life, even as death approached someone whom we loved and honoured.

I was asleep when death came to the Chief Wulfred. I think I was woken by my love laying my head gently down onto a sheepskin. I opened my eyes and saw his family all standing around the bed, and I knew the time had come. I did not move, but stayed lying in the dark, and it is natural that I thought then of the loved-ones of my own family that had died. Usually, I dreaded to think of my mother's death, because of the darkness of soul that it always brought. Therefore, it was very strange to me, that I found I could no longer visualise the scene of her killing. I knew every moment of it, indeed I would never forget. But I could no longer see it in my mind's eye. Thus, no force of terror crushed down upon my heart. And, thus, for those moments, I had no need of my strong spiritual talisman – my true warrior quest - to strengthen and protect me. As I lay there in the dark, I felt a deep sadness for Chief Wulfred - an old friend passed now. But I felt something else too: not terrifying, but raw and disturbing nonetheless. It stayed in the shadows of my mind, and it was some time before I would allow myself to give it any true notice.

As the news of Chief Wulfred's death became known, all the people within the walls of Beornwine rose from their beds and took torches into the night in his honour. I was glad to be released into the cool, fresh night, so long had I been within that close and smoky house. Kyneth stayed there with his family, just touching my hand in farewell and nodding for me to leave. I went to find Aldyth, who was still in her day-dress, having been kept active with guests wanting food and drink into the night. We took torches each and went outside. Everyone was walking in a great circle widdershins around the inside of the Beornwine walls and then out of the gates and around the outside of the walls also.

"It is like a feast or rite," said Aldyth sadly. "Yet it seems wrong that he, who was at the centre of all our festivals, cannot be here to lead us now."

I nodded and squeezed her hand, but could not speak.

After the procession, the night was coming to its end and I went to a hill between Beornwine and Flytun from whence I could see both places. It had been a cloudy night, but now the sun rose in glory between the land and the edge of night. I watched as the great light dissolved the cloud and warmed the ground. It was going to be a beauteous day. I knew Mother Werberga and many others of the old religion would see this as a tribute to the old Chief and a portent of a great new era, but I felt only sadness for my old friend. Suddenly, there was fear and puzzlement and loneliness in my heart. I wanted Kyneth and Archibald and Ethela and my sisters of the Women's School; I wanted my family. I turned with tears on my face and went down to find people who loved me.

The Chief's dead body was lain upon a pallet, decked with rich cloths and sacred herbs, for another day, and then he was buried outside the walls. Father David came from Ufer Hall, carried all the way on a litter, for he was not well enough to ride so far. Brother Carau attended him and helped with the ceremony. A pit the size of a small room was dug, and the Chief's body laid down inside it. Father David and Brother Carau made Christian incantations over the body and then moved aside respectfully as Mother Werberga told an old prayer over the Chief and laid a stone carved with runes next to his heart. The Lord Wulfirth then brought his father's great ceremonial spear and shield that Wulfred had carried at special feasts. These he laid beside the body. Finally, Brother Carau handed him two small golden Christian crosses, and, weeping openly, Lord Wulfirth laid them over his father's eyes. The little room was roofed with wood and earth, and a small mound raised over it, covered with turfs. And the time of Beornwine's Chief Wulfred was over.

All of Beornwine and Ufer and the farms and settlements and tuns all around were in mourning for seven days, until the moon was new. No building work was done, nor did I take part in any training at Ufer Hall. Of course, normal work of farm and dairy had to be done, but Kyneth stayed among his family and I stayed at home. I made myself be patient, knowing Chief Wulfred warranted this time of stillness to let his spirit find its way to heaven. I did take myself off to the woods to shoot off a clutch of arrows and make a few throws with my javelin, but I did that in honour of the old Chief, thinking of his long life. And then I found a better way to honour him; I wrote a story of his valour as a young man, one that I had heard told about him leading a small band of ill-armed men to battle with a great army. They fought in the forests and were helped by magical forest-sprites, who made them invisible. Thus, they killed a great number of enemies and Wulfred became known as a great captain of fighting men. I wrote the story as though I was Wulfred himself, and said how it had been to meet with the king of the sprites and what advice he was given concerning forest warfare.

It came to pass that my story was well-liked among Wulfred's family and people. I was charged to read it many times; people learned it by heart, and some added particulars that had not been in the original. Even within a few moons, my tale of *Wulfred in the Forest* became a fireside story and was held to be true. Thus, I played my part in honouring the memory of Kyneth's ancestor.

48

A New Governor for Beornwine

I heard my parents talking.

At that time I still had a room, partitioned off next to theirs. Once, when I was perhaps thirteen winters, the outside walls of the house had been remade and there were many changes inside the house. My little room was enlarged at that time, and Hereward made for me a table and chair so that I should be more comfortable when I wanted to study or scribe alone.

That evening, I had been working on my Wulfred story, but my candle was gone, so I put myself to bed, pushing Spin to one side so I could get in, for he was asleep long before me, sleep being his preferred occupation in those days. I, however, could not sleep, for thoughts and uncertainties were itching at my mind, compelling me to scratch at them with anxiety. This did not help, only making the matter worse. I knew action would help me, but I had shunned action for the mourning period. So I lay, sleepless. That was why I was awake to hear my father come home from a gathering of elders at Ufer Hall. I listened as he made his tired footfalls across the loft to Elanor's room. I heard her voice greeting him sleepily and, by soft sounds, I knew she rose to pour a drink for him from an ewer that she kept there. Then, in low tones, they began to talk.

"Has it been decided?" she asked.

"Wulfirth will not do it. I knew he would not. He cannot run Beornwine from Ufer Hall."

"What of his brother?"

"Yes, Alfred has been called for. He will come full soon, I doubt not, to make tribute to his father. Wilfirth says although Alfred has inherited lands through his wife's kin in the west, he might yet be willing to return to his old home as governor."

"He was a pleasant youth, I remember, but given more to action than sober thought and command."

Father gave a short, muffled laugh, "We men of action learn to curb our urges as we age. But Wilfirth is concerned that the right man is chosen. That is more important than that he should be of the Chief's kin. He asked me to give thought to it."

Elanor spoke again, but I could only hear the words, "… respect and maturity".

Father then said, "It would be a privileged position, but constrained."

I lay stiffly, staring into the dark. All the talk at Beornwine had been that Wulfred's younger son, Alfred, was to return, and take his father's place as governor of Beornwine. But if he had extensive lands of his own in the country of his wife's kin, how could he also live here? If not, who would be chosen? It was a new thought and a rousing one: could it be that my own father might be made Chief of Beornwine?

The next morning, a messenger came from Ufer Hall, saying that Wulfirth's brother Alfred had arrived, and to summon my father to attend him there. I spent the day with Elanor, helping her with household tasks and listening to her concerns.

"If Alfred refuses to be made Chief of Beornwine, then your father might be asked take that title," she confided to me, "The honour would be great, but I fear he would miss the freedom he has here on his own tun, with the forest nearby."

"He would be able to hunt from Beornwine," I said, "And Hereward and Fritha could move here to care for our farm. Hereward mostly manages our farm anyway."

"I cannot see it … I cannot see it being right for him – or for any of us." Elanor mashed the yeast, added it to the water and flour and put it next to the fire to prove. I made a brew of camomile and peppermint and poured a beaker of it for each of us.

"Father would love to wear the purple robe," I said.

She met my glance, and we laughed together. "He would love it." She took a sip of brew, then said thoughtfully, "I would miss the household here, and the farm and garden."

"You will have a garden at Beornwine, and Kyneth will make a fine house for you; there would be no need to live in the old Chief's house."

She nodded, "That is true. Besides, old Mordeth will not leave the old house. Nor would anyone wish to disturb her." But she looked distracted and neither of us noticed that she had over-proved the bread, so the loaves would not rise.

"What a waste!" she cried, when we discovered the error, "I have not made that mistake since I was a girl."

"It was my mistake too," I said, for she seemed much distressed, "I kept you talking. But do not fear, bake the loaves anyway. We have plenty of milk; I shall crumble the hard bread and mix it with milk and honey and apples. Everyone shall do without bread but have apple pudding at supper tonight instead."

Elanor nodded. "That is good," she said, "For we might have cause for celebration."

There was no sign of Father by supper time so Elanor supposed he would be eating at Ufer Hall. She ordered the household to take our meat without him. She was helping me to lift the bowls of apple bread pudding to the table when Heath's son Pepin raised his head, listening.

"Horses," he said, going to the doorway. He was back in a minute, "It is Lord Finric," he said, "with Kyneth."

They entered the house together, and Father's eyes were shining as he dipped his hands in the herb-water beside the door. Then he strode up to Elanor and took her hands.

"Well, wife," he said, "Beornwine has a new governor."

Elanor stood and kissed him, "It is an honour that you deserve, husband," she said.

"That may be true," he said, "But the honour is not mine, and I am glad of it."

I stared at my father, and saw in the straightness of his back and the brightness of his face that a great weight of trouble had been lifted off his shoulders.

"That honour goes to another who fits it far better than I."

And my father turned to Kyneth and clapped him on the shoulder. "Behold," he said, smiling broadly, "Beornwine's new Governor – Kyneth Wulfson."

49

Echo of Orin

Everyone was happy. Beakers were raised to Kyneth and to me as much as him, as if it was I who had been chosen as the new Chief of Beornwine and was to wear purple robes at every feast.

When my father had made yet another pretty speech, and Kyneth had taken enough old mead to be almost beyond sitting upright upon a horse, he decided that he would be wanted at home.

"Father and Mother will expect me," he said, anointing my hand with a wet and mead-scented kiss, "But I could not let the day pass without bringing this news to you myself."

I was not unconscious of the tribute he paid me thus, and I imagined his parents would not be best pleased at his riding away to me on the very day he was made Chief of Beornwine, especially as his uncle was just arrived.

"Can somebody ride with him?" I asked quietly.

"I'll go," said Heath, with a kind smile to me. I gave him a quizzical look, wondering if he was in any better state than Kyneth, for I had seen him raise his beaker many times that eve. But he looked sober enough and I reflected that Heath's powerful frame could soak up more ale than most other men. I nodded and Elanor said:

"Ride steadily, Heath; deliver him safely to his family."

"I will, Lady."

"And stay there until the morning."

Father was slumped happily in his chair. He raised his beaker again, "Farewell, Chief Kyneth!" he called drunkenly, "Farewell son of my heart!"

They needed no torch, for the night was clear and the moon was waxing high. "Hold on to your horse's mane," I advised Kyneth as Heath loaded him onto his horse.

Elanor was outside with us, making farewell to Kyneth, as Father was safer left in his chair. "Come and eat with us soon," she said, "When your visitors have departed."

"I will," he said, "I long to be with you again, even but I have not yet left you." And he shook his head drunkenly and stared in wonder from Elanor's face to my own as though we were a matched pair of unicorns, offering to make all his dreams come true.

I watched Kyneth ride away, looking less like any new governor than did young Pepin Heathson, who was only ten winters but at least sober.

Elanor did not seem to be enfuried at all by the men's drunkenness. When we had seen Kyneth and Heath out of the gates, she turned to me and embraced me tightly. "Oh, daughter of my heart," she said, "What a happy day is this!"

As we walked back to the house, Spin came out looking for me, walking stiffly on his old legs. I bent down to pet him, putting my face close to his. "Come," I told him, "Let's go to bed." He approached the ladder stair determinedly, but slipped after the first few steps. "All right, Spin, my sweet one," I said, and took him in my arms, not even calling "God's night," to the household, for Elanor was in Father's lap, kissing his face, and nobody was taking any notice of me.

I slept ill that night, finding no peace in dreams, and waking before cock-crow. I lay wide-eyed in the dark until the first faint glow of morning light crept into my room. Then I rose, leaving Spin asleep on my bed. There was no activity in the house below, only a few of the unmarried men snoring on the benches or the floor. I took a couple of spoonsfull of cold apple pudding, which I had always thought of as a fine breakfast, and went to get my horse. Dancer was pleased enough to see me, for she had not had a run for two days. She was expecting us to take our usual road to Ufer Hall, but I turned her in the opposite direction, galloping her when I could, until we passed the walls of Beornwine. There I dismounted for a little while, and Dancer ate some grass, while I paid my respects at the turfed mound under which Chief Wulfred lay. Soon, we were away again and passing the Flyfrith tun where Hereward was out tending his cows. I waved and he called out, "Take my good wishes to her!"

"I will!" I cried, and headed my horse in the direction of the distant copse of trees that led down to the river.

She was outside her house when I arrived, shielding her eyes from the early sun.

"I think you always know when I am coming!" I said.

"I listen to the earth, child," said Mother Werberga, "She tells me when a rider is near."

"Of course," I dismounted and embraced her, keeping my arms around her for a little while.

"It is good to see you, Edith," she said, putting me at arm's length and studying my face, so that I could not meet her eye.

"So," she said, "How does Kyneth's news sit with you?"

"How did you know?" I was amazed that she had already received information that could not yet have even reached Beornwine.

"How did I know that Kyneth would be made Chief of Beornwine? Only by my good sense that told me they would be fools to choose any other."

I only stood there, looking into her eyes; and there I saw the truth in my own heart. Kyneth was well loved and of an honoured family; a great planner and maker; a great master of men; kindly, honest and true. What better man could they choose? Why had I not seen it myself?

"I … I only thought he would be too young," I stammered.

"Too young? He is twenty-three winters, has lived at the King's Court and ridden with the royal mounted huscarle. He has been granted his own land, beyond the gift of his family, and has the true loyalty of all his own father's huscarle." She stopped and bent to pour out a beaker-full of herb-draught which had been steaming on her little fire near the house. Passing the beaker to me she said, "That is a powerful man."

I sat down on one of the log-seats outside her house, and she took the other one.

"He is always so kind and … and ordinary to me. I did not think …"

"You think of him as ordinary because he is not a great warrior." She did not say it in an accusing manner, but gently, as though she feared to hurt me with a plain truth that might be too sharp for me to grasp.

"No," I said, in some anguish, shaking my head and spilling my drink on my riding dress. "I honour him; believe this, I do honour him. I love him indeed."

"It is good that he is loved. It is his right. Shall you marry him?"

"We were to be wed at next summer's Grain Rite. He will have finished Father's new house by then." I sat, blinking into the fire while new matters - which I'd had no idea of until last evening - assembled themselves in my head. "And, he is to build a new hall at Beornwine also. I had thought he might build one for his uncle or even for my father. I had not thought it would be for himself."

"For himself - and for you. He will build it for you, because he graces you by making you his choice as Lady of Beornwine."

I bowed my head, conscious that she was making clear to me what should have been obvious to a simple child. But now I felt ashamed of my own previous expectations. I said ruefully, "I had thought we would ride together to fulfil my quest."

"I know you thought that, child."

I looked up at her, "But how can he do that, if he is to be Chief of Beornwine?"

She did not answer me, but began to speak of Archibald. "Your brother saw all of this," she said. "He had grown beyond his need for quest, yet he went because he wished to save you from your own. I told him that he could not do that, and I believe he understood the truth of my words. Yet his care for you is beyond wisdom."

Bewildered, and becoming angry, I said, "How can he have grown beyond his quest-vow? It was his true warrior's purpose!"

She did not answer me, only saying, "Do you remember your own quest-vow?"

I nodded, my eyes blazing at the notion that anyone might accuse me or my noble brother of forgetting or putting aside any such solemn pledge. But I recalled it was Mother Werberga before me – she who was not capable of conscious insult. Certainly, she was too much respected by myself and everyone for me to even imagine venting my anger on her. I kept my voice down, but it was still clear with honest indignation, "My quest-vow - and my brother's – is to avenge our mother's death."

"And, that being done, would your quest end?"

Her words surprised me, and I found I could not answer her. I reflected on the wondrous, shining quest-vow that had kept me from terror for all these winters. That vow was to avenge my mother's death. If there was to be a clear plan, it must be to find and kill Orin, but no such plan stood solitary and complete in my mind. I had thought first of making myself a warrior of skill and courage – of joining a band of fighting men, proving myself worthy of their company and, eventually, fulfilling my quest vow and finding honour thus. It was surely not possible that the vision of valour and nobility I had hoped for myself should be dependent on the death of one evil creature.

Mother Werberga got up from her seat and began to prepare a dish of food – crumbling day-old bread into milk and warming it on the fire. "Stay and eat with me, Edith," she said, "I should be glad of your company."

Her voice quavered a little and I watched her as she moved stiffly to make the meal. She was very thin and I realised that her face showed a great sadness that had no connection with my own troubles. Suddenly, I remembered her gentle and attentive nursing of Chief Wulfred on his death-bed and I realised she had lost a dear friend.

"Thank you Mother," I said. "It will make me very happy to stay and eat with you." I got up from my seat, "Let me help you, I pray."

"It is only bread and milk," she said, "I need no help in making such a simple dish for a welcome guest, but I would thank you to help me gather fire-wood later. I can walk and cook as well as ever, but bending again and again to gather firewood begins to be a trial for my old back."

I looked and saw that her store of firewood was completely gone, and I vowed silently that within another day I would fetch good, dry logs for her from my father's own store. But I straightaway jumped up and quickly gathered a bundle of kindling and a number of fallen branches, enough to give her what fire she could want for a day and a night. By the time I had finished, the dish of bread and milk was ready and I sat down with her again, refreshed by the exertion, thanking her kindly for the bowl of food she put into my hands.

We began to eat and after a while I said softly, "I made tribute to the Chief Wulfred at his grave on my way here."

She looked grateful that his name had been spoken between us. "Did you leave flowers there?" she asked.

"I wish I had thought of it," I said sadly, "For I saw daisies in the long grass near our woods. I could have brought them to him. I only stood and raised my spear before the grave, paying tribute to his name."

"That is well," she nodded, smiling kindly, so that I should not feel blameworthy that I had not brought flowers to the Chief. She took some more food and then said, "Wulfred was the last friend of my youth. Our mothers were sisters."

Mother Werberga continued to surprise me. So she was not only kin to the Lady Leoba, but also to Chief Wulfred and, thus to Kyneth too. "Oh, Mother," I said, "You are sad, and I should have known it. Forgive me for thinking only of my own troubles. Chief Wulfred was a good man and full kind to me. I miss him."

She nodded. "He visited me here often. I am not sad for him, because he lived well and died among those who love him. I am sad only for myself, and that has no importance."

I sat and gazed at this beautiful, noble woman who had been teacher, friend and guardian to me for so much of my life. My love for her overflowed from my heart and I wished fervently that I could ease her sorrow. "But your sadness *is* important, Mother," I said. And I went on my knees before her and took her hands in mine. "Your sadness honours him. It is right that you see him pass with sadness, because your memories of him are happy ones."

As she looked at me, her eyes softened. "I thank you, Edith. Your words comfort me." She smiled, "It is true, as I agreed with Leoba when we discussed your future. You have natural wisdom which has grown with you."

"I do not feel wise," I said, "I do not even know what to do with my life. Of all the ways I could choose, there is none that seems right, none that will not hurt others."

I raised my eyes to her. Beyond her, Dancer was grazing on a bit of grass. Suddenly, my horse raised her head, twitching her ears. And a man was standing in the opening to the copse. My bow and quiver were at my feet. In one movement I had stood and had an arrow notched in my bow.

"Stay, Edith!" Mother Werberga's hand was on my arm, preventing any chance of aiming true. The man had disappeared, but my heart was beating like a forger hammering steel. The man had been huge, with long hair and a plaited beard, and dressed in warrior-gear.

Garth! Ten winters had passed since he had chased me into hiding in a cart that had taken me to the Holywell Abbey, yet I knew for cèrtain it was he.

"Mother, you must come now on my horse with me," I spoke urgently, with all the assurance of a young person who tries to advise someone much older and wiser. "That is a dangerous fighting man. I doubt I can protect you from him. We must flee!"

"No, Edith," she said in a clear voice, "You leave me now. I am in no danger from a traveller who has come across my little home in the woods. There is nothing worth stealing here."

The urge to escape was great in me, and my agitation was affecting my horse. She snorted and stamped, ready to run, but I could not leave Mother Werberga. I felt sure that Garth was still close by – watching us from the trees. I called Dancer and she came to me in a moment. Mother Werberga took Dancer's harness and spoke to her gently, also putting an arm around my shoulders.

"What two nervous creatures are these!" she laughed. "Edith, you must not fear for me. I have more guests and see more travellers here than you can know. People come for herb-remedies and to sit and talk to an old woman.

"But that was no ordinary traveller!" I cried, "That was Garth. He tried to kill me years ago – after the Grain Rite at Beornwine."

"He tried to kill you?" She looked astonished and concerned.

"Well – he chased me." I thought back to a memory which was as clear as though it had happened only the previous day. I remembered there had been something in the nature of the huge man's face that had echoed in my memory. It had discomforted me then, and the same discomfort disturbed me now. At once the thought struck me that Garth could have been one of Orin's men, which was the reason he disturbed me so. But I knew I could not explain this to Mother Werberga or anyone else, because it shamed me. My only response to this first inkling of a connection with my quest – this first echo of Orin - was to flee. And I was ashamed.

"I have heard of this Garth," said Mother Wergerga, "by repute he is a fierce warrior, but nothing has been said of him murdering children at public Grain Rites." She spoke respectfully, but her mouth twitched as though she would like to laugh. "Now, come Edith. It is time you returned to your home."

I found myself trembling with shame and bewilderment and lack of sleep. If I had been confused when I first came to Mother Werberga that day, I was now more so. She put her arms around me and I shed a few hot tears into the cloth over her thin shoulder. "Do not fear," she said. "I doubt I am in any danger." She kissed me. "But wait now. I have something for you."

I waited by my horse, stroking her neck for comfort, while Mother Werberga went inside her house. She returned with a small flask, sealed with a leather plug. "This is a brew I made especially for you," she said, handing it to me. "It will help you to find calmness of spirit and self-wisdom in this time of uncertainty. Take two drops of it with chamomile brew at night and peppermint in the morning. And let it do its work; do not look either for troubles or for resolutions. Only strive to live and love and be happy. Then the answers will come."

When I passed through the copse on my horse a little while later, I had the certain sense that eyes were watching me. But I kept Dancer to a slow trot, refusing to display any fear, only knowing that my bow was easily to hand and that my aim was true and well practised.

50

Making Ready

The days went by as I took Mother Werberga's remedy and her advice. And as my passions settled into tranquillity, the truth became clearer. Although I loved Kyneth and longed for him with my body, still my mind was happiest when I was practising archery and sword-action, or discussing texts with Father David and Carau. I could not see myself as a wife and mother, wiping the faces and arses of a family of children and keeping charge of the oven and dairy in a prosperous household. As the moons passed and the new apple blossom had set to fruit, I believed that at last I knew my mind.

Kyneth had now almost completed the building of my father's new home. He had made it nearly as large and beautiful as the one at Ufer Hall, and seemed to come to the work more keenly and with more pride than when he was building the Lord Wulfirth's own house. Indeed, it was Father himself who bade him take a few strides' length off the hall. "It is not meet my house should rival your Father's," he told Kyneth, and later I heard Father murmur to Elanor, "Wulfirth would not care much, I believe, but his wife would likely have me banished from the land with my ears cut off if my wife's household were finer than her own."

"Do not speak so of Cwena," whispered Elanor, although she laughed at him.

"Kyneth is certainly the ardent bride-man," said Father, "bestowing such a gift upon the family of his bride." And Father gazed proudly around the new hall with its benches and big fire-pit and shutters covered with oiled velum to let in light even when they were not open.

While he was building the hall, Kyneth stayed with us in Flytun, sleeping by night on a bench in our house, or in the single men's sleeping quarters. When he began work on the new hall at Beornwine, I saw him less. Although oft-times he would ride over to us for his breakfast, I was often already gone to Ufer Hall by the time he arrived. There I would visit with Carau and Father David, and afterwards practise with Eben and the

313

huscarle. In that company, I found that few could match me at mounted archery, and Eben said that even Archibald would be hard pressed to do better. However, Eben would still not allow me to take part in hand-to-hand tests, and I curbed the rage and resentment I felt, for any warrior under command must respect his arms-master's decisions.

All virtuous actions have their reward, and such was the case for me as I gained control over my frustration, and learned self-discipline. One day, I had been riding my horse hard in the thick of a practice mounted huscarle charge, wheeling and turning and holding her back to the pace of the other horses. Afterwards I watched as some of the huscarle performed hand-to-hand tests against each other. I always put myself at the front of the watchers, because I wanted a clear view of the tests, and I was shorter than most of the men. I watched avidly, trying to imprint every movement and mistake of the fighters upon my own body's memory, as if I had performed them myself. When the tests were over, the winner announced and the contestants having any wounds and hurts tended, I went alone to return my sword to the armoury. There I hung up my borrowed leather breast-plate and cleaned and checked the blade of my sword before stowing it. As to that, I reflected discontentedly that it needed little attention, for I had used it for movement practice only, not for any true testing against another.

The guard that day was Orworth, and I stopped to pass a few words with him when a powerful figure appeared in the doorway.

"Master," I said, standing straight and bowing my head, for it was my arms-master Eben Freeborne, and until I left the armoury I was still under that day's command.

"Come, Edith Fly," he said, "I wish to speak with you before you leave." He had begun to call me 'Edith Fly' during my training time (I liked it better than 'Lady Edith') and I knew therefore that he wanted to speak to me about my conduct on the training field. I feared that some unconscious fault of mine had caught his notice and I followed him with some unease.

He matched his pace to walk side by side with me and I waited for him to speak, feeling some pride to be thus beside him, even though it might be to hear his censure.

"Edith Fly," he began, "I have been watching you this day, and I find you above all others in horsemanship. You are already proved the best archer in our ranks, despite being the smallest. What am I to do with you next?"

I flushed with surprise and pleasure to hear this unforeseen praise. I did not answer him, but turned my face to the ground in discomfiture, for a warrior should not show his feelings so easily.

"You would ask to be put to the tests?" he said.

"I would, but you have forbidden it," I said without rancour, for I had learned better than to rail against his decisions.

"There is one I might test you against."

"Who?" I glanced at him sharply, expecting he might suggest some untrained boy.

He tapped the centre of the heavy leathern breastplate he always wore. "Myself," he said, returning my glance and giving a stiff smile which soon changed to a laugh as he saw the astonishment that must have been apparent on my face.

In a moment I was laughing with him, for I was immediately delighted as well as shocked by the idea of such a challenge.

"In this way, I can guard you while you test yourself against me," he said.

But I shook my head, "I doubt I could raise my sword against you, master." Indeed, my respect and loyalty to Eben disallowed the idea of treating him as an enemy.

"You will have to Edith Fly," he said dryly, "Unless you wish to be thrown on your back in the mud before your huscarle brothers."

I glanced quickly at him again, and in a moment saw that he had his shield up. I was completely defenceless, encumbered by my bow and quiver about my shoulders, yet without my shield which was left with my horse. All I could do was to twist away as the weight of Eben's shield came against me. But the edge of it caught my hip and sent me tumbling. I rolled onto my hands and knees. Eben was standing over me, laughing, with his hand out to help me up. Cautiously, I took it and he pulled me to my feet.

"Don't believe me to be an easy opponent because I have a care for you," he said. "And don't fear – I shall not surprise you unarmed again. But prepare for tests against me. I believe you will have to work hard." He nodded a dismissal and walked away from me.

Thus began the best training of my life when, perhaps four or five times in a moon, my arms-master allowed me to pit myself against him in an arms-test. This taught me more about defense and attack than any amount of theory or observation could have done. He was true to his word, in that he never inflicted any dire hurt on me. Yet, as I became more skilled, he needed to work harder to defeat me, and I was often badly winded or bruised by the force of his effort. I felt at last that my skills were growing alongside my brother huscarle, and I was more glad of it than I could speak of.

51

The Ordering of Lands

There was much talk between Kyneth and Father, Elanor, Hereward, Alvar and their wives about Kyneth's own tun. Alvar was no farmer, but Hereward was much interested in the land. "The soil is good," he said, "It should yield plentiful grain and the grass will make fine summer fodder for your cattle. Your dairy and grain-store should be rich."

"Will you take it Hereward?" Kyneth said suddenly, "Will you take over my tun as your own and work the land as it deserves? I cannot, for it is a long distance from Beornwine. I shall have to give it up."

Hereward flushed like a girl at this generous offer, but he shook his head, "I am needed here," he said. "The Flytun and the Frith lands take all my time. I cannot leave them."

"And I cannot spare him," said my father loudly.

Kyneth nodded, "I could offer it to my brother Osred, should he have enough of questing when he returns from the east with Archibald. But he has spoken of going to Court and joining the Royal Huscarle. Besides, he is only just fifteen and has never shown much interest in farming, although he likes hunting well enough."

I nodded in agreement, "Osred is a warrior at heart," I said.

"What of Archibald?" said Alice, "He has spoken of working land and making a household."

Several heads nodded, and Elanor said, "Archibald would be glad of such a site for his household, for he will marry, I think."

I stared as if I was in a nest of madmen. Archibald was a great warrior and hunter. How could so many of his kin believe him to have a calling to the land?

Kyneth shook his head, "I deem Archibald's plans will take him elsewhere."

And I was glad that Kyneth at least was in accord with me. I opened my mouth to voice my agreement in strong terms, but the talk had moved on and no-one's eyes set on me. It was as if I had no place in that family discussion. Indeed, I felt strangely invisible there. Indignation agitated my limbs and my thoughts turned to Dancer grazing in the nearby paddock, waiting for my call. I might as well go for a ride and perhaps hunt a hind or two for my brothers to take home with them when this gathering was over, which I wished fervently to be soon, for talk of farming was not a topic that interested me much. I guessed I could leave without giving offence for no-one was taking any notice of me, and I was about to get up from my seat when I heard the name of one I loved.

"… Heath." Hereward paused: he had everyone's eyes on him.

Father was frowning, "Can Heath be spared?"

Hereward sighed, "I can never spare him as brother of my heart. But I know of no other who has better judgement in matters of husbandry. I always consult him. He could be trusted with your land. I know of no-one else I could recommend so highly."

Kyneth turned to Father with a curious look. "Is Heath a kinsman to your family?"

"He came into my family when he saved my daughter's life."

Then the tale had to be told of my rescue by Heath from the iced pond when I was a little child. I thought I might tell it, for I was at the centre of it. But, although I sat there before him, Father took less notice of me than of the piece of meat on his plate, as he related all the details of how Heath preserved the life of Kyneth's bride for him.

"So, Heath is not bonded to you; he is free?" asked Kyneth.

"He bears my name. I made him my son," said Father.

"Then if Heath Fly will have it, Kyntun will be his to order as he will."

It was a magnificent honour for Heath, who was sent for straight away. And I was glad that I hadn't ridden off for I would have missed the look on his face when he was given the news.

So Heath and Bebbe and their children, all of whom I loved greatly, were to move from their small house in our homeyard to the handsome hall at Kynton. All of our family were glad of it, for they deserved such luck. Elanor herself went to give the news to Bebbe and to bring her back to the house. I remember dear, beautiful Bebbe standing at the doorway with tears in her eyes, declaring that she could not leave Elanor or Father or me.

"But we shall visit with each other," said Elanor gently. "Kynton is less than a morning's ride from here. It is not so very far."

Thus the order of things at Kyntun were settled and Kyneth could turn his mind to matters at Beornwine. I often visited the site of the new hall there. It was set quite close to the old Chief's house, on the field that was formerly used for boy's tests at Grain Rites. The hall was grand enough – of a size with my father's, and was painted outside with the coloured devices of the old Chief Wulfred. They included a spear, a wild boar and wheatsheaf. Kyneth was pleased with the workmanship and skill with which they were painted and was eager to show them to me.

"See," he said, "I have not changed anything, but ordered the addition of the holy cross and a horse – which is in honour of your family."

I was glad to see the shape of the holy cross, filled in with red paint, and was much impressed by the horse, which was white like my father's present steed.

"As Chief, my house has to bear the device, to show that this is the heart of Beornwine," he said, "It is not for my own fame, but that of the land, and of my honoured grandfather." Kyneth went on to tell me that his duties would concern the ordering of land, the hiring of men and the division of offerings to the Holywell Abbey. He would also stand in judgement in the case of disputes and preside at feasts. "I know that I may call upon my father in need, for he is first Lord of the region, and any final decisions are in his hands. But I wish to show him that I am capable of ordering matters and keeping a peaceful community here. I believe I can do it."

I observed Kyneth's face, which was as handsome and animated as if he was planning a new hall, or even the seat of a King. I reached up and softly touched his face. Immediately, he took my hand and kissed it.

"My love," he said, "It will be responsible work, but if you believe in me I know I can do it well."

"You will do it well," I said, smiling, "But who will you leave in charge of everything when you are away?"

"My grandfather's trusted freedman, Jaren Mead, is a capable man," he said, running his hands over a smooth joint in the doorframe, "I can trust him to carry out my orders well enough."

"Will he be trusted enough to leave as ward to your household when we ride to quest?"

I saw a faint veil of irritation cross his face, but he looked down at me and his expression became kindly and wistful-looking. He said, "But I don't know when that might be, dearest, for my responsibilities won't allow me to leave my household for many a long time, no matter how trusted my principal servant."

I looked into his eyes and nodded, at last understanding how it was between us. Kyneth would never ride to quest with me. His own true quest was here – in the ordering of men and lands. I knew it – and I could not expect anything more from him. I put my arm about his waist and turned my head to his breast, for I loved him greatly and could hardly contemplate letting him go. But as he responded to my embrace, and I tightened my sword-arm around him, I had the sudden knowledge of the strength in my arm, which had lately grown muscular in my tests with Eben. I stood in Kyneth's arms, my eyes closed against the mix of anguish and gladness that filled me. At last he pulled back from me, kissed me on my forehead and then on my mouth. And then our kisses were fierce, our bodies hard against each other, and if we had not been standing before the house of the new chief, and if there had not been a crowd of men and women about the place, I believe our embraces might have developed to their natural conclusion.

52

A Leave-Taking

The torch-light wavered and jerked with the movement of horses. There was nothing else to see by, for thick cloud obscured both moon and stars. It was a poor night for travelling indeed, yet travel we must. I could see little beside strange shadows cast on the riders who bore the torches riding ahead and to the sides of me. Dancer carried me gently. I guess she knew the condition of my mind, for I was hardly capable of directing her. She followed the other horses calmly while I shivered uncontrollably, although the summer night was not cold.

Where were we riding with such urgency that disallowed awaiting the daylight? To Ufer Hall. And what was the reason for the journey? Father David asked for me, and Father David was dying. That news was the cause of my shivering. I had not the comfort of Elanor or Father on the journey, for Father was on his regular visit to the market at Holywell and, rarely, Elanor had accompanied him, taking Bebbe with her. There had been no time to fetch one of my brothers, and Heath was gone to Kynton overnight. The messenger had ridden on to Kyneth at Beornwine, but I would not wait; I rode back immediately, alone but for the messenger-guard from Ufer.

The courtyard of Ufer Hall was well lit as we arrived and the Lady Cwena herself came out to greet me.

"Will you take refreshment, Edith?" she asked, her voice and expression all kindliness, "Or will you come at once to see him? He is weak indeed."

I was glad of her gentleness, which I saw only rarely, although I knew her capable of it.

"Let me come to him, my Lady," I said, my voice wavering as much as my body shivered. I got unsteadily from my horse and Cwena took off her own cloak and wrapped it around me, holding me close for a moment most kindly, as if I was one of her own children.

321

"Be courageous for his sake Edith," she said, "Do not let him see you grieve too deeply."

Now I was close to her, I could see she had been weeping, but she wiped her face and led me steadily to the chapel-house and thence to the room beyond where Father David and Carau had their living place. The Lord Wulfirth was there also, with Lewitha who bore the marks of tears on her face. A herb-wise wicca-woman of the household sat nearby and there were others that I knew, but I could not acknowledge anyone, for I thought only of the one I had come to see. Although the Lady Cwena and her bondswoman had entered the room with me, Father David looked only at me, and Carau got up immediately to bring me to the bedside.

"Edith, my child, bright joy of my heart!" said Father David in a soft voice that was little more than a whisper. He reached out a hand to me.

I rushed to kneel at his bedside, took his hand and kissed it. "God's eve, Father," I said, "How is it with you?" In his presence, my voice did not waver, nor did my hand tremble in his. There seemed to be nothing of death about him; he appeared to me entirely present and alive, though his body was thin.

"I am well, child," he whispered, "But my body fails."

"But it will rally Father, and we shall study together again."

"Perhaps not again Edith."

"I have stories to show you."

He smiled and made to speak again, but paused to cough a deep, terrible cough that threatened to shake the very life out of him while I watched. I looked about me in panic, but Carau was there, gently propping up the old man with a feather pillow and his own body. Father David gave another cough and as he did so, a stream of blood, black in the torchlight, flooded from his mouth, over the cross at his throat and onto his breast and bed-cloths. His eyes widened once, but then the life went out of him even before another thick mass of blood filled his mouth and poured out over the bed.

I found myself backing away from the bedside, my hands covering my mouth in horror and my body once more trembling violently. When my reason came back to me, everyone in the room was silent with shock, except for Carau, who was trying to wipe the blood from Father David's face with his own robe, calling to him and sobbing pitifully. It was Carau's distress that brought me out of my state of horror. I went and put my arms around him, drawing him away from the bed. "He is gone, my friend," I murmured, "Father David is gone to his Lord. He is gone."

"No, not yet. He will be well again," Carau pulled himself away from me and went back to Father David, dipping a cloth in a bowl of water nearby and using it to wipe at the blood. I turned to Cwena, my voice shivering with my body:

"Might we have more washing-water, my Lady?"

Cwena immediately ordered bondswomen to bring water and cloths, and this seemed to break the deep shock and stillness in the room. The sound of weeping began, for everyone present had loved Father David. Lord Wulfirth came to stand over the body. He put his arm kindly around Carau's shoulders and spoke to him in a low voice. This seemed to bring Carau back to his proper mind, and he knelt at the bedside. After a spell of quietness, he began to chant a sweet Christian incantation to the dead, which I had never heard before:

"Father of heaven, bring this thy fair son to his last home in thy heart. With love we offer up his soul freely to fly from the earth to thy heaven."

This Carau repeated many times, while he continued to clean his master's face and body. Bowls of steaming water were brought in and the wicca-woman cast herbs and drops of certain precious oils into the water, then began to help Carau in his work. Carau's chant was taken up by everyone in the room. Softly, I joined my voice with the others and slowly it calmed me. Then I took up a cloth of soft wool, dipped it in a bowl of water and helped to wash Father David's body. By the time Kyneth arrived from Beornwine, coming straight to the chapel-room wearing his riding gear and kneeling at the foot of the bed, Father David's body was pure and clean, dressed in a fresh robe and laid on a rich bed-cloth, brought from the Lady Cwena's own chamber.

I know not how long I stayed there, praying to release Father David from my heart so that his soul would be free, but daylight was full again when Kyneth and Carau led me out into the courtyard. Carau was quite calm now and he gave us both a blessing.

Kyneth put his arm around Carau's shoulders, saying, "You are free now, brother. He will not need you any more."

"I had wanted freedom," Carau answered, "but now I only want the presence that bound me to this place. He was full wise and devout and kind. What is freedom to me without him? I am lost without his guidance."

"Not lost, brother. Are you not strengthened and blessed by knowing him?"

"That is true Lord Kyneth. But I know not what I shall do now."

"My mother and father would gladly have you stay here as priest."

But Carau raised his head to the morning breeze and I saw the desire for freedom writ on his face.

"Father David should be buried at Holywell," I said. "You will escort him. There you can consult with Lord Tobias and Lady Leoba. Perhaps they will advise you to follow the mission to the north."

"Holywell," he looked at me. "Yes, I must take Father David's body safely there."

At once I knew that I also would go with Father David to Holywell, so that I would bid him final farewell at the sacred place where first I encountered him. "I shall come with you," I said. I went to get my horse, but Kyneth followed me to the stable.

"Dear one," he said gently, "You cannot travel to Holywell this day. Stay here in my father's house and take comfort and rest before your journey. You had little sleep last night, and Carau had none. He is to stay here today and set off at daybreak tomorrow. My father will provide an escort. It will take a day for everything to be arranged properly, so there is no reason for you not to rest."

I nodded, but then a thought came to me, "What of Elanor and Father?" I said. They will return from Holywell today. They must be told."

"I shall ride straight to your father's house now," said Kyneth. "I'll break the news to them, and explain about your journey. Then I have to go on to Beornwine, for today has been set for the choosing of men and women for the new household. Jaren Mead has charged many to come and I must be there, though I would far rather be with you."

So Kyneth's horse was made ready and I bid him farewell. "Rest now, my love," he said, kissing my hand. "I suppose you will return at the first-quarter moon?"

I nodded and watched him ride away. Then I was guided to a chamber in Ufer Hall and the Lady Cwena herself brought me a beaker of hot cordial. It was full sweet and helped me to drift away to sleep despite my sadness.

By day-break the following morning, I had eaten and was on my way to the Holywell Abbey. Carau rode beside me with Father David's body on a light horse-cart, all piled with herbs and wrapped around with a soft sheepskin. We were escorted by a band of Lord Wulfirth's mounted huscarle.

Thus we travelled, without haste, and with every step of my horse's light feet, I heard in my head the sweet incantation that Carau had made:

Father of heaven, bring this thy fair son to his last home in thy heart.

I spent the time of mourning for Father David at the Holywell Abbey, returning to Ufer Hall some eight days later. The night before my return, the Lady Leoba invited Carau and me to sup with her in her private chamber. We spoke with her well into the night. At last, she took Carau's hand, saying:

"The time of your freedom has come, Brother Carau. I have letters from the north mission which will guide you to their settlement." Then she turned to me, "As for you, Edith, my daughter, you think you have come to know your true mind, and I respect that. My only caution to you is this: you are young; even a few moons can bring new understanding that you do not think of at the present time. I charge you now to go home and speak to your mother of this."

"To my mother?" I was surprised, for I thought my decision should be known to Kyneth first.

"Yes." My Lady gave me a sober smile, "It is Elanor who will be most affected by your actions."

"But what of Kyneth?"

"Kyneth might have another wife," she said, "But Elanor can have no other daughter."

"My brothers have wives. All are full fond of Elanor."

"Yet you are the daughter of her heart, more so than any other."

It was these words that I thought about most as I journeyed back from Holywell, riding among the mounted huscarle, and as I pondered I found it true that Elanor was the one to whom I must trust my confidence, and the one to whom I most dreaded giving it.

I waited not long at Ufer Hall, only resting my horse and paying my respects to the Lady Cwena; then, I ran Dancer at a slow gallop back to Flytun. Guards had seen me coming; the gate was flung open and there was Elanor, hurrying to meet me with my father not far behind her. I realised suddenly that no-one save Archibald loved me as Elanor did, and it was Elanor I would miss most should I ride away to quest. When I saw her dear face, I nearly fell from my horse at her feet, and she wrapped her cloak around me and drew me into the house as, for the first time, I wept properly for my beloved Father David.

53

Enchantment

I slept deeply that night and into the next day, being weary from travelling and sadness, and when I came down into the house, breakfast was over and the men gone. Bebbe was there, chattering eagerly with Elanor about her new household at Kyntun and on the table-board was a host of new cooking pots, fire-irons and torch-shafts, together with loom-hooks, cards of needles, and other packages. I guessed Elanor had brought these back from the market and that they were for Bebbe. As I stepped down the stair, Elanor came to kiss me. "God's Day. Did you sleep well, dear one?"

"God's Day. Yes, I slept too well, for I have missed breakfast!"

"Come then," said Bebbe, "there is new bread and meat and eggs. You shall have your fill."

"Kyneth was here," said Elanor, "but I sent him away, saying you needed to sleep. You shall see him this eve, for he comes to eat with us."

I ate, and they displayed to me some of the household purchases they had made.

"Look," said Bebbe, "This pot has two handles so that it can be moved safely straight from the fire." And she proceeded to demonstrate how this could be done.

"You will need good, thick protectors for your hands though," I advised.

She immediately showed me some mittens, made of a double layer of sheepskin, with a cover of thick pigskin. "Elanor has a pair also," she said.

"I could not resist them," Elanor chuckled.

"Oh, may I try them?" and I put on the mittens and lifted up a pot of water that was bubbling on the cooking fire. It is true that my hands stayed marvellously cool inside. "They are as good as forger's gauntlets," I said, wonderingly.

"Well, I bought a third pair, as I knew you would like them, and you will have your own household soon. There they are." She pointed to a small pile of packages on the beaker-board against the wall, and there amongst them was another pair of the mittens.

"Thank you Mother," I said wistfully. I was thinking how pleasant it was to be discussing with these beloved women the ordering of a new household, and how difficult it would be to tell them that my own household would never be.

Elanor must have read my expression as one of disappointment that I had not been to market to buy my own mittens, for she said, "There will be plenty of time for you to go to market to choose things for yourself, dear one. But the merchant who sold these had few of them, and did not expect to be at the Holywell market for another year."

"I do not mind you buying them for me, Mother. It is full kind of you." I laughed, saying, "I could never mind receiving gifts!"

They laughed with me, then Bebbe's youngest little girl, Daisy, peeped shyly inside the house, then trotted inside, followed by a small gathering of her little friends. "Look, mama," she said. In her little fist was a baby chick, gasping for breath. Bebbe got up with a cry and went to rescue the little creature. "Come, child," she said, "We will return him to his mother. Chicks are not play-things."

Elanor and I smiled at each other as Bebbe led Daisy out of the house, and I reflected on the mothering that inevitably proceeded from marriage. Most women took to child within a few moons of betrothal. Some bloomed and grew to strength in bearing and nurturing children. Bebbe was one such. Elanor also was a model of fulfilled womanhood: running a large household and raising Archibald and me so that we never missed the mothering of the one who gave us birth. Even now the house was rarely bare of children, for all the offspring of our household were welcomed and loved by Elanor who had never given birth, but had given life to me, as surely as the best of mothers.

Some of Daisy's little friends had gone with her to witness the reunion of chick and mother-hen, but a few others had remained in the house, their big eyes staring around, for the new house was still a novelty in Flytun. Elanor held her arms out and they ran to her, expecting a treat of honey-cake or cordial, for it was her way to be kind.

She looked up at me now, her arms full of children and such a light in her eyes that was a joy to see. "Oh Edith," she said, her voice blithe with happiness "I am so glad that you are to join with such a fine man as Kyneth whom you love and who loves you so well. And you shall have your own household – so close to us! I think I shall see you as much as I do now, and when your children are born they shall be ..."

327

She paused and her eyes brimmed with sparkling tears in which I felt all my resolution weakening, failing, drowning.

Now her voice was low and hesitant – half full of doubts, "My Edith, my daughter, would it be wrong to feel they will be my own grandchildren, even more than your brothers' children?"

How could I answer these words from she who had rescued me from terror as a tiny child? She who had loved me, nurtured me, given me the priceless gift of letters? How could I answer her but with my eyes and hands to raise up her spirit as she had raised mine through all our years together? So I went to her, kissing her hands and her face. "My Mother, my dearest Mother; of course they shall be yours. Who else's indeed!" I laughed, bringing a merry smile to her face.

"And now, dear one," she said, "We shall talk of your wedding dress." She got up and took the children to the honey-cake jar, letting them choose a cake each and then shooing them out of the house. She could not therefore have seen the dismay that must have appeared on my face as I realised that the subject of my marriage and household and offspring was becoming more and more a reality against all my intentions. She turned to the beaker-board and came back to the table with a leathern bag from which she took two soft, flat parcels, wrapped in linen. Unwrapping the larger parcel, she revealed a length of fine woven cloth, dyed a vibrant blue the colour of cornflowers, the like of which I had never seen in my life. I gasped with admiration and an unexpected pleasure that I saw reflected in Elanor's own face.

"Does it please you, Edith?" she said softly. "Would it not make for a fine wedding-dress?"

"Oh, Mother, the finest," I cried, and, beguiled by blue, I forgot my fears and troubles for a space as I imagined myself dressed grandly in a robe made of the wonderful cloth.

"See how fine and soft the wool is," she said, unfolding an arms-breadth of it. I touched it, folding it around my hand and stroking the surface of it. It was indeed softer than lambswool and yet strong in the weft and weave.

"What is it?" I asked, for I had never handled cloth like it.

"It was brought by an eastern merchant and is the wool of a mountain animal from a far off land. It was costly, but your father would spare no expense for his daughter's wedding." As she spoke, she took up the other parcel, which was smaller than the first. She passed it to me. "Unwrap it," she said, smiling. Inside, folded in a leaf of white parchment, was a finished head-cloth of dazzling green like sunlight on new grass. I took it in my hands and its texture was soft as goose-down, thin as water, light as a breeze. I had seen such a thing only on the head of the Lady Cwena at the highest festivals.

"It is silk," breathed Elanor and she took it and placed it over my hair.

"How is it on me? Does it look well?" I asked eagerly, all thoughts of questing flying off to the outskirts of my mind.

"I knew!" she said. "I knew it was just the colour for your hair!"

Now Bebbe came back into the house with Mythwyn and some other of the bondswomen. Bebbe clapped her hands when she saw me wearing the green silk head-cloth and all exclaimed at its beauty and that of the blue cloth also. "Has she seen ... the other?" Bebbe asked Elanor.

"Not yet," Elanor shook her head, laughing.

"What other?" I asked, "What more could there be than this?"

Elanor reached into the leathern bag again, bringing out a bulky parcel wrapped in sacking and a carved wooden box. She pushed them across the table-board towards me. I unwapped the parcel, revealing a pair of green leather shoon, most soft and elegant. I tried them on immediately and they were just of a length for my feet.

"They will be far too good to stand on the ground with," laughed Bebbe, "We shall have to carry you when you wear them!"

"Look how the colour matches with the head-cloth," said Mythwyn and there were more cries of wonder and admiration. I turned now to the carved box; I was curious to open it and found inside a whetstone about the length of my hand. It was made narrow and straight, light enough to carry easily at the waist. The end of it was carved into the shape of a horse's head. I was mighty taken with it and thanked Elanor greatly.

"It was time you had a new one," said Elanor, examining it happily. "Since your father gave you your new houseknife."

I nodded, glancing at the knife at my waist, which was no houseknife, but a full-sized freeman's seax. I wondered what Elanor would think to call the warrior's sword from the Ufer Hall armoury that I had been using for practice these last moons. A cooking spit or flailing staff perhaps? But I did not wish to trouble her with such truths, so I just smiled and wound a strap around my fine new whetstone, ready to tie it to my belt.

There was the sound of voices outside and then Fritha and Alice, Gytha and Aldyth arrived. I was glad and surprised to see them.

"I invited them to cheer you, dear one," whispered Elanor, "and to see what I brought back from my marketing trip."

We made sweet herb-brew for everyone and sat together speaking first of Father David and then of Gytha's baby, whom she had set to sleep in one of our cradles.

"Thank gods he sleeps now," she said, "For he usually feeds all day and screams all night."

"Travelling here on the cart has calmed him, no doubt," said Fritha, "Eldric was just such a fractious infant, and I could always settle him with a long walk, or by pulling him in a hand-cart when he was too big to carry. I did the same with Hylda, but she was a much easier child."

"Is that so? But does not the cart make them sick?"

"Indeed no; it is the motion that stills them."

"But what of the night-time. I can hardly walk abroad in the pitch dark. Ham has moved to the men's dorter because the boy's cries keep him awake. I am at my wits' end for trying to bring the child to sleep."

There have been times in my later life that I have wished I listened then as Fritha, Alice and Mythwyn all joined in with advice on the calming of a restless infant. But at the time it held no interest for me and I felt my attention slipping away. I drew the blade of my seax, intending to remake the edge with my new whetstone. However, my movements were noticed:

"What a fine-looking whetstone," said Aldyth.

"Yes, Elanor brought it for me from the Holywell market."

Alice looked up at this. "Oh yes, do let us see what you bought, Elanor," she said and everyone gathered round while the blue dress-length, green head-cloth, whetstone and shoon were brought out for everyone to admire. I was made to stand still while the blue cloth was hung about my shoulders and fixed with clasps. Then Elanor made bride-braids of my hair with green ribbon intertwined with blue cornflowers and fastened it back over the silk head-cloth.

"See how the red lights in her hair glow against the green," she said.

"Now," said Bebbe, "Let her put on the shoon," and she made me sit while she tied them around my feet with more green ribbon.

Then Elanor rushed upstairs to fetch her bronze mirror and a string of rich beads of her own. She fixed the beads to the clasps at my shoulders and held up the mirror so that I might see how I looked. And indeed I looked and felt like a queen of brides, with all my maids about me, their kindness and good wishes showered upon me like so many hands-full of summer flowers. I felt happy then, at the centre of these women, for once accepting my place among them joyfully in a way that never occurred again until these recent times, when I find myself in a peaceful place, content within a community of women again.

"This is well," Elanor muttered as she measured the blue dress-length with her eyes, "Well indeed. All needed now is for me to cut the robe to length and hem it, and to embroider the edges and neckline in green."

Then the shoon and beads and silk head-cloth were taken from me to be wrapped and stowed in Elanor's chest in her room. The blue cloth she took from me, cutting it there and then to robe length and beginning to work on it without delay. Elanor did no cookery or other household work for the rest of the day, but sat stitching that dress with the most delicate and skilful embroidery while the other women prepared food for the evening. Nothing seemed required of me and so I took Spin out for a walk. He looked at me doubtfully at first, as he was not pleased to be taken from his rest, but when I lured him with a morsel of honeycake he trotted stiffly after me on his poor old legs.

I had thought to take a walk to Beornwine, but I reflected that would take me to Kyneth, and I did not wish to see him. Besides, I doubted my dog could walk so far. Instead, I took him to the woods a little beyond our gates, and found the clearing where I had previously spent many an hour practising with bow and javelin, in the time before Kyneth had arranged for me to train with Lord Wulfirth's huscarle. There in the sunlight I sat with my back resting against a tree while I stroked Spin and remembered what Kyneth was to me and how much I was in debt of kindness to him. I had been avoiding him simply because to be close to him was to love him with my mind and my body. I did love him, but to marry him, I now understood, was to forsake my quest-vow. I thought ruefully of my own behaviour among the women, exclaiming over the gifts that Elanor and Father had brought for me. It had been a sweet relief from my sadness for Father David to think of beauty and companionship and love. One thing was certain – it was not possible now for me to admit to Elanor or anyone else that I would not marry Kyneth. It was hardly possible for me to admit it to myself.

The truth was that from the moment I laid eyes on that beautiful cornflower blue cloth, I had become enchanted: I was enchanted with the notion of myself as a bride; I was enchanted by the pleasure I could bestow on my father and Elanor by marrying the Chief of Beornwine and son of Lord Wulfirth; I was enchanted by the possibility of surrendering to my desire for Kyneth.

When I returned to the house, preparations were well forward for the evening's meal. Elanor had ordered that there would be a small feast for our family and household to greet my return. "It is well that we came over early," said Alice, "For Elanor can think of nothing but that dress."

I found Elanor in her private room at the back of the house. She was sitting close to the open shutter, where the light was good for stitchery, and had completed part of an embroidered wreath of leaves across the neck-line of the dress. She looked up as I entered:

"Come and see, Edith. Is it to your liking?"

"It is beautiful. You are greatly skilled."

"See this ..." and she showed me a tiny white embroidered unicorn with a green horn that she had worked at one shoulder of the dress. "You loved the unicorn when you were a little one," she said, "And they so often appear in your stories. I thought it meet you should have one on your wedding dress."

I was charmed and touched at her thoughtfulness. "Thank you Mother. I have often thought that, should I have my own colours at arms, I would paint a unicorn on my shield."

She did not look up from her stitchery, but only frowned a little, saying, "You did have such notions a little while ago, Edith, before you were a woman."

I looked at her with a puzzled smile, wondering what she thought of my daily arms-practice at Ufer Hall. My skills were well known, yet rarely spoken of in my own home. I guessed Elanor did not think of it at all, because it would be disturbing to her. Such interests are, after all, out of kilter with a life of domestic responsibilities that should more properly occupy the mind of the bride she thought me to be.

I walked softly from the room, feeling strangely unreal as if I might be a maiden in one of my own stories, with no will of my own, only destined to be what the writer chooses.

Because of the planned feast, some of the men arrived early for the evening. Aldyth, who had brought a cask of ale from Siric in her hand-cart, set to serving out beakers to all who wanted it – and many did. I took one myself, for Siric's ale was known to be good and I needed refreshment. It cheered me, and I set myself to being useful to my sisters, making ready the table-board for the supper. Soon Father arrived and, with him, Kyneth and my brothers, and I went to greet them. I had not seen Kyneth since the night Father David died; it seemed a much greater time than the seven or eight days it was and I was shaken to my heart to see his beautiful smile, which seemed only for me. But I blushed, for his glance, taking in the bride-braids in my hair and – no doubt – the bride-dream in my eyes, had more of admiration, more of desire, than I think I had ever seen before. I returned to my work of preparing meat and sweets for the table – suddenly wanting to impress Kyneth with my housewifely skills. And, as I worked, I blushed again and again, for whenever I looked up, his eyes were upon me. I saw him talking with Father and Elanor, knowing by their smiles and glances that I was the subject of their words.

Now, you might well ask where had gone my urge to quest – my passion for a life of action that, only two days before, I had told the Lady Leoba I had chosen above love and marriage. And I cannot give you an answer. Only be advised that a woman's body (and that of a man also, I trow) will not always follow the urgings of her heart. The waters that flow in a woman's body are strong and, when swollen by flattery, persuasion, desire or even grief, can break the banks of her reason and swamp, for a time, the heartland of her dreams.

But tides turn, flood waters recede, and a vow that is set with honourable intent cannot so easily be overcome. A story is at the mercy of its creator to bring to joy or disaster, but a vow will take on very life of its own, and can of itself burn off, without pity, the false mists of enchantment.

54

Another Death

We sat to eat with my brothers and their families and all the household. Father had placed Kyneth next to him, and I was sat near, on the other side of the table. Father began the feast by raising his beaker to Kyneth, saying:

"Here's to our guest and our son, Kyneth Wulfson, Lord and Chief of Beornwine. You are greatly well-come to our home and our household."

Now, this was a formal well-come that Father had never extended to Kyneth before, although he had been amongst our family and household very many times and had, of course, built the very house in which we all stood. Father's words, given in such a way, signified a change of manner and status.

Everyone raised their beakers, crying, "Well-come to Chief Kyneth!" As I made to drink, looking over the rim of my beaker into Kyneth's eyes, he reached across the table-board, took the beaker firmly from my hand and drank it himself – every drop. He then walked round the table to me and presented his own beaker of ale to me, feeding it into my mouth by his own hand. This action affected me with such a sweet weakness in my body, as he gazed into my eyes, that I was almost fainting. All around the table laughed and applauded loudly and I found myself laughing with them but with my face as red and hot as an ember. For it is well known that, when a man drinks with such ceremony from a woman's cup and then feeds her from his own, he takes upon himself the right to lie with her. I well understood this, and knew at that moment that my father had given Kyneth permission to drink from my cup and, therefore, to lie with me.

That night the household ate finer food and drank more ale than was usual on any but the highest feast day. Father was at the fire-side, giving out tales of his fighting youth, and there was much cheering and singing, the married women were talking together near the food-fire and watching over sleeping infants, for even Gytha and Ham's little boy seemed to be slumbering peacefully amid the revelry. Some of the bondspeople were putting certain valuable left-over foods into jars and baskets, to be eaten by the household the following day. Others were sitting on the earth-filled benches, or – wrapped in cloaks and sheepskins - dozing contentedly on the floor. I found myself in a shadowy corner, listening with feeble attention to my father, not but that I would ever be tired of hearing his stories, but Kyneth's arms were around me, keeping my awareness nearly entirely with him. At length, he whispered closely in my ear, "Come outside, dearest. Let us look at the stars together."

"It's raining," I said, smiling, "There will be no stars, and we will get wet."

"Not true; the rain has stopped. I swear to you there will be stars."

So I got somewhat unsteadily to my feet and went with him, believing that few people noticed our leaving. And it was true, the clouds had rolled away and the sky was a meadow of stars, as crowded as a harvest field with cornflowers. Then Kyneth demanded a kiss from me, saying I had wagered a kiss that there would be no stars. This was most untrue, but I cared not, being only too glad to have an excuse to kiss Kyneth. Soon I wanted no excuse, and I would have eaten him if I could, or poured my own body into his, so urgent was my desire to be as near to him as his own heart. I knew that the household were all very likely aware that we were together, and this might have discomfited me on another occasion, but I was well sluiced with strong ale, which always had the effect of making the unlikely or prohibited seem perfectly possible and allowable. So I kissed Kyneth and felt his hands upon me inside my dress with nothing but the purest pleasure.

After some time he drew back from me, saying, "Come, come with me." And, taking a torch from a stand, he drew me towards the men's dorter.

"We cannot go in there!" I exclaimed.

"Yes, we can, Edith," he said softly, opening the door. "No-one is here; no-one will come. We shall be alone; your father has seen to it."

Again I had the strange consciousness that my actions were beyond my own will; again I did not care. The scent of ale on Kyneth's breath was strong as he held me tightly against him and kissed me hard on the mouth. This was not exactly pleasant, for it hurt my lips and I could not breathe very well. I struggled out of his grasp. "You're hurting me!" I complained in a loud whisper.

"I'm sorry!" He backed away a little with a very winning - if guilty-looking - expression on his face, then he giggled – and I knew he was drunker than I. He swayed towards me and kissed me again, very much more gently. His arms came around me again and I let myself lean against his broad breast. That was a mistake, for he was already off balance, and we both went tumbling to the floor. Fortunately for me, he was underneath so I had a soft landing.

"Kyneth, are you hurt?" He did not stir and I moved over him, stroking his head, suddenly very concerned, for his eyes were closed and his body limp. "My love!" Now I was alarmed and, in a fright. I began to examine his head for injury.

At last he opened one eye, "Oh Edith," he said with no real attempt at pretence, "I am *so* hurt! I shall need you to kiss me until I'm well again."

I laughed with relief and gave him a smack for scaring me. But I hated to hurt him and so I had to kiss the place I had smacked, and then more than a few other places on his head and body that he imagined were hurt. Where would all this lead? To the place you might expect; and it was not long before we were doing what a man and a woman do best together. It was my first time, but not painful or frightening, for I was with one I liked heartily and desired much. None could ask for better.

Afterwards, I slept deeply, close against him underneath the fleece he had pulled over us. Later, I woke and he was at the doorway, I guessed coming back from relieving himself outside. Over his shoulder I could see the old moon as a narrow sickle, just rising before the morning.

"Edith!" he whispered. I knelt and opened my arms to him. He came to me then, with his friendly smile and sweet, beautiful body, and we were together again thoughtlessly in the gladness of our youth. Before we slept again, he stroked my face in the flicker of the failing torchlight. "Dear Edith," he said sleepily, "Will it not be a fine thing if you are with child on our wedding day?"

I was so sated with bodily joy that I did not immediately grasp the full import of his words. Then it came to me – a picture of myself keeping house with two or three little children at my feet. It was not an unhappy picture, and so clear and true that I fully believe now it was a vision of a future that I could not then have had any notion of. But there, in the presence of he to whom I was promised, I thought it to be the image of a much nearer future, and I stiffened with the realisation of my lost hopes. I glanced at Kyneth's face in the dim light, but he was asleep again and would not have seen the deep apprehension which must have been written large on my face.

Before the dawn was more than a faint glow in the east, and while the thin old moon still hung overhead like a chink of light from an almost-closed door, I stepped out of the men's dorter and across the home-yard to the main house. Inside, it was dim and warm with the fire burnt to embers, spilt ale and sleeping bodies, for there was quite a crowd of young men without their usual beds that night for the sake of my coupling with Kyneth. Deep in ale-fuelled slumber, none stirred as I stepped by. Only Spin, who was tethered to the table-leg, sniffed at my foot and gave a sleepy wag of his tail to greet me as I passed. I released him and, taking a candle with me, I carried him up the stair to my loft room. Within were all my familiar belongings from my childhood and growing years. Looking around at them, I felt, unaccountably, as a traveller returned after a long absence. I took Spin on my lap and wrapped my old childhood bed-cover around my shoulders, while Spin licked my face, for he seemed to think I needed comforting. Although my head was dull with ale, I perceived a deep sense of loss in my heart. There was discomfort between my legs – but it was not sufficient to trouble me bodily, only to make me aware that my maidenhead was broken. Much more than the flow of my first moon-blood, this made me realise that my life as a child was truly lost. It was like another death.

Too absent-spirited to weep, I lay down on my side, with Spin making himself comfortable against my back. My eye fell on the corner of my little room, where lay the full-sized wooden sword that Archibald had gifted to me when Father bought him his true sword. I had kept it for sentiment's sake and should now offer it to my nephew Eldric Hereson. I thought of Archibald and what we were to each other. I thought of him now, freely riding to quest with the blessings of his kin and his Lord, supported and encouraged in the company of brother-warriors, having the opportunity of using all his skills: I thought of myself, confined to a woman's place in life by my woman's body and by the expectations of all who knew me. And I felt a deep, abject envy - blacker than the darkest night - for my brother. And, for the first time, resentment quite overpowered my love for Archibald.

I wept then, silently and hopelessly, despite Spin's concerned whimperings; I wept for my lost childhood and my lost dreams; I wept for Father and Elanor because I was not the daughter they deserved; I wept for Kyneth because I could not be the wife he deserved. I wept for the child which might have been quickened in my belly that night, because its mother did not want it. But I wept mostly in self-pity and despair. If I did not marry Kyneth I would let down nearly everyone who loved me. If I did marry him, I would commit myself to a life of confinement and drudgery, for I knew without doubt that my husband would never ride to quest with me. Thus, I would deny the vow that had kept my spirit true for so many years. Should I leave and ride alone to quest, how could I live? Where could I go? I would have to set out without blessing or support or any word of guidance. I would have to run and hide like a hunted hare, for they would surely search for me and try to bring me back.

I feared indeed to go unaided into the unknown. But, more than that, I feared to stay – to not even attempt the fulfilment of my vow and my dreams. The thought of that made me shiver with dread, and the dread stilled my tears and blackened my heart still more until the shivering exhausted me and I slept.

I slept out the dawn and most of the morning. Even then, nobody came to waken me. It was the sound of hooves coming into our home-yard that woke me. Hooves and the voices of men calling and speaking urgently, and of women wailing, and men too.

I came down into the busy morning household, with breakfast over and the fire built up for more bread-proving. I came down with my eyes swollen from sleep, my legs beneath my dress streaked with dried maiden-blood and the flow of Kyneth's seed, my hair half in and half out of green-ribboned bride-braids. But there was nobody in the house; a cauldron of water boiled unchecked on the fire and half-made dough shrank coldly on the table. I went through the threshold and stood at the edge of the door. In the yard I saw Archibald's old horse, Swift, panting and riderless, a great wound over his back, caked with dried blood. I saw two men dressed in the Lord Wilfirth's colours, dismounted from horses flecked with foam; one of the men was Kyneth's brother, Osred. I saw Elanor kneeling in the dirt with Bebbe leaning over her; both were keening and weeping. I saw my father's face blanch white as he turned and caught sight of me in the doorway. He swayed and almost fell, but Osred grasped his arm to support him. Father righted himself – his face grey and ill – but his back and shoulders straight with warrior courage. Alone he walked towards me and alone I went down to meet him.

"It is Archibald," I told him in a clear voice. "Archibald is dead."

55

Warrior Maiden

How I passed that day I cannot tell you. Try as I might, I can find no memory of it, only of terrible inner suffering. I knew I had denied Archibald in my heart: resented, perhaps even hated him in the dark night when envy overcame my love for him. Had that darkness somehow carried itself to my brother and caused him to fall? All envy was gone now, and my fullest, most tender love for my brother returned to torture me as I entered into the dreadful agony of grief.

What? Had I really imagined that Archibald's quest was without dire danger? Had I really not prepared myself for the worst end? I was not a fool: I knew he was riding to confront death. But this knowing was in my head. My heart had never contemplated the sundering from his own – the finality of never hearing his voice again, of never finding myself in his eyes. And my spirit broke, for it did not know where to belong. And my heart pleaded, every minute, for my brother; and my heart was told – every minute - *Archibald is dead, Archibald is dead.*

Over the next days I knew the taste of bitter herbs that made me sleep beyond dreams. Often, I thought Mother Werberga was with me, her old hand cool on my brow, her eyes searching mine for some truth that I tried to hide from her. My moon blood ran and I was washed and changed and tended like a baby. I only knew such things vaguely. When true consciousness raised itself in me and I remembered my loss, I cried out for Archibald, but my best comfort lay in the bitter herbs and oblivion.

~ ~ ~ ~ ~

Archibald's body lies deep in undergrowth. And if the story be true, it might lie undisturbed for a thousand years or more, the bones bare, gradually crumbling back to earth, the belt-knife rusting as leather and wood rots, only the circle of pure gold that decorated its handle remaining – a crisp foil of brightness that might be found by some hunter with a treasure-seeking wand in an unthought-of future. And should such a thing never be found, then let it lie, pure and untarnished as the reputation of a man not destined to fulfil the promise of his youth, pure and untarnished as the love of his sister.

~ ~ ~ ~ ~

It came to be that at last I awoke in quietness of soul. Opening my eyes I saw that Mother Werberga was indeed with me. Her back was towards me as she opened the roof shutter next to my bed. I saw it was evening, and the bow of the new moon graced the western sky, taut and true as Archibald's own bow. The three days of darkness were passed and I knew the truth of my brother's love for me and mine for him. For love transcends anger, envy and resentment; love transcends death. I forgave myself for those dark emotions because I knew Archibald would forgive me for them.

Mother Werberga turned from her contemplation of the new moon and saw that I was awake. She gave me a gentle look that was yet full of pain, and I was able to return her smile.

"You have been caring for me," I said.

"But now you are well again."

"Can I ever be well without him?"

"You are not without him, child." She sat down beside me, not touching me but soothing me with her eyes. "We are never without those we love, whether they walk this Earth with us or fly to the heavens."

Quietly, she spoke to me of what Osred and the other mounted huscarle had told of Archibald's death. "They were set upon at the end of the day when the light was dim and they were tired. They had no time to arm themselves. Archibald was slain and the others rode for cover before making themselves ready and turning to fight. They won out and Osred recovered Archibald's sword and shield, which had been stolen by the enemy. Osred slew the thief and brought the arms back to your father."

"Where did they bury him?" I murmered.

"They searched, but could not find the place where they were first attacked. They had seen Archibald fall with terrible wounds to the head and body, for he was in the vanguard and bore the full force of the attack, but the country was forested, with much undergrowth. They could not find his body."

I whispered, "Oh." Grief could not pierce me more deeply, but it was a new sadness to know that his body lay without the honour of a grave.

We both turned to look at the moon's beautiful silver curve, sinking now as the evening faded, and I could no longer see Mother Werberga's face when she turned to me again and took my hand.

"They will marry you to Kyneth at the full moon, and not wait for the Grain Rite. A Holy Father will be sent for from the Holywell Abbey to make the wedding by Christian and Land Law. They have decided that will help you more than any other thing."

I nodded, but did not speak. My mind was without thought; the knowledge of my brother was clear and transparent before me.

Mother Werberga held a beaker to my lips. "Sleep," she said, but all the beaker contained was pure spring water. I drank thirstily and then she left me. "Kyneth will come to you in the morning," she said, "I cannot keep him away from you any longer."

That night I entered sleep not as previously, hungering for oblivion, but as one who eats for strength. And I had a dream.

In my dream my spirit left my body and floated close to the ground, swiftly over the dark land until, finding a stream, I followed its silver thread until it entered a dark thicket. Not restricted by any barrier, my spirit entered in and found there the pale body of my brother. I reached out my hand to wake him but heard a kind voice, warm and dry as brown moss:

"You shall not wake him Edith."

I looked up eagerly, for it was the voice of my mother, but I could see nothing but the unicorn standing in a shaft of moonlight.

The unicorn spoke, "This is the one you told me of?"

"Yes," I said, "He is my brother". And I made to step forward.

"You shall not wake him Edith."

And I awoke in the earliest gleam of dawn, with the echo of my mother's voice still ringing in my head. Clear of thought, I knew that Archibald's body would never be brought home. This knowledge liberated me, for with no grave, honouring my brother could not bind me to any place, but only give me freedom to roam as his spirit might roam. Now my way ahead was clear; there was no trace of dilemma left in my mind. I was no longer torn between a childish dream of questing and my simple woman's desire for Kyneth. Now, my doubts were gone; now neither my dreams nor my desires held any power over me. With Archibald dead, it was my duty to fulfil his quest and mine. My vow stood firm and true, mightier than myself.

Thus liberated and strong, I rose up from my bed. From a thick bed-cloth I made a bundle and put into it Lady Leoba's prayerbook, a wrap of needles and some other useful items, then strapped on my own sturdy belt with its hangings of knife, spindle and whetstone. Then I took up my bow and quiver of arrows, and stepped quietly down to the silent house.

In the feeble light cast by the earth-banked fire, I saw a high board set up across the head of the table, covered with a rich velvet cloth which I recognised as Elanor's most costly cloak. Reverently upon the cloth was laid Archibald's sword and his scabbard and heavy shield, all cleaned and polished to a gleam. Quickly I took up the sword and pushed it into the scabbard, which was almost new – its raw wool lining resisting the thrust of the blade. I would need a good sword for my life to come. It was meet I should take Archibald's sword to complete his quest and so I did take it, notwithstanding the anger of others. I knew I would carry Archibald's blessing and a measure of his valour as I carried his sword. It was heavy – heavier than the one I generally borrowed from the Ufer armoury – but the muscles of my arms rejoiced in its weight, knowing a time would come when sword and shield would seem but an extension of my own limbs, so naturally and easily would I wield them. I took them without any trace of guilt in my heart, but in the full knowledge that taking them was the mark of no-return in my resolve. Quickly, sword and shield in hand, I left the house.

Spin was in the yard with the other dogs. He greeted me joyously but, at my bidding, made no sound. With him at my heels, I entered the stable and saw Dancer tethered there. She whickered in pleasure to see me and I thanked my luck that she had not been put out to pasture. She stood still, only trembling a little as she always did before the promise of a run. I made her ready, tying on the sword and shield to the saddle-straps and throwing my cloak over her back to conceal the sword. Then I knelt and took Spin in my arms for the last time. Gladly would I have taken my dog away with me, but in those days he was old and stiff of limb, much given to sleeping, and by no means fit for questing unless it be for honeycake. I kissed him and shed a tear onto his old muzzle before tying him well to a stable-post and giving him a rag of my own clothing to guard, as I always did when riding out for the day without him. Then I led Dancer out of the stable and mounted her, turning her towards the gate.

In those days, at my father's order, there was a constant watch-guard over our home-yard, which was fenced all around, with a ditch on the outside and a sturdy guard-gate. Ina the Welshman was on the watch that dawn, with old Worik, who was still hale and great of voice. They both greeted me with warm and sympathetic expressions.

"God's morn to you Lady Edith," said Ina in his lilting way.

"God's morn," I gave them both. "I have been too long mourning within walls. I am riding out today to visit Mother Warberga and thank her for her care of me."

"It is good to see you well, little one," cried Warik with a tear in his eye, which I knew was for me and for Archibald. I was always "little one" to Warik and no-one expected him to call me 'Lady Edith'.

I stopped my horse next to him and reached down to touch his hand. "Thank you, dear Warik, old friend," I said.

That was my last farewell to my childhood home. They unbolted the gate to let me out and I cantered Dancer over the open pastureland beyond. I was glad to be free, glad to have my quest ahead of me – my reason for banishing my terror and grief at my brother's death.

I made a wide path around Beornwine and Hereward and Fritha's house and, as the day broke, I rode down towards the wood where Mother Werberga lived. She was standing on that narrow road, half hidden by the bushes, but I saw her. I slipped from my horse's back and ran into her arms.

"I've been waiting for you," she said. "Come, take food and drink before you travel on."

"I told the watch-guard that I was come to visit you," I said, feeling a little guilty to be involving her in my escape.

"And so you are visiting me," she said. "I shall not see which way you turn when you leave me." She smiled and led me to the little fire that was always burning just outside her house. We sat there as we had so many times and drank a fresh and delicious brew that she had steaming there on the trivet.

"I fired my oven as soon as I returned from your father's house last night," she said. "There is fresh baked bread and new eggs; we shall have a feast before you leave!"

But I shook my head, "I cannot wait, Mother. I took Archibald's sword and shield. As soon as they find them missing they will know my purpose."

Mother Werberga got up immediately from her seat, "Your father will hunt you," she said. "He will not tolerate your action. You are promised to the Chief of Beornwine. Finric Fly will think it a matter for shame that he cannot fulfil that promise."

I realised this was true and my heart sank, perceiving the depth of my father's anger. "I had not thought of that," I said. "I only feared hurting him and Elanor and Kyneth."

"You have a choice: to ride immediately back to Flytun or to go with all speed away."

"I am going."

"Then you shall go properly equipped, and a short delay is allowable. Come into the house with me." She took a light from the fire and I followed her into the little house. Setting the light into a holder on her table, she turned to the sturdy-looking chest that was standing upon two beams next to the table. Opening it she took out a pair of boy's breeches, a shirt and short coat, and something else that was large and quite heavy. I thought at first it was a shield, but then saw it was a thick leathern breast-plate, such as warriors wear.

"These clothes will fit you, I think, and the breast-plate too. Put them on quickly."

"But how did you come by these things?" I asked, already half out of my own clothes, for there was no time to spare.

"You have been talking for these years about riding to quest. Do you think I would let you go without doing my best for you? I have been preparing for such a time as this. You will be safer travelling as a man."

I stopped in my fumbling with the clothes. "How did you know I would come?" I said. "How did you know I would choose my quest?" I whispered the words, for my voice failed me at that moment, in the knowledge that this dear friend had kept her belief in me and cared for me at my darkest hour.

"I did not know, my daughter. But I have commended you to the Goddess these last days. I asked for nothing but Her blessing on you, knowing you would leave or stay, as only you could decide."

I was dressed, and she lifted up the breast-plate, showing me how to strap it on. It was bowed out slightly at the front and quite stiff, but not uncomfortable, for it was thickly padded with wool inside and at the shoulders. "This will hide your breasts," she said. "Wear it whenever you can. You will get used to the weight of it." She stood back and looked me over. "Only your hair needs cutting now and you will pass anywhere for a warrior-youth." She took a pair of shears and cut off my hair above the shoulders, making a man's fringe over my eyes at the front. More than the man's clothes on my body, more even than my theft of Archibald's sword, it was the cutting of my hair that made me feel I had taken an action that was beyond withdrawal. I felt free and light-headed with my hair swinging at my shoulders like Eben Freeborne's. I could not help smiling, and Mother Werberga smiled with me.

"Do I look like a man, Mother?" I said.

"You do indeed – like a young man. But try to remember to keep your voice as low as you can. Now, you must go in haste. There is no time to lose." She ushered me out of the house, "Make your horse ready. I will come to you now."

I tightened Dancer's girth-strap and then took Archibald's sword in its scabbard, threaded my belt through the carriers and tightened the belt around my waist. Mother Werberga came out of the house, bearing a small bag of coins, a full leathern water-bottle and a wax-sealed jar which she stowed in my bundle.

"The jar is full of my sweet-biscuit," she said, "baked especially for your wedding or your leaving, whichever was to be."

The little clearing by the river was awash with morning sunlight as I took my leave of her. It was not until I was seated on my horse that she handed me a small purse.

"Travel north and then west," she said. "Cross the great river and keep the sea to your left hand."

I was startled and searched her face. My hand was on the purse, arrested in accepting it from her. "West?" I asked, "West, to the Welshlands?" Would she send me into peril so soon?

"In this purse is a powerful rune of passage," she said. "Show it when you are challenged and say you bring a message to the Brenin Math."

I stared at her, "What is the Brenin Math?"

"It is the name of a king. Remember it, Edith. In the purse is a written message also."

I snatched the purse and opened it. Inside was a folded piece of soft leather and a dark, smooth stone. The stone had a carving upon one side in the shape of a horn; on the other was a curved line, turning back upon itself. I looked again at Mother Wergerga, "A horn and a dragon?" She gave me no answer and I unfolded the piece of leather. Upon it was scribed close-handed writing. I studied it, but it was neither Christian Latin nor Anglish. "What is this?" I said.

"It is written in the Gymraeg – what the Welsh call their language. The Brenin Math will understand it."

Once more I stared at her. I had known Mother Werberga for most of my life, yet she never ceased to surprise me. I knew full well that she was wise and learned, but she had never told me of any connection with the Welshlands or knowledge of its language.

"It has been secret," she said. "But now, in your need, I shall help you. Do not lose these things."

I nodded and tucked the purse into my tunic, tying its strings securely to my belt.

She gave me her last blessing for my journey and I clasped her hand, but could find no words of thanks fine enough. Dancer had taken no more than two steps away when Mother Werberga called me again with a note of urgency.

"Edith!"

I stopped and turned my face around to her once more.

"Edith, you will need to take a man's name now. Have you thought what it shall be?"

I had not given it any thought, but now I looked back and nodded as I urged my horse away, "Archibald," I called, "Archibald Fly!"

I saw her smile and raise a hand and I waved back, then turned my horse to the north, away from my home.

Despite the need for haste, I could not but turn before entering the forest to take a last view of the country I knew. Where the land rose between myself and Mother Werberga's woods, two riders appeared on the hill. I froze, but they were motionless whilst they seemed to look in my direction. I reflected that they would not be able to see me so well as I could see them, for they were silhouetted against the sky, whereas I was in the valley, with the forest at my back. If I stayed still, they might not notice me. One of the riders turned and, raising himself in his saddle, pointed away to the east. The other looked and set his horse off in that direction. Before following, the first rider turned again towards me. Many times had we seen each other on horseback from afar; always we had known each other, even from a great distance. He raised a hand in salute and, without waiting for any response, rode away. He was Kyneth, Chief of Beornwine.

I rode my horse on, keeping the forest to my right, with my sword at my side and my bow on my back, although I had no need to use them, for I saw not a soul for the rest of that day. I should have been lonely or sad, for I was leaving behind all who loved me, but it was without regret that I rode, at last ready to pursue and willing to encounter my quest. I believed that I had luck on my side, and blessings too; I believed I would find Orin and avenge my mother's death; I believed my own deeds would one day be made into stories and that, through them, I would bring honour to the name of my noble brother Archibald.

Lightning Source UK Ltd.
Milton Keynes UK
UKOW050643160612

194525UK00001B/32/P